WITHDRAWN

THE

FATIGUE ARTIST

a novel

LYNNE SHARON SCHWARTZ

SCRIBNER

New York   London   Toronto   Sydney   Tokyo   Singapore

SCRIBNER
1230 Avenue of the Americas
New York, NY 10020

SCRIBNER and design are
trademarks of Simon & Schuster Inc.

Designed by SONGHEE KIM

Manufactured in the United States of America

10 9 8 7 6 5 4 3 2 1

Library of Congress Cataloging-in-Publication Data
Schwartz, Lynne Sharon.
The fatigue artist: a novel / Lynne Sharon Schwartz.
       p.   cm.
I. Title.
PS3569.C567F38   1995
813'.54—dc20   94-48009
                                                    CIP

ISBN 0-684-80247-3

Any disease introduces a doubleness into life—an "it," with its own needs, demands, limitations.

Oliver Sacks

"Hey, I wish I had a picture of this," said Tim. "I didn't think of bringing my camera."

1

The Tai Chi teacher has barely changed in seven years. It's still hard to tell his age—a youngish old man or an old young one—except that over time he's developed something of a pot belly. He carries it proudly, for beneath its layers, deep in his center, is the *tan tien*, "field of the elixir," he says through the interpreter, where the *chi* gathers, the vital energy enhanced by breath, to flow through the body, strengthening bones, animating flesh. Like many Chinese terms, *chi* is hard to define: the presence of *chi* in the body, the teacher tells us, is what makes the difference between life and death.

He does seem to have very resilient bones, as far as I can tell through his jeans and T-shirt (in winter he wears a flannel shirt and on very cold days an old gray down jacket), but his general appearance is not muscular but soft, a compressed softness like a bale of rags which, coming at you unexpectedly, could send you reeling.

He addresses the class in Chinese, giving his instructions through the interpreter. You'd think after years in New York he'd use English, but no. I guess for his purposes he doesn't need it. He teaches mostly by example and, except for the anecdotes, his instructions tend to be laconic, though I suspect not quite as laconic as the interpreter makes them.

They take less time in English, and as a result I don't quite trust the translation.

"Continue," he says after bidding us good afternoon. He never says, "Begin." Always "Continue."

"Again," he says after one round of the form, "and this time paying attention to breathing. Make the breath thin, long, quiet and slow. Start with slow. Sink the weight into the legs. Be heavy. Continue." All this through the interpreter, of course.

So we start all over again. It's easy to sink and be heavy since my body, these last few weeks, feels like sand in a sack. We're in the park at five-thirty—despite my exhaustion I ordered myself out like a drill sergeant—a dozen of us plus the teacher and the interpreter, practicing amidst the trees, near the sunny playground, not too many children at this hour; the swings wobble in the hot breeze while beyond us the river drifts lazily down from the resplendent bridge. Morning and late afternoon we're here, not all of us each time, for few people can manage to come twice a day or even every day. For a flat fee we come as often or as seldom as we choose—it's all the same to the Tai Chi teacher. He accepts our money with the air of accepting a gift ("thank you" is one English phrase he feels comfortable with) and apparently keeps no records, though who knows, he may have detailed ledgers at home, wherever his home is. As in a play, the cast changes but the spectacle remains the same. Breathe, sink, feel the feet rooted in the earth, stay balanced, over and over.

I used to watch, enthralled, from the living room window when Ev and I first moved into the apartment overlooking the river: a motley group of all ages, mostly in shorts or jeans but a few in business suits, their jackets and attaché cases on a nearby bench, doing a slow-motion dance in unison, yet not quite a dance. A ritual, a meditation, I didn't know what. One afternoon I went down to see for myself and followed along as best I could. Every few moments, as we held a posture, the teacher would come around to fix us, adjusting a shoulder or arm or hip, rounding out sharp angles, uncurling tense fingers, the interpreter following along. "The body moves in one piece, head, shoulders and torso in line," he'd say, or "The foot clings to the pull of gravity like iron to a magnet," or "Most important of all, relax, use hand force." It was habit forming. I even thought I might learn Chinese by exposure and by matching what I heard with the interpreter's English, but that, alas, didn't happen. Other things happened. My leg muscles hardened, my feet sank roots deep in the earth. I began to move like a cat, and like a cat could anticipate the movements of others, but out of vanity I resisted letting my stomach droop into a pot belly.

The second time I came, the teacher demonstrated push hands—the martial art aspect of Tai Chi—with an advanced student. Face to face and standing very erect with one leg placed forward, their hands before them at chest level, palms together, they bowed to each other. Then they stepped closer, and deftly shifting their weight from one leg to the other, began to touch at the forearms and elbows, turning slightly now and then. Nothing much seemed to be happening—mostly I felt their intense absorption. Suddenly the student tottered forward; the teacher reached out an arm to break his fall. They did this several times. The student never seemed disconcerted but smiled and began again. The teacher remained impassive.

"Yield," he said to the student. "Stop relying on strength. Just try to adhere and stay balanced. You will fail many times. It doesn't matter. You are making an investment. You're investing in loss."

"Righto. No complaints whatsoever," the student said, and everyone laughed as if at some private joke.

They continued, and soon I saw that it was the teacher's drawing back slightly, yielding to the weight brought to bear on him, which threw the student off balance. When they were finished they faced each other once more with palms touching and bowed.

The teacher turned to the group. "What was the most important posture in what you have just seen?" He nodded at me.

"The bow," I said.

It was the right answer. After that he always favored me. He gave me a

9

slim book outlining the philosophy behind Tai Chi—a physical expression of Taoism—with diagrams of the postures so I could study the basics. He told me to read the Samurai's creed at the back of the book. This was puzzling because I couldn't see what I might have in common with a Samurai warrior, but I read it anyway. "I have no principles; I make adaptability to all things my principle," it said, among other things.

Now he nods to me, to do push hands with him. I step forward and we bow. I'm quite relaxed since I know from experience that I cannot overcome him; strength and effort are of no avail and are to be shunned in any case. I also trust that he'll break my fall.

We continue. I stagger and reel a couple of times, but nothing much is happening. "What's the matter today?" he asks through the interpreter. "Very little *chi*."

"I have no energy. I'm feeling very tired." As if I have a perpetual flu, but I don't trouble the interpreter with that. He translates into Chinese, and I have to trust that he's repeated my words, or some facsimile of my thought.

"Relaxed is good, but not limp. Like a cat, alert, vital, in a state of readiness. Don't resist but try to sense my energy and stick to it. Continue."

I try harder. I even try pushing him though I know it's futile. Wherever I apply my weight, he is suddenly not there. It's like grappling with a shadow. I press, and his substance vanishes, he's elusive, he's elsewhere. I keep stumbling through the space he's vanished from and he catches me before I fall. He regards me with disapproval.

"I'm investing in loss," I attempt to joke.

"You're investing in nothing," he says, and we bow.

At the end he makes a little speech. "My fellow students, the *chi* of the ancient Tai Chi masters was so powerful that they could repel an attacker with a look alone. They didn't even need to use their bodies. The energy was all concentrated in the glance." He glances my way and indeed I find myself stepping back slightly, at which he smiles. The interpreter never smiles.

The class is over and breaks into small chatty groups. I sit down on a bench next to a new woman, Grace, who's come only once or twice before. She's rubbing her calf muscles. I know how she feels; it's quite hard on the legs at first. It never really eases but you get used to it. A student once asked when his legs would stop hurting. "Never," said the teacher. "If your legs stop hurting, then it's not Tai Chi."

"It's all a matter of discipline, isn't it?" she says. "I thought it would be easy because I'm used to that kind of discipline in what I do, but this is different."

"What do you do?"

"I'm a performance artist." She's slightly older than I, mid-fortyish, a holdover from the late sixties, dressed all in black, with short dark hair nicely streaked with gray. Soho, I bet. Gay, I bet, from something carefree and staunch in the way she moves and speaks.

"Oh, my stepdaughter is very involved in performance art at school," I tell her. "She's always describing the bizarre projects her group does. Do you do theatrical pieces?"

"Not exactly. What I do is more a cross between theatre and visual arts. But really the best thing is to erase the line between the two. Erase all the lines. Forget the idea of a product, a beautiful object. Lots of times we don't come up with any products. We might just take a piece of ordinary life out of context and exaggerate it." She pulls off her sneakers and curls her legs under her on the bench. "For instance, someone I know lived in a cage without speaking to anyone for a year. He also lived outdoors for a year. He's into tests of psychological endurance but he's also doing social commentary. Like about homeless people, you know?"

"Living outdoors by choice is different from being homeless, though, don't you think?"

"Sure. That's what makes it art. It's a metaphor for a real condition, not the thing itself. It calls attention to the condition. By the way," and she lowers her voice, "doesn't this guy speak any English at all?"

"It doesn't seem so. Except thank you and good-bye."

She looks dubious. "I bet he understands what we say. He looks very

1 1

tricky. I've heard some of these Taoist guys do magic. Has he shown you any magic?"

I shake my head, no.

"I don't know," Grace goes on. "I heard this was great but frankly I haven't the faintest idea what it's about, all these people paired off and sticking to each other like he says, pushing each other around and feeling each other's energy."

"Don't worry about it. It takes months even to begin to do what he's asking."

"You know what the pairs remind me of? The couple-tied-together piece. That was a while ago. The guy who lived outdoors had himself tied to another artist. For a whole year they had an eight-foot rope looped around their waists, with about four feet of slack between them. The woman was into Zen. She was a nun for a while, too."

"Was that performance art, being a nun?"

"I think so. But I'm sure she was a sincere nun. That's the whole idea."

"Odd," I comment, "that a nun would have herself tied to a man for a year."

"Oh, she wasn't a nun anymore, at the time. Besides, it wasn't the way you're thinking. Just the opposite—the discipline part was that they weren't allowed to touch for the whole year. They had to do everything together, cook, shop, walk the dog, go to the movies, you name it, without touching. They kept a chart of the times they accidentally touched. They had everything in the apartment arranged so they could manage. The desks were near the kitchen so one could cook while the other worked. He did more of the cooking. He was very good at Chinese dishes."

"What was the point?"

"The point?" Grace stares at me in surprise. "It's about awareness. Training the mind. You begin to notice all the daily little things—where the borders are between people, and where they can connect or merge. Plus the dynamics of gender in domestic life. They did it for so long that it became their real life. Of course, there were a lot of places they couldn't go, and they decided not to sleep with other people—more trouble than it was worth, I suppose. Personally"—Grace sighs—"I think the greatest danger would be getting bored to death with each other."

"Not necessarily. Not if they weren't bored with each other to begin with. I can imagine a couple of people I could be tied to and never get bored," I say.

You are the only person, Q. told me so many times, who never bores me. You never know, I said. Someday I might. No, he said, never. And what would happen if I bored you? I asked. It's academic, he said. It could never happen.

"The couple tied together," says Grace, "didn't complain about being bored, but they did say they dreamed a lot."

"Did they dream of being alone or of touching?"

"I don't know. That's a good question."

The teacher, who's been chatting with a few students, passes by. "Good-bye," he says in English, and the interpreter adds, perhaps on his own, "He hopes you feel better next time, Laura. Eat watercress."

"Watercress? Okay. Thanks a lot. See you soon."

"I don't see how you could ever defend yourself on the subway with Tai Chi," says Grace as we trudge up the hill, away from the river. "Always yielding? How would it work with a mugger? Do you think you could do it?"

"Probably not. But I'm not in it for self-defense. The teacher says it's the one martial art you have to know very well in order to use. Otherwise it's a risk."

"I'll bet. Some performance artists are into risk. They design dangerous projects to make a point. There was a show downtown where a man covered the floor with broken glass and slithered through it on his belly with his hands tied behind his back."

"Did he have clothes on?"

She gives a throaty laugh. "Yes, I'm pretty sure. You have to realize, the whole thing is a metaphor."

"I get it, yes." I can imagine other projects performance artists might try as metaphors: surgery, or at least a prolonged hospital stay. Divorce. Getting fired. It's a fertile field for anyone with imagination. Everything, seen in the proper light, can become a metaphor. The trick is finding, or being found by, the right ones.

I dropped my keys on the way in. That's the latest symptom: things leap from my hands. Mostly small slippery things, bottle caps, paper clips, the pen, as I write this, but often larger things as well—magazines or socks or fruits I'm squeezing at the open-air market. Thoughts, too, slide from my grasp, but that's another story.

The very next morning, it was a commonplace glass from Woolworth's. I had groped my way from bed to the kitchen, cursing the car alarm just below my window, and was about to pour some juice when the glass wantonly escaped, to plummet three feet through the air. The instant it took to reach the floor was time enough, even in my stupor, for me to envision the results. The thud and smash, shattering me awake. I'd reach for the dustpan and brush above the sink and sweep up the chips around my slippered feet. Shuffle into the pantry for the electric broom—I could hear its ominous rumble waiting to be summoned into existence—and let it suck up the shards that elude the brush. Even so, I'd keep from walking around barefoot for a while, to be quite sure. I thought of the man Grace mentioned, who slithered on his belly through broken glass. For art's sake. Obviously I wasn't daring enough for the avant-garde.

I'd have to warn the others in the house not to walk barefoot . . . wait, there were no others in the house. Ev, my husband, was dead and had been so for more than two years, though when half-awake I tend to forget this, then promptly remember not so much with grief any longer as with astonishment. His children, my stepchildren, Jilly and Tony, don't visit very often (Tony almost never, to tell the truth), and when they do they naturally wear shoes.

Days from now I'd be seeing slivers glinting from corners, sharp reminders that if not for the fortuitous slant of light, a misstep might have sent them journeying through my bloodstream to pierce a vital organ. Heart, lungs, liver, spleen and kidneys are the vital organs in Chinese medicine, the Tai Chi teacher says, each corresponding to one of the primal elements—fire, metal, wood, earth, and water, respectively, which came into being out of nothingness through the coupling of yin and yang—and to a primal emotion: joy, sadness, anger, will, fear. I could ill afford that sort of damage.

All this I foresaw as the glass plummeted to the tile floor where, happily, it didn't break (cheap and sturdy) but bounced twice, rolled a few feet—the floor in this old apartment building is slightly sloping and halted at the edge of the refrigerator. At that instant the car alarm abruptly ceased.

A good omen. I've been worried lately about the things dropping, the supernatural exhaustion, the hypersensitivity to noise, not to mention the more mundane signs—sore throats, headaches, stomach cramps. . . . Oh, and not minding the heat. Everyone complains that the weather is tropical, unbearable, but I haven't noticed except in a mental way—I hear bulletins on the radio, I check the thermometer. It's because I myself am so hot. Not my skin, especially, but inside. No sudden waves of heat such as my former editor, Gretchen, a case of early menopause, would describe when she phoned to prod me about my books, but a steady heat steaming out from the center with each thump of my heart, clouding me with mist. Feverish people say they're on fire, but I feel like the cauldron itself, containing a stew—those vital organs—that simmers dully along. Or like a bag of sand left out in the sun. Between the outside weather and the inner is no disparity; the weather is merely my projection. They say illness makes you solipsistic, the world a mere projection or translation. If this is illness. It could be any number of things. I'm not eager to find out.

Pathetic, to take so unremarkable an incident as a good omen. Superstition is a symptom, too.

Friends who've noticed my symptoms tell me to go to a doctor but I'm reluctant. Not only for the obvious reason, that he or she—but it seems usually to be he, doesn't it?—might find something really wrong. My previous visits have been a powerful deterrent. "Our private conversations," as Joel Cairo says in *The Maltese Falcon,* which I saw last month with Tim, "have not been such that I am anxious to continue them."

Nine or ten years ago, I must have been thirty-one or so, I consulted a doctor, let's call him Dr A., about some white specks on my tongue. They were disturbing out of all proportion to their size, the tongue being the organ by which we taste and speak, take pleasure and shape language. Moreover, the mouth is the gateway for the breath, which is palpable spirit and is also the place where we live, notwithstanding Freud. A few small specks on the tongue can be as uncomfortable as a grape-sized lump on the hand, with which we write and grope our way through the world, or on the foot, which gives blessed mobility.

"Stick out your tongue," said Dr. A., and I became a child again.

He was very tall and straight, with a military bearing, so although I was in the higher seat, a large leather chair, and he on a small stool, we were face to face. Quite close, our knees nearly touching. He was older than I, with a pink Buddha-like face, a huge bald dome of a head with a fringe of dark hair, and serene gray eyes that seemed too static, trance-like, as he studied my tongue.

"I'm afraid I must ask you a very odd and perhaps embarrassing question," he said, and paused to allow me time to retract my tongue and prepare myself. "It is this. Have you sucked any strange penises lately?"

I was unprepared. I had to control the urge to giggle into the looming pink face. They're all strange to us girls, was the response that sprang to mind, but that would never do.

"No," I said truthfully.

Not even my husband's, I might have added, which would have been the least strange in the sense of the word I took him to mean—unfamiliar, illicit—since he's away covering the conflict in Nicaragua. And Q., short for Quinn, the only other man I occasionally sleep with, Doctor A., since you ask (though one doesn't do that specific act every time, speaking for myself at any rate—it's hard to say in general and I for one never trust the answers people give on those sex surveys), is in Minneapolis doing a season of repertory with the Guthrie: *All My Sons*, I believe, and God, I don't envy him that; Creon in *Antigone*; something by Molière, I forget which; and something very current. Besides, flustered as I am at the moment, Doctor A., I can't even recall whether Q. and I are in a lovers' phase or a just-friends phase—it changes so erratically. Immaterial anyway. Come to think of it, I just spoke to my husband, Ev, on the phone two nights ago. It's hard for him to make personal phone calls so I was pleased that he made the effort and succeeded, and although after telling me a little bit about the situation in Managua—very little, you understand, the phones are bugged—he did say something mildly erotic on the order of how he wished he could hold me in his arms that night, while I on my end was thinking more or less the same thing, nothing as localized as sucking penises was mentioned. I didn't even entertain the notion, in case the power of suggestion has anything to do with my ailment, nor, I would imagine, did Ev, who was preoccupied with the political ferment around him, the kind of volatile situation I presume could take a man's mind off his penis for a while, though I couldn't swear to it. Anyhow, that was two days ago and the specks on my tongue had already erupted.

Naturally I didn't say all this. I know how to behave in a doctor's office.

"Well." Dr. A. pushed back from me on his wheeled stool. "I would say it's probably nothing to worry about. Chances are they'll disappear as mysteriously as they came." He stood up and turned to his desk with a slight air, I think, of disappointment.

Oh, dear, had he been hoping for a good story? Did I let him down? So sorry, try me another day, I might have said.

In a few days the specks did go away as mysteriously as they had come and I regretted visiting Dr. A., whose odd question would now have a permanent and unwelcome place in my memory, the data bank, as my friend Mona calls it with disapproval. The visit confirmed my instinct not to consult doctors but rather to wait.

Years later, just after Ev was killed, I developed a bad sore throat. I waited and waited but it didn't go away. It got worse. People—my on-and-off lover Q., my stepdaughter Jilly, my cousin Joyce—urged me to see a doctor. It might be strep, it might lead to something worse. I was a brand-new widow and everyone wanted to take care of me. Oh, all right, I agreed. But Dr. A.? After that odd question? For two days, while my throat worsened, I debated whether to return and risk being asked other odd questions (yet how much odder could they be?) or go elsewhere, flying to evils that I knew not of. In the end I decided on Dr. A., unwisely, you may think, but when feeling sick one isn't wise. He couldn't possibly remember my tongue, I reasoned. He probably wouldn't even remember me after eight years—so many patients, so many tongues, who knows how many odd questions. And this was a plain sore throat; innocent children get sore throats all the time.

Of course he remembered me, said Dr. A. genially, and as he sat on his wheeled stool and examined my throat he asked how I had been in the intervening years, to which I could reply only with a gagging noise. No way to tell him my husband had been shot to death in the interim. No inclination either. Dr. A. had the same entranced gray eyes and Buddha-like expression, though unlike Buddha he had visibly aged; his skin was not so pink and babyish any more. As he retrieved some fluid from my throat on a cotton swab, I felt pleased with myself. I would find relief, come away with a prescription like a sensible person. I had not been daunted by a question perhaps posed in the line of duty, however gracelessly.

He walked across the room to put the fluid on a slide. With his back to me he said, "I not only remember you but I remember that the last time you were here I had occasion to ask you a very odd and possibly embarrassing question. Do you remember?"

"I certainly do."

I might have added that today his odd question would be even less pertinent, since Ev had died two months earlier, killed on a Bronx street in a drug bust. A bystander, more or less. And Q.? Well, yes, Q. had turned up a few weeks later. He walked in with a suitcase and a bag of groceries, all the foods he knew I liked, and stayed for a month. He warmed the bed, but the love we made for that month was of the consoling kind. Q. managed everything, solicitous, treating me like a bereft child; no question of much on my part. I was passive until the last moments when I would erupt in tears as well as pleasure. Q. was magnanimous as only he can be, especially when nothing much is expected of him. Despite the irritation at my marriage he had shown on and off over the years, he was in no hurry to appropriate me now that I was "free," the way, when a New York City parking space becomes free, the next occupant is already waiting, motor humming, to slide in before it cools off. Long ago, when I was in love with Q. in a less ambiguous way, I had had fantasies that if Ev were to disappear (God knows I never envisioned him shot, I just thought he would tire of me), Q. would rush to my side as the Prince rushed to Sleeping Beauty or Snow White or countless others, sweep me up on his horse and carry me off, even though I was neither sleeping nor held captive. But this didn't happen, and after a while I stopped imagining or wishing it. I tried to live my divided life.

In any event, my tongue was fine today and my sore throat, however painful, felt ordinary—unless it was punitive, my own retaliation for sleeping with Q. so soon after my husband's violent death. But I hadn't suffered much guilt while he was alive, so it didn't follow. . . . Well, never mind all that. An antibiotic would do the trick.

I didn't say any of the above to Dr. A. Indeed, I spoke not another word, quite as if my once-offending tongue had been cut out. I listened to his instructions about the antibiotic, accepted the prescription from his cool, dry hand, and left. In a week I was better. I resolved never to return to Dr. A. and perhaps not to any doctor ever again.

19

WHY NOT GO BACK TO BED FOR A WHILE, I thought after I drank the juice from the sturdy glass. I see the bed as my true home, my home within a home. Whoever invented it deserves as much renown as the inventor of the cotton gin or the steam engine, those inventions taught in school. People have always stretched out spontaneously on anything handy, yes, but I mean the combination of elements forming the bed itself. The raised platform, which makes climbing in a decisive event. The mattress and box spring, inspired notions lovingly wrought. The feather pillow and the quilt are to repose what champagne and chocolate mousse are to diet. Amazing, really, that such luxurious sensuality is available to all strata of society, except of course the homeless who swarm the local streets and sleep God knows where, niches, doorways and sections of Riverside Park they've appropriated as campsites. Even so, many of them drag around shopping carts stuffed with puffy bedding.

My bed, a modest double, nothing kingly or queenly, has become more than a haven or refuge. It's a lover. At my most exhausted moments I sense it reaching toward me like the vibrations of the universe, for the Tai Chi teacher says the universe is a great system of vibrations we draw to us by our feelings: fear draws fear, love draws love. I almost hear the bed whispering to me to come, the way you might feel a lover longing for you miles away, and I come readily, falling onto the waiting mattress, firm but yielding as an accomplished lover, the strong coils beneath the stuffing like reliable bones beneath the flesh. I lie down as eagerly as did the princess worn out from her wanderings, except under this mattress is no irritating pea. No, the bed is a perfect and perfectly welcoming lover. The pillow sinks benignly under the weight of my head and rises mildly around my hair. I pull the sheet over me to be utterly surrounded, voluptuously embraced. It folds coolly around my legs as a lover's skin may be cool at first touch, but it quickly warms up from my body's heat, creating a tube of warmth. As the bed presses gently along the length of me, I let go. Every cell yields to the embrace which of late I find satisfying like no other. Totally understanding, the bed accepts that I have nothing to offer but warmth, which I have in abundance. I need not respond or embrace in return. The bed seeks nothing for itself—its pleasure is to wrap me in pleasure.

I WAS ROUSED by the sound of the door opening. Tim. Since I gave him a set of keys last month, I've had to get used to that sequence of sounds all over again, the key slipping into the shaft, metal grating against metal, the door thrusting past the wooden frame. His arrival and the light filtering through the drawn shades told me it was early evening. Slept the day away. Just as well—things pick up for me around twilight. My blood stirs and moves a bit faster. I hauled myself up to greet him.

Standing in the hall, tired and apparently dazed by the heat, his tan suit jacket slung over his shoulder in the manner of middle aged professionals in summer, Tim held beside him, like a cane or a crutch, a five-foot-high narrow gray object, curved at both ends, with two holes cut out as if for eyes.

"What is that?"

"What does it look like, Laura?"

"It looks like the bumper of a car."

"It is the bumper of a car. Your car."

"What is it doing here?"

"I guess you haven't seen your car lately. I passed it as I was coming up the street, and this had fallen off."

"How?"

"Oh, probably during the daily stampede to park by two o'clock, someone backed into you, and your car being the piece of junk it is, this fell off."

I ignored the insult to my car, which I'm fond of, a little white Geo which Tim says resembles, in looks and performance, a golf cart. "When I moved it around one-thirty there was someone in front of me with a few feet to spare. I wonder how this happened. Luke would have let me know if he'd seen anything."

The super of the building next door, with whom I've had an amiable flirtation for some time, is our block's de facto mayor, of the Fiorello La

Guardia type. Luke knows everyone, keeps close track of local develop-
ments, sizes up newcomers and acts as public relations and peacekeep-
ing officer. He alerts us to cops or meter maids in their drab brown
uniforms—a cut below the blue—writing out parking tickets, and will
even ring doorbells to shout a warning through the intercom, at which
we race down and drive around the block until the menace has passed.

"There's no one in front of you now. But someone must have done
this."

"Well, put it down, for God's sake. It must be heavy."

"Where do you want it, ma'am?"

"Anywhere. Leave it over there against the wall. Wait, let me help you
drag it."

Tim shook his head and raised the bumper high in the air with the
slow, triumphant gesture of a weight lifter.

"What are you doing? It's a bumper. Put it down."

"Here, you try."

I was expecting to lift a heavy weight, so I almost dropped it. "My
God. Isn't it metal?"

"Plastic. On some cars it's metal, but not on yours."

"So what do you think this weighs?" I leaned it against the wall.

"Maybe four pounds."

"Four pounds?"

"Yes, it's shocking, isn't it? When you think that this is what stands
between you and an oncoming car. Well, I'll put it back on in the morning."

"Is that all? You mean I don't have to take it to the garage?"

"I doubt it. It's probably some kind of hook-and-eye affair. I just
didn't want to bother right now. So how about a reward? Give us a kiss."

I went closer. "Thanks, Tim. I dub you Sir Tim for that deed. It looks
sort of nice against the wall, doesn't it? Like sculpture."

He let his jacket slip to the floor and put his arms around me,
checking here and there as if to make sure the vital parts were still in
place. Maybe finding the bumper detached had unnerved him. "Any

chance of getting a cold drink?" he murmured in my ear.

Besides rescuing my bumper, he had rented a movie we could watch along with the Chinese food I would procure by telephone. The sort of evening that could not have taken place in the pre-electronic age but now took place virtually everywhere, even in the little seaside hamlet that was the setting of the novel I was trying, in my few waking hours, to write. The movie in Tim's briefcase was *Anthony Adverse,* which he assured me I would enjoy since it was based on a book and contained everything important: love, war, travel, betrayal and loss, music, suffering, and scenery.

After we studied the Chinese menu, Tim went off to take a shower and I made the call. Our local restaurant operates with the efficiency of the FBI. I needed only to recite my telephone number, and all my required data popped up on their computer screen, including my previous purchasing record. Tim is the sort of man who doesn't find this unsettling.

While he is in the shower, a word or two about Tim might be in order. Not that his excellent qualities don't deserve lengthier consideration—I appreciate him and show it, believe me—but I have a feeling he may not be a crucial character in this particular story, however it proceeds. I'll be patching bits and pieces as I go. Even in real life, I sometimes feel I'm making Tim up. He is so useful for the moment and appeared so opportunely in my solitude.

Tim is a lawyer. An attorney, I guess he'd prefer to be called. He draws up contracts between parties—people or corporate entities. He presides over their arduous creation and frequently over their arduous destruction. He is familiar with the byways and crannies of accommodation, which makes him a good companion. That's all I know about that part of his life. He doesn't like to talk about his work, unfortunately, since I love hearing people talk about their work: I store it all in the data bank. Ev was invaluable that way, with sagas of crime, war, and derring-do he picked up as a reporter. He tended to dwell too long on political systems and physical settings, but I was willing to wait for the intrigue, the moral turpitude and outrageous behavior I liked. That source, alas, has dried up.

Tim is one of those people who divide life into work and recreation, and I fall into his recreation category, especially as he doesn't associate me with children or family obligations, which he has elsewhere. He's divorced, gradually growing less bitter about it. So far I've been willing to be his recreation. What he offers me in return, aside from companionship and the usual male handyman skills, is an entrée into ordinary middle-class life, where I can carry on my researches. Tim is my analogue of Ev's press card. Since Ev died I've become reclusive, living on the margins. Through Tim I get to spend an occasional weekend out of town, to attend parties and go on excursions I wouldn't seek on my own.

In the gatherings Tim has taken me to, sooner or later, after discussing the number of miles they log each morning to outrace mortality, or the relative merits and demerits of butter and margarine, people get around to "serious issues"—the destruction of the rain forests and the depletion of the ozone layer, the aimlessness of the younger generation illustrated by examples from their own children, the scourge of illiteracy, and, inevitably, why is it that some ethnic groups, *e.g.,* Koreans and Jews, have been able to lift themselves out of poverty onto the plateau of the middle class while other ethnic groups, *e.g.,* blacks, have not?

Four possible approaches are taken to the issues, and they generally appear in fugue-like form: Bemoaning is the opening theme, followed by Blaming the parties involved; next comes Defending the parties involved by examining the problem in its social context—a kind of counterpoint melody—and finally, some form of Temporizing, usually offered by a peaceable person thus far silent. The four themes can go on indefinitely until they're resolved in the harmony of grateful good-nights. I've often thought that on arrival the guests might choose placards representing their positions—for in the nature of things these positions are fixed in advance.

For the dozen years I shared Ev's bed, I, too, was diligently concerned and well informed. Ev knew the etiologies and interrelations of all the issues and their positions in the issue hierarchy as well as the range of possible opinions, and where did all his knowledge lead? The data of that conscientious brain spilled on a Bronx street in a shootout. Ever since, I can't seem to concern myself with issues. It's not a political reaction. The issues remind me of him and of all the things he didn't talk about, also spilled and lost. The hollow tunnel of our life together that I'm trying, now, to fill belatedly with words.

Anyway, Tim is more fun alone, and as I listened to the pleasant brooky music of the shower, I found myself thinking, This is not so bad. Not bad at all. So what if Ev is dead? And Jilly miles away and Tony doesn't like me. So what if Q . . . No, leave us not even think of Q. at a moment of relative contentment. So what if something is wrong with me, so wrong that I'm too tired to write a sentence of the modern-day fable I'm struggling with, set in an idyllic town washed by the sea and lulled by the rhythms of the tides, a salty-aired benevolent town where, aside from the explosive vagaries of nature—gales and storms—nothing ever goes much awry, a keen contrast to my city, guarded by rivers and shaken by car alarms and shrieking sirens. And if I don't write a few sentences pretty soon I'll run out of money. I have this clever, well-built man splashing around in my shower in that energetic way they have. Later in my bed. I don't love him except in the mildest way and chances are he doesn't love me no matter what he professes in bed. So what? We behave well to each other. Surely that counts for something? He rescues my car, he brings a good movie. Soon we'll be eating steamed dumplings in garlic sauce, shrimp in black bean sauce, sesame chicken, and the little extras like toasted pecans and oranges they throw in to beat the competition. No complaints whatsoever.

I set up a couple of stacking tables in the living room so we could enjoy our feast while watching *Anthony Adverse,* featuring the young Fredric March.

"All set?" asked Tim, his finger aimed at the Play button. His graying blond hair was smoothed down, and he was less formal in shorts and a striped T-shirt.

"No, wait a minute. Something's wrong here." I was undoing the cardboard cartons, putting aside the fortune cookies and teabags. Some packets of soy sauce and mustard slipped from my grasp. "Shit, I drop everything lately. Maybe I have a brain tumor."

"Nonsense. What are you fussing with?"

"Come and look. This isn't shrimp in black bean sauce, is it?"

"No, it looks like lamb or beef."

"And this. It isn't sesame chicken."

"It could be." He smelled it.

"No, I know what their sesame chicken looks like. Little nuggets. This is sesame something else. Let's see what that other one is. We can certainly tell if it's dumplings."

"It's sesame noodles," said Tim.

"That's a bonus. Open this. Maybe it's the dumplings."

"Spare ribs."

"Oh, for Chrissakes. They sent the wrong order. I knew this would happen one day. It's because they've got everything on the damn computer."

"Why don't we eat it anyway? It looks fine. And it all tastes more or less the same."

"But it's not what we wanted. Someone else is having what we wanted."

Tim faced me wearily. "Would you like me to call and have them straighten it out?"

"Oh . . . no. I guess it doesn't pay. You're very hungry, aren't you?"

"I could wait, if it's important to you."

"Never mind. You're right, let's eat it. That's the secret of life, isn't it? To like what you get."

"I don't know about life in general, but this looks okay to me. Come on, Laura, don't take it so hard." He filled his plate eagerly. "And now for the show."

"Tim, you'd make a great Buddhist. You remind me of a story my Tai Chi teacher tells. It's become sort of a joke in the class."

"So, am I going to have to beg you?"

"I wasn't sure you'd be interested. Okay. Long ago there was this Japanese woman who was known far and wide for her wisdom and integrity. Another Buddhist—this one was not so calm—traveled for days to consult her and when he arrived he said, 'What can I do to put my heart at rest?' She told him, 'Every morning and every evening, and whenever anything happens to you, say, "Thanks for everything. I have no complaints whatsoever." ' Well, the man went home and did that for a year, but his heart was still agitated. So he went back, very dejected. 'I did exactly what you said,' he reported, 'but nothing has changed. I'm just as discontented as ever. What should I do?' She said, 'Thanks for everything. I have no complaints whatsoever.' And then, naturally, he was transformed by her wisdom and lived happily ever after."

Tim chuckled. "Very good. I'm in total agreement. No complaints whatsoever, at least about the food."

Ten minutes later he nudged me with his foot. "It's good, isn't it? Admit it, it is good."

"The movie or the food?"

"The food. You're eating it, I see."

"It's tasting bitter," I muttered.

"What do you mean? What's bitter?"

"Nothing. You're right. It's good. But it still isn't what we wanted."

The movie was superb, offering all Tim had promised plus opera, Napoleon, the evils of the slave trade, and many stars in their youth. Afterward we cleaned up the remains of the wrong Chinese dinner and went to bed and made love. "I love you, I love you," Tim whispered. That was quite nice. It always adds something to hear it, even if I was fairly sure he was only temporarily deluded. Or else saying it out of courtesy, a sense that it was necessary or expected. I didn't expect it. Q. rarely said it at those moments but rather when we were up and about. In bed he said other things.

I felt a bit ungracious. "I love you, too," I whispered back. When in

Rome. . . . Don't get me wrong. It was fine making love with Tim. Just fine. Not bad at all.

We lay in each other's arms for a while. Outside, a whirring motorcycle tore through the night. "Did you happen to bring the paper with you?" I asked. "I thought I might read for a while."

"It's in my briefcase. Aren't you sleepy?"

"I slept on and off all day."

"Did you call the doctor yet? Well, what are you waiting for? It's not like you to sleep so much. When was the last time you saw a doctor?"

I shrugged. No point bringing up Dr. A.

"You should get some blood tests and find out what's going on." He shifted around. "Come on, put your head here. I'll hold you and you'll fall asleep and in the morning you'll call a doctor."

Other times he had lulled me to sleep. Tim was good that way. Not tonight, though. "I want to read the *New York Times*," I said sulkily.

Ev and I often read the paper after we made love. Companionably—neither of us felt rejected. The dire events of the day were more palatable in a sexual afterglow. Sometimes after the page-turning and exchanging of sections we made love again.

Tim seemed to be asleep. I got the paper out of his briefcase and took it into the dark living room, where I stood at the window gazing at the park and the river. At first they were indistinguishable masses of shadow, but soon I could make out billowy treetops and ripples in the water beyond, and above that the Palisades, and above that the night sky punctured with stars. I enjoyed the rare stillness and the night landscape taking shape as my vision cleared, and I would like to say that a feeling of peace descended and penetrated me, but it didn't. Peace didn't enter me but drew me. I wanted to drift through the screened window, rise and be part of the night, just another puff of darkness dispersing. I even stood on tiptoe, as if waiting to be lifted off my feet. I wondered if this was what Jilly had felt last year when she burrowed into my chest—as she used to do long ago, frightened of monster shadows on the wall—and moaned that if Jeff, her boyfriend, died after his motorcycle accident, she would like to die, too. I doubt it. It didn't seem something a girl of eighteen could feel. I had had enough, that was all. I wanted an assumption. When Ev died I hadn't wanted to die. I was stunned and listened mutely to what people around me said. The gist of it was, Don't be afraid, you're strong, you'll manage. After a while I began repeating to myself, You're strong, you'll manage. I think now that true or not, it was the wrong message. I don't know what the right message would have been, only that that was wrong.

Suddenly I heard scraping, scratching noises from the south wall, where a streetlight cast a lurid glow on the glass of the French door. Ev used to keep plants on the narrow ledge outside, but they had died shortly after he did. Now the ledge was strewn with leaves, for in summer the building was draped in ivy, and in the leaves a squirrel rustled. I could barely make it out, but the glass reflected the hunched shape and the tiny, distinct hairs of its tail. The hairs shimmered in the light with the stirring of the air. The squirrel's reflection in the door was clearer than the squirrel itself, as if reality were a subsidiary order of things, whose use was to provide the stuff of images.

Squirrels often darted across the ledge with a sense of purpose and destination, perhaps the park across the street or all the way to the river beyond. If they lingered, I had only to tap on the window or the screen and they would skitter off—I don't want them to start feeling at home on my ledge. This time when I tapped, the squirrel looked about bemused, like an old scholar at his desk perturbed at the interruption. Then it walked logily back and forth across the ledge. I thought of those indecisive suicides in movies, tottering while eager spectators gather below. The squirrel was bald in places, its fur patchy and matted. Only the tail was full and plump, like a plume richly feathered in every shade of gray. I had to tap several times before it slunk off.

I sat in the armchair facing the river, with the newspaper on my lap, remembering another rodent skittering across the window ledge, the west ledge, seven years ago. It was spring, soon after we'd moved into this apartment high above the water. I was on the phone with Q. I hadn't spoken to him in months; he'd been away on tour. His voice—Laura, my love—spread through me like honey. Warm, viscous. I took the phone to this same chair and curled up. I wanted to feel through every sense: to bask in the voice and be embraced by the soft chair and fill my eyes with the trees, newly green and spread like lace over the gray, gleaming river. Ev was at his desk in the study; when he worked I didn't exist for him, but that didn't matter now. He, too, had ceased to exist. There was only Q.'s voice, this time from California. I leaned back and gave myself up to its spell.

I've been thinking of you, came the voice. I miss you. All the time I was away, I thought of you.

He told me stories of his travels. He had been to China, to Japan, to Hong Kong. They were doing *Antony and Cleopatra*.

The Chinese stared at us on the street, he said. They kept wanting to take pictures of us. Do you know the two things I longed for most? A glass of orange juice in the morning and the sight of a woman in a short skirt. They do Tai Chi in the parks in the morning, Laura, just like you. You would like that. You could join in. Whenever I saw them waving their arms and legs in that serene and powerful way I thought of you. What did you once tell me it was supposed to feel like? That nice image?

Like pulling silk from a cocoon, I said. One smooth unbroken motion all the way through. If you pull too hard, the teacher says, the strand breaks. You lose the rhythm and the flow of energy breaks.

Yes, yes, I like that, said Q. That's how they all looked. *Proprio così.* Like they were pulling silk from a cocoon.

As he went on and I basked, a rat ran across the window ledge and burrowed in a corner. Not a squirrel; its tail was long and thin, not rich and bushy. I hated it because it distracted me from my pleasure in Q.'s voice.

I went to Tokyo, the voice murmured. I took a bath with hot coals heating up the water. There were piles of fresh towels and a robe waiting for me. I ate in a noodle shop. I watched them cut up the sushi. They are amazingly quick with the blade. Flick, flick, flick.

Normally I would have been horrified at the rat. I would have dashed over to bang on the window and shoo it away, but now I tried not to pay attention. Besides, Q. had called me serene and powerful, more or less. Go away, rat, let me enjoy this.

I went to a Zen temple and tried to meditate, he said, but I can't meditate. I just watch the others. I can look like I'm meditating but I'm really not. I wonder if the Zen masters can tell. What am I saying? Of course they can tell. That's why they're masters.

Make that rat go away, I prayed silently. Not a Taoist prayer, which is a simple affirmation of the way things are, but the ordinary kind, a personal demand. The rat skittered away. It had been there only two or three minutes, time enough to adulterate my pleasure. I wanted to tell Q., so as to rid my mind of it, but I also didn't want to interrupt the spell of his voice. It had been so long since I'd heard it.

I did Antony again in Hong Kong, he said. Everyone there speaks English, you know. It's a British territory, for a little while longer, at any rate. They loved it. They were rapt. When I died there was a hush in the theatre like I'd never heard before. It was my best death ever. The streets are a maze. The whole city is like a carnival. Honky-tonk. Hongy Kong. I miss you, *cara*.

When are you coming to New York? I asked.

I don't know. Next month, maybe.

Did you fall in love lately?

No. I'm never in love. Or always—it's the same thing. He laughed. Not right now. Someone is in love with me, though, a young woman working on the sets. Believe me, I never encouraged her, I don't want any part of it. . . . Her boyfriend is in the cast, which makes it all rather—

Oh, don't, I said. It's just too boring.

You're right. Look, Laura, I want to talk to you. In person, I mean. I have so many things to tell you. I want to hear everything about you. Did you get pregnant again?

No.

Do you want to?

No. I don't know. I'm not sure.

You don't still blame me for that? You know a miscarriage doesn't happen that . . .

No, of course not.

What's the matter? Why are you so quiet? Speak to me. Tell me things. Anything. I want to hear you speak. Is your husband around, is that it?

No, it's that a rat just ran across the window ledge.

A rat? So what? He was on his way somewhere.

It distracted me. I'm starting a new book. It's about a child.

I told him all about the book. As I spoke, its shape began to work itself out, the way a shape in a developing photograph gradually dislodges itself from the void of the background. All I would need to do now was write it down. Because he listened and concentrated, the book took shape. It would be a good book, I could tell, and I rejoiced. With Q. I could do anything.

It sounds wonderful. Write it down just the way you told it to me and it will be perfect, he said.

I know.

Silence.

Sometimes, he said, I think we made a terrible mistake. Or I did.

Yes, you did. Maybe not me.

Is it too late?

I don't know. I think so.

(But I thought the opposite: No, come back, carry me off. Don't ask, just do it. You ask so that I'll release you. But it's you who have the spell. Or is it? Who keeps us this way?)

Don't say that. It makes me unhappy, he said.

You've earned it. Till next time.

I think of you.

I hung up and sat for a long time looking at the river. Finally I walked to the window ledge and saw that in a corner, the rat, or maybe rats, had built a small nest of twigs and hair and lint and ivy leaves. I'd have to clear it away. Not now, the rat might still be in the vicinity. Tomorrow.

Ev came in and paced about, taking a break.

"There's a rat's nest on the ledge, Ev. I saw a rat run across just a few minutes ago."

"Are you sure it was a rat? Maybe it was a squirrel."

I looked at him with bitterness. Q. never doubted me. "I'm sure. I can tell the difference. It had a thin curly tail."

"Sounds like a rat, then." There was no danger that he would ask who was on the phone. He rarely asked me personal questions.

Early the next morning while Ev slept, I got up and put on rubber gloves. Remembering Q. on the phone, I swept the rat's nest into a plastic bag, tied it securely and dropped it in the kitchen garbage can. Ev would take down the garbage. He always did. I suspect his mother trained him, for he seemed to regard the garbage as his particular responsibility, like a dutiful child. After I was done I washed my hands of the rat.

I NEVER READ the paper on the night of the wrong Chinese dinner, but went back to bed after a while and fit my body against Tim's. A cooling wind was rising off the river. When I woke it was almost nine—too late for the Tai Chi class—and I was alone. I thought I recalled Tim kissing me good-bye but I wasn't sure. It might have been a dream, or a memory of some other morning or other kiss. Time no longer feels like a fluid medium carrying the world along, but has become the collapsible, teasing dimension scientists say it truly is. This morning's kiss or some other kiss wasn't the important distinction it once was (though whose kiss still mattered as much as ever). Nor do sleep and waking feel like very different states: they drift close and merge like clouds, blurring boundaries. I walk sleepily through the apartment, and asleep in my ardent bed I dream of writing: long passages about the seaside town where life is, or seems, simpler and more manageable than in the city, the book I'm writing for solace and as a kind of quest, a book for Ev. A book of more words, maybe, than we ever spoke together. I work out intrigues between the characters, little hurts and betrayals, secret loves among the librarians and schoolteachers and fishermen, the Moth Agent, the Constable, the Surveyor of Lumber, the Town Hall Janitor and the one Social Worker. Trysts and confrontations. None of this can I remember when I wake. Sometimes it feels pleasant to have sleep and waking no longer opposite states, just as it was pleasant to discover, as I grew up, that many accepted dichotomies are false: passion and reason, flesh and spirit. But this merging was not the product of mature wisdom. Sleep and waking are different. This was just one more symptom.

On the kitchen counter was a note from Tim. The only other evidence of his passage was the clean glass, the plate he must have used for toast, and the coffee mug resting in the dish rack. His notes to me while I sleep are businesslike, telegraphic; he's used to dealing with secretaries. "Took the bumper to attach on my way, also your screwdriver, just in case. Dinner with clients tonight, I'll phone when I get home, probably late. *Call doctor.* XXX Tim." In style they compare poorly with Ev's; Ev was, after all, a writer. Could he see me from on high he might feel some slight shame that I was seeing a man with no writing style to speak of. It wouldn't help to cite Tim's intelligence and many virtues. To Ev, the notes would be conclusive.

I switched on the radio, my lifeline. No television—I could make my own images. What I needed in the empty house was sounds, voices. Something sprightly and Baroque filled the air with the humming vibrations of the universe. Still there, beyond my private fog.

Then I called the doctor Ev used to see and made an appointment for two weeks off, the earliest they could fit me in. The moment I put the phone down I felt sicker—weak, achy, lost in mist—as if by making the appointment I had granted reality to the illness. It felt more like some evil spell, though. Could Q. be nearby, perhaps at Peter's place in Chelsea, his spirit inhaling and sucking in my energy, that old black magic turned malignant with too much use? I hoped not, for his sake as much as mine, poor Q. He never intended any harm. A prince of a man.

From the front window I could see the Tai Chi class breaking up into small groups in the park below, the teacher and the interpreter walking off together as always. I checked the side window ledge. As I'd feared, the squirrel was back, nestled in a mound of dried ivy twigs and leaves, His body looked unusually hunched, even for a squirrel. My taps on the screen sent a wave of shudders over his rounded back, yet he didn't skitter away. Couldn't, or didn't care any more, or both. He simply peered over his shoulder, showing a beady eye. Did he see me, and if so, what did the sight signify to him? I kicked but not too hard, for fear of breaking the screen: what if he climbed into the living room and settled in? I shuddered, too.

WHEN I DRAGGED MYSELF OUT TO MOVE MY CAR, Luke was leaning into the open hood of his polished maroon Cadillac with the sober, absorbed air of men inspecting their engines. Just as I was about to speak, he straightened up and turned. Like the Tai Chi teacher, he can sense people approaching from behind; it's a matter of feeling vibrations.

"I'm doing okay," he replied to my greeting, "specially now that I have a fine woman like you to rest my old eyes on."

So it was that mood. You never knew. He was quixotic: now preoccupied with business and now paternal; angry at some local injustice or, bound for church Sunday mornings, gravely dapper. I appreciated his flirtatious mode though I was aware that Jilly and her friends would roll their eyes. Unless they'd find it acceptable on the grounds of cultural diversity.

I smiled wanly. "Something wrong with your car?"

"Nah, I'm just looking like I'm tinkering with it because they's giving out tickets early today. They ain't got no mercy lately."

"It must be because the city is broke. They're trying to raise money."

"The city is broke? Well, we's all broke," he commented. Luke never looks broke, though, especially on Sundays in his double-breasted gray suit and gray fedora, ushering his three-generational, elegantly dressed family into the Cadillac. It was in this guise that I met him years ago when I was a newcomer to the block. He introduced himself formally

3 5

and shook hands. Stocky, black, mustached, winning. Mid-fifties or so. (Over sixty, he confided later on.) The local community leader, possibly? Unnervingly good-looking, whatever he was. Days later I saw him in his navy blue super's garb. He also minds cars, that is, moves them from one side of the street to the other at the appointed hours—a thriving business with weekly cash payments; his belt hangs heavy with keys. On most streets this complex auto dance is anarchic, every man for himself, but on ours it's masterminded, as strict as a minuet.

"I saw your boyfriend putting the bumper back on this morning."

"Yes, that was a new wrinkle. He found it lying on the ground. Did you see anyone back into me, by any chance?"

"You know I'da rung your bell if I had, Laura. I was away for a while, had to bring my car in to check the carburetor. These strangers come by, don't know how to parallel park."

"So, you said the cops are lurking?"

"Just round the bend. You better sit in it for a while, it's still early. You're lookin' mighty sweet today."

"Thanks. You don't look so bad yourself."

"Ah, I'm an old fellow now. You shoulda seen me forty, fifty years ago."

I wished I had. Luckily, halfway up the street, a history professor from next door was just pulling out in a very respectable Chrysler. When he saw me he waved and waited. We locals have developed a sensitivity to the gait of people scurrying to move their cars, one of those traits nurtured by environmental demands. I waved back gratefully and moved as fast as I could. How were his wife and daughter, I wondered. Months ago, he'd told me they had some mysterious illness. An epidemic? He looked cheerful enough, so they were probably still alive. I must bear that in mind. I found the bumper securely fastened, looking as if it had never left its post.

Once more to bed, compliant as a milk-filled infant put down for her afternoon nap, as a besotted bride gently nudged yet again onto the mattress. Suddenly came the high-pitched beep of a truck backing up. Like a metronome it beeped with murderous precision, the sound waves oozing through my skin, setting every cell pulsing in response like an audience clapping in rhythm. The beep became my heartbeat, pulsebeat, bloodbeat. Like the muted cooing of pigeons, the electronic beep has something of the toneless, sneakered approach of death. "Man goeth to his long home," read a graveyard inscription Ev showed me up on the Cape, "and the mourners goeth about the streets." The beep was their dirge. My flesh beeped, my skin beeped, I was distilled to a mere echo, and after a while I didn't even long for it to stop. I was wedded to the pain of it, and wonder of wonders, I fell asleep in it and dreamed in it. Q. dreams.

DREAMS BROKEN CLOSE TO MIDNIGHT by the phone. My parents down in Florida in an overturned car, my father's precious glasses shattered? Shouldn't they be tucked in by now, watching Arsenio? I reached out a sandbag arm and picked up.

"Hi, Laura."

"Jilly!" I hadn't felt that spurt of love at the sound of a voice for some time. "Where are you?"

"Let me see. If it's Tuesday this must be . . . Seattle. Yes, I'm pretty sure. I'm in my friend Chrissie's apartment, I know that much."

She was spending the summer going through the country by train and, I feared, hitchhiking, stopping wherever she had friends from college, or friends of friends. Why? To see. To flee. To stay in motion.

"So what's it like, all alone on a train? Do you talk to people?"

"It's great. I've been all over. Colorado, Montana, Washington. I've met lots of people, though there are some you'd rather not talk to, if you know what I mean. Some people are, like, too friendly?"

"I hope you know how to take care of yourself."

"Oh, it's not that. It's not men. Most of the men are with their wives anyway, and they're old couples, fifty, sixty. They want to take care of me, you know? What's a young girl like me—that's what they call me, a young girl, like I was six—doing traveling all by herself? One couple from Wyoming wanted to take me home with them. Then for about three days there was this other old couple sitting behind me. The man was compelled to say everything twice. 'Colorado sure is beautiful,' he would say to his wife. 'Yup, Colorado sure is beautiful.' In the morning when everyone's getting up: 'Honey, have you seen my razor? Honey, have you seen my razor?' And then after he came back from shaving, 'Just look at that bridge! Will you just look at that bridge!' By the time we reached California I was so exasperated I wanted to turn around and say to him, '*Must* you repeat everything twice? *Must* you repeat everything twice?' Anyway, in San Francisco I met my friend Barry. I met my friend Barry. He had his father's car. He had his father's car. We went—"

"Stop!" I laughed. "Enough! Enough!"

"Actually, this guy gave me an idea for a performance piece we could do in the fall at school. Take a play, any well-known play, say, *Hamlet* or *A Streetcar Named Desire*, and perform it with all the lines done twice. After every line there'd be this echo from offstage that would represent, sort of, how after the actor speaks the line, it echoes in the audience's mind? What do you think of that?"

"I think it could take an awfully long time."

"Oh, we'd have a food break, you know, sell sandwiches in between or something," she said blithely.

"Or you could do it with a simultaneous translation into some other language, so it becomes a bilingual version. The way they do with sign language for the deaf."

"Except no one knows languages anymore. Though that might make it even better. So how are you doing, Laura?"

I told her the truth, the whole truth, complete with fevers and chills and all the rest.

"Oh, you poor thing. That's awful."

Ah, joy! Barely into my forties and already longing to be mothered by my child. Not technically my child but I like to pretend she is. My feelings are more simple and easy than a true mother's, and no wonder—I've had mostly weekends and summers, the good times. Jilly doesn't get along very well with her actual mother, which is common enough at nineteen, but I never bad-mouth Margot. It's not so much decency on my part as pragmatism. Someday they'll be reconciled, and I don't want to be rejected in turn as the anti-mother.

Aside from the doctor, Laura, you can do a few things for yourself. Don't smoke, for starters. Eat right. Clean up your act."

Jilly was always big on cleaning things up. Even as a small child, when she came to spend weekends with Ev and me she would straighten her room and make the bed on Sundays, leaving hardly a trace. It was as if she wanted us to think her visit only a happy dream, I used to tell him, from which we must wake sadly on Sunday nights. Or maybe she resented his new marriage as much as Tony did, and was making it clear this wasn't her home. But Ev said ruefully that it was nothing so elaborate, she was just very neat, like her mother.

"It sounds like you might have one of those chronic fatigue viruses," she suggested. "Find out about it. First of all, get a book. Go into your local—"

"Jilly, I know how to get a book. That's one thing I do know how to do."

"A book from a health food store," she continued. "Don't do everything the book says, just what appeals to you? Like, don't give up everything you like to eat. That can be very depressing. For instance, you could go on a macrobiotic diet but I know you, you'd bitch about it and cancel out all the benefits. And while you're there, buy some stuff for energy. Ginseng. Bee pollen."

"Bee pollen?"

"It's very good for you."

"You sound like a witch."

"The Women's Studies program offers a course in witchcraft but I haven't taken it yet."

"I would think it'd be in the chemistry department. It so happens I was in a health food store a few weeks ago. I was passing by when I got these sudden hunger pangs. I thought if I didn't eat something that very minute I'd die, so I got a little box of apricot cookies and ripped them open right there. This terrible musty odor rose up, sort of like dried manure. They were the most awful cookies I ever had. I can't imagine what was in them."

"That's because we're so used to the artificial smells of processed food that we're turned off by the natural smells. Your hunger is probably hypoglycemia. You have to eat often, in small amounts. Take a banana wherever you go. Listen, Laura, I have a great idea for us. Next month we'll go up to the Cape. Grandma and Grandpa promised themselves a break from the tourists this year, so they're going away to some Elderhostel thing, whatever that is, it sounds like a summer camp for senior citizens, and they want someone to take care of the house. I said I'd do it but my mom doesn't want me staying up there alone, so this'll be perfect. Wouldn't it? Remember all those summers?"

Her voice caught and stopped, leaving a silence vast with the night breath of mountains and prairies between us. She was thinking, as was I, of the summers we used to spend there on the sandy soil Ev's family had rooted in for generations, Portuguese immigrants gradually taking on the look and sound of Yankees, losing their men to the sea, and of how her father would plunge the umbrella into the sand as if, like his ancestors, he were staking out a claim, then carry her into deep water and hold her above the waves.

"The ocean has great healing powers," she said, recovering herself. "It's the salt."

Yes, that I could believe. And it smells good, too. "It would be lovely. But they haven't asked me. Maybe they'd feel . . . " Maybe I'd feel . . . is what I mean. Ev's old house, his room, his town, his everything.

"They'll feel fine. They would have asked you sooner or later. You know how they leave things to the last minute. I'll find a waitressing job up there. Or if not I can always pump gas another summer. They hired two extra guys but it's sure to be busy." Ev's parents had a gas station and small convenience store on Route 6. We'd all taken our turns pumping gas. "Come on, say yes. Then I won't have to stay home with my mother and that wimp she married. He keeps cross-examining me about—"

"Uh-oh. I don't like the sound of this, Jilly. I have a feeling your mother won't like it either."

"No, she'll be grateful whether she knows it or not. It makes her tense, having me around. Besides, somebody has to take care of you. I bet that lawyer isn't any use." Outsiders interfered with Jilly's storybook vision of her father and me. She'd be horrified if she knew about Q. She also had no idea how hopeless Ev would have been with illness. He'd have managed to get sent to Peru to cover El Sendero Luminoso rather than act as nurse.

"He does what he can." I told her how Tim rescued my bumper but she seemed unimpressed.

"Okay, we'll figure out the details later. I've got to go. That's Call Waiting."

The sea. A month with Jilly. A future that mirrored the past. Would I be able to swim or take long walks or ride a bike as we did in our early days? Ev taught Jilly to ride the waves. I taught her to float in the salty bay. We watched the tides move in and out in their comforting motion, always the same yet always slightly different, an inexhaustible range of nuance as in a dance—same steps and pattern but each performance unique, depending on the breath and energy of the dancers and the mood of the air embracing them. I'd watch the tides again, this time without imagining my future mysteriously contained in their patterns, unknown and thrilling, sometimes frightening. That future was the past now.

I could work up there, gather data for the book about Ev's town. It wasn't coming to me at all here in New York, but on its home ground it would invent itself, from the taste of the air and roll of the water, the history and the hills. Like the Samurai creed in the book the Tai Chi teacher gave me: "I have no design; I make opportunity my design."

An eerie stiffness crept up my arms and legs, as if they were slowly sinking into a granular state. I pictured the inner landscape, its clotted waterways. Not quite stone. Pre-stone. Sand. I tested each arm and leg to make sure they still moved. Yes, but they were astonishingly heavy. A sandbag woman, body on its way to stone.

41

The phone rang again. What now?

Laura, my love. Did I wake you?

Q.

It's been bedlam here at Peter's. That's why I'm calling so late. I'm sorry if I scared you.

He'd been in town for three days, working, staying as usual at his ex-brother-in-law's place in Chelsea, and he had an excellent excuse for not having called sooner—only a venial sin on his permanent record card. Chaos and grief filled the apartment. Peter's lover, Arthur, was in the hospital, dying.

It's dreadful, Laura. I mean, Arthur, of all people. I've known him so long. He and Peter lasted longer than Susan and I did. I knew he was HIV positive—remember, I must have told you—but he'd been okay for years. . . . Then it hit all at once.

That's awful. Is this really the end or can they keep him going awhile?

I doubt it. I haven't seen him, they're not letting visitors in, but Peter says he won't be coming home. He's in a wild state. He says he can't bear the apartment without Arthur in it. He found a place a few blocks away and he's packing madly. Maybe it's a way of avoiding his grief.

Oh, the apartment. I always thought of it as ours—I mean years ago.

I know, said Q. I can't imagine not having it to go to either. But maybe we could get used to the new one. He cries while he packs, and hurls things around, you know, photos, mementos, stuff like that.

It doesn't sound like avoidance.

I guess not. In between packing he goes to the hospital. He's neglecting the store. When I come back at night I have to hold him in my arms while he cries some more. It's very unlike Peter. You know how he is.

(Yes, I do. Close-mouthed. Prim, the pair of them. Over the years I'd run into them when rendezvousing with Q. Not often, though. Peter owns a rare-books store and Arthur was an editor at a business magazine, so that Q., when he visited, had the place to himself most days. Still, we were careful. When they turned up we managed to be drinking tea in the living room, conversing decorously. Only once was there a close call. Shit, I forgot, said Q. as we tore off our clothes with one hand each. Peter's coming home at four. Oh, I said. And what time is it now? He climbed over me to pull a watch out of the night table drawer. Twenty to four. We'll manage, I said cavalierly. But Laura, he moaned, it takes time to get dressed and make the tea. About six minutes, I said. He set upon me, laughing and grunting. He'll be here in ten minutes, he moaned. Peter's compulsively prompt. So what? I said. The door is closed. I'm shy about these things, said Q. I was married to his sister, remember. And he's so proper. Don't rush me, I said, giggling, it sets me back. Less is more, as in art. Oh, shush, Laura. *Basta.* This is no time for intellect. Think porn.

(At four o'clock Peter found us in the living room, dressed and reading from a script. There hadn't been time to make the tea. We often read. I would be Q.'s straight man as he went over his lines. *Happy Days,* I believe it was, in which Beckett, though it was surely not his primary intention, captures the essence of latter-day marriage: the women is buried up to her neck in sand and the man seems not to notice.)

I can't describe what's been going on here the last few days, said Q. Friends are in and out. Plus the movers, giving estimates. But listen, Laura, come tomorrow. No, wait. Not tomorrow. Susan is coming to see Peter. You don't want to meet up with her. The day after.

I'll have to call in the morning and let you know if I'm up to it. I can't say definitely.

Please say definitely, Laura. I need to see you and my dance card is getting all filled up, as it were.

Your dance card. Your dance card! Are you telling me you're going to have to fit me in?

It's just an expression. Come on, don't get on your high horse. I'm dying to see you.

You can just die then, and they can bury your dance card with you.

Jesus, you're touchy. More than ever. What's wrong? Are you sick?

I'll tell you when I see you.

Tell me now.

No.

All right, forgive me, then. It was an unfortunate remark.

I forgave him. I knew his needs. Like a giant doomed to eat damsels, Q. must fill a vast daily quota of attention and adulation from varied sources. In a small town he might run out of people, but by keeping in constant motion, he's in no such danger. The only danger is to those suppliers of attention who expect some continuity of response, who fail to understand that for Q. people are an inexhaustible natural resource for his sustenance and delight, like air or water or sunshine. You are my sunshine, he sang to me in jovial moments; not for a long time did I realize he meant it literally.

Okay, then, you'll come. Because I must tell you about this movie I'm in. It's silly but fun. I play a righteous cop. Can you imagine? I never played a cop before. I have to get into a cop mentality. You can help me.

Me? I'm no expert on cops. Just because of—

No, no, I didn't mean because of that. I mean you're strict. You have principles. That's a start.

Q threads through my life like an unusual color in a tapestry or a swatch in a cape of many colors. Or I might say Q. is the wild card in an otherwise ordinary deck. Or, with Q. I lead a life parallel to my visible one, of another order of reality, metaphorical, where people do not speak in quotation marks but fluidly, tongue to tongue, no translation required.

Q., as you know, is an actor. Not a star, but familiar to people who care about the theatre and remember the actors. Years before I met him, he played bit parts and picked up money as actors do, working as a tour guide, a carpenter, a bouncer. Fortunately his wife, Susan, was a kindergarten teacher with a steady income. Since we met, he has rarely languished for want of work. He thinks I brought him luck by some witchy power, and also watered his talent, but I make no such claims.

Anyhow, if I called him by his complete and multisyllabic Italian name, you might recognize it and I don't want that. To his friends he's Quinn, which is his middle name and his mother's family name. He was born of the highly volatile combination of an Irish mother and an Italian father who met in Milan, where his mother was studying opera. She had a splendid voice, Q. tells me, and he's inherited a musical bent, though his voice is not splendid, only large and serviceable. His father was in the diplomatic corps (Q. has inherited the diplomatic gifts, too) and was posted to Washington when Q. was about ten. There they remained. When he's angry at the government for its aggressions and intrusions, he'll say he's not really American and wants no part of it, but it's not true—anyone here over forty years is part of it.

His mother was often traveling with small opera companies and his father was busy with whatever diplomats of friendly, comparatively powerless nations find to do in Washington, so Q. considers that he brought himself up as well as his younger sister, Gemma. For all his diplomacy and charm, he does have the improvisational behavior of the self-taught—mobile, adaptable, a relativist. I call him unreliable. He says he lives in the moment.

He speaks English like no one else, and that uniqueness is one of the traits which kept me spellbound. You can't quite call it an accent; English is, after all, one of his mother tongues, his mother's tongue. But there's a hint of a brogue along with a slight foreignness, not in the pronunciation of words but in their cadences. He's rarely at a loss for words, but when he's very tired, or very passionate, a wisp of an Italian accent will creep in, ghost vowels hovering around the edges of the audible syllables. With such fluidity he can do any sort of accent, which directors appreciate.

I like calling him Q. as I write, not simply because Q. stands for question and in my life he has always been a question in the sense of a riddle or something unfinished. He's also a question in the sense of an issue. More vulgarly, he's a questionable character; his behavior is questionable and by association, mine has been, too.

But his success: why, when so many actors are out of work, is Q. always working, aside from any spells I unwittingly wrought? Talented, no question about that, but no more than dozens of unemployed actors. The answer is that Q. can turn himself or be turned into nearly anyone. He's big and tends toward the beefy—good for fathers, businessmen, royalty, workmen—but he can slim down at a week's notice to become a romantic hero or sober schoolteacher or earnest politician. Delicate and fey, no. Never Richard II. Bolingbroke, yes. He's dark but not too dark, with large assertive features (they can be toned down with makeup). His coarse hair, once chestnut, is peppered with gray, but that's easily fixed. He can be made to resemble most any ethnic type (Othello, Zapata, Lopakhin). He has an antic disposition and can do farce—Vladimir in *Waiting for Godot*—more naturally than tragedy, but *Lear* is his dream. He sings and dances. Buffalo Bill in *Annie Get Your Gun*, a cowboy in *Oklahoma*, though Poor Judd would have been more in his line. In grade-B movies he's frequently a gangster, a bartender, or a lawyer in an expensive suit who's fought his way up from the slums. He's been a surgeon, though not, I think, very persuasively, as well as a ship's captain, a union organizer, and once a priest. Enough, you get the idea.

I wanted to be on the stage, too. I was twenty-five, avoiding my own words by speaking the words of others. This, to his eternal credit, Q. pointed out. He was the lead in a Noël Coward–like comedy; I wore a uniform and carried in a tea tray and probably wouldn't have gotten much farther. I didn't like him—too loud and insistent—but he won me over. Plied me with cups of tea. Phoned at all hours. Wooed. He taught me how to say my lines and how to move and carry the tray. Endlessly, in my walk-up apartment in the Village, he demonstrated my small role, transforming himself into an Irish maid while I laughed. But he was right, he knew exactly how it should be done. I was grateful. I fell under his spell. And finally, finally, when I was wondering if he'd ever get around to it, he kissed me. I never dreamed he was married; he had all the time in the world, never dashing home like some married people in the cast.

I was the woman he had always dreamed of without knowing it, he said. We were halves of an egg. He loved to hear me talk, he said. Plus he had to tell me everything that happened to him. (This he still does.) It would be agony, he said, but he would leave Susan. Don't think a person can't love two people at once, he said as we lay in my bed, exhausted, as many surfaces touching as possible. There were no questions, then. We were tied together, like the performance artists experimenting with boundaries. It was as if I had waited all my life for the rope. Except we touched. How we touched. It kills me to remember. Not because it was a crazy way to be—what do I care for craziness? Because I had that once and lost it.

Under his spell I understood that this would be my last little part in a little play. I started writing. Because of what he showed me, he is mine forever. I can forgive him almost anything.

And what did I do? Freed him, he said. From what, for what? If that's true, then it was a bad piece of business I did.

He would leave her. But it couldn't be done crudely, abruptly. No, ever the gentleman, a prince of a man. There were the children, too. Four, good grief. All girls. Teenagers, for he was old, at least he seemed so then, pushing forty. I didn't care about them. What were children? I cared only about having him.

He would leave her. But not when her younger brother was drowned in a boating accident. And not when Carla was going through drug therapy or Jessica was applying to college or Renata, only fifteen, needed an abortion. For two years he waited for the right moment until one day I hit him. I need my life, I said. You're holding on to it so I can't use it. Get out, I screamed, I never want to see you or hear your name again. He didn't hit back. He went, skulking like a whipped dog, closing the door very silently. I felt my heart crack but paid no attention. How could I have loved that contemptible creature! Get that dog out of my life.

I made an ill-considered marriage, as might be expected. First of all, he was much too thin. That thinness or sparseness was the clue to what was wrong about our marriage. There wasn't enough of him. Enough for him on his own perhaps, but too meager to give any away. It was as if what was missing, the weight needed to flesh out the bones, was somewhere in the ether waiting to be summoned into material existence. Very thin people make me suspicious. I suspect an unwillingness to absorb and assimilate what life offers. Though literally speaking, Ev ate enough; it just didn't seem to add to him. I didn't think much about any of this when I married him. It was like making an investment on a hunch that the stock will grow, because you're eager to start the money working for you. Then the hunch turns out to be mistaken. I really didn't think at all and married out of desolation and spite.

It was at a party held to celebrate my first book that I noticed Ev, a party I couldn't enjoy because my heart had broken. I knew the precise moment it cracked, the way a rib or an elbow cracks—when I threw Q. out and he skulked away, shutting the door behind him ever so quietly as if he were afraid to increase my wrath. The crack occurred at the sound of the door softly clicking into place. So at the party I was moving gingerly: the two halves of my heart, which I pictured as the jagged halves of a greeting-card Valentine, would hold together only if I was careful not to jolt them. Still, I intended to pursue my life. I was twenty-seven, far too young and strong to retire on a broken heart. I gazed around and spied a man whose head rose above the others so that I thought at first he might be standing on a chair. He was pale and gray-eyed and bearded. Good, different from Q. Though like Q. he seemed fired by energy, a convoluted energy, directed inward.

"Who is that tall man?" I asked my editor, Gretchen, a curly-haired motherly woman known for her austere and exacting literary tastes. She kept bringing me little bits of cheese and broccoli on cocktail napkins and urging me to enjoy myself.

"I don't know but I'll find out." She scooted away and returned in three minutes. "His name is Everett Acosta. He used to write for the Boston *Globe* and is supposed to be very good. Just moved to New York. He's married"—she gave an exaggerated pout—"but recently separated from his wife," and she smiled goofily. "He's here because Joe Barton is courting him. Wants him to do a book about Cuba. He's covered El Salvador and Nicaragua. To these boy editors, El Salvador, Cuba, it's all the same."

"How did you find all this out so quickly?"

"Nothing to it. Want to meet him? Come along."

I left the party with him and we had dinner, one of those long, late, slightly tipsy dinners when intimate details flicker unexpectedly like fireflies on summer nights, glimmering, tantalizing. Everyone knows it's easy to confide in a stranger you may never see again. If it happens that we do see the stranger again, that we even make him a friend or lover, it's just as well to have gotten some secrets over with early, when we're less likely to be blamed or judged for them. I think now that Ev was offering a few easy confidences so he wouldn't have to offer much in the future, if there was a future, and could coast comfortably onward. For the rest of his life, as it turned out. That first dinner might have been our most intimate time together.

He seemed a sad man. He instinctively bent his head at the doorway of the restaurant even though it was high enough to accommodate him. Yet attractive, too, as sad men can be. I assumed he was sad because he had separated from his wife only three months earlier and left two young children, a girl of four and a boy of ten. He smiled seldom and when he did it was a rueful half-smile, but speaking of his children he smiled, at last, without the aroma of rue. That was a point in his favor. I was already totting up points and hoping he would come out with well above a passing grade.

I did, at that first dinner, what women invariably do and will no doubt do forever, regardless of feminist theory. I got him to talk of what he cared about. Sometimes this takes some groping, but with Ev it was easy. Politics. He described his trips to Central America. "You get used to seeing children in uniforms guarding public buildings with machine guns at their hips," he said. I was impressed. I romanticized it—not the children, but Ev's familiarity with such sights. I imagined that from getting used to such sights he had deep knowledge. He did, of a sort. Of politics, that was all. Nothing romantic.

In college he had been a runner. The track team, he told me as we sat in the restaurant, called him the Flying Feather. Because he was so thin and so tall, I was curious about what he might look like without his clothes, and as if he could read my mind, I tried to suppress my curiosity. I was used to Q.'s reading my mind and reveled in it. Reading each other's minds had been an antidote to the common notion that we live trapped in our solitudes, a notion I'm sure Ev held. I never told him I had proof to the contrary. I didn't know, when I thought furtively about what he might look like without his clothes, that Ev had no interest whatsoever in reading my mind, indeed wouldn't think of another's mind as something that might be read or that one might wish to read.

"Why did you and your wife separate?" I asked.

"She didn't want to go on with it," he replied, delicately spearing the meat out of the claw of a lobster. I liked watching him eat the lobster—he didn't refuse to accept that particular one of life's offerings. But he didn't eat red meat. He was fastidious, I later found, not moralistic. He didn't like the look of blood. I think he must have regarded my roast beef, that first night, with distaste, though he was far too polite to comment on my tastes, ever. I don't think he ever knew my tastes, as a matter of fact, or thought of people as collections of tastes, as I tend to do.

"Why not?"

He looked at me forthrightly, the whites of his eyes clear and innocent as porcelain. This, too, was good. It bespoke candor and simplicity. Q. also was candid, God knows, but hardly simple. "I don't know."

That should have alerted me, but I was young and walking around gingerly to keep the pieces of my heart together instead of using my brains. Later, when I learned his wife was a psychiatrist, I was willing to bet she had told him in analytic detail exactly why she didn't want to go on. Perhaps he didn't understand her reasons, or understood but didn't consider them sufficient to end a marriage. More likely he didn't care to tell me. I actually never knew what he felt about anything and sometimes suspected he didn't either, or didn't want to know. Maybe he lost sight of her reasons, in the mist of sadness.

"Are you still in love with her?"

Again the candid look. He was standing up well under my deliberately indiscreet questioning. "I'm not sure," he said with an awkward, self-deprecating smile. After Q.'s theatrics and virtuosity at dialogue, I found Ev's hesitations, even his sadness, trustworthy signs. I made many such mistakes. I thought anything that was not Q. would be salutary. That is how blind and broken I was.

"She used to say that every appetite passes in twenty minutes," he volunteered, grinning again, and I grinned along with him.

"Is that so? What else?"

"Let's see. She arranged the bathroom so that nothing was visible except the absolute essentials like soap, towels, toilet paper. She even found a little contraption that hid the toilet paper. All the everyday stuff, toothpaste, deodorant, was in cabinets, so it looked as though we had no bodily needs."

I was entranced. Those were the early days of my data bank. I pushed on, but that was all he had to say.

He insisted on taking me home in a cab. I didn't ask him in and he didn't seem to expect it. As I undressed for bed I reviewed what I liked about him. His tallness, his awkwardness, his devotion to his children, his politics, the clear whites of his eyes, and his skill in extracting the meat from the lobster, perhaps from having grown up on Cape Cod. Above all, he didn't seem awed by my having written a book or by my possessing opinions and delivering them forcefully. (Q. hadn't been put off by that either, except that those latter qualities, he once explained, deprived me of magic. Women, I gathered, were supposed to be mysterious. I could never figure it out. Q. loved to hear what I thought, he implored me to tell him, but when I obliged, there was no mystery left. Or so he said. I never felt mystery was a matter of words.)

Was that list enough to like? Sure. Not for marriage—I wasn't dreaming of marriage then—but for diversion. Recuperation. If he called. I wasn't sure he would, nor did it matter much. Just an evening off from brooding over Q. Practice for a future.

He courted me with shy, fumbling grace, like someone who doesn't quite know the steps to a dance but tries to follow, faking a bit. When I realized what he was attempting I helped him along, since my instinct is to help in socially awkward situations. I made it easy, led him through the steps. I was fascinated when he peeled off his clothes, like peeling a banana. He looked like a Mannerist rendering of Jesus about to be hoisted onto the cross. Beautiful in his way. We made such an incongruous pair—I'm not the austere type—that I wanted to call up Q. and joke about it: Hey, I'm sleeping with this guy who looks like Jesus Christ. A man of sorrows. But of course telling Q. was unthinkable. I never wanted to see him again, the dog. Who could foresee that in years to come Q. would do just that, call to tell me about his latest loves. In character, I should point out, Ev was nothing like Jesus Christ, only in appearance, angular and sorrowful.

Months later, meeting his parents, I decided he might be congenitally sad. They came down from the Cape to spend a few days in New York, tall and thin and sad just like Ev. Not sad in the sense of morose or displeased. Sad in a deeper way, as if nothing they did or saw could distract them from the sad truth of life's ultimate futility. And when Ev took me to see the house where he grew up, in the town washed by the sea and the bay, I learned one reason for the sadness, a good enough reason in itself yet so far in the past that I thought it should have lost its force. Maybe it wasn't the real reason.

His parents visited us several times after we were married, and I tried to make them happy by cooking good dinners and taking them to musical comedies and for walks along the river, but though they said they were having a fine time, nothing could dispel the sadness beneath. Listen, I wanted to tell them, we all know about life's ultimate futility. Surely you can put it aside for a few hours and enjoy yourselves. But apparently not. After a while I decided that whatever the reason, it was their pleasure to be sad and they had passed it on to Ev, and why should I presume to interfere? He was an only child, born after his parents had been married many years, and maybe their cellular exhaustion made him sad as well, in which case each new sadness that befell him was added to the original store, spreading itself through the entire long length of him.

He moved wraith-like everywhere, yet attracting attention because he was so tall. I once asked if it didn't hinder him as a reporter, being so noticeable, and he said, with the half-smile that tinged his simplest remarks with the aroma of rue, that maybe it did, surely it would were he on a secret assignment, that is, pretending to be other than a reporter. "I suppose I couldn't be a spy. Spies should be nondescript." "But would you even want to be a spy?" I asked. "No. Not with the world as it is." He paused, as always, between sentences. Did he mean if the world were otherwise he might want to be a spy? I often had cause to wonder about those pauses, and decided he was formulating his next thought, for he rarely spoke without thinking first. Yet his next words might be matter-of-fact, nothing that required formulating. "I think I'd make a good spy, though, otherwise." Implied but unsaid was the question, What do you think? "Yes, an excellent spy," I said obligingly.

He moved wraith-like through our marriage, through his life and his death. I was surprised, I am still surprised, and affronted, that the bullet was able to find him. He seemed too unsolid to be a good target, but then he wasn't a target; he was hit by accident. I've often pictured the bullets whizzing on the grubby Bronx street where the cops staged an impromptu helicopter raid, swooping down on drug dealers, and where Ev was investigating a story about those dealers. In my visions I make him turn sideways and offer his papery profile, eluding the bullet. In reality, he must have looked around with his startled, monkish air, squinting in alarm. He must have presumed he could be a spectator, since as he liked to tell me, his life was undramatic. His death made up for that.

It wasn't an awful marriage, simply a marriage that didn't begin to explore what marriage might be. If Q. and I were lashed by some invisible rope, Ev and I were divided by the finest of screens. He's more vivid dead than alive because the screen—his screen—is gone: he can't keep from being seen. I insist on trying to see him, inventing a life for him. Guilt, you may say. But not guilt over Q. I don't hold that conventional view. Guilt because I didn't insist on seeing him, on tearing away the screen, while he was alive. I was preoccupied elsewhere.

So I can't say I knew him very well. I was married to him for eleven years, until he was shot in the street; I tried to know him, and then at some point I stopped trying.

It wasn't a marriage without love, either. It was an affectionate, functional union. I loved him not just for appealing qualities like his tallness or his decency or his exemplary politics or his respect for my privacy, but because my life was attached to his, and young as I was, I knew it is essential to love your life or else change it. I couldn't or didn't wish to change it so I willed myself to love it. For years we sat companionably working on opposite sides of the room. I would go off to a closet-like room to write, but I could read and prepare classes with him nearby. He liked my presence and could work under any conditions. Only sometimes the silence got to me.

He never asked much about me. He rarely asked questions when he wasn't working, maybe because as a reporter he had to ask so many, and time off meant not asking any questions. I told him a few things nonetheless, out of courtesy. Fairness. If he lived with me, there were a few things he ought to know about. Such as Q. Besides, I understood later, I liked to shape stories about myself and Q. I liked the idea of being part of a story. The version, especially, in which I played the role of wronged innocent—snared, enchanted, held prisoner by a spell—made it possible for me to live with the outcome. Or what I thought then was the outcome. I couldn't foresee that there would be outcome after outcome.

I didn't tell Ev his full name because I thought that, working at a newspaper, he might recognize it. I didn't want him attaching my story to a specific known quantity, for that might weaken my version of it.

He heard me out patiently, occasionally giving his rueful half-smile. That was all. And the silence grew, broken by the children, Tony and Jilly, who came down from Boston by train every fourth weekend. Ev or I or sometimes both of us would pick them up at Penn Station on Friday nights. Tony was eleven when the trips began, and they continued for years, until he refused to come anymore and Jilly had to manage on her own. They would step off the train, two valiant children, glancing around for us. Tony was protective of Jilly, who was just five; he gripped her hand firmly and sometimes even carried her to keep her up out of the crowd. He looked apprehensive, not of the strangers or the escalator or the bustle, but of the responsibility vested in him. I told Ev they were too young to travel alone, but he and his ex-wife, Margot, the psychiatrist, thought otherwise. She planned the trips carefully, as she did everything, packing healthy snacks and thermoses of apple juice. She gave Tony money for emergency taxis and phone calls, and tucked some bills in Jilly's pocket, too, in the unlikely event that they got separated, along with a slip of paper with Ev's name, address and phone number. She even gave them instructions about going to the bathroom. If Tony had to go, he was to ask a nice lady nearby to keep an eye on Jilly. If Jilly had to go, he was to stand in the corridor outside the unlocked door, because doors on train lavatories are tricky and Jilly was afraid of getting locked in places. With all those precautions, I still thought it wasn't a good idea.

Often I have wondered if it was the strain of those monthly trips that made Tony dislike me so, for he must have believed, erroneously, that if not for me his father would be living in Boston. He didn't complain much (though when he did it was at the most inopportune moments, such as while I was cooking dinner), but I could read resentment in the set of his shoulders. Jilly always looked eager for adventure: she had a round rosy face and dark curls flopping around her head, giving her the look of a wild child. I was surprised, from what I had heard of her mother, that the hair was not smoothed down and disciplined by barrettes. Her eyes gleamed with intrigue, as if she would willingly go off with any of her fellow passengers at the merest suggestion.

We had a room fixed up for them and spent the weekends doing what we hoped they would enjoy, but because Jilly was so small it often happened, especially in winter, that Ev took Tony on excursions while I stayed home reading her stories and baking cookies and playing with clay and beads, or watching her prance around in my hats and high-heeled shoes, gobs of makeup anointing her face. We acted out fairy tales about witches and princesses and fairy godmothers, and when Ev and Tony returned from their wanderings I'd be faintly abashed to be discovered hunched as a crone, a shawl draped over my head, locking Rapunzel in her tower room—an armchair piled with pillows—or tucked in bed while Jilly tripped about with a red scarf for a hood and a basket of fruit on her arm. We could have used someone to play the Prince or the wolf, but Ev only smiled vaguely and ruefully, his eyes tearing from the cold, raw pink patches on his pale cheeks, and Tony, lean and ascetic like his father, glanced at us with disdain while streaking blackened snow across the floor.

One Sunday evening after we'd taken the children to the station we went to a movie, and there on the screen briefly flashed Q., to my shock and dismay: I was so out of touch, I didn't even know what he was doing. I, who used to know everything! He was playing a pastry chef in a fancy restaurant.

I couldn't keep still. I nudged Ev. "That is the man," I said. "The actor I told you about. The prince who turned out to be a frog." I spoke impulsively, as I tend to do. I was feeling full of life, free of the past. Maybe I thought, too, that I'd get a rise out of Ev, for I was getting frustrated at his impassivity but not yet grasping where my frustration came from.

"Mmm," he grunted.

I felt myself deflate, as if my clothes were caving in around the space that used to hold my body. I temporized. He didn't like to talk during movies. It was gauche of me to blurt it out. He was more sensitive than he appeared. Jealous? Q. didn't show up to advantage in his white chef's hat and silly accent. Was Ev jarred to find that this was the man his wife had been so foolish about?

There rose in me a gust of desire to defend Q., to declare how magnificent and inspiring he was, even to boast of how women were drawn to him, not a quality I had ever before considered an asset. Surely he was not to be judged by a bit part in a comic murder mystery. But I kept quiet. Ev might be waiting until later to ask what it meant to me, seeing him loom so unexpectedly on the screen. Was I shaken or stirred or infuriated or what? And I would say no, none of the above, merely startled, for it was all over with Q., and in any case it was Q. playing a role, something he did so well that the real man was barely discernible. All I felt, besides admiration for his skill, was amusement at seeing a pastry chef with the familiar lineaments of Q.'s face and body.

But after we left the theatre Ev said nothing. I understood, then, that he would say nothing most of the time. He would listen; he would never ask. If I complained of his lack of curiosity, he'd call it politeness, discretion, as if any fool should appreciate that.

I didn't appreciate politeness or discretion. I wanted what I had had with Q. A form of neurosis, a boundary problem, Ev's ex-wife the psychiatrist would no doubt call it, but it made us happy. In the end, Ev's not asking about Q. drove me to thoughts of him which the image on the screen alone had not provoked. And the silence grew.

Do something about it, Jilly said. The nearest health food store is a few blocks down Broadway. Its windows flaunt posters about foot massages and aids to flawless digestion and sexual virility. As soon as I'm well inside, strolling down the aisles of grains and rainbow-hued juices, the odor of sanctity—flat and dusty, earthy but without earth's moist, loamy richness—makes me want to rush out and sin. It's a flimsy, stingy smell, like a wasps' nest rotting behind a wall or a mess of cobwebs tangled on the mop. A smell that may signify the freedom guaranteed on many of the labels: wheat-free, sugar-free, yeast-free, fat-free. Freedom, my generation was told, means nothing left to lose, and here the lesson has been learned well. The smell calls to mind a style of writing practiced by some of my colleagues: metaphor-free, emotion-free, meaning-free, form-free, suggesting that the writers are knowledge-free and talent-free.

"I'd like some vitamins, please," I announce to the young woman behind the counter: dark skin, hair in impeccable corn rows fastened by colorful beads, taut shoulder and arm muscles. The picture of health, a fine advertisement for the wares, but her eyes as she reluctantly looks up from her book—such rage can't be healthy.

"What kind?"

"I'm not sure. A pill that has all the vitamins together. Something to give me energy."

"What you want is a multi," and she turns, reaching a long balletic arm behind her to pick a brown jar off the shelf and set it before me. Near the cash register is a small placard lauding the strengthening effects of bee pollen. That has a nice sound to it—nectar, honey. Yes, Jilly mentioned it.

"Is that bee pollen any good? For energy, I mean?"

"Sure." She shrugs.

I take a jar; it's in tablet form, not sticky, as I imagined. What next? This isn't going as well as I'd hoped. A stranger in a strange land, I'm not finding succor. The hollow smell of health is making me slightly woozy. No place to sit down except the stool behind the counter where the clerk is perched with her paperback copy of *Beloved,* and I'd rather not ask her. I try rooting my feet as the Tai Chi teacher counsels, to feel the rushing spring from the earth. Surely it can penetrate the floorboards of the health food store.

After a while I find a rack of books and pamphlets against a back wall. Aha, not a strange land. Let's pretend it's a musty library. Most of the pages are given over to recipes—ingenious ways of disguising tofu. But here's one book, *Take Your Health in Your Hands,* that's recipe-free and moreover includes a chapter on Creative Visualizing. Well, fine. That sounds like something I can do. The gist of it is that you can conquer or at least weaken whatever plagues you, from the common cold to AIDS or cancer, by envisioning your body's good warrior cells destroying the bad invading cells in a pitched battle, using little swords or little bombs or machine guns or whatever toy implements strike your fancy. What a curious leap. We've been instructed about the dangers of seeing illness as metaphor, and now here's cure as metaphor, too.

I skim the examples of efficacious visions, bits of a microcosmic *Iliad,* and the writing isn't half bad, either. I wouldn't go so far as to buy the book, especially as it's the sort of thing that drives my work out of the marketplace, but I read enough to get the idea.

Outside, the sun is aglow in a radiant sky, the streets crowded with people in scant, brightly colored clothing. Plenty of Saturday afternoon traffic, and a red light catches me in Broadway's center mall between northbound and south. What a falling-off. I can't easily defy the flashing Don't Walk sign and dash across in front of oncoming cars. These are honorable skills in the quintessential New York game of driver versus pedestrian, and losing them is ignominious, like losing teeth or hair or potency. Waiting for the light to change, like a tourist!

On my left, three homeless people sit on a bench, perhaps feeling as sick as I do. One man wears heavy winter clothes and drinks coffee from a Styrofoam cup. Another is curled up, shirtless and barefoot. A woman sits apart, gripping a shopping cart that holds a bulging plastic bag. There's some room on the bench. No, not yet. Give it a few months.

Suddenly we're all jolted as a glossy black convertible thunders down Broadway, crammed with teenage suburban jocks slumming in the city, the radio blasting voices and drums from hell. The buildings on either side tremble at the sound, the shop signs sway, glimmering in the sun, the asphalt of the street quivers and the traffic light swings on its cable. Louder, I can't hear it, I'm always tempted to shout. But we don't. We don't know what they might be carrying in the car or what they might be on.

I don't shout. Only silently, from the battlefield under my skin, I shout, Die. I hope you die. It echoes through the channels and caverns of my body. Just for the hell of it I wish all the other drivers dead, too, for the crime of moving blithely along in fine health while I wait for the light to change. Die, so I can cross the street. It's so energizing that I wish it on everyone in sight, from the beggars at the newsstand to the young mothers pushing strollers and licking frozen yogurts. Why don't you all just die and get out of my way.

I'm a little horrified, not so much at the vengeful wishes but at how easily they come, how I take them in stride. All at once I stiffen, recalling the strange case of Dr. B.

I met Dr. B. shortly after Ev was killed. My sore throat had passed, thanks to Dr. A.'s antibiotics, but it left a tightness, as if something were stuck, something I couldn't swallow or bring back up either. Ev's old doctor sent me to Dr. B., who he said was a South American photographer-doctor, to get pictures of my esophagus in action. Wearing a powder-blue paper robe, I shivered for so long in a curtained cubicle that I thought I'd been forgotten. At last an acolyte led me into the presence of a tall, elegant man who looked so much like Vargas Llosa, the renowned Peruvian novelist, that for a moment I thought Vargas Llosa, who after all had recently had an abortive career in politics, might now be trying medicine as a sideline; we might even discuss his novels. He shook my hand and in his suave accent said, "I am going to mix you a little cocktail. It looks like a strawberry malted."

The cocktail was made of barium, and the idea was that as I ingested it, sip by sip, he would take pictures of its swift and slippery progress down my esophagus.

"Now take a sip. Now hold it in your mouth. Now—swallow! Swallow, swallow, swallow!" he commanded again and again.

I did my best to obey as Dr. B., behind cumbersome machinery, snapped away.

"You're not swallowing right," he snapped. "You have to try harder!" He was undergoing a transformation: his charm was evaporating and he was definitely not Vargas Llosa. He was rather like those chameleon continental types in movies—Charles Boyer comes to mind—who can turn menacing in the space of a breath. "Swallow exactly when I tell you, not before and not after. Now! Sip, hold it in your mouth—swallow! Bigger sip. Big sip and . . . swallow! Swallow!"

Dirk Bogarde, the fashion photographer in *Darling*, also snapped pictures of captive Julie Christie at an alarming rate: Now smile, pout, toss your head, good girl, smile! Quick, quick, more, more! And Julie Christie tosses her wonderful hair, pouts, narrows her eyes; everything she possesses, all her blood secrets, come rushing to her face like a blush, making her lips swell, darken, and tremble; her eyes glint; the lush sleek hair sings arias.

I, however, was not a professional.

"Swallow, and . . . swallow! You're not cooperating! If you don't cooperate you'll have to drink more," he threatened.

"I'm doing my best. Tell me how you want it done and I'll try to do it." I imagined neophyte prostitutes saying those words to far-out customers.

"Yes, well, all right, never mind. You can get dressed now."

On the bus ride home I wished something bad would happen to Dr. B. I didn't specify, just something that would cause him discomfort and mortification.

A week later a secretary called to say I would have to take the test over because the pictures hadn't come out right.

"Aha, how do you do?" Dr. B. shook my hand, all charm again. "So you enjoyed our little cocktail party so much that you decided to come again?"

"Look, there's something I must say before we begin. Last week you made a big fuss about the way I swallowed. Now, I don't know if that's why the pictures didn't come out or if there was some other problem. But as you must know, swallowing is partly a reflexive act which I can't totally control. The way I swallow is the way I swallow and I don't wish to be scolded for it. Maybe the problem that brought me here in the first place is the reason I don't swallow to your satisfaction. Have you thought of that?"

Had such speech ever been spoken in a doctor's office? How proud I felt, like young Stephen Dedalus complaining to Father Dolan of being wrongfully paddled when his glasses were broken, except I was even braver—I confronted the perpetrator himself. On the other hand, Stephen Dedalus was seven at the time and I was almost thirty-nine.

After my speech, Dr. B. managed to behave like a man of science, despite his frustrations about my swallowing or his equipment or anything else in his life. I left feeling satisfied with us both: let's hear it for civilized behavior, *ententes cordiales,* rah, rah. I took back my malevolent wish.

What the pictures showed, Ev's old doctor informed me a week later, was ambiguous: a minor problem or more likely a mechanical glitch in the camera. He seemed to be hinting that I let the matter drop, although he couldn't say so openly in case I later died of cancer of the esophagus and in the process took it into my head to sue him.

"The doctor seemed to be having trouble," I said. "He kept complaining about the way I swallowed. It became quite an ordeal, as a matter of fact."

"He died. Dr. B. just died of a cerebral hemorrhage."

I gasped. "Oh, my. I'm sorry. I'm really shocked." And he was so good-looking, too.

"Yes, it was very sudden."

That was excessive, I whispered to the powers that be. Much more than I intended. At least I had not destroyed a famous novelist.

"What's that?" said Ev's old doctor.

Had I spoken aloud? "Nothing, nothing. That's too bad."

I didn't investigate further. The tightness in my throat was easing, in any case. Perhaps it had come from shouting or smoking or weeping; any number of common daily activities might have caused it.

So I wonder, do malevolent thoughts have power, riding the vibrations of the universe? The Tai Chi teacher calls it the great symphony, of which we hear only snatches of melody, those melodies we ourselves summon, like vibrations drawing like: anger drawing anger, love drawing love. There might be something to it. *E chi lo sa?* as Q. would say. Even my mother, surely no Eastern mystic, warned me against bad thoughts and bad words. Not nice. If you can't say something nice, don't say anything at all. If you can't think something nice, don't think. . . .

AT THE ELEVATOR DOOR, clutching my paper bag of bee pollen and vitamins, I almost collide with my downstairs neighbor, Helene, and her shopping cart, which she takes out daily, like a pet. Helene is a retired schoolteacher. Many of the locals have passed through her exacting classroom.

"You're looking rather peaked," she declares. "What's the matter with you?"

"I don't really know. I'm awfully tired. I'm having some blood tests next week, to find out. My stepdaughter thinks I might have one of those chronic fatigue viruses."

"Are you sure you're not just depressed? All those newfangled illnesses, they sound like depression to me. What we used to call down in the dumps."

"Well, you're looking just fine, Helene." I'll let her live, simply press the button to slide the door closed, erasing her robust presence.

I stumble into the empty apartment. Ev? Ah, yes. My keys miss the table where I toss them and jangle to the floor. I open windows, look through the unpromising mail. If I'd kept the answering machine on, there might have been a friendly, chiding message from Tim: what a good time he was having at the shore, I should have come.

Behind the screen at the French door are clumps that might be leaves or shadows. No movement. Gradually I make out a shape that is not leaves or shadows, a trembling, rounded shape with tiny bristling hairs catching the light. He's curled up for an afternoon nap. A wave of weakness hits, making me sway. I don't tap on the glass—too harsh for a sleeper—only give a low hiss against the screen. Nothing.

The squirrel is clearly sick, too sick to respond promptly as squirrels do. What's more, he'll die here, he has chosen this place to die, and tomorrow or the next day I'll find his body festering in the heat, perhaps with flies or bees hovering round, and I'll have to raise the screen and lift out the body, wearing rubber gloves, of course, since squirrels are reputed to carry disease, even rabies, then place it in a paper bag—I know the procedure well, from the rat—and take it down to the garbage cans in the basement. The bag will smell, maybe like damp rotting leaves, maybe flat and stubborn like a decaying mouse under the floorboards, or worse. And suppose on the way down to the basement I get stuck in the elevator, for this happens from time to time and normally doesn't frighten me, someone always hurries to the rescue, but to be stuck holding a dead squirrel in a paper bag with the stench filling the cubicle, to be trapped with the smell of death. . . .

Stop, calm down, be sensible. The dying squirrel is just a coincidence. Unless it's one of those angels or good witches who turn up in fairy tales in hideous disguise, testing the heroine's character: does she offer hospitality or turn the wretch away?

I sink back in the easy chair, facing the river. Now is as good a time as any to test Creative Visualizing. I'll picture my innards as a battleground, the organs as the killing fields. A very intimate landscape, with strategic valleys and waterways.

Recalling the instructions in the book, I conjure up the bad cells racing rampant down my bloodstream. Malevolent and alien, they'll be blue, since few things in nature are blue except for bluebells and blueberries and, of course, the sky. (Though the blue of the sky, scientists say, is not true blue but a result of the refraction of light, as well as of our own desires: l'azur was the dream of the French Symbolist poets, who deepened the blue of the sky by sheer longing.)

The bad blue cells come into focus, resembling speckled M&M's. The good cells, hot on their trail, are flat red disks with squat pointy spears around the circumference, like gears. I imagine regiments of good red cells—my heart pumping them out as efficiently as a draft board—flowing down the channels of my blood, protectively colored, hunting out the enemy. As the reds roll along, up-ended, their spears pierce the blues, which shrivel into empty crumpled skins like the skins of rotted grapes, to be washed away with other waste.

This seems a harmless little fantasy, yet my heart's pounding at the very notion of such mayhem under the skin. I'm used to the subtle contest of push hands in Tai Chi. I don't like being a battleground. I let the vision go, and it's abruptly replaced by a vision much closer to home, another battle against an intruder.

I had set a new kind of mousetrap, a flat, white plastic rectangle about three by four inches, coated with a honey-colored, gummy paste. The plan was that the mouse who invaded our kitchen at night would stumble onto the rectangle and stick. Like most weapons of destruction, the trap was a metaphor, maybe from some inventive mind who couldn't find work at the Pentagon: victim stuck in place, straining to tear free. (Mouse foot in aspic—could be some chic new delicacy from a bistro on the cutting edge.) I assumed the misstep would occur at night and hadn't thought any further, for instance, what to do with the rectangle holding the stuck mouse. I was a wife, then, with a wifely outlook: Ev would take care of it. And to be frank, I was terrified of the mouse, or not so much of the mouse itself as of its sudden darting appearances, its scuttling shadow. I might not have minded had I been warned in advance, or had it moved more slowly. All the more peculiar that I wasn't terrified by the rat scuttling across the window ledge as I spoke to Q. on the phone years earlier.

Jilly was in for the weekend. We sat in the dining room lingering over coffee while she told me the plot of a crime movie in scrupulous detail; she could act out the dialogue so well that I didn't need to see the movies themselves. Ev was out. Ev was out much of the time. Even when he was in, it felt like he was out.

"So then she puts this personal ad in the paper. That's to make you think the killer was after women who put these ads in, but that's not it, because he's really—"

Yelps came from the kitchen. We dashed in.

The mouse was stuck on the rectangle, beside the garbage can. Admirably, if unwillingly, rooted. In its vain struggle to get unstuck, legs straining and torso wriggling, it gave the illusion of forward movement, like those vaudeville dancers in top hat, tails and cane who affect a strutting motion but stay in place. I, too, felt glued to the spot.

"Kill it," said Jilly. "Put it out of its misery."

"How?"

"I don't know. Knock it out."

I hastily grabbed a broom from the closet, though there was no need for haste; the mouse wasn't going anywhere. It kept squirming and yelping as I flailed again and again.

"Forget it, I can't do this," I cried. "I'm a pacifist."

"Since when?"

"I never told you before. I wasn't sure. Now I know."

"Never mind that bull. Just kill it. You can't leave it there squirming."

I closed my eyes and battered blindly until the yelps stopped. Opening my eyes to slits, I swept the trap into a paper bag and stuffed it in the garbage, then leaned against the counter and took a few deep breaths. Jilly watched. Adolescents love to watch.

"It's easy to stand there looking contemptuous. Why didn't you do it, since you're so cool about it?"

"It's not my mouse," she said coolly. "It's not even my house." And she sauntered off toward the guest room.

She was right, I wasn't really a pacifist. It wasn't the brutal killing I abhorred, only its proximity. (Maybe I should use a stun gun on my bad blue cells, then administer a lethal injection that would work while I slept.)

When Ev came home I said, "It's funny, I didn't mind poisoning them, remember, a few years ago? I left the stuff out and in the morning it was gone and that was that. I guess they crawled back into their holes to die. I never thought about it. But battering it to death was vile."

"There's no difference whatsoever," he said with the same coolness as Jilly. "It only feels different because everyone here is so sheltered. You've never seen killing except on a screen. We used to bomb whole villages at once, but when the Vietcong sneaked up in the dark and slit a few throats we called them barbarians. If you're going to kill someone or something—and I personally don't care what you do with the mice—you should at least do it in such a way that you know what you're doing. That it's for real."

"Well, aren't you the pompous one. How convenient that you were out at the time so you could keep your integrity."

"I had to go up to the Bronx to see someone."

Then the phone rang, and it was over. His words shook me up because that war was one of the things he wouldn't talk about. At our first dinner he'd mentioned being there, as if it were a secret to get rid of fast, and then never again except once, early on in bed, when I teasingly demanded an account of every year in his adult life, where he had been and with whom. It was a terse account. Mid-'sixties, Vietnam. He was drafted right out of college—drawing a low number—then wounded after two months and sent home to a desk. He never spoke of it and never wrote of it. He wrote about the other wars of the last twenty years, but never the one he was in. One of his silences.

A few days after the mouse incident, Ev was dead. Trying to run but caught in place by a bullet. Certain visions require no effort and no instructions from a manual. Such as slamming the cab door despite the sign on the window, Please Do Not Slam the Door, barreling through the revolving door where I almost tripped a Korean woman carrying a baby, homing in on the path as if I were led through the hospital maze by an invisible Virgil, forcing my way through the swinging doors of the Emergency Room—not there, no longer an emergency—past flustered nurses and two old men in wheelchairs and a bearded security guard—door after door like Chinese boxes, to the final revelation—until too late, too late, the ripped body, the gaping throat, not meant for the next of kin. The blue shirt I had chosen, stained purplish-black. "That shirt looks like it's seen better days," I'd said, wifelike, just a couple of hours earlier. "Why don't you wear another?" "I'm only going up to the Bronx to see my drug dealers." "Still. Drug dealers dress pretty well, don't they? You should fit in." He was in a good mood. He peeled off the old shirt. "Okay. Which do you suggest?" "This one." I picked out a blue one I'd given him.

I tried to close his mouth and the jagged hole in his neck. My hands got sticky. I fixed his hair but it was no use. He was beyond repair. The room was crowded with hospital staff. How could I leave him there, so helpless, with strangers? I thought of ways I might get him home and fix him up. I knew he was dead, I just had this compelling urge to fix him up, close his neck and wash him and put clean clothes on him. But they didn't let me.

"What happened?" I asked the cop who pulled me out into the hall. I was in that peculiar calm state that goes with shock, much calmer than I'd been about the mouse.

"I'm terribly sorry for your loss, ma'am. I know this is a great shock—"

"Tell me what happened."

"Well, uh, it's a complicated situation, ma'am. It's not really clear, I mean, to explain at this point."

"Try me. I have a high IQ."

"There was a raid. We came down in a helicopter, see, to get the dealers. It was part of the plan."

"A helicopter. In the Bronx?"

"Uh-huh. But things got out of hand and there was some shooting. Three people were shot, including a cop. Your husband, now. Seems like he was up there hanging out with the dealers—"

"For Chrissakes, he's a reporter. He was doing a story for a magazine. He's been working on it for weeks."

"Uh-huh. Dangerous work. Could be the dealers thought he was a ghost."

"A ghost?" If he were a ghost, maybe he could hear us. I strove to stay cool as Ev would do—I'd seen him at work, very smooth, very controlled—so his ghost would be pleased with me.

"A ghost is a kind of undercover cop. You know, he helps set them up."

"I see. Well, who shot him? Maybe one of you."

"Ma'am, I'm real sorry about your loss. I know you have a lot of questions, and there'll be plenty of time to answer them down at the station. Maybe this isn't the right moment. . . . Can I call anyone for you?"

It's not true that bureaucracies are cold and faceless. The cops and assistant DAs I got to know over weeks, months, couldn't have been more courteous and sympathetic, especially after I flashed Ev's press pass to show he wasn't dealing or buying, Ev, who couldn't smoke a goddamned cigarette without turning green. The trouble was, all they ever said was how sorry they were for my loss, over and over like the refrain of a song until I wanted to shout, Fuck my loss, you motherfuckers, just tell me which of you did it.

Naturally there was an investigation. My friend Mona's brother Carl, a public interest lawyer, helped me. The case went to a grand jury. The grand jury threw up its hands and exonerated everyone, dealers and cops alike.

"I don't believe it. How can that be?" I asked Carl. He was chain-smoking, looking almost as weary as I did.

"Not enough hard evidence. Everyone shooting at once."

Not Ev. He had no gun. "What the fuck do they need? They've got bodies all over the place."

"Laura, these DAs throw so many facts and so much chaos at the jury that in the end they say, A plague on both your houses."

I pushed. I played the holy crusader. A tabloid headline read: "Slain Reporter's Widow Seeks New Probe of Bronx Shoot-out." I wasn't well cast but I pursued it until even Carl told me this was not a movie; in real life there were more unsolved murders than not. I would never get the truth about the bullet that tore Ev's neck apart. He was dead and I was dead-tired, especially tired of spending so much time in the company of uniformed men, the cops' blue and the DA's gray suits.

I conducted my own kind of probe, sitting in this very armchair facing the river. As soon as I closed my eyes the vision would flash on the undersides of my lids, looking like the movies Jilly used to recount in such minute detail: Ev standing on a dismal, narrow side street lined with tenements, some of them boarded up, a few sullen teenagers leaning against cars, bags of garbage breaking at the seams and leaking orange peels, pizza crusts, and yellow McDonald's wrappers onto the street. Ev's wearing the blue shirt and washed-out jeans, very beanpole-ish with his jacket slung over his shoulder—it was an unusually warm mid-March day—talking to a couple of skinny men who keep glancing furtively about. He's not taking notes; like me, he remembers everything he hears and writes it down later. It's sunny, but Ev and the dealers are in shadow, near an open door they can dart into just in case. (Why didn't they?)

Down the block, other small groups of men stand around smoking nervously. Now and then a passing car slows down and a hand gestures out the window. One of the men walks over, turns and goes into a building, goes back to the car. Meanwhile, around the corner on the avenue are busy shops, women pushing strollers, old people inching along, a few gripping walkers with string bags swaying from the handles. Suddenly comes a rumbling, not the familiar subway rumbling from down below but a sound that seems to come from everywhere at once, a wartime rumbling few people recognize since they haven't seen war except on a screen. From above, from the helicopter, it must look like a meadow of upturned heads, flowers seeking the sun.

The blue and white helicopter is slowly descending, hovering over the low buildings, but to the skygazing shoppers and walkers it seems incredible that it will actually land on a Bronx street on a sunny afternoon. The drone itself is an assault. People shriek and scatter. On the side street, for an instant, they're too stunned to move. Then they scatter, too. The logical thing would be to run through the open door into the shelter of the building, and in most of my visualizings, that's exactly what they do. But maybe the dealers know better: in the building they could be trapped, maybe it makes sense to stick to the streets. The cops come leaping from the helicopter floating a foot or so above the ground and give chase, their guns drawn.

But in the official version the dealers don't run into the building, Ev along with them, and don't run down the street either. They run right toward the cops as toward an embrace. They attack the raiding cops. A curious choice, that.

Well, I've run it many ways, I assure you, more ways than I could repeat. And I've come to think that Ev didn't talk about the war, the one he fought in, because he knew how hard it is to distinguish between what really happened and "creative visualizing." Could it matter to the dead?

One thing is the same, though, in each vision, or version: Ev baffled, dazed, turning sideways—on the street or in the hallway—to elude the bullet as he eluded me, as if his thinness could save him, making him an impossible target. But the bullet, cleverer than I, knows how to reach him, finds its way right into his papery profile, the left side, just below the collarbone, into soft flesh (oozing a stain on the blue shirt), then another bullet (what for?) higher up, in his neck, and he collapses as if someone's let go of the strings. A ghost. Drifts out of life like a phantom. He was like a phantom in it, sometimes. And the pain I felt and feel without him is the pain amputees feel in a lost limb, phantom pain.

I heard about a new method of photography, Kirlian photography, which makes visible the energy field left by an object recently removed. A leaf, say. Cut away half a leaf along the central vein, take a picture immediately of the half remaining, and the completed photo will show a shadow perfectly reflecting the missing half. If they photographed me with that special lens, there'd be a shadow beside me, tall, lean, bemused at the dramatic fate he'd felt so unsuited for.

A few days after the shooting I went through his desk looking for pages to give his editor. Alongside the typed notes about the dealers' lives, I found scrawled marginalia in an unfamiliar lingo. Nickel bags. Solid gold. Aphrodisia Cruz. American Eagle. Checkmate. Benny Bluecaps. Crazy Eddie. Tonto and Cisco Kid. Yellows, blues, purple sage. Drug talk, the editor said. Street names. *Noms de guerre.*

I used to wonder why he was so intrigued by the drug trade. It wasn't drugs or trade that intrigued him. It was war.

When he saw the helicopter he must have thought for a wild moment that he was back in the war. A chopper picked him up when he was wounded, that much he told me. And maybe between the time the bullet entered his neck and his last moments, struggling on the hospital gurney to stay alive for me—and God knows I ran, I gave the driver fifty bucks to speed—he was back in the jungle, inhaling terror, not spirit, with every hard breath, sure he'd never get out alive. Though I can't say, really, what or how he'd think. If marriage is the endeavor to know the other, I failed. Unlike with Q. That's why I stuck to him. I had to know someone.

Three weeks after the funeral Jilly came down for the weekend as she'd come regularly for twelve years. At a little after one, she rang the bell then turned her key in the lock. She had a pack on her back. She wore a long flowered peasant skirt, old sneakers, a white T-shirt and a motorcycle jacket, and her hair was up Grecian style with wisps dangling around her cheeks, as if she were trying various identities at once, keeping all options open.

"You're here," I said.

"Sure I'm here. You look surprised."

"I didn't know if you would be."

"What do you think I am, Laura?" She slid her pack to the floor and came and put her arms around me.

"I was thinking if you didn't come I might go up to the Bronx to see the street. I have this great curiosity but I haven't managed to get myself—"

"I'll go with you."

"Are you sure? I could go another day."

"I came to do whatever you feel like doing."

It was and it wasn't as I'd visualized it. The garbage, yes, but the tenements weren't boarded up and the street wasn't lonely or grim but lively. Children and teenagers streamed in and out of the houses, and girls in tight, bright clothes stood holding their babies and chatting. A couple of supers swept the sidewalks outside their buildings. A cluster of men played dominoes at a card table in the mild early spring. In between spurts of traffic, boys played soccer in the street. A small-town Saturday afternoon. I was wrong about the angle of the light. The side of the street where Ev had stood was drenched in sunlight, not shadow. On the corner was an old movie theatre showing films in Spanish, several letters on the marquee missing. Next door, along the avenue, was a dingy supermarket with a pyramid of paper towels in the window. A tiny botanica crammed with painted statues of Jesus and Mary and the saints. An OTB parlor with the usual seedy patrons studying the *Racing Form*. Across the street was a clothing store selling polyester maids' and nurses' uniforms.

Bicycle repair shop. Pizzeria. Hardware store with a hand-lettered sign outside: Boxes, Tape, String. At the fruit and vegetable stand were piled hairy brown yuccas, plantains, puny oranges and gorgeous overripe eggplants striped white and purple. I wanted to steal something and run. The yuccas, maybe; they looked like grenades, or the sex organs of something very big, bisons. It all told me nothing.

Jilly and I walked back and forth along the stretch, mourners indeed, going about the streets, then turned the corner to stand once again in front of the building. The door to the basement was closed—maybe he couldn't have run in after all. Or I might have gotten it wrong and it was an open window he'd mentioned. We scanned the sidewalk for the chalk marks outlining the bodies, but there'd been heavy rains during the week and the few faint traces might have been just another hopscotch game. All the while, people stared at us. I guess they knew who we were. People do, in tight neighborhoods. I wanted to talk to someone but what would I say? Are you by any chance one of the drug dealers my late husband was interviewing?

At the subway entrance, a yellow-faced skinny man in a brown suit thrust a copy of *Awake*, the Jehovah's Witnesses' pamphlet, in our faces, and I waved him away. Back on our own turf, we went to the local Chinese restaurant and snickered over the errors on the menu. "Listen to this," I said, " 'Fresh sliced chicken scared to a crispy, various kinds of seasonable vegetable cook in the wok.' Or how about 'Egg drop soup served in a large bowel.' " "Thanks but no thanks," said Jilly. "Look, Laura, it says 'We can alter the spicy according to your taste.' How do you like your spicy?" We giggled like schoolgirls. Jilly was in fact a schoolgirl. " 'Cho Joan chicken, first time served in U.S.,' has been on the menu ever since we started coming here," she said. "Should we try it?" It tasted bitter.

The trip was a letdown. We were relieved and disappointed that it hadn't been more painful, more of a revelation.

That street never left me, though, like a litany you're forced to learn in childhood, the catechism or the four questions: it no longer means much, but in idle moments your mind will take up the words the way people fiddle with crumbs on an empty table. I see the street and murmur like a chant: movie, supermarket, botanica, OTB, clothing store, bike rental, pizzeria, hardware, vegetable stand with hairy, phallic yucca. Sometimes it's in vivid Technicolor, and sometimes faded and wan. We can vary the spicy according to your taste. But it still tells me nothing.

I DIDN'T GO to the Tai Chi class for a long time after Ev was killed. I watched from the window, missing the teacher and his pithy commands. I read the Samurai creed to remind me of him: "I have no design; I make opportunity my design. . . . I have no friends; I make my mind my friend," but to tell the truth, the teacher didn't seem a Samurai warrior any more than I did. I knew he must wonder about me at times, however detached he pretended to be. I even missed the translator, in fact I never pictured the teacher without him alongside. I remembered their phrases about standing firm and rooting my feet in the earth while keeping my body soft and pliable yet alert. But these were words with no meaning anymore and might just as well have gone untranslated.

Then one afternoon in gray, mild October, I forced myself down to the park. If only he wouldn't ask where I'd been, just say a casual hello. . . . Spare me the gems of wisdom about yielding and accepting. If he told the joke about having no complaints whatsoever, I'd have to flee and never go back.

The class hadn't yet begun; people stood around in small groups. When he saw me, the teacher's face brightened with surprise and pleasure and he came straight over, the interpreter following along.

"Laura, how good to see you," the interpreter translated. "I've so often wondered what happened to you. How have you been? Have you been away?"

"No, I haven't been away. I've been . . . busy."

He waited. I assumed he didn't read the tabloids.

"A difficult time."

His face darkened as the interpreter repeated my words. Again he waited for me to go on, then prompted. "What? Did something happen?"

"I . . . well, the fact is, my husband was killed a few months ago. Shot in the street."

I saw it then, clear as day. The instant I spoke, before the paling but unruffled interpreter had a chance to translate, the shock registered in the teacher's eyes. The muscles of his face went slack and he moved closer to take my hands.

"That's so bad! Terrible. I feel so sorry."

"You speak!" I cried.

As he realized what he had done—the master himself, who anticipated every move, caught off guard by plain human sympathy!—he let out a small gasp.

"No, no," he said through the interpreter. "Only a few words. Not really. I'm so sorry to hear this. Please, tell me how it happened."

"No, first you tell me why you pretend not to understand."

"Pretend?" the interpreter said for him. "I don't pretend anything. I understand a word here and there. How are you managing, Laura? Are you all right?"

"Speak to me yourself." I had learned the lesson well. You need only stand firm and stay balanced. Never resist, just persist.

The interpreter kept translating.

"Please," I said, turning to him. "Don't repeat what I'm saying. I know he understands. It's not fair. It's a deception. Now, tell me," I addressed the teacher, "what this is all about. Is it some kind of trick? You want a mysterious aura, right? Or some kind of power? You want to keep your distance from us. What is it? You're not into any hokey business, are you? Do you really believe all the things you tell us?"

"Hokey?" he repeated.

"Tell him," I said to the interpreter, "what hokey is in Chinese," and he did, or I had to assume he did.

The teacher smiled lamely. "No," he said. "No hokey business. I speak badly. I can't say right what I want. In all things I say true."

"It's pure vanity? I'm surprised at you." Though he did in fact speak badly, with a thick, clumsy accent. Struggling with English words and inflections, he lost all authority.

"No vanity. Not for me, myself. Say to her," he implored the interpreter, "what I mean."

"He means it's not personal vanity. It's for the discipline. It's important to express the principles correctly."

"Not correct only," the teacher interrupted. "To be. . . ." He made fists in frustration and continued volubly in Chinese. Suddenly the two of them, the mutual muses, were engaged in a kind of verbal push hands, partners yet adversaries in a tongue I couldn't understand, though I knew the teacher was explaining to the interpreter how he wished to be translated.

"Thorough," said the interpreter. "He needs to be thorough, and he feels he can't be in English. Thorough and eloquent. With the right imagery."

"Right," said the teacher with a slight bow to the interpreter. "Thank you. Thorough and eloquent."

"Okay. Okay. I'm a writer. I can appreciate that. But you could at least show that you understand. You don't need to have him translate every little thing we say. Don't you see, there's something not right about it. . . . Oh, if you don't see then I can't explain it."

He smiled. "For unity and smooth."

"Consistency," put in the interpreter.

"Ah, yes," I said.

"Laura, enough this stupidness of words. Important what happened to the husband. And you."

"He was a reporter. . . ." I told the whole thing, the police helicopter, the shooting, the neck wounds, the hospital, the blue shirt, the grand jury, while the two stood frowning and shaking their heads. Even the interpreter cared, I could see. He was a person, too.

"Terrible. I wish to say more but in the English as you demand I have no right words. I feel very bad for you."

"Thank you. You can't say it any better than that."

"Me too," said the interpreter.

"Thank you."

"Any help needed please ask. A valued student." He handed me a card. "You should return before."

"You know why I didn't? I was afraid you would tell me to invest in loss. Or that I should have no complaints whatsoever. Something like that."

"You crazy? Your husband killed and I tell you not grieve? These which I teach are things in books. . . ."

He struggled for a word and finally turned in irritation to the interpreter, who said, "Parables."

"Parables, yes. We here are to lead life with woe. Tasting bitter."

"Woe? That's a pretty good word. You have a lot of potential. Woe. Yes, well, it's interesting that you see it that way."

"Time for class. Laura, you are not telling the secret?"

I laughed. "Oh, all right. It's a little foolish, though, don't you think?"

"Maybe a lot foolish, but how I do."

"One more thing, while we're at it. How old are you?"

"Forty-three. Why?"

"I was curious. So you're just like us." Not a well-preserved hundred and ten, I meant, or a precocious seventeen.

As he spoke in Chinese, even his posture seemed to change. "I never said otherwise," the interpreter translated. Then, "Continue," he called, and the groups broke apart, the students assembled.

"Head erect and suspended from heaven, feet rooted in the earth, arms carrying the ball of energy. Breath thin, long, quiet and slow. Move as if you're drawing silk from a cocoon, never breaking the thread." He was the master again.

THERE WAS Q., of course, settling in with his suitcase and groceries not long after the funeral. To take care of me, he said. (Except on Jilly's weekend when I made him leave, in case she turned up.) He came, he

*"Head erect and suspended from heaven, feet rooted in the earth, arms car-
rying the ball of energy. Breath thin, long, quiet and slow. Move as if you're
drawing silk from a cocoon, never breaking the thread."*

cooked, he was full of labors, like Lear's faithful Kent, whom I'd seen him play memorably.

He even danced and made me dance. Imagine. On my husband's grave, practically.

Nonsense, said Q. We've always danced, don't you remember? We're just doing our thing.

He put on a sexy reggae tape and started dancing by himself, twirling, snapping his fingers, exaggerating his hips and shoulders to make me laugh. He looked so unabashed and silly all alone that I got up to join him, and soon we were jiggling and slithering around the living room. I thought of how my great-aunt Bess, close to eighty with knees so stiff from arthritis that some days she could barely walk, nonetheless at my cousin Joyce's first wedding rose from her chair like a Lady Lazarus, hooked her cane along its back and inched to the dance floor on the groom's arm, where she kicked up her feet and stepped nimbly across the polished wood, shaking her hips and mighty shoulders while he did his shy best to follow. As a young girl she had been famous for her dancing, and at last I could see why. Head held high and lips parted, she breathed in the music, sending it through her torso and arms and legs the way the Tai Chi teacher told us to breathe in the air, transforming it into energy, motion. Dancing is the body's song, and Bess sang. Years fell from her, her pinned-up white hair fell, until Joyce and all the others ceased their own dancing to clap and urge her on, as if the collective will could keep her song from ending. She stopped abruptly between beats, glued to the floor, overtaken by stiffness. "Okay, enough already with the dancing. I'll pay for this tomorrow." Hobbling toward her chair on the arm of the groom, she aged instantly, as if the edge of the dance floor were the border of Shangri-La.

How did she do it, I'd always wondered. Dancing with Q., I understood. Once in a while the pain falls asleep on the job, and the experienced sufferer knows enough to seize such moments swiftly and without thought—for when we realize we're actually dancing, the jolt of joy wakens the pain.

I can't believe I'm dancing, I said to Q. Am I really? Is this me?

Don't believe it, don't spoil it, just keep doing it.

And we did, until we collapsed on the couch.

I can't imagine dancing now. But it could happen that one morning before the little blue cells are fully awake, a good dance tune will come on the radio and my hips will start twitching. Soon I'll be dancing around the kitchen as I used to do, for the sheer pleasure of it, until I remember I'm sick for reasons I can't sort out and maybe shouldn't even try to: this can't be me dancing.

After a while Q. went away, like the wind, blowing as it listeth. The time wasn't right, anyway. Much too soon. What did I feel? Grateful, hateful. Did I want him to stay or go? Neither, both, I don't know. I wanted the intervening years not to have happened. I wanted us to be other than what those years had made of us, or we of them.

4

Much as I want to have lunch with Q. (not least because I'm curious to see what he'll come up with—he's as ingenious in the kitchen as he is ingratiating in the bedroom), it appears, after the morning Tai Chi class, that I will not move anymore today or perhaps ever again. My head aches, my eyes burn, my arms and legs have given up, and my face in the mirror has a grayish cast. The bed, across the room, calls in its unmistakable lover's croon, Come to me, come, only I can make you truly happy, oh, how happy I'll make you, don't resist, remember how you moan with pleasure the instant we touch. . . . Every cell yearns for that voluptuous embrace. Why deny myself?

I lower myself onto the bed, sinking as a stone sinks, then slowly bring my legs up over the edge and lie back. Once my aching shoulders hit the mattress the ache turns sweet. Ah, the relief, the luxury of not having to bear my own weight. At a time I never expected it, life has sent me another great love. I no longer care whether I'll ever hoist myself up to visit Q., or write about the seaside town, inventing benign intrigues for the Wire Inspector, the Tree Warden, the Oil Spill Coordinator, the Shellfish Constable. . . .

I don't feel like sleeping, though. I've been awake only a couple of hours. A flick of a switch on the bedside radio summons the vibrations of the universe. Often I pretend the sounds riding the airwaves are for me alone; they offer personally designed little messages in the form of music or news, chance comments, snatches of interviews. Now the sound of a solitary violin trickles out, making a long, cajoling speech. It's taking time off from its orchestral duties to develop an ascending theme, an extended narrative, a message of . . . what? Hope? Cheer? No, more like complexity and patience. The complexity of patience. The need for it. It sounds like a voice addressing the blue ether, or soothing an injured child. My morning news. It carries me into the melody, lulling me to a half-conscious state in which only my ear is awake.

When it's over, I find I can move. I switch off the weather report—hot, hot, hot—and inspired by the violin, put on a tape of Mozart's *Exsultate, Jubilate.* Slip on sandals, comb my hair, make the little motions of preparation while the music's splendor reminds me that somewhere people have reason to exult and jubilate, and before I know it I'm walking down the broad way, Broadway arrayed for summer with crowds of vendors: the street is a vast carnival, a performance, the stage set with books, bracelets, rows of sunglasses reflecting dozens of suns, racks of cotton dresses skimming on a breeze, pyramids of oranges and dark avocados, oh, life is abundant. I stop to buy red grapes and fancy cookies for Q. since he's fussing over lunch, then descend into the subway.

My mind may be dulled but my senses are abnormally alert, and the subway chafes each one in turn. First the eyes: a world of grays. The walls are creamy gray and the floors dark, dust making them soft as suede. The trains are steely gray, the papers at the newsstand pale and wilted. All the faces and clothes dissolve in grayness. The passengers truly look like mourners going about under the streets. The roar of the train erupts out of the long pit, spilling onto the platform like audible lava held in check by the gray walls. At the far end of the car I enter, some unseen but surely gray person has a box blasting heavy gray music. No one suggests he turn it off. People have been killed for less. We're savvy, we're grateful he has the box to advertise his rage. Across the aisle a toddler in a stroller drops his pacifier, wails, and his child-mother swats him across the head. Here comes a beggar—another kind of performance artist—delivering a robotized soliloquy about his plight. Three teenage girls giggle hysterically and yank at each other's trizzed hair, while the old man next to them snores. Warm impersonal thighs press on either side, compacting me. The air smells of grime, sweat, plus something remotely, rancidly burning—probably one of the dozens of fires on the tracks each day. A few yards off, a stuporous man sprawls on three seats; the passengers have left a discreet space around the smell rising from steamy sores on his shins. My tongue tastes bitter. I swallow hard and study the ads but they're not much distraction. For the most part, they're exhortations to health, as if the whole city were stubbornly sick, a vast hospital where individual immune systems conspire against the body politic. Ads for acne doctors, for bunion doctors, for anal fissure and hemorrhoid doctors, for hernia doctors; ads for gynecological clinics, for family counseling, for psychiatric services; ads urging a test for HIV, ads for condoms ("If you're going to play around, play with condoms"—a photo of merry teenagers tossing inflated condoms like balloons); ads for detox programs—"When You're Ready to Get Off Your High Horse," appropriate for Ev's dealers up in the Bronx. And many more. There's metaphor, I could tell Grace. Not a moment too soon, I climb back out into the clean heat of the sun, my little spurt of jubilation all fizzled out. I can't remember the sound of Mozart or why the soprano exulted.

The walk to Peter's apartment leads through a construction site lined with trucks and dumpsters. It's looked this way for years, as I recall, heaped with rubble and chunks of concrete. Hard to tell if they're building up or tearing down. An elevator bearing a load of caged workers creakily ascends the scaffolding. Since the street is impassable, I slink through a narrow plywood walkway plastered with a row of identical posters showing a gun aimed straight at me, then emerge into a crowd of men in hard hats, their drills set aside as they lounge on the sidewalk, eating lunch.

"My wife didn't make my lunch," one man says to his companions, "and she took her pocketbook with her, so I couldn't get any money. . . ." I'm out of earshot for the rest, but it makes me wonder again what Q. will come up with, maybe something Italian. I wonder, too, whether he might have attached some innocent woman to himself, a woman soon to be innocent no more. Over the past ten years or so, when Q. has fallen in love, I've been gnawed by jealousy yet felt supremely safe. His energies were occupied, he would stop preying on me like a Siren with his voice, his conversation, his repertoire of pungent lines from dramatic literature. Stop asking me to write a play with a role for him. Wouldn't that be marvelous, Laura—voice booming, face beaming, shedding his fireworks—a play by you with me starring? Oh, yes, he'd like that. I don't write plays, I told him over and over. I like to write the stuff in between the dialogue. The narrative, we call it.

Q. greets me with open arms and I sink into them, more from fatigue than love. We do our special kiss, the between-friends-and-lovers kiss. Handy, since we never quite know, these days, how the occasion will turn out. It's almost like an equation in algebra: will the product of passion times affinity prove greater than that of remorse times resentment? Aside from any possible love in Q.'s errant life, the new unknown today is my exhaustion. That can probably outweigh any other factor.

He waves his arm at the surroundings: half-packed cartons, mounds of books, shoes and pots.

We'll go out, he says, somewhere close. I just couldn't manage to get lunch together in this mess.

I look around, think it over, judge. He's right, I'm always judging him, deciding whether or not to take offense and mark his permanent record card. The apartment is a shambles; the chaise I like so much is piled with stuffed shopping bags; anyone would be hard put to move around in that kitchen. Okay, exonerated this time. I needn't have bothered stopping for the fancy cookies and grapes, though, which I hand him without a word.

How lovely. Thank you, *cara*. We'll come back and eat them later. Listen, do you remember that little Mexican place we once ate in? We had such a good time there, didn't we?

I look at him in shock. Yes, we did, I agree.

We could get a cab and be there in ten minutes.

No, I say. I don't want to go back there.

How can he even think of it? Something special happened there. Truth. Clarity. Even if they've since receded, the memory has to be kept pristine. But not, it seems, for Q. He lives for the moment. He wants an exhilarating experience. Even a warmed-over revival would do. The motherfucker just wants an experience.

Not back there, I repeat.

All right, never mind

We walk in the opposite direction from the construction, so I never learn what happened to the man whose wife didn't make his lunch. Had I known how things would turn out, I could have given him the grapes and cookies. After a block and a half, there's a café with tables and colorful umbrellas outside, crowded with jolly young people dressed mostly in black. To Q., who was a small child during the war, black shirts mean Fascists. His shirts are white or striped. Without consulting, we step inside, where it's dark, cool, and empty except for a middle-aged blond woman washing glasses at the bar.

Anywhere you like, she waves. We sit in a corner. A waitress appears, dressed in black, too—short skirt, spindly legs, blue and orange spiked hair.

"Love your hair," says Q.

"Thanks. Do you want to hear the specials?"

For Q., a hot roast beef sandwich with trimmings and for me, a green salad.

A few leaves of lettuce? he asks. That's all?

I can't eat anything heavy. It upsets my stomach.

So tell me what's wrong.

I make short work of that subject. Yes, he claims I could never bore him, but listing symptoms is certainly walking the edge. It bores me, at any rate. Besides, speaking takes too much effort. Sitting upright is effort enough.

Have you been to a doctor? he asks. I want you to go to a good doctor and get this checked out. I really mean it, Laura.

I'm going, Q. I have an appointment.

If I get him talking, I can rest and nibble on my greens, lulled by the spell of his words, his voice. And with a small prod, hardly more than How've you been? How are the children?, he's off and running.

The girls are fine, he reports. Graduate school, jobs, travel, marriage. His second youngest, Renata, is even pregnant again and this time she'll keep it.

Mostly I've been alone a lot, he says. I love it. It's wonderful, being alone. Do you know, I think that after everything, I'll probably end up alone.

(Everything: we know what that means. Including me? Am I part of everything? I was the first, the one who jolted his settled life and launched him on this picaresque career.)

It struck me the last time Ann left me, he says. Remember Ann? You do know she came out to stay with me? That lasted six weeks.

Of course I know. Remember I called while she was there and you couldn't really talk and then you called me back later from the theatre?

Oh, yes, he says. Oh, yes—assaulting his open roast beef sandwich with gusto, washing it down with sips of beer. Well, he goes on, so she left again. Again we decided it wouldn't work. She was going back to the commune. I drove—

The commune? I didn't know there were any left.

Sure, there are quite a few.

What kind of commune?

Q. hesitates. Could he be embarrassed? This was a women's commune, he says, in California.

I almost laugh, but manage not to. I don't believe it, I say. Do you mean she was choosing between that or you?

He shrugs. I didn't set up the alternatives, Laura. It wasn't my idea to live together. It was hers. She got hung up on it. It put me in a ridiculous position, as you see. If she chose the commune, as in fact she did in the end, it wouldn't be good for my self-esteem, to say the least.

Not an easy choice, I comment.

Thank you, my love. So where was I? *Dunque* . . . I drove her to the airport. I came back to my apartment. I walked through the rooms. I looked in the closets. Her clothes were all gone. I lay down on my bed and took a long nap. I got up and took a long bath. I played a tape. Mendelssohn, I think it was. I read a book. It was wonderful.

I laugh. He's entertaining. No pain at all in Q.'s loving solitude. I like it, too.

I saw her once more after that, he says. She called a few weeks later in semi-hysterics so I flew out to meet her in Santa Monica for the weekend. I stayed in a motel near the beach. We had lunch and sat for hours on a patio overlooking the Pacific, watching the dolphins. It's warm there all the time, you know. Those people don't know what suffering is. No wonder the movie industry started in Southern California. It could never have happened in Minneapolis. Anyway, we sat talking for so long we almost forgot to go to my motel for the obligatory half hour of making love. She told me astonishing things. Her parents didn't let her speak at the dinner table. They said it would do her good to listen to adult conversation. They also had silent evenings a couple of times a week. They were clearing or perhaps it was cleansing their minds.

Maybe that's why she likes communal life.

Hmm. I never made that connection. They made her do most of the housework, too, laundry, cooking, vacuuming, while they watched. They seemed to think it was cute, a game. They told her she was playing maid, and sometimes they even pretended to pay her.

Pretended? Real money, fake money, or what?

I think real. I didn't go into it. I'm not a novelist. She also told me things about her ex-husband that you wouldn't believe. She said he was really a woman.

I don't get it. An actual woman? Someone from the commune?

Just then the waitress comes by. "Everything all right here?"

"Superb," says Q. "*Ottimo.*" They ask that, he murmurs, so later if you get ptomaine poisoning and sue them, they can say they asked if everything was all right and you said yes.

A woman? I repeat.

Oh, Laura, my love, you're always so literal. He waves his hand in a cavalier way I like, almost knocking over his beer bottle. No. He's a man. Technically. A swimmer—he almost made the Olympic team. I saw him once in a supermarket in L.A. Muscles, mustache, all the secondary sex characteristics. Works in a bank, drives a big car, very manly. But deep inside he's a woman, she said. At home he dresses up in women's clothes, at least he did when they were married.

I suppose that could drive you to a women's commune.

When they made love, Q. continues, she had to pretend he was a woman. She had to call him Roberta or some such. His name was Robert.

What do you mean, had to? Did he put a gun to her head?

I'm speaking loosely.

Actually that's not as unusual as you might think, I contribute. I saw a TV program once about men who dress as women at home. Married men. I was in a motel somewhere, on a book tour. I always watch those morning programs when I'm in motels. That's how I learned who Geraldo was. They didn't go into what they do in bed, though. Was it like two women making love, or did she have to pretend to be the man?

I don't know, love. It was a long time ago and she didn't go into detail.

Did he wear a nightie?

Q. laughs. I don't know if he wore a nightie, Laura.

(What I should say is, Why are you telling me this? But I'm intrigued. I think of the data bank. I remember the men on the TV show quite well; maybe one of them was this Robert.)

How would a man pretend he's a woman? I inquire.

Do I know? You have to imagine it. Well, for one thing, she wasn't allowed to touch his cock.

She wasn't?

No. Off-limits.

I thought she didn't go into detail.

Well, just that. That was all.

I was under the impression men liked that.

Yes, well, they do. You're correct on that score. *Senz'altro*. But she wasn't allowed to.

Didn't she find anything odd in this?

Of course. I don't suppose they did it very often. And eventually she left.

So how did she act with you? (Am I actually asking for more?) Did she pretend you were a woman? Out of habit, I mean?

No, no, she was perfectly normal. There was just one thing, though.

The waitress appears again, running her fingers through her spiky hair, and asks if she can take our plates. I have some salad left and Q. is chewing his last French fry, the fork still in his hand.

"No, would you mind leaving them?" he says. "I like to sit awhile with the empty plate in front of me. It feels more like home."

She rolls her eyes and sidles off.

They're always in a hurry to take the plates, he says. It's the fastidiousness of modern life. They want to destroy all evidence of physicality. Puritan America—as if the sight of leftovers were too sordid.

What's the one thing?

I could never tell when she came. You know how with women you can always . . . I mean, even if they don't make a lot of noise there are physiological signs. . . .

(Funny how he can look me in the eye and say these things. He wouldn't be so clinical with a woman he'd never slept with, or with a woman he was currently romancing. How useful I am. Irreplaceable.)

Yes, I'm aware of that, I say.

Well, with her I could never tell. One time things were very quiet and I said, Did you come? And she said, Sure, I came six times.

(Did you come? One of those little jokes. When after a great display, things had calmed down, Did you come? he'd say. Sometimes I'd punch him lightly. Sometimes I'd say no.)

Six times? I echo. My dear Q., with all due respect, I don't believe that. Researchers have found that some women who never have orgasms think all the nice little feelings along the way are orgasms. If she came six times you'd be able to tell, believe me. You know, what's truly curious is that she picked you. Because you're a woman in a way, too, so maybe for her it wasn't so different from her ex-husband, not to mention the commune. I mean it as a compliment, you understand. You talk, you listen, you do all those womanly things.

Yes. Q. laughs. But I also let people touch my cock.

(As I well recall. But let it go.)

So, did you ever get to the motel for the obligatory lovemaking?

Yes, we finally went. She stayed for an hour. After she left, I stretched out on the bed and gazed out at the ocean. Then I took a long bath. I turned on the TV and watched the news. By that time it was evening. I watched the sunset out the window. I read a book. It was wonderful.

Tell me something. Do you talk about me, too?

You? He looks shocked. Never. I've never spoken like this to anyone about you and me. You know I wouldn't.

Why? Because I'm not weird enough?

Because the way I love you is too important.

I see. Listen, Q., I just can't sit up anymore.

Come, we'll go back so you can lie down. I'm sorry I went on so long. He waves for the check. I got carried away, he says.

I encouraged you. It's grotesque that you tell me these things and I listen. It's not even titillating. Or only intellectually.

He takes my arm and we walk back to the apartment, into Peter's bedroom, a maelstrom of clothing, suitcases, books and papers. Still, the bed is welcoming. One is as good as another—I'm promiscuous about beds. I shove things over and flop onto it. Q., too.

Oh, are you going to lie here with me?

Well, where else? Do you want me to sit in the living room and we'll shout back and forth? Unless—and suddenly he's not ironic but considerate—unless you really want to sleep?

No, I don't want to sleep, just rest.

Lying on a bed with Q. is not restful. Many nights we spent together left me frazzled: as a sleeper, he could be jumpy and clutchy or aloof, hunched in a corner. How could I have imagined sleeping a lifetime with him? I would have died young from sheer exhaustion. Yet I'm exhausted now in any case.

Lying next to any man generates sexual vibrations, but with Q. they're fraught with ambiguity. Since the day I threw him out, that is, and he closed the door so silently. . . . After that, I was always bitter over history while he was bitter because I married. Each of us too proud to show a need, waiting for the other to make a move. At least I think that's how it was. Why else would he pursue me over the years, always wanting to lie down? Just to be lying beside a woman? It's also true that he's happiest with his feet up—probably low blood pressure. I'm the same way. Why stand on ceremony, after all we've been through?

With such a tangle of pride and need, it's a miracle we've made love through the years. How does it happen, if neither of us can yield (a bad example of push hands, the Tai Chi teacher would say)? It happens. We touch, we fall together, and it's happening. It's ready to happen at a touch. Then it goes on for a while until something else happens, a hasty word, a flare of anger, a love affair—his, not mine, after all, I was married. . . .

Today, though, is different. I want only to lie still. Let's hope he doesn't come too close, so I don't have to back off and hurt his feelings.

He senses how I feel and doesn't come too close. My feelings are hurt.

On my way here I stopped in Cleveland to see my sister, he says, rolling onto his side, head propped on his elbow to face me. I hadn't seen her in almost a year, *Madonna*. Not since her latest divorce. I went over for dinner, saw the *ragazzi,* that was fine, the usual teenage pandemonium. Nice kids. All different fathers, but they get along. The next night I took her to dinner at my hotel so we could talk. I was staying downtown. The seventeenth floor was all they had, with a little balcony.

You know how I feel about heights, Laura. Anyhow, that night Gemma was totally different. Like Mr. Hyde. Ms. Hyde, I should say. She was getting hysterical in the restaurant so we went up to my room. It's this man she's in love with. He's married, what more need I say? She wept and moaned and tore her hair. She wanted me to tell her what to do. Me, of all people! Why? Because I'm still the big brother. Gemma, you know, is a woman who lives for love. She's spent her whole life searching for love. *Amore.* In between that, she's a CPA, as you know, but in actuality she lives for love, not figures. This man, though, also a CPA—he's in her office, no less—sounds like a CPA to the bone. He doesn't live for love, I'm sure of that. He sounds very practical. I tried to tell her that. Gemma, I said, for all the wild passion, this Herb sounds like a very practical man. He's not going to leave his wife. When it comes right down to it, they don't, most of the time. They stay where they're comfortable. That is the nature of the beast, says Q., changing his position and leaning closer. I can feel the warm stream of his breath, slightly beery, not unpleasant. I could fall asleep this way, if I let myself.

She wept more and more, he goes on. She wept and moaned so much that it got very late and finally I said, Look, Gemma, *cara*, it's very late. Why don't you just sleep here in the extra bed? You're in no state to drive. Call the *ragazzi* and tell them—they're old enough to stay by themselves, they'll be fine. So she stretched out on the bed and I lay down on the other bed and turned out the light. Like the old days. Then just as I was falling asleep I heard her starting all over again.

Gemma, I said to her in the dark. I was trying to be patient. Gemma, everybody has gone through this. We've all had our love affairs and gone through our pain and heartbreak. That's all it is, nothing unusual, just pain and heartbreak, *magari*. I didn't know what else to say at that point. I was down to the rock-bottom truth. Isn't that the truth? Finally I fell asleep. When I woke early in the morning, six-thirty, she was gone. She didn't even leave a note. How do you like that? The first thing I did was, I went out on the balcony to see if she had thrown herself off. I was terrified to look down. Besides how I feel about heights, I thought I'd see her body spattered there in the middle of downtown Cleveland.

But it wasn't, I say.

No, *grazie a Dio*. I called her at the office a little after nine just to make sure she got there. She was fine. Ms. Jekyll. As if it had never happened.

Jilly once told me, I say drowsily, about a performance artist who jumped out of a window and managed to have photos taken of himself in midflight. A second-story window—he didn't really mean it. It was for art, you know. The seventeenth floor would be more than an artistic gesture, I guess. But you'd have more time to get the photos.

I don't think it's artistic from any floor. At least I wouldn't want to see it. I honestly thought she was capable of it, though.

So you've seen her secret life, I say.

It's everyone's secret life. But why do they tell me?

Because you listen like a woman. Or at least a hermaphrodite.

Huh! I'm improving. Other times you said I was a frog.

That, too.

Dropping off to sleep, I picture Q. slipping into his male costume each morning, hairy skin complete with musculature and genitals. Maybe he keeps on talking while I doze, it's not impossible. When I open my eyes, Peter is packing clothes in suitcases with Q. following along, trying to help.

"Hello, Laura. Stay where you are, it's all right. I'll work around you."

I used to dread Peter's finding me in his bed. Or on it, as now. Today I don't care. How will I get home with my eyes hot and my legs clogged with sand, is what I care about.

"Hi, Peter, it's been quite a while. I'm so sorry about Arthur—how's he doing?"

"Still dying. What about you, Laura? Quinn tells me you're not feeling so well."

"Oh, it's nothing. Just a little tired."

The relativity of suffering is a problem. No objective standards of measurement, we're all entitled to our own—so say the experts. Yet in the face of Arthur's dying I can hardly complain of my sandbag body, or the little things that slip from my grasp, or my inability to stay upright for more than a few hours at a stretch.

I thank Peter for the hospitality of his bed, and Q. accompanies me downstairs. Peter is moving in two days, he says, holding open the front door. I'll be working here for a couple of weeks. I never got to tell you about the movie. You wouldn't by any chance have any room for two weeks, would you, Laura?

(Ah. That's what the frogs always say in the stories. It's not enough to have me in your garden, you must keep me by your plate at table; it's not enough to have me near your plate, you must keep me on your pillow.)

Won't they put you up somewhere while you're shooting?

Queens. He gives a pathetic grimace as we head for the corner.

I'm sorry, Q., but I don't feel well enough for a guest. Besides, I think our time for living together has passed.

Since when am I a guest? I'll take care of you. I've done it before, Laura, don't you remember? Whatever you need. I'll make you soups. I'll rub your back. In fact I'll rub anywhere you say. You just name it.

It's too hot for soups. It was April, last time. Look, don't you have any women here these days? Or have you been away too long?

Nobody. You have the wrong idea about me.

Really. Nobody on the set?

There's someone who interests me but she's much too young.

(It's easy to imagine her, assuming she really exists. I know just what he likes. So well that I could earn a finder's fee. Elegant women, but not ethereal. Not too thin, firm, not fragile, with a certain grace. A touch of earthiness. Never coarse or crude, yet with an ineffable, barely discernible hint that they might be crude at the right moments. Intelligent, but not quite as intelligent as Q.—there's my failing. Vastly tolerant, optimistic women.)

How young? I ask.

Never mind. Too young. She'll be ready in about ten years. Besides, she's in the motel in Queens, too. He pauses. You know, Laura, you make me say these things. You deliberately provoke them.

Do I? Did I provoke you to tell me about Nadine?

Nadine? Who's Nadine?

The sexual savage from El Paso.

Oh, Laura. *Che sciocchezze.* I forgot all about her. It was nothing.

Maybe. But you told me unprovoked.

I thought I could tell you anything. You were the one person. . . . It was amusing. But I see I was mistaken. I remember now. You hung up.

(Indeed I did. It was during a spell when we, more likely he, had decided it was too difficult being lovers; we should be "just friends," an arrangement that left him free to confide his escapades—after all, I was his best friend. The damnedest thing happened in El Paso, he said over the phone. We did M. *Butterfly,* and afterwards there was a cast party given by—

Which one were you? I interrupted.

I was the diplomat. What did you think?

I thought maybe you were the mistress, you know, the man who pretends to be the woman all those years.

No, that has to be an Asian.

They could always fix you up.

There are limits. I'm too big. That kind of actor has to be able to look delicate. Anyway, why do you think that?

Because, I keep telling you, you're a woman at heart. I think you'd be great in that role.

Well, I wasn't. So anyway, the Chamber of Commerce gave this party and I was introduced to one of the county judges and his wife, Nadine, her name was. She looked young, especially to be married to a judge, but he was a young judge. I guess out in El Paso there's not a huge supply so they take them younger. Now, you know I'm not captive to Hollywood standards of youth and beauty. That kind of thing means nothing to me. To me a woman is a woman, a person, not flesh at a particular stage of ripeness. I'm definitely not American in that, I'm glad to say. You were the youngest, I'm pretty sure, and you're not so much younger than I. What is it, ten, twelve years? Well, anyway, this nubile Nadine must have made up her mind the minute she saw me—she was a character, I'll tell you—because as soon as she got the chance she literally rubbed up against me. That's the only way to put it. There was definitely some . . . chemistry, *magari*. I didn't think much of it, it was just droll. After all, the judge was right across the room, and at this point, well, I'm not one for quickies in hallways and things of that nature, not that I ever was, much. But before she left she asked me my room number at the motel. Expect me, she said, just like that. Wouldn't you know it, later that night there's a knock at my door. Circe of the Sunbelt. Not a word of explanation, how, what, anything. There wasn't time, frankly. It was one of those wild, once-in-a-lifetime things. This woman, Laura, was like a savage. I've never seen anything so uninhibited in my life. Q. chuckled. What could I do? She brought out the beast in me.

I pressed my finger soundlessly on the button, then kept the phone off the hook for a while, holding my breath, as if it required my total rigidity to break the connection. A few seconds after I replaced the receiver, the phone rang.

What happened?

We were cut off, I said.

Oh. That's odd. Well, where were we?

You were in El Paso. Look, I can't stay on. I'm expecting a call from my editor. It's important.

At this hour? Okay. Did I run on again? Sorry. So, I'll talk to you soon. I'll call you in a couple of days.

I didn't tell him I found him loathsome. That would only have strengthened the bond. No words could weaken it. His spell thrived on words, exchange. The way out was silence.

Months later when we were lovers again I wanted to ask, What did she do? Maybe I could learn it. I'm willing to learn. But Q. seemed very content—he himself was not what I'd call savage—and I never got around to asking.)

You're afraid to have me stay, aren't you? he says, still standing on Peter's corner.

Yes.

What are you afraid of? That it will start all over again? That might not be so bad. You never seemed afraid before.

I hail a taxi cruising up the avenue about two blocks south. In less than a minute I'm out of here, out of danger. Did I really hear what I just heard? For a moment the mist clears, my legs are light. I could, maybe, fall into Q.'s arms and erase the past dozen years. . . . Oh, God! It takes the last dregs of my will to master the impulse.

Yes, I'm afraid it might start all over again, I say. I'm also afraid it might not. Or start and stop again.

Q. looks at me with utter comprehension. Maddening. If I leaned forward two inches, . . . No, he just wants a comfortable place to stay for two weeks. With me in it. The taxi pulls up.

Anyway, I say, I have a friend who's around a lot.

Oh. A man, you mean. You didn't tell me.

I open the taxi door. No, I say, you're the one who tells stories.

(So many stories, fed to me like lotuses, that he makes me forget the story of my own life. Well, this time I'm heading home.)

Who is he? I want to know about him. What is he to you? Tell me, this is important.

I've got to go now. (I'm in the cab, I give the address, but Q.'s holding the door open.)

You're very hard on me, Laura, he says, leaning inside.

Hard? I say, as the meter clicks on. Because I can't fit you in?

Because you expect me to be what I'm not. This is who I am now. I can't change at this point.

How I wish I had it in me to make some perfect gesture, kiss him hard on the lips and say good-bye forever, memorably, or cast a glance so filled with *chi* that he staggers off in retreat—anything to mark this moment when I am actually standing firm and refusing Q. what he wants, not out of wisdom but some animal instinct of self-preservation. Instead I drop my purse and Q. deftly reaches in to pick it up.

"Well, Missus, we are ready?" asks the turbaned driver.

We never ate the grapes or cookies, I say.

Oh! Q. smacks his forehead dramatically. And they looked so good. Thank you for bringing them.

Eat them with Peter. 'Bye. I pull the door closed, leaving him disconsolate on the street.

Does this mean I am "getting over" Q.? Does the onset of one sickness obliterate the previous sickness? Or is it all the same sickness translated into different symptoms, behaving metaphorically? Whatever it is, I'm not fond of this new-found sanity. In the stories, the princess always risks it and takes in the frog. Two weeks of unadulterated Q., at my table, surely on my pillow, like being stoned. Yes, and then what?

As we slog through ear-splitting traffic, motorcycles being gunned and puling car alarms, plus the occasional pneumatic drill cracking the pavement, I lean back and stretch my legs in what might be the last Checker cab in New York. A clutch of police cars and an ambulance block the entrance to the Port Authority, and the next thing I know the taxi driver is tapping on the glass to rouse me. "Missus, missus! You have reached your destination. You are okay, missus?"

I can hardly wait to get back to bed, the only trusty lover. And to my squirrel.

It's no longer there. I didn't think it had the strength to leave. The last few times, it hardly responded to my taps, as if it no longer cared about such minor nuisances. Could his friends have carted him off to a sacred burial ground? Ants, they say, do something like that. Why not squirrels? Unless it simply decided to die elsewhere, on some other ledge, if you could call it a decision. But when I look closely I see that like his cousin rat, the squirrel has built a little nest of ivy—leaves, twigs, and pale-green berries—along with clumps of hair and scraps of tissue, suggesting he plans to return. I haven't seen the last of him. I'll have to clear out this nest as I did the other, the rat's. Later. When I'm stronger.

5

"Call the doctor at ten o'clock Monday morning for the results of the blood tests," Cindy, the receptionist, said as I left.

"The doctor isn't in now," she said on Monday morning at ten. "You can call back at eleven."

I took out the stack of pages I'd been working on, about Ev's town, but couldn't concentrate.

At eleven: "The doctor isn't in now. Try him in an hour or so." The voice sounded awfully stern for Cindy. It sounded like Cindy's mother, or a Cindy considerably aged and hardened over the past week, like cheese.

"You told me to call at eleven."

"He's out on an emergency. Try at about one."

I forced myself at least to read over what I'd written—an easy part, about the family house I'd soon be staying in with Jilly.

"The house rests on one of the town's many low, rounded hills with the air of someone settled in for a long stay: an old Cape Cod house more roomy than it appears from outside, its lines as simple as the houses children draw in their first pictures, with square boxes for windows and a brick chimney rising firm and squat from the A-shaped roof.

Through gales and hurricanes and the intermittent sun of over a century, its shingles have weathered to a gray soft as cloud, and in the misty early mornings, the house seen from a distance seems no more than a denser patch of mist. Toward mid-morning, as the sun burns off the fog and brightens the salty air, the color of the house darkens, so that by early afternoon it stands clear against the deepening blue of a broad sky. The soil around the house is thin and dry, covered by low drab shrubs with here and there a cluster of flowers springing up as if by accident, blazing tiger lilies or daffodils or impatiens. Farther back is an ancient toolshed, upright and neat, and behind that the brush dissolves into woods. Similar houses nearby are screened from view by the trees."

Not too bad, but I was in no state to judge, couldn't quite get my mind around it.

"The doctor isn't in yet," said the voice at one-fifteen. "Try again at about four-thirty."

"But at four-thirty I'll be out. I have an appointment." Querulous. Very poor strategy.

"Well, keep trying, that's all I can say."

"Can't you tell me the results?"

"No, only the doctor can do that."

Could be pretty bad, if she wasn't allowed to tell.

I pushed on. "Though it was built in 1877, the house is well sealed and well heated. It was built for comfort and tended to, despite the legacy of sadness that seeped through the family generation after generation the way damp seeps into the walls of other houses, making them moldy and chill. Indeed, the damp is hard to avoid, what with the sea to the east and the bay to the west and the river, as a bonus, running through the already watery town—the Pamet River, named for the Indians whose place this was before the Pilgrims landed some nine miles north."

Pilgrims and Indians seemed very far away, maybe too far for my purposes. It was a relief to give up at four o'clock and join Mona at our favorite local hangout, the Café Athena. Every few days we would sit lengthily at one of the scarred wooden tables beside the open windows and watch Broadway's passing scene; if friends went by we pulled them in to join us. The food was mediocre at best, in fact patrons had been known to bring their own. It took skill to catch the attention of the help—actors and graduate students so engrossed with their chatter at the kitchen door that they had to be coerced to stop by. The Athena had a collection of two tapes, repeated in alternation all day long: *The Four Seasons* and Handel's *Water Music*. Outside, buses lumbered past, beggars lurched.

"Remind me," I told Mona, "at four-thirty I have to make a phone call."

"Okay. Speaking of phone calls, I just spoke to Madelyn Prescott yesterday. She's coming to New York pretty soon and she's going to stay with us for about nine days."

"That's a long time for a guest. Do you mind?"

"Not at all. She's an ideal guest, a real pro. Last time I hardly knew she was there. She goes out in the morning and stays out all day and most nights doesn't even show up for dinner. When she does she often makes her own food because she's a vegetarian. She's living near Santa Fe now. Raising llamas."

"Llamas? Like in *Doctor Dolittle*? Listen, let's try waving at them. I'd love an iced tea."

"Why don't I just go up and ask. It'll be quicker." Mona slithered off in her feline way. "Yes, llamas," she said, sitting down again. "It seems they're very sweet and people do quite well raising them."

"What for?"

"Well, people rent them for treks in the mountains. That sort of thing. But she's not that far along yet. They're very expensive and she's starting small, with just two, I believe. The idea is that when they're ready she'll breed them. They're cuter than camels or mules, she says. Oh, she's also a Buddhist now."

"That figures. Llamas. Tibet. There are Buddhists in Tibet. The Dalai Lama. Remember we went to hear him speak at Columbia last fall? Compassion, he said. Overcoming anger."

"Yes, that's all well and good, but the kind of llamas she raises are from Peru, it so happens. How's it going?" she asked Daria, the anthropology student bringing the drinks.

"They're closing us in two weeks. Didn't you see the notice on the door?"

"No. How come?" Mona's usually composed face was stricken.

"Cineplex Odious is buying the movie next door and the whole building and they want everyone out. It's not that they're actually throwing us out, just, like, quadrupling the rent. What's happening all over town."

"Isn't there anything we can do?" I asked. "Protest or picket, like in the old days?"

"I think it's too far gone for that," said Daria.

"I'll ask Tim. A friend of mine, a lawyer. Maybe he can suggest something."

"I doubt if Tim would be much help," said Mona with asperity. "He's a corporate lawyer, remember? He's on the other side."

"I always forget. It must be denial. How about your brother Carl, then? Does he do cases like this, or just violence?"

"Thanks for the sentiment," said Daria, "but I think it's a done deal. You could speak to the owner, though, and find out for sure." She nodded toward the carrot-haired balding man who usually sat in a corner drinking coffee, reading thick books and taking notes in a steno pad.

"I will," said Mona. "What will happen to you?"

"I'll go across the street to the Indian place, I guess. The only trouble is, you really have to work there." She slouched away, pulling up her sagging jeans.

"This is very unsettling," I said. "Two weeks! It's like being evicted. We'll have to find someplace else. So, about those llamas, can you also shear them for wool or am I thinking of alpacas?"

"You're thinking of alpacas, Laura. I thought I might make a little dinner when Madelyn's in town. Invite some of the people we used to know, see what they're up to. Sort of a reunion."

The downtown group where I met Q. We also did a season of summer stock on the Jersey shore—old favorites: *Mrs. Warren's Profession. Guys and Dolls. Peter Pan*. I was an Indian. I can't remember who Madelyn was. Tinker Bell? Mona did the costumes, but left the theatre soon after—impossible while raising children, she said, with the husbands coming and going. She started her own business. Let Me Dress You was now a thriving concern with the lowest possible overhead; one room in her apartment held the treasures she gleaned from thrift shops all over town. She talked at length to her clients—wealthy East Siders to working-girl types newly arrived from the provinces—like a therapist doing an intake interview, took their measurements, then went out and found wardrobes to suit their desired identity. Help Recycle, she advertised. The Most Painless Makeover in New York. Most of the time she herself wore jeans and a T-shirt, as if scorning a busman's holiday, but now and then she would turn up looking like one of Cleopatra's handmaidens or Madame de Staël's guests. "Identity is fluid," said an Art Deco poster hanging in the alcove she called her dressing room. No inconsistencies bothered her, a postmodernist let loose in the world of fashion. Low fashion.

"So what do you think, Laura? Would that be fun? A little dinner?"

"Sure, very nice."

How nice was questionable. I preferred to gossip about Madelyn rather than see her. Still, dinner at Mona's was always worthwhile since she was a gourmet cook. And it seemed only fair that one should pay for unrestricted gossip (llamas!) by actually seeing the person, which in turn would provide more material for the data bank. . . .

Mona, the provident, checked her watch. "It's four-thirty, Laura."

"Oh, thanks." The doctor was in! Yes, I'd wait. The phone was on the wall across the room at the bar, where the sounds of buses and car alarms were less acute, but three seated men were bellowing over some baseball contretemps, while the gang of graduate student and dancer waiters tittered over someone's audition for *Miss Saigon*, not to mention the Vivaldi tape. *Autumn*. When the doctor came on I could barely hear him.

"It looks like you do have something," he began.

"Leukemia or hepatitis?" I wanted to say it first myself. "AIDS? Lupus?"

"No, nothing like that." I caught something about mononucleosis. Not mono itself but a relative of. Often its aftermath, like the dessert. This doctor of Ev's was a poet *manqué*, another metaphor maker. My just deserts?

"But I never had mono. Not that I know of."

"You had it sometime in the past. You have the antibodies. You just weren't aware of it."

So much for my powers of awareness, in which I took such pride. Still, what a relief. Just then the espresso machine began roaring and I strained to hear. A little-understood virus, I gathered.

"It usually takes about four to six months." His next words were pulverized along with the Colombian coffee beans.

"I'm sorry, I can't hear you very well. Could you repeat that, please?"

"I said, don't be surprised or alarmed if you get strange aches and pains or feel very fatigued."

"Oh."

More fractured words. I felt rather heady, knowing I had something mysterious and tenacious though not fatal. Neurasthenia, it sounded like. All those Victorian heroines we thought were stifled by the patriarchal system—was it just a virus? Would this discovery bring down Women's Studies?

"I'm sorry, I'm having trouble hearing. I'm in a bar. I tried calling earlier several times, but I couldn't reach you."

He didn't say—or perhaps he did for all I knew—If you're so sick what are you doing in a bar?, but he might have thought it. Standing firm and persisting, I thought in reply. Continuing.

I caught something about "titers." Or was it "'taters"? Should I eat potatoes instead of watercress? Was he Southern? Irish? My titers were high, he seemed to be saying. I didn't know what titers were but I couldn't ask him to repeat again, not that it would have done any good, what with the *Four Seasons* and the waiters and all the rest. I'd look it up later. Or ask Tony, my stepson. Surely he was a doctor by now, or far enough along to know the lingo. I hated to ask him anything, seeing that he'd been angry at me since he was eleven, but this wasn't much.

"Is there anything I can take for it?"

"I'm sorry to say there isn't a thing I can do for you. We don't know enough about this. Take good care of yourself. Get plenty of rest and wait it out. It'll pass. Don't treat yourself like an invalid. On the other hand, don't overdo things. And don't let anyone try to tell you you're malingering. It's really a virus. Your titers are very high."

No, it definitely wasn't about potatoes.

I couldn't help feeling a kind of pride about those titers, whatever they were. "Thank you," I said, as if he'd paid me a compliment. But he sensibly took this as a close to our conversation.

"Call me if you have any other questions."

Happily he had no odd questions himself.

"So?" inquired Mona.

She was both skeptical and concerned. A bonus: she knew about titers. She'd been a chemistry major in college, a tidbit I hadn't known. Good for the data bank.

"They keep diluting your blood—titration, it's called—and the number of titers is how many dilutions in which the blood still shows traces of the virus. Or of the antibodies, to be precise. So how many titers did you have?"

"I couldn't hear the number exactly. It was too noisy. In the low two hundreds, maybe? Does that sound reasonable?"

Mona's green eyes widened. I didn't really care how many. I was more intrigued by the wonderful metaphor. How many dilutions would it take to get the image of Ev's bloody neck out of me, or Q.'s vacillations, or Tony's resentment, and a dozen other sickening components? If I put myself through a wringer would I come out dry and pure, an amnesiac like Ronald Colman in *Random Harvest*? (Tim and I watched that a few weeks ago; he has a flair for choosing old films.)

Mona didn't say anything soothing or encouraging. That wasn't her style. But she did invite me to come home with her and stay for dinner.

"If you don't mind having dinner with my mother, that is. She's staying with us for a few days. Actually I should get going. It's close to five, Dave's away, and I've left her alone long enough. Okay?"

"Sure, thanks. How is Evelyn these days?"

"You'll see for yourself," she said curtly.

Evelyn was asleep in the guest room when we arrived, and I, too, took a nap on the living room couch while Mona went to work her magic spells in the kitchen. Hours must have passed; when I woke the light was waning. I was sitting near the big picture windows gazing out at the river when I heard shuffling steps—Mona coming from the guest room, half pushing, half leading her mother as if she were a large package on a dolly. I had met Evelyn several times over the years, before the Alzheimer's had set in; she used to sing, I recalled, in amateur theatricals and church choirs. She looked a bit dazed now, but no more so than someone just awakened. She was a slender, olive-skinned woman with hazel eyes and silvery hair stylishly cut. In her light print dress with a wide belt (surely not one of Mona's acquisitions), her white sandals and rose-painted toenails, she might have been a fashion model for *Modern Maturity*.

"It's Laura, Mom. Remember Laura?"

"I'm not sure we've met." The hand she offered reluctantly was cool and limp. "Are you Mona's friend from the flea market?"

"No, I'm a writer."

She sat down beside me and looked out the window. I followed her westward gaze, where the purple light was deepening, with a greenish tinge.

"Don't worry if you don't get a response," said Mona. "She tunes out a lot these days. Come, dinner's all ready."

At the table beside the window, she had set out a feast of roast chicken with rosemary, green rice and salad. Mona sat at my left, her back to the river and the view, facing Evelyn. She put food on Evelyn's plate, and every so often Evelyn speared a morsel and brought it absently to her mouth. Meanwhile, the lights across the river gradually came on—a follow-the-dots puzzle—and the lordly Hudson took on a sheen. Beyond it, to the south, glittered a magical little enclave resembling Oz, which Mona informed us was actually Hoboken, New Jersey.

"If it's a nice day tomorrow I think we'll drive out to the country. How would you like that, Mom, an afternoon in the country?"

" 'Take me out to the ball game,' " Evelyn sang, and I suppressed a giggle.

"It's all right, you can laugh. She doesn't mind. A little lower, Mom, okay?" Evelyn was belting out, " 'I don't care if we never get back.' "

"How about some iced tea?"

Evelyn nodded. " 'I'm a little teapot, short and stout,' " she sang. "That's what you used to sing in school, Mona." She held the glass quite steadily, I noticed. She might have lost her grip mentally, but things did not leap from her hands as they did from mine. I was being quite careful with my glass and silverware and napkin.

" 'Here is my handle, here is my spout.' " She did the hand motions just as Jilly used to do.

Suddenly a streak of color exploded outside and I sat upright to stare toward Hoboken. "Fireworks!" I cried. "It's fireworks across the river. Look!"

"Well, well," said Mona. "Quite a display, isn't it?"

Evelyn clapped her hands with delight, then turned to me and smiled. It was a professional show of splendidly cosmic proportions, loud and brilliant, one of the rewards of living in this decaying yet exuberant city. The noise suggested a major battle taking place just out of sight, with the lights its visual expression. The best moments were the suspenseful dark times before the outbursts, the waiting for unimaginable wonders.

"This is fantastic," I said. "It must be for July Fourth. But that's a few days away, isn't it?"

"It's coming from Hoboken. Maybe they've been misinformed over in Jersey," said Mona, swiveling for a brief glance. "So about my little reunion party when Madelyn's here. . . . I'll have to start calling people.

Too bad Quinn isn't around. We could use someone like that, to hold forth, tell stories."

"He's in town, as a matter of fact, but I think he'll be gone by then. I just had lunch with him. I forgot to tell you. He was full of stories, yes. Mostly about love. He's compelled, like the ancient mariner. He thinks love in any form is the most fascinating story." I didn't add that I thought so, too. So did Evelyn, apparently.

" 'Oh, my man, I love him so,' " she sang in a beautiful contralto, " 'he'll never know. . . .' "

"It never lets up with you two, does it?" said Mona. "It's like a soap opera where the actors have a lifetime contract. They have to keep writing scenes for them."

Outside, a huge purple dandelion erupted over the river, scattering light like seeds. Evelyn grabbed my hand and squeezed it. "Isn't this fantastic?" she said. "It's better than in the old days. A few things are better than in the old days."

"The Chinese invented fireworks," I said. "They used it at all their great festivals, my Tai Chi teacher once mentioned, to scare off the demons that come out at night."

"Is that so?" said Evelyn. "And what happens when the festivals are over? Do the demons come back?"

"I guess so. I didn't ask. Actually, I've decided that what Q. really is is a flasher," I told Mona. "Oh, not literally," I hastened to amend, as Evelyn blinked and sat up straight with a disapproving frown. "Not a weirdo. He's every inch the gentleman—Laurence Olivier as Hamlet is his idol. A prince of a man. I mean an emotional flasher. He has to give you a quick and shocking peek at who he is and what he looks like underneath. And while no one likes a real flasher, this kind has a certain appeal. To judge from the results, at any rate."

"That's quite good," Mona remarked, as if I had constructed a minor work of art, as certain conversational gambits are. A scaled-down version of performance art. "Very good, Laura."

"Thank you." We paused for another magnificent shower, blue and yellow petals strewn through the sky. Faintly, in the distance, a fire engine wailed.

Evelyn, who had been crooning to herself, rang out, " 'He isn't true, He beats me, too.' "

"Oh, no." I turned to face her. "It's nothing like that. You've got the wrong idea."

"It's only a song," said Evelyn. "Don't get all worked up. Look, the stars are coming out. What was the rhyme you used to love?" she asked Mona.

" 'Twinkle, twinkle, little star.' "

" 'How I wonder where you are,' " said Evelyn.

" 'Up above the world so high, Like a . . . Like a   ,'?" Mona coaxed.

"Diamond!" said Evelyn at last. " 'Like a diamond in the sky.' " She rose abruptly and began striding haughtily across the room.

"Hey, wait, Mom. Where are you going?"

"I have to make a phone call. What did you think? I'm not totally out of things yet, you know."

"Who are you calling?"

"A friend. Do you mind?" From the back, as she turned into the bedroom, she seemed girlish, the frothy dress fluttering about her slim legs.

"The reason I asked," murmured Mona, "is that she's taken to calling people she hasn't seen in years, sometimes in the middle of the night, to tell them what she thinks of them."

"You're very patient," I said. "It's a wonder you get any work done."

"It's not so difficult yet. When I'm working at home she can stay here with me, and the rest of the time I have people with her in her apartment. No, the worst is to come. Actually I find it easier to talk to her this way. I tell her things I wasn't able to say before. She was nothing like she is now. Very businesslike. Believe me, I'm more maternal to her than she ever was to me. I don't know where all the nursery rhymes and getting thrilled over fireworks are coming from. What's the matter, are you okay?"

"Just tired. I'll help you clean up and then I'd better go home."

"Never mind that. Shall I walk you? It's a nice night."

"Walk? Are you kidding? No, I'll take a cab. Thanks. I'm sorry to cut this short."

As soon as the doctor offered his diagnosis I began feeling sicker, as if official recognition, like election to political office, had granted my virus a license for all sorts of bad behavior.

A real illness. Not grief or guilt in translation, not urban decay or environmental pollution, witchcraft or the movement of the tides. A man of science ought to know. Don't let anyone accuse you of malingering, he said.

Little did he know how much I'd like to malinger, but I can't seem to get the hang of it. I keep shuffling to my desk to work on my book, give Ev a better destiny. I leaf through notes or old Town Reports, tinker with a phrase here and there, until my brain short-circuits. Lights out. I sit holding the thin manuscript on my lap like a mother in a famine-struck land with nothing to offer her baby, hoping it will grow from love alone.

There are a few things I can still do, though, such as buy groceries. The first strategy in the face of danger is to keep to routine. Persist. Flexibility is all very well, but not until called for. I've heard what happens to people who let go, especially if they live alone. It starts with not going out to buy food. Soon I wouldn't bother to dress or comb my hair, would even leave off washing. I wouldn't make the bed, since I'm so often in it or on it. Yes, it is my lover, but in time lovers stop preening for each other and allow themselves to be seen in disarray, even dishevelment.

With no food in the house I might stop eating altogether, though more likely, not being of an anorexic persuasion, I'd languidly lift the phone to order a pizza or Chinese food (my sallow tinge and yeasty smell shocking the young fellow who bikes it over to the door), then leave the remains—burnt crusts, white cardboard cartons with soy sauce dripping out the bottom—wherever I happened to be at the last bite, probably in bed, where one day I'd be found—Mona or Joyce or Jilly or even Q. having prevailed upon the super to open the door since I'd given up answering the phone—my hair matted and my face gray, my eyes dimmed and my fingers on the coverlet making the faint clutching motions of the dying or the mad, the apartment musty with cobwebs and Mozart's *Exsultate, Jubilate* all unraveled on the tape player. As Q., years ago, unforgettably described finding his father in his Georgetown house, after Aldo was widowed and had retired from the Italian diplomatic service. Q. never dreamed it was only the beginning. Since then Aldo has been in and out of mental hospitals more times than I can count. Depression, the experts call it. He's lost his *joie de vivre*, is what Q. says. He and his sister Gemma are summoned to Washington at crises to confer with doctors, defrost the refrigerator, air out the house and buy clothing in different sizes, for Aldo's weight fluctuates wildly when he's at his worst. At the hospital where he's been carted off, they jump-start his life with pills. What else? says Q. That's definitely not performance art.

So my kitchen is well stocked, not the larder of a person who daydreams of jumping from windows, for art or for real.

Then there's the telephone, after the radio my other lifeline. I really ought to call my cousin Joyce but I'm afraid. She might be so concerned that I'd end up having to console her. The delicate calibration of sympathy is, like cooking, an art everyone dabbles in but few, alas, do to perfection. Scrumptious though it is, sympathy must be offered in exactly the right tone to be effective, and in exactly the right proportions, like salt or spices. Too little leaves you deprived or dissatisfied, while too much can make you gag.

Joyce's sympathy can be boundless, a flash flood sweeping off everything in its path on a tide of commiseration. Her praise is the same, wildly exceeding its object. When I appeared in my first walk-on, two-line role in a gritty church basement theatre on an East Village street of abandoned buildings, she was as proud as if I'd done Lady Macbeth at the Old Vic. "Stop it," I hissed, "you're embarrassing me." "What do you mean?" she protested in her symphonic tones. "I'm so thrilled I could weep." "Well, don't," I warned. What if I really were playing Lady Macbeth? She leaves no margin.

Joyce herself knows no bounds, a lushly unkempt, radiant woman whose tremulous musical voice pours from her throat like liquid gold, an anthropologist who has attached herself and her professional future to a small tribe in West Africa (though she tells me I must call it an ethnic group or, even better, a native nation). She blossomed out of the ruddy, good-hearted girl I played with growing up. I was an only child and Joyce became the self-styled big sister, the point man, so to speak, for perilous ventures into the steamy jungles of adolescence. Didactic, protective, she got everywhere five years ahead and passed along the word on menstruation, sex, and filling out college applications.

"Oh, that's awful," she said soothingly over the phone. A mild molassesey tone. "I had a feeling all wasn't well when I didn't hear from you in so long. But look, you'll carry on. I'm sure you'll be fine. Tell me if there's anything I can do."

She meant it, too. It was she who appeared, scarves whirling, to take me to the hospital in a cab the long-ago night I had the miscarriage. And later when Ev died, she arrived promptly, bracelets jangling, to manage everything. Still, I kept a wary distance.

"I will. Thanks."

"You sound very low. I can hear it in your voice. But look, you're strong, Laura. You'll rally. Look, I don't know whether this would help, but you could try my physical therapist. She does excellent massages for aches and pains."

"I'll think about it."

"I really feel terrible for you. What a thing to happen. I'd be utterly devastated. Not to be able to—Oh, I can imagine how—"

Ah, here we go. The waters had been gathering slowly. I started to say good-bye before they split the dam of self-restraint. We arranged to have lunch as soon as I got back from the Cape.

"If you like, I'll come by for you in a cab."

"No, thanks, Joyce. I can manage."

I KEEP GOING. Continue, as the Tai Chi teacher says. Persevere in my own being, as I once had a brave heroine who knew Spinoza do in the face of adversity greater than my own. How easy it is to have characters behave with pluck and virtue. I admire her more than ever, that fantasy of mine.

Weeks ago I'd promised to speak at a panel discussion honoring a great Italian woman writer who recently died, and dammit, I'd get there. I didn't prepare any formal remarks but I knew the subject well. Words, as usual, would come to my aid. More important was what to wear.

Before rummaging through the closet, I switched on my friendly radio, which obliged with just the sort of diversion I craved. An Italian city official from Verona was being interviewed, through an interpreter, about the search for a woman to answer the many letters addressed to Juliet Capulet, since the person who for years had been answering Juliet's mail was retiring. The dress fell from the hanger as I stood entranced. Letters came from all over the world asking Juliet's advice on *problemi di cuore*, which the interpreter translated as "relationships." Even with the meager Italian I'd picked up from Q., I could bet that *problemi di cuore* were not "relationships." Verona needed a person who could write back with warmth and understanding. Well, this certainly qualified for the "nice work if you can get it" category. I'd gladly learn Italian. Q. could help with the finer points over the phone. But would I qualify otherwise, with my history, that is? In prompt response, the interviewer asked how come so many people seek Juliet's advice, seeing that she did not fare so well in her own relationship? Evidently, replied the Italian through the interpreter, the letter writers feel that despite if not because of that fact, Juliet would be sympathetic to their *problemi*.

It was painful to tear myself away from this discussion, but I managed to get downstairs, waved to Luke reading his paper in the calm of early evening—he gave a suave approving nod at my efforts to dress for the occasion—and climbed into a taxi.

The driver was Greek. Before long we found ourselves discussing the Greek origins of democracy (never mind the slaves and women, save the energy for the talk), as well as Socrates and his cohorts in the agora, the hemlock and so on. Very nice to sit back in an air-conditioned car, shielded from the horns and sirens, hearing almost firsthand about classical antiquity. Not at all a bad way to pass the time, though it soon appeared I might be spending the entire evening: the driver, notwithstanding his Attic wit and learning, couldn't find a thread through the labyrinth of lower Manhattan and I wasn't much help. Factor in the late rush-hour traffic and the trip took twice as long as it would have done by subway. We parted with genuine regret, and I went woozily through the auditorium toward the room behind the stage.

"Just in time, Laura," the moderator greeted me, a rising young literary star with the aplomb of a talk-show host. "You can leave your bag here, the ladies' room is back there if you want it, but hurry up because we're going out there pronto."

"Fine. Can I just sit down for a second?"

The others were pacing around, gossiping, glancing at their notes, adjusting their bra straps. I sank into a chair and a veil of gray descended over my eyes. Then the floor was rising to meet my face. I dropped my head down to my knees.

"Laura, are you okay? What is it? Stage fright?" It was Charlotte, a kindly older writer I'd shared a stage with twice before. She bent down and patted my shoulder.

"Nothing. I'll be all right in a minute."

"Why don't you go and arrange chairs or something, Vicky, so they know we're on our way. And someone bring Laura a glass of water."

The faintness passed. I tried to sit up straight but hadn't the energy to raise my head. My arms and legs were turning to sand again. "I don't think I can do this, Charlotte."

"Your face is pretty gray." She waved the others off. "Here, drink this. Maybe you're getting that flu that's going around."

I tried walking a few steps but it was no use. The couch across the room beckoned irresistibly and I fell onto it.

"Charlotte, come on," the moderator called. "Laura, I'll start and say you're late. Come in when you're ready. Ten, fifteen minutes."

"No, don't say I'm late. I can't go out there. I'm sorry to do this to you—" I was so sleepy I could barely get out the words. The figures of the others, hovering, concerned, faded into a mist and I closed my eyes. Through the patchy film of sleep I heard intervals of applause as the panelists were introduced. So this is how it's happening, I thought. With a drifting sigh, with a whimper.

After a while I got up and someone from backstage helped me outside and hailed a cab. A light rain was starting. This driver had no conversation but he maneuvered quickly through the slick, darkening streets, and when I next opened my eyes the car had stopped. Somehow I got to my door and made straight for the chair overlooking the river.

As darkness took hold and the rain got heavier, my body stiffened. The streets, the car, had been a shield. Now I was alone with it. I had failed. I was no good for anything. Useless. Finished. I couldn't pretend to fight it, whatever the doctor called it. The virus could take on the shape of any emotion, and it became a virus of dread. As I was the illness, so I was the dread. The aches started in my shoulders, moving down the skeletal chain to invade every joint. Fear translated and made tangible. Like the Samurai warrior in the book, I had no friends. Could I make my mind my friend?

I sank deeper into the chair, imagining the future, the vibrations this very moment rolling my way. Evelyn. Mona's mother lurked in my mind like a dream not yet dreamed. What could it be like, being Evelyn, gradually shedding everything but manners and habits of unknown origin? Soon even the songs would vanish. Maybe I should write down the facts of my life before I began to forget. So much sleep might obliterate memory, like a pillow pressed down on the brain. Jilly once told me about a conceptual artist who kept minute chronicles of every daily activity, from grocery shopping to chance encounters to making love, all painstakingly inscribed in color-coded charts and graphs. But her goal was to heighten awareness of daily life as a form of art, not to lasso memory.

I could envision myself years from now, not as lucky as Evelyn. No loyal daughter looking out for me. For all her affection, I doubted that Jilly would take it on. Too young. No, I'd be in a nursing home, a fairly decent one, let's say. Let's say I can talk almost rationally, I'm not a social disgrace. But I'm pastless. Forgotten the facts of my life, forgotten I was a writer, forgotten the books themselves, right now as unforgettable as my ears or skin. I do remember a few people who visit—Jilly, Joyce, Mona (not Tim, Tim is long gone)—though I've forgotten how their lives intersect with mine. I recognize them only from their visits. One day a visitor brings me my own books to cheer me, hoping perhaps to touch a nerve that might restore my life the way a second blow on the head restores to Ronald Colman in *Random Harvest* the life which the first blow on the head sent to oblivion.

The visitor arrives—most likely Joyce—toting a foot-high pile of books. For I've done what James Baldwin said is the writer's task, steadily, methodically filled an empty shelf with books. The visitor brings books I haven't even written yet: maybe a high-class thriller, and a comic novel set in the future, and the book which right now I find so intractable, the revised vision of Ev's life that keeps him safely in his seaside town so he doesn't end in a pool of blood on a Bronx street but grows old and hoary.

There are my books, handed to me one by one, and the pity is that I don't recognize them as mine, not even with the name and the photos (of a youngish, fairly elegant, interesting if not quite beautiful woman). When I'm told they're mine I don't understand. Nonetheless in my better moments, alone in my austere little room, I read them. Not straight through—I haven't the concentration for that—but passages here and there and . . . I like them. When the visitor—hopeful Joyce—returns, if I'm in one of my better moments, I say, Yes, I enjoyed the books but with certain reservations. I liked the part about the college years and the marriage, but why did she have to make the children die? That was cruel. Or, That was outrageous, about the adolescent seduced by the doctor. And presented so nonchalantly! And that seaside village: what was the author getting at, spinning quaint fantasies about the Moth Agent and the Shell-fish Constable's wife and the Surveyor of Lumber? Contrasting the peaceful town with the havoc of the city? What for? Everyone knows that already.

It's clear that my mind, what's left of it, has grown very ordinary. Or, rather, only the ordinary part remains; the radical imagination is gone. And I wonder why my visitor's eyes fill with tears.

Maybe I even read this book, long ago completed and published though now it lies dauntingly before me, and I say, Well, I liked it all right but why did she dwell for so long on the scene with the pool, wait-ing for the pool to fill up (a scene not yet written, its exact place uncer-tain)? What was the point of that?

WHEN YOU'RE TRAPPED IN A ROOM WITH FEAR, when the fear is trapped in you, it seems a reasonable response to the world. Given the certainty of death, primordial mother of fear, and the mystery of how she will greet us, it's a wonder we aren't paralyzed all the time.

I felt a hunger to hear my parents' voices, an infantile longing for them to rescue me, long distance. I reached for the phone, envisioning them in their sleekly landscaped Florida retirement community, which resem-bled a futuristic prison or orphanage outdoors, and indoors an unending airport lounge where they seemed content to wait out the remainder of their days, which might be many since they were barely seventy and in good health despite my father's complaints.

"Hah," he said on hearing my own complaints. "Everything they don't understand they call a virus. Get a few good nights' sleep, you'll be all right."

"Sleep is not my problem. I could sleep all day if I let myself."

"Maybe you should get a job, then. Get out more. At least you're not in pain. I'd take a virus any day over my arthritis. Listen to this. Our next-door neighbor here—he feels great, out on the golf course, plays cards every day, goes for a routine checkup and they find colon cancer. Bad, right? What everyone dreads. They take it out, a month later he's back to normal and out on the course again. He hardly felt a thing. Meanwhile they keep telling me this damned arthritis won't kill me, but I can't do what I like to do, like go bowling or play golf. . . ."

"Golf? Since when have you played golf?"

"I never did, but now that I'm retired I might like to."

"People seem to walk around golf courses very slowly. I bet you could manage it. Or ride in one of those carts."

"I'd be afraid to swing the club. I could throw my back out and then where would I be? Besides, my vision is so poor, I don't think I could see the ball. Listen, what you need is to get out of yourself a little. You're still a young woman. You could marry again. You could even have a baby, it's not too late. Nowadays lots of women do it at your age."

"Is Mom around?"

"We just want you to be happy."

"I know."

"Laura?" My mother took over. "You've heard of Dr. Atkins on TV? Listen to him. He knows all about these kinds of things. Get a pencil, I'll tell you when to watch. I watch him all the time."

The rain had stopped as we spoke, but the night sky was overcast. I could barely distinguish the trees from the river or the sky. The only clear thing in the blackened windows was my own face, artificially lit, staring back as if from the other side of the glass. What was that look? Stony? Bewildered?

My father used to laugh affectionately when we drove through tunnels and I cried, Get me out of here! When I was very small I cried it in panic, then as time passed, with less panic, until it became a joke, a ritual performance. For he always did eventually get me out as promised. Now is different. I'm not in a scary, closed-in, seemingly endless place. That dark place is in me. Get here out of me! I want to cry to him.

It's no performance, either. It takes discipline, yes, but unlike the projects Grace describes, it's not a discipline I've chosen. The man who slept outside for a year wasn't really homeless; he chose to behave as if he were. Though maybe he didn't feel he had a choice, any more than I feel I chose the books I wrote, or am writing. They chose me for their translator and I had to stick by them every waking moment, as the interpreter sticks to the Tai Chi teacher.

The eyes in the dark window glinted unnaturally; the corners of the mouth turned sourly down. Bitter, fearful and confused, not a face I'd like to present in public. It came to me that this was a juncture—since my father was not going to rescue me—when life begged to be lived as art. That way, it could be tolerated.

Very well. For a start, I put a better face on the face trapped in the glass. We've all heard of the hunger artist. I could be the first fatigue artist. Give it my best shot.

Too bad my performance would never resemble the lone violinist's I heard on the radio, or the soprano singing Mozart's *Exsultate, Jubilate*: they draw you in to surround you with feeling, a transforming embrace. My performance, born from constraint not freedom, would be a smaller, less generous thing. The audience would witness it, but only I would feel it. If I did it badly, no one would ask for a refund. If I did it well, only I would appreciate the craft required.

"Relax the thumbs. The thumb is the grabber. In Tai Chi there is no grabbing. Only relaxing. Yielding."

The teacher is chipper this afternoon. The hotter it gets, the more energetic he gets. He probably has some theory about the vibrations of heat drifting over the river stimulating the flow of the *chi*. For him, maybe. Not for the rest of us.

"Head erect, suspended from heaven." He moves through the group like a fish gliding through water—another of his favorite images—adjusting our postures. Most people are in shorts, except for the two stockbrokers, their shirtsleeves rolled up and ties loosened. "No, no. No weight on the front foot in this posture. Never equal weight on the feet. No stasis in the universe. With the weight on one foot you're always poised to move, in a state of readiness."

Grace breaks from the agonizing posture we've been holding for several minutes to rub her calves. "Shit," she mutters, "my legs are killing me." Assiduously, the interpreter translates, and the teacher approaches her.

"Learn to take pain," he says somewhat harshly, for him. He's generally forbearing. "Tasting bitter, we call it. Get used to the bitter taste." Chagrined, she resumes the posture. Her face isn't relaxed—she looks as though she has something bitter in her mouth.

"No, don't sit down," the teacher says to a student moving toward a bench, the young Dominican who works in the pizzeria on Broadway. I've seen him twirling the dough with a look of serene mastery, very like the Tai Chi teacher's look. "Never sit while doing the form. Relax, but don't sit."

His rounds finished, he returns to the front and allows us to rest. "Good, very good. Everyone's tasting bitter. You'll feel the pain less if you remember the rushing spring. Yes?"

We nod obediently.

"The energy from the earth bubbles up into the foot, the place just behind the ball of the foot, where you're rooted. That's why it's called the rushing spring. Concentrate on that energy and your legs won't hurt as much. Now for some push hands."

He pairs everyone carefully, large with small, athletic with delicate, old timers with newcomers. What matters is not size or muscle but pliability, as well as a feel for the oncoming energy in the partner's body. If you can get out of its way, become an elusive shadow or ghost, as the teacher calls it, your partner will stumble through his own momentum. Large with small so that neither will be tempted to use force—needless for the one, futile for the other. He pairs me with a big paunchy man called Marvin, who's been studying for a year or so, not nearly as long as I. We're not meant to be adversaries—we're in this together, like dancing partners but my malaise and crankiness get the better of me, and very quickly Marvin has me tripping around on the concrete.

"What's going on, Laura?" The teacher comes over, the interpreter at his heels as always. "Why do you resist him?" He demonstrates with Marvin and catches him before he falls. Marvin is gracious about it, I must say, and for a large man he successfully avoids using the strength at his disposal, not that it would do any good. In real life Marvin manages a local video rental place, and when I drop in, we exchange a complicit glance and a few words if he has time. How're you doing, I ask, and he answers, No complaints whatsoever.

"Continue," the teacher commands. Again Marvin becomes a shadow and I totter through the vacated space.

"Don't fight him, Laura, but stay with him. Adhere, follow his every move. Know what he's going to do before he does it. Never resist, but persist."

"This is just not my day, I guess."

"What's the matter?"

I answer with a shrug.

"Continue. Listen to his energy. Listen."

But I stumble again.

"How can you listen," the teacher says, "if you're so busy thinking and doing? Stop trying to do. You think nothing will happen unless you do it?"

I shake my head and move off to sit on a bench. He leaves me alone but appears worried. Even the interpreter looks concerned—I'm usually an apt student. What will he suggest this time? Chicory?

After a while he calls through the interpreter to those of us who've left the field. "Come back. I have a story to tell you. I see you all think this is very hard, the push hands. Hard to yield, hard not to use strength, hard to stay balanced. It's not hard if you do what I tell you. Do nothing. Let the other do it all. You think there's some secret power but it's no secret at all. Listen. Long ago, Lao-tzu, the Taoist master, and one of his disciples, Du Be, were walking with a student and they came to a river. Lao-tzu and Du Be stepped into the river and began walking across it, apparently walking on the water. Like your Jesus Christ, ha ha. When the student tried to follow them he found himself in deeper and deeper water. Lao-tzu, already on the other side, said to Du Be, 'Maybe we should tell our student where the stones are.' And now, thank you."

The class is over, and as usual we rest on the benches nearby. Grace sits rubbing her legs.

"I've been wondering about your work," I say. "Can you really make a living doing performance pieces?"

"Oh, no," she says with a laugh. "Most of us have to do what's called real work. I work for a women's co-op gallery downtown, running the business end. It's an okay job, but I could really use the time to develop new projects. It's amazing how much preparation they take. My Take Back the Night costume took weeks."

"What was that?"

"About three years ago I constructed this very chic outfit out of metal, a long dress with boots. It looked like a medieval suit of armor, and I wore it every time I went out at night or rode on the subway. When strangers asked me why, which of course they did, that was the whole idea, I explained it was to illustrate the feeling women have of being threatened in the city, sort of like a walking Expressionist painting. Right now I'm planning a dental show. I need some root canal work, and it occurred to me how a visit to the dentist's office is a formal ritual everyone goes through periodically. This new dentist tells me the equipment they use in dental school nowadays is very different from the old—they've got high-powered drills that make an excruciating noise, and you can't even buy the old kinds of chairs anymore. In the new chairs the patient lies down and the dentist sits. He's unhappy about this—he likes to stand—and we should be, too, because it makes the patient more powerless, and you know how at the dentist's office you're powerless enough as it is. So I thought I might have a show of the new equipment in a gallery, like a trade show, and actually have my dental work done on it in public. My dentist says he'd be willing to perform in front of an audience. I might even ask members of the audience to volunteer to have their teeth fixed as part of the show. It'd certainly be cheaper. And people would become aware of the social and political aspects of the process."

"What's so funny, Laura?" It's the Tai Chi teacher and the interpreter passing by.

"You should ask Grace. She's a performance artist. She's telling me about her work."

"Go ahead and laugh. I don't mind," says Grace. "Lots of people laugh. Listen, I laugh myself sometimes. Our kind of art," she tells the teacher, "what my friends and I do, is more of a process or a discipline than product-oriented." She stops considerately for the interpreter but he nods to her to go on; he can translate large segments at once, though God knows what he makes of them. "We're against the commercialization of art as a commodity to be shown in museums or sold in galleries. Our art is part of our lives, a way of life, political, social, personal. We don't compartmentalize."

This comes out rather shorter in Chinese than I would expect.

"In China in the old days, art was also not a career or even a profession but a way of life," replies the teacher. "The artist expressed the harmony of the universe through the five excellences, painting, calligraphy, poetry, medicine, and of course, Tai Chi Chuan. He would never have dreamed of selling a painting or a sample of calligraphy. He gave it away as a token of regard."

"Well," says Grace, "then we're part of a similar tradition. I'm not familiar with China. But the Western tradition goes way back. Diogenes, for example. Do you know about him?"

The Tai Chi teacher shakes his head.

"Diogenes was a Greek philosopher from the fifth century, B.C. The legend goes that he traveled around with a lantern in search of an honest man. But that's not the half of it. He spent his whole life acting out his beliefs, making gestures we'd consider absurd. He pretended to be a beggar and begged from statues, he walked through the streets backwards, he glued shut the pages of a book. Once when he was invited to give a public lecture he got up on the platform and just stood there and laughed. In the same vein, I have a friend who walked around Soho barefoot when the women's movement was in its heyday, with pots and pans hanging all over her body, to make a point. About women's lives, you know?"

"Very interesting," says the teacher after a pregnant pause. "But not exactly what I was thinking of. Chinese art did make beautiful things, poems, paintings, pottery, all of them with a great deal of empty space. The empty space represents the inner life, what is most important but unseen. Like the breath, which is invisible but sustains us. They say the ancient Tai Chi masters could live on air. Eat air, that is. Of course, I'm sure they preferred food, but in an emergency . . ." He smiles, but the interpreter doesn't smile, just keeps translating, as if the teacher is his muse. Or perhaps it's the other way around. Who is whose muse here?

"The space in a bowl, for instance," he goes on. "You use the clay to make it, and that is the part you see, but what makes the bowl useful is the space within. That metaphor is from Lao-tzu, to give proper credit."

"Yes, well . . ." murmurs Grace. "Eating air. And here we're always dieting. What is the cost of the classes, by the way? I've taken four now and haven't even paid you yet. I assume you're not giving them as a token of regard."

"No, unfortunately, here we all have to earn a living. We cannot eat air all the time."

They step aside to discuss her payment and I head home on sandbag legs, to work. But how can I get to work if I can barely get to my desk with the waiting pages about the idyllic town, rocked by the tides, where Ev grew up? I read over my pages in bed—the house, always the house:

"From the bedroom windows you can see the curving bay a half mile off, shimmering still waters where far out rest the blackened remains of a sunken ship, mast sticking up lonely against the sky. At low tide, when the bay is nothing but mud for a mile or more, parts of the hull are exposed, but at high tide only the mast and a few tips of wood or metal sway in the breeze. The easy way to the bay is to drive down the dirt road to the paved road that cuts through heathery fields and hushed, melancholy marshland, but a better way is to walk the narrow path through the woods, then through open brush tufted with blueberry bushes, gradually becoming sand dunes, and over the dunes to the beach itself, where clumps of black seaweed in orderly rows mark the reach of the tides."

Even in the bed's snug embrace I couldn't grasp the images tight, they whisked through my head like blown dust. Blown by fear.

As I lay back against the pillows, the warm, faintly stale smell of bed—of me in bed—rose up in a little invisible cloud. If it had a color, it would be amber. A homey smell like old-fashioned cooking, roasting meats and sweet pies in farm kitchens, but not quite as fresh. The bed and I smelled slightly overcooked, not yet distasteful. Was it me or the virus, that smell? Or are we one and the same?

Outside, the coming night was cool and uncommonly quiet. I could see the moon rising, also amber, a few gray wisps like stray hairs across its placid, indifferent face. Even with the windows open, the smell gave the room an airless feeling. Better to smell of the red sand in my veins, clean and dry as a desert. Then came the stiffening that used to alarm me so at the beginning. I waited for the sensation to shudder its way along my limbs, and once it passed off, I began very slowly to move through the apartment like a newborn animal testing its legs.

The lights going on over in New Jersey shimmered on the river and silhouetted the trees. I checked the French door for the reflection of that rich, defiant tail, its hairs quivering in the imperceptible night breeze. Nothing there. This was my moment.

I fetched a paper bag and a knife to cut away the ivy, and put on the orange rubber gloves I had used for the rat's nest that long-ago morning after Q. told me how much he'd missed me in China. I raised the screen, gathered up the damp clump of leaves and other debris bearing the contours of a recently occupied bed, perhaps as languorous and welcoming as my own, stuffed them in the bag, then gathered up stray leaves and twigs so as to leave a clear and, I hoped, uninviting space. I fastened the screen firmly but left the window open, for it was oppressively, deliciously hot. I thrust the bag into the kitchen garbage can, washed my gloved hands, then removed the gloves and washed again. I felt like a mortician, though I had not touched or seen the body. I was one of those women in old villages the world over who clean up the remains, while the mourners go about the streets. Then I took the elevator to the basement, where I deposited the bed in its final resting place.

Mona was not entirely correct about the llamas, I learned at her party. She was so rarely wrong that I took a secret pleasure in her small error. Madelyn, her houseguest, wasn't breeding the llamas, at least not yet. She had two, yes, but male.

"A female is very expensive, about ten thousand dollars. If I had ten thousand dollars I wouldn't use it to buy a llama but to go around the world," she explained in her thin, even voice, like a novitiate instructing a sixth-grade class. Madelyn paused a lot when she spoke, as Ev used to do, but her pauses seemed deliberately spaced to set off the words in a mystifying halo. Maybe I should have tried that with Q. from the start, to be more mysterious.

Madelyn was looking serene, tanned by the Southwest sun and draped in a long dress of vaguely Indian design and autumnal colors which made her pale face rise as if from one of Rousseau's tropical jungles. She no longer had that air of faint disapproval, as though nothing in the vicinity quite met her standards. Life, or the llamas, had mellowed her.

"So what do you use them for?" I asked.

"For backpacking."

"You rent them out to people who go into the mountains?"

"No, I go into the mountains myself. The mountains are full of mystery. I meditate."

What did she do with the llamas while she meditated? If they were Tibetan and hence Buddhist, perhaps they would meditate also. But since according to Mona they were Peruvian in origin, I imagined Madelyn tethering them to a tree like a cowboy securing his horse while he lolled around the campfire or poked through the sagebrush.

"Another thing is, I keep combing them out, hoping to get enough wool to make myself a sweater, but I haven't gotten there yet. A sweater takes an awful lot of wool."

"I thought so, about the wool. And you—" I turned to Mona—"you said I was thinking of alpacas."

Mona frowned, barely altering her intelligent, deadpan expression. When she permitted it, her face could be astonishingly fluid, revealing a hidden powerhouse of emotion. No wonder she kept it guarded.

I studied Mona, lanky, sleek and dark, quite splendid in one of her thrift shop finds, a 1920s dress covered in fringes, suggesting an antique lampshade. Strange that I trusted her so thoroughly, while most thin people made me suspicious. Though my trust was wavering: not only had she been mistaken about the sex of the llamas and misleading about the wool, but this was not the little reunion dinner she had promised. The room was filled with people who for the most part were standing, not sitting, the mark of a full-fledged party. It was informal enough to join groups without an introduction, yet large enough so we'd be eating on our feet, buffet-style. Mona's husband, Dave, was already carrying in platters from the kitchen. I'd have to be careful not to drop things.

I was in no shape for a party but had done my best, coaxed my body from bed and into festive attire, adorned my face with dangling earrings and makeup to mask its tense, bewildered look. The walk down the Drive was graced with one of our magnificent smoggy New York sunsets, creamy purple, amber and pink suspended over the river like a slice of melting spumoni. The kind of sunset that engenders, albeit briefly, faith in the world, love, redemption and every other good thing. Why sunsets should inspire such feelings, who can say? It must be a genetically programmed response to enable us to face nightfall, an appalling event, when you think of it—everything gradually losing color and outline to sink in blackness. Imagine how the first humans must have felt when they saw the night coming on. Maybe what made them human to begin with was the willing acceptance of night, the dawning of faith that light would return. I would have worshipped not the sun itself but its light. The sun is monotheistic, but light appears in infinite forms, the gods and goddesses in their protean moods.

I had arrived infused by the sunset, eager to watch its finale from Mona's high-ceilinged and benign apartment, and found this decorative crowd of theatre people. More spruced up and shiny than an ordinary crowd. Loud and expansive, with grand gestures and embraces, mannered pouts and raised eyebrows, smirks, snarls, and laughs of every sort. I'd always liked that atmosphere. It was no more artificial, really, than common social behavior, only more colorful. I might have taken on those manners had I stayed in the theatre. But just now it was daunting.

"Shit," I'd greeted Mona, "it's a real party."

"Well, yes, it grew," she said. "There were more people in town than I thought, and everyone wanted to bring their current loves, so here we are."

I should have brought Tim—something tangible to show for the intervening years—but Tim had a meeting to attend, and not being a wife, I hadn't dreamed of pressing him.

"The really lucrative thing about llamas, though . . . , is their manure," Madelyn was saying. "It's miracle manure. You can use it to grow just about anything, even in the desert. It's like rabbit pellets, very dry and cohesive . . . only larger, of course. I've given some to my neighbors. They put it on their gardens and the results are astounding. Things grow miraculously, even in the dry soil we have."

"Too bad you can't package it and sell it," I said.

"Oh, but that's exactly what I'm planning to do. I hope to start packaging it next winter. After all, people love to buy Santa Fe things—Santa Fe jewelry, Santa Fe food. . . . Anything with a Santa Fe label has this incredible cachet."

"Santa Fe shit," said Mona, and my trust was fully restored. Never mind the size of the party or the error about the wool or her disconcerting thinness emphasized by the fringed green lampshade dress.

I hastened to click on the tape machine in my head, which fortunately could work retroactively, picking up the previous ten minutes and then running for about half an hour. This had to be transcribed for the data bank. It had the aura of usefulness, though I wasn't sure why.

"It must be a beautiful place to live," I said, setting her up and rolling the tape. "I remember last time I saw you, oh, four or five years ago, you were hoping to live there someday. It's great that you've done it."

"Yes, well, I wandered around for a while first. . . . I lived in Tibet for almost a year. I wanted to study a certain kind of folk music, which I did, and I lived in an ashram. You know, in Tibet . . . it's amazing, people don't have our notion that the individual is central, only the group. You'd never have a phenomenon like that Madonna movie, for instance. People in Tibet would be baffled at why . . . anyone should choose . . . such display of self."

"You don't have to be Tibetan to be baffled," murmured Mona.

"In Tibet," said Madelyn, "they feel themselves part of a community. Living in that atmosphere helped me get my priorities straight. At this point I feel . . . I have my life all worked out. I have the work I want to do. I live where I want to live. I get up in the morning and look out and see those wonderful mountains. I go to feed the llamas and gather their droppings and . . . I feel terrific."

After a near-sacred hush, she added, "Mona told me about your husband. I was sorry to hear that. What a terrible experience it must have been. The city is such a violent place."

Mona exchanged a meaningful conjugal glance with Dave, who was arranging silverware on the buffet table across the room. Here in our rotting but alluring city we were humble. We didn't presume to work out our lives. If we get a meal nicely organized for thirty people, we feel it's been a good day.

"Yes. Well, thank you," I said. "It was a . . . a bad experience, as you say, but after two years you begin to—

"Dinner!" called Mona loudly, saving me from myself and swiveling to face the guests, her fringes following along diagonally like a well-ordered regiment. As she turned back and faced me she rolled her green eyes.

Madelyn slipped away, the folds of her jungle dress disappearing behind someone's somber slacks.

"So what did you make this time?"

"A new recipe. Llama molé," Mona said.

I drifted off to say hello to people I hadn't seen in years, not since the cast Halloween party where Q. assaulted the stagehand. Many of the same people were here—I wondered if they remembered it. We were in love in that savory adulterous way and Q. was going to tell Susan very soon. He came as Superman and I as Cleopatra—love makes you grandiose. So much so that not for a moment did I think of Susan at home with the flu, God forgive me. One of the stagehands showed up as a Nazi storm trooper—boots, belt, holstered gun, and a swastika on the sleeve of his uniform. As he goose-stepped around the room, people stared open-mouthed, a few trying feebly to laugh. Q. stalked over, puffing out his chest with the big red S. "That's not funny," he said. "In fact it's vile."

"Oh, come on," the fellow answered, "where's your sense of humor?"

"I have no sense of humor, that's right." The others tittered nervously; Q. was known for being funny. "I'd rather have no sense of humor than no brains." More words. Knave, beggar, coward, pander, and the son and heir of a mongrel bitch, "one whom I will beat into clamorous whining if thou deny'st the least syllable of thy addition." Words to that effect, more or less. We had just done Lear—Q. was Albany that time. Eventually Q. did start pummeling him as Kent did Oswald in the play, until the others tugged at his Superman cape and pulled him off. The knave got up, brushed off his uniform, and left. Q. was a hero but uncomfortable. "For my next number I'm going to fly," he said awkwardly, and downed a glass of bourbon. I loved him so then. For the awkward remorse as much as for the attack of righteousness.

I made my way into the crowd for the hugs and shrieks. Thank goodness no one would offer condolences about the shocking death of my husband, since no one else here knew I had married him.

"What about Quinn?" asked Sonia, a broad-boned woman who was once Ophelia in *Hamlet*. Today she'd have been cast as Gertrude. "Are you two still in touch?"

"On and off. I had lunch with him a couple of weeks ago. He was in a movie they were shooting in Queens."

I turned away, stumbling into a discussion about why women in concentration camps survived better than men. Because women are accustomed to mutual help and camaraderie, someone asserted. Did they survive better? I hadn't known. The question was not unimportant; it was not even tedious, which was more than could be said for global warming and adolescent anomie, but as usual I couldn't get interested. I kept thinking of all those newspapers Ev used to read in bed and how I had encouraged him to talk. I required conversation, and since he didn't talk about personal matters I became very knowledgeable, even about global warming, which was just coming into its own as a topic when he was shot.

"I always felt sure you and Quinn would get together one day," said Sonia, equally unable or unwilling, it appeared, to focus on the serious issue at hand. "I mean marry. Or something. But you never did, did you?"

"No. Not Quinn."

"Are you married?"

"Not anymore."

She smiled knowingly. "Me, too. I just divorced my second. It's an epidemic. So how are you? I know you've done okay. I've seen your books in stores. My mother reads them."

"To tell the truth, I'm feeling sick. In fact if I don't sit down pretty soon I'm going to fall. Excuse me."

Before I could move off she hustled me into a chair. "Sit. This minute. I knew it." She placed a comradely hand on my shoulder even though we weren't in a concentration camp; it wasn't a question of outlasting the Nazis, just a pleasant little summer party. "I knew it. When you came in the door it took me a minute to recognize you, you were so changed, and it wasn't only the years. I thought to myself, she must be sick. That is one sick girl."

Despair. All my efforts, my frisky clothes and ornaments, to no avail. I looked hideous. A spectator at life's banquet (not so bad were it really llama molé). An invalid tolerated at merry parties out of pity. Invalid, meaning not valid.

"I'm going to get you some food," said Sonia. "You stay right here. You'll feel better once you eat. You can eat, can't you?"

"I can eat just fine. But please don't bother. I'll get it myself in a few minutes."

"Uh-uh. I'll be right back." And she was. Like a hospital orderly, she presented the plate and bade me eat; all we lacked was the wheeled tray across the bed. Poached salmon, potato salad with leeks, that was a new one for Mona. Tunisian carrots? My, my. I raised the fork obediently.

"Now, what is the matter with you?"

Like a fool, I told her. Too demoralized to make anything up—the very same problem I had at my desk.

"Ah, so that's it. Listen, I must bring Greg over to meet you. He had that and he's fine now. He'll tell you exactly what to do."

She zipped off and I immediately rose, fortified by a few bites of excellent salmon. I'm no good at keeping distress to myself. Despite all those years with Ev, or perhaps because of them, I always rush for solace.

Dave, an ideal husband in Mona's view, the culmination of her hectic love life, was eyeing the array of food, possibly wondering if it was time to refill the platters.

"Tell me, Dave. Do I look sick? Sonia says I do."

He studied me as judiciously as he had studied the table. Dave was one of those comforting people who seem at ease in their lives without making any fuss over it. It wasn't hard to see his appeal to a woman whom love had frayed. He would never have announced that he had his life all worked out, yet he seemed to have done just that. Husky, round-faced, graying, he suggested a friar in a medieval monastery. I had to remind myself that he was not a friar but an industrial engineer. He knew no more about emotional blight than anyone else.

"You look very nice, Laura. I like that purple shirt. Is it one Mona found?"

"No, it's new. I mean, from a real store. Thanks, but that's not what I meant. Sick. You know, fading away?"

He studied me some more. No trace of irony. Mona had enough irony for both of them. "Not at all," he said levelly. "You look tired, not sick."

Nice, but not nice enough. I wanted enthusiastic conviction. Something a woman might give. I wanted one of the theatrical types to fall all over me with reassurances.

"Oh, Sonia's just a bitch," he said in his placid way.

"Is that your considered opinion?"

"Yes, she—"

I touched his arm in warning, for Sonia was closing in, pushing before her a youngish man. Her hand on his black shirt sleeve, fingers slightly bent to keep a grip, suggested property recently acquired. Chiseled face, blond, muscular. Vanity surging through his veins. Too much hard upper-body strength, the Tai Chi teacher would say; he'd snap like a stiff branch. The picture of health, though, which boded well. Sonia presented him as a fellow actor.

"Laura, you must talk to Gregory. He'll tell you how to get better."

Smiling, she moved off with Dave. Was I expected to congratulate her later, the way you tell new mothers how stunning their babies are?

He didn't seem eager to impart his knowledge. "What are your symptoms?"

I had a flicker of anxiety, as when reciting symptoms to doctors, who always looked skeptical at my performance. Gregory might make a suitable doctor if the acting didn't work out. When I finished he kept staring.

"Well, how did you recover?" I asked. "You look fine."

"There is a way to cope with this disease if you're willing to try it. I myself went to a homeopath, an Austrian down in Chelsea. You do know what a homeopath is?"

The mental Rolodex turned up homosexuals and psychopaths, the mind of a writer being nine-tenths ear. "Sure." They were an alternative to doctors, at any rate. They fought fire with fire, in small doses.

"Have you ever been to one?" Gregory asked tauntingly.

"No."

"Well, if you've never seen a homeopath, you have a surprise in store." He waited, with a slight smirk, but I vowed to wait him out, enjoying the certainty that I could send him reeling across the room if I chose. Into the silence came Sonia's throaty laugh a few feet off, and Dave's answering grunt. At last Gregory yielded. "He'll make all sorts of tests and ask you lots of odd questions, then depending on your answers, give you the appropriate herbs. You have to take these herbs at weird and very specific hours. . . . What do you do, anyway?"

"I'm a writer."

"That's good. If you worked a regular schedule you might have trouble following the instructions. For instance if you worked sixty hours a week in an investment brokerage firm. But with your lifestyle you can do it. Aside from the herbs, the other part of the cure is massive intravenous injections of Vitamin C. Not everyone can do this. It all depends on whether you want to go down to Chelsea twice a week and lie on this guy's cot for an hour in a darkened room with a tube in your arm. Some people can deal with this and others can't."

Clearly, we both suspected which camp I fell into. I ate morsels of the dinner to provide ballast for the Scotch I was planning to drink as soon as Gregory finished describing his course of treatment.

"But it's the way to recover, for sure," he said.

"How long did it take you to get better?"

"Six months or so."

"Six months, eh?" I didn't puncture his smugness by saying the obvious. I was once smug, too. He wasn't much older than I'd been then. Smug about Q.'s wife Susan, first off. He loved me more, *ergo*, he would have to leave her. Gregory would be unsmugged soon enough. I almost felt sorry for him: what a long way to fall until he reached the porous soil of humility. For most of us the drop was not that great, so we didn't sink as deep.

"Well, I'm glad you're better. Thanks for telling me about this." Thank you for sharing, as they say in the support groups which had also been suggested to me, where you sit around and talk about your symptoms as my grandmother and her friends used to do over mah-jongg. At least they had the sense to play a game along with it.

"I can give you his name and number if you like."

"Why don't I think it over and then maybe call Sonia to get in touch with you, okay?"

"No problem. Good luck." He was off.

I finished what was on my plate, poured a Scotch and sat down on the couch near the window. It was fine, sitting alone in Mona's living room, slowly sipping Scotch. Very comfortable. Maybe Scotch was the cure, though not, to be sure, intravenously. I envisioned lying on a cot in a dim room while a tube pumped orange juice into my veins. What would Q. say?

ALWAYS AND EVER, what would Q. say? He does it, too, invokes me in his mind, he's told me. In this case it gets me nowhere. He'd say what I say. Orange juice through a needle?

Forget Q. I'll ask Tony, my stepson. Ex-stepson, I suppose. He may resent me but he'll give a trustworthy opinion. And civilly, too, for Ev's sake. He's a thoroughgoing doctor now, as Jilly recently pointed out when I referred to him as a medical student. "He's doing his residency. He goes around the hospital on his own and decides how to treat people. That's a doctor," she said with pride. How confidently she rested in his boyish arms as he carried her off the train those many years, coming to spend weekends with Ev and me. She was the brave one, on the lookout for adventure. Adventurers can afford to take risks because they're rooted in safety: Tony was her root and stem, she the flower sprouting from the firm branches of his arms.

Yes, I'll call him. The chill in his voice won't hurt all that much. And I'm entitled to a question. I've earned it, like the disciples of Taoist monks: haul the firewood and buckets of water for twenty years and you can ask one question. Years of weekends. Picked glass out of his foot when he dropped the crystal decanter arthritic Aunt Bess gave us as a wedding present, then took him to the emergency room to get out the rest. Let myself be tackled time and again in football on the beach with far more force than was needed, but I never protested, it was only sand. Stripped the guest-room bed of sheets bearing his wet-dream stains. Corrected essays on *Romeo and Juliet*, *Great Expectations*, and *A Farewell to Arms*, even typed a few, when he complained his visits made him late with homework. I could go on and on. (Twenty more years and the monk's disciple is entitled to a second question, an option often passed up. If the first twenty years of carrying buckets is ample time to formulate a proper question, the next twenty can cure you of the desire or need to ask another.)

There's still time after the party. It's early evening in San Francisco. Saintly Dave insists on walking me to my door, for this is not the sweet seaside hamlet of my imagination, where violent crimes never happen. . . .

"Don't worry, you look fine, Laura," he says as he turns to go. "Get a good night's sleep."

Right, but after I speak to Tony. Interrupt his sunset. Can it be as fine as the one that accompanied me along the river hours ago? Why on earth not? No limit to the splendor and democratic distribution of sunsets: custom-made, fashioned to locale.

I mustn't forget he's married now. Sara, Sandra, Phyllis? Sophie. Also a medical student. Doctor, sorry. I could get a second opinion for the same quarter. Not that I've had the pleasure of making her acquaintance. I wasn't invited to their wedding, held about a year ago in Boston. A very small wedding, Jilly assured me, blushing with vicarious shame. Well, never mind all that.

The voice—its familiar pitch and diffidence—gives me a phantom shiver of pleasure. The next instant I see the gash in Ev's neck running from just below the left ear across the throat to the collarbone. I got there so fast when the police called, they hadn't yet fixed him up. Fixed his appearance, that is, since they couldn't fix him. Not fast enough to speak to him, only fast enough to see the damage. I never told the kids how he looked. I accept it. I don't ask to have it excised, only I would like, someday, that it not be the first image I see when I think of him.

"Tony." I announce myself. "I hope I'm not interrupting. . . ."

I'm touched, disarmed, when he says, "Not at all. Is everything okay?" until I realize it's Jilly he must be thinking of.

Doctors hate being asked advice after hours, don't they? I plod ahead with my mission.

"Are you sure it's not just depression? I mean, even a long time after a trauma. . . . There's a chance it might be psychosoma—"

"Tony, please. I know how you feel about me but don't give me that shit, okay? At least not for openers. Do you think if it were 'just' depression I would call you of all people in the middle of the night, at least here it's the middle of the night—"

"Laura, calm down, will you? I only meant it was a possibility. I know you've been through a lot and . . ."

"Listen, Tony," I say carefully, "all I really want is to ask you a very specific question. I heard—"

"Wait, Laura. Before you, uh. . . . What you said before, that you know how I feel about you. Maybe we should . . ." He's shaping phrases with the diligence of a toddler jaggedly piling up blocks, knowing they will very likely fall but not knowing why, unable to align them properly. "Maybe we should talk about this."

Go ahead and talk, kiddo. I'm not your mother, I don't have to help.

"You're mistaken about how I feel about you, Laura."

"Am I?"

"Yes. I—well . . ." Some throat-clearing, then a swallow. Coffee? Beer? "It's true I used to resent you but . . . but not as much as you think. I mean . . ."

"Oh." Happily, one faculty my virus has not diminished is my sense of the ludicrous. That seems to have been enhanced. I also hear something dimly familiar, not just in the words but in the tone. In the earnest groping for a certain unobjectionable diction. Is it marriage? Has Sandra, I mean Sophie, had a feminine, tenderizing effect? They must talk over childhood wounds in bed. Well, that's sweet. What's her secret? Ev would listen but never contribute, and it doesn't work as a one-sided game. No, beyond Sophie, it's . . . ah, yes. Therapy. The unmistakable accents of working things through. He must have gone when Ev was killed, sure, that sort of blow could send even the most taciturn. He has been urged to examine his feelings and settle unfinished business, preferably out in the open.

"Do you want to define exactly how much you resented me, then? Is that the point?"

"That came out all wrong. You know what I mean. I mean, I know I gave you a hard time but I had my reasons."

"People always do."

"I blamed you for my parents' breakup."

"I know. You've told me that before. When you were twelve, the first time. How could I forget? I was trying to make a soufflé."

"But I see now . . ."

I have to admire his doggedness. Perhaps it's good for him to encounter resistance. His feeling of closure will be all the more thorough. His therapist will be proud of him when he reports this conversation.

"I see now that you weren't really all that responsible."

"I told you that several times. When I met your father your parents had been separated for months."

"I suppose I wasn't ready to hear it. I always thought he would have come back if . . . if not for you. Because when he left he told me it was only temporary. Like a—a trial. I thought it was sort of like one of his trips, so then I was really blown away when—"

"Oh. Well, that's something I didn't know. That he told you it was temporary. I thought you understood."

"He said he might be back. I'm almost positive he said that. But then you came along."

"He wouldn't have been back, regardless of me."

"Are you sure?"

I hope he's not going to cry. Poor Tony. A grown-up doctor but suddenly reduced to a boy of eleven. I really should help him out. I might reap some benefit. He might drop by next time he comes East, and truth to tell, I'd very much like to sit in a room with him—tall, lean, austere—hearing his voice at close range, feeling a wisp of Ev drifting my way.

"Yes, I'm pretty sure, Tony. Do you know it was your mother who asked him to leave?"

"I don't know that. No. She never really explained. All she—Well, she did sit me down and explain that they couldn't get along or live together but it wasn't my fault or Jilly's. Like, straight out of the book."

"Oh. He was difficult to live with, it's true."

"Difficult how?"

How indeed? How to explain that absent presence, that silent wrestling with a shadow? "This is enough for one night. I'll tell you some other time. Nothing outrageous or gory, don't worry."

"But you see . . . I'm married now—" an embarrassed pause for the wedding I didn't attend—"and . . . and I don't want to be difficult in the same way, whatever it was."

"No, I don't think you will be." You're too dull, for one thing. You're like him in many ways, but he wasn't dull. I would have had an easier time if he were. "How is Sophie, by the way?"

"She's fine. She's doing her residency in pediatrics."

"And you?"

"Internal medicine."

"Good. Well, that reminds me of why I called. I just met someone who suggested that I have massive doses of vitamin C pumped into me intravenously. It sounded strange but you never know. What do you think? Would there be any bad side effects? I mean, would my blood turn to acid or anything like that?"

"I've heard about good results in some cases." He eases into the professional tone. "But I myself . . . well, I wouldn't advise it. There's not much data on the long-term effects. I don't know enough to say definitively, but the point is, no one really does. This is a very conservative opinion, I should tell you. You could find doctors who'd say go right ahead. But I'd hang on unless you've exhausted everything else or you're unable to function. How bad is it?"

"I get around a little. But mostly I lie down, or I want to be lying down. I've heard of worse cases."

"You can try large doses of vitamins. Orally, I mean. Some people say magnesium. The few specialists each have some magic solution that works for a handful of people. The problem is, the immune system is off, and nobody understands enough about it to start it up again. There're theories going around about hormone imbalance, brain inflammation, you name it."

"What about modern life?"

"Listen, no kidding, that's got to be part of it. The environment's messed up, the air, the food . . . there are people who claim it's a variant of the AIDS virus—not to scare you or anything—but just so you know it's taken seriously."

Thank you, thank you. I don't really need Tony to make that clear. It's quite clear. I can feel it in the general systemic refusal.

"Stress, too," he goes on. "Frankly, the best thing is to get yourself a book by somebody who's had a lot of experience with it. Diet is important. Stuff like that."

"That's exactly what your sister said. And she didn't even go to medical school."

"I'm sorry you're sick, Laura. But it'll probably pass in a few months. And I'm sorry . . . I'm sorry I gave you such a hard time, all those years."

"Do you think you ever would have called me to say so?"

"Sooner or later, yes. Or knowing me, I might have written you a letter." He gives a short laugh. The crisis is over. All those years of bad behavior wiped out by confession. Clean slate. "By the way, if you want to talk to someone . . . Sophie's mother, Hortense is her name, had the same thing a few years ago. She was treated by an herbalist out here. In California, you know, that holistic stuff is taken much more seriously. You could call her and see if she has anything to suggest."

"I'm not sure. Sometimes it's better not to know."

"Oh, but she came out of it just fine. She had some surgery recently but that was completely unrelated. Let me give you her number. You never know, it might be helpful."

He sounds quite lighthearted now, relieved of his burden. The young are resilient—well, they need to be. I, on the other hand, feel too weighed down to budge, and may just go to sleep in my party clothes. Better yet, toss them in the direction of the nearest chair. I miss, but there's no one to mind the clutter. Now, since the phone's right here, why not try this Hortense in crepuscular San Francisco while the inquisitive mood is on me? How to introduce myself? Oh, words will come. They always do.

She has a weary, mildly aggrieved voice—What now?, her hello suggests—but at the same time sounds well-meaning and capable, a woman resigned to being asked questions, even proud of the role. I invent her from the one word: a mother of many children who keep in close touch, with their increasingly complex demands. The sort of mother who could always be relied on for lifts in the car, last-minute houseguests, hurry up and iron a dress for the interview, homemade birthday cakes, mediation with teachers or Dad, and God knows what all else. They are still relying, not having noticed her weariness. She's a pretty woman, stout, a bit unkempt, always running late. Over the years she's cultivated a few minor indulgences. She goes to the manicurist once a week and prizes her well-groomed nails. She buys lottery tickets often, at different places, when the urge comes over her. In bookstores, she leafs through soft-core porn but never buys any, just recalls key scenes when she needs them. The grievance in her voice is not aimed at her children or even at unknown supplicants like me, but at something far more general and diffuse. How long, O Lord, she whispers at night, into the dark.

"Well," she sighs, "to tell the truth that's far from my mind now because I just had a mastectomy six weeks ago."

"Oh, I'm so sorry to bother you. I had no idea. Tony mentioned some surgery but he didn't say . . . why don't I call at a better time, in a few weeks, maybe?"

Shit! That Tony has a lot to learn. How much more therapy would it take before he'd warn me? Some surgery!

"No, we might as well talk now because we're leaving for Hawaii tomorrow and I'll be away three weeks, so . . ."

"How are you doing? I mean after the mastectomy?"

"Okay. As well as can be expected. In between the chemo, that is. The chemo is a killer but it's only one week a month. We had to time our trip. I'll tell you, this really wreaks havoc with a relationship."

Wreaks havoc with. How long since I've heard anyone say that? It dates her. To be Sophie's mother she might be fifty or so, but what if Sophie is the youngest of the demanding brood? It also establishes Hortense as fairly literate, otherwise she'd say "wrecks havoc," as autodidacts tend to do. An odd word, "havoc," to apply to a "relationship," by which I assume Hortense means a marriage, though you can't be sure of anything these days. "Havoc" evokes a jumble of things thrown up as if by a tornado, while a "relationship" has only two components. She's referring, of course, to all the physical and emotional facets of a "relationship," an abstract entity like a corporation. "Wreaks" I'll have to look up—it's an incentive to get out of bed. Sounds like Middle English, possibly Anglo-Saxon? I ought to know this stuff. Drum me out of the writers' union if they could hear me.

This takes no time at all. With scarcely a beat lost, "I'm sorry to hear it," I reply. "I hope things are better soon."

Hortense, no sympathy hound, moves right on to business. "Yes, well, I had what you have. I was sick for three years and they were the worst years of my life, bar none."

Bar none. That's intriguing, too, but my professional interest in diction has abruptly lapsed. All I want to do now is get off the phone. My heart is pounding like mad. The fear is a heavy sack pressing on my chest.

"The very worst," she drones. "I forgot what it was like to feel well. My body was a stranger. I felt I aged twenty years. I moved like an old lady. The slightest thing was a major ordeal. I thought it would never go away, and I didn't know how I'd get through the rest of my life. I was so depressed, I mean as a result of the illness, not a cause. Don't let them tell you it's depression. Believe me, before that I wasn't any more depressed than the next person. If you're simply depressed, you don't lie in bed planning all the things you'll do as soon as you get up, and then have to lie right down again. If you're simply depressed you just lie there wanting to die."

I move the phone two inches from my ear.

"It was as if my life had been taken from me." I hear her fine even at a distance; she has a firm, clear voice from all those years of domestic administration. "I felt hopeless. I think maybe the most frightening symptom was the memory loss and the loss of motor coordination. Do you have that?"

"No. Not yet. At least I haven't noticed. Maybe a little."

"Things would slip my mind, I mean more than they normally do. And my fingers didn't work right. I've always made all my own clothes, and I began to lose control. I couldn't fit pieces of fabric together or thread the needle. And then, for example, making phone calls, I'd press the wrong numbers. It was terrifying. But it passed, little by little."

She mentions a number of things I might do. Not do, to be precise. No caffeine, sugar, or alcohol. "Alcohol is the worst."

Too bad. But all right. There are magic herbs that help, she says, but no, I can't get them by mail. I should see an herbalist in New York.

"Drink ginseng tea, but it's very important not to brew it in a metal pot."

"Why not?"

"I don't know. Just don't. And no salad."

"What could be bad about salad?"

"I don't know, but for some reason it's not good for you."

Toenail of frog. Eye of newt. As soon as decently possible I thank her and wish her a complete and speedy recovery from her mastectomy.

Is this—tonight's research—what's called taking control of your life? I can't say I find it especially exhilarating. Or empowering, as they say. Quite the contrary. My heart is still racing, the sack of fear growing heavier.

At the window, I stare into the dark until the river grows distinct from the sky and trees. There's a wind; the water's rippling. And there's the squirrel. I'd almost forgotten about him, approaching his death in slow motion. I wouldn't have thought he could get any sicker without dying, but he's dying like Zeno's arrow, moving through an infinity of interme-diate positions. His bed is fully restored. He probably feels as enamored of the little nest of twigs, leaves and lint as I do of my bed, and bitterly resents finding it cleared away every few days. Well, I doubt if I'll be doing that much longer. Soon the arrow will reach its target and then, for the last time: brush, pan, gloves, bag (heavier with his weight), elevator. I tap lightly on the window, not really hoping or expecting to dislodge him, more as an acknowledgment, even a greeting. Of course there's no response. He seems to be in some kind of coma, breathing evenly, a slow rise and fall of the curved back.

I ATE NO SALAD FOR A COUPLE OF DAYS, but nothing changed and I missed it sorely. So I went and strolled down the sweet-smelling, boun-teous aisles of the outdoor market, our urban farm, and carried home a bag full of earth's harvest, including watercress. I even went to put some lettuce out for the squirrel, but he wasn't home and I was afraid to leave it in case the old rat returned to feast. I laid out my riches on the dining room table as a still life, from which I plucked a few tidbits each day. I love especially the bitter greens, perhaps the way the Tai Chi teacher loves the ache in his legs, the ache he calls tasting bitter.

"Today we're going to do a little exercise," says the Tai Chi teacher, in an expansive mood. "We're going to feel the air like water. In Tai Chi you move through the air feeling its texture the way you walk through water feeling its resistance. You all know how it feels to walk through water. You go to the beach on these hot weekends. You feel the water's pressure as you move in it. That's how you should feel the air around you when you do Tai Chi. That's why we call it swimming in air."

The air does feel very much like water this morning; the humidity is in the nineties and even the teacher is wearing shorts, longish ones—a small bit of exposed thigh and rather nice knees. He demonstrates how we must walk through the air-like-water, lifting our knees high and moving our arms in opposition with each step. "Feel the density around you. One drop of water is nothing, no power at all, the softest thing. But massed in a tidal wave, everything gives way before it. The same with air. What's a little breath of air? Nothing. But massed in a tornado, whole towns crumble in its path."

I have to hand it to that interpreter. He can translate into poetic, vivid prose on his feet; never mind the grammar. It's what I need to do in my book about the seaside town—translate straight from the inner shapes of emotion to the words.

"That's the strength you're walking through. It's also the kind of strength you'll develop, if you practice."

We walk around in a circle, pressing our way through the air, conjuring up the texture of water. Swimming in air. In the adjacent playground the few children eye us as if we're a band of escaped lunatics kept in good order by our leader. The teacher walks among us nodding and smiling, the interpreter at his heels. It's a good chance to look at the others. A couple of new people, graduate students, I'd guess, escaping from the library. Marvin's getting in a class before he opens the video store. There's the pale, plump sixtyish woman I often see on Broadway, pushing her ancient mother in a wheelchair—lessons in standing firm must help her. There's the pizza spinner. The pair of dazzling young lesbians who arrive on bicycles and work in television. Grace has made friends with them, too, though I can't imagine they share her views about art. A black stand-up comic who's the soberest in the group, a retired Irish police detective, a former ballet dancer—her obstinate turnout gives her away, no use at all in Tai Chi.

We walk around maybe five or six times when the teacher says, "You'll get dizzy this way. Who said you had to walk in a circle? Walk wherever you want. Make a random pattern."

I'm walking through a thick sea where each step takes effort. A foretaste of my trip to the Cape with Jilly, rehearsal for the real sea. It's mesmerizing, yet I can't help wondering how long he'll keep us at it. Each time he smiles and nods, I expect he'll tell us to stop. Now? No. I think of prisoners, chain gangs. Okay, you've made your point. Walking through water induces a trancelike, meditative state. So enough. But still we walk. Swim. Until there comes a new stage: I don't care anymore. I stop longing for release. This must be the real lesson beneath the lesson. Fine, I'll walk through this water forever if need be, raising my knees high with each step, dimly seeing the others around me making a random pattern. And after a while, just as I've come almost to enjoy it, accepting that life will hold nothing more than this walking around in the park with a group of familiar strangers, he says, "Stop. Enough. Very good."

We're dazed and giddy. We gaze around at each other as if we've traversed an ocean together and emerged onto a fresh new continent. We giggle and rub our aching legs. Tasting bitter. No complaints whatsoever.

"Next time, don't forget the breath while you walk. Thin, long, quiet and slow. How you breathe is important. The breath is spirit."

Oh, come on, give me a break.

"Do you know about Marcel Duchamp, what he said about breathing?" asks Grace, made bold by the flood of endorphins.

The interpreter translates and the teacher shakes his head.

"A great surrealist artist. But after a while he gave up making art and just lived his life as a surrealist. Meaning that the way he did whatever he did, even if it was nothing in particular, was his art. He once said he liked breathing better than working, so he could consider every breath a work of art. Not art for an audience, but for himself, and just for an instant. You can see how that would be the logical result of his attitude."

"Marcel Duchamp," says the teacher. "I must look him up." He repeats the name to himself and nods pensively. He seems to prefer Marcel Duchamp to Diogenes.

When we do push hands he says something I never thought I'd hear him say. "There's such a thing, Laura, as too relaxed. Yielding doesn't mean limp. It means pliable. A palm tree sways and bends but doesn't fall or droop. Or think of a cat. Alert, vital, ready. No, now you're tensing up. How do you feel today?"

"Terrible, can't you tell?"

After class he comes over with the interpreter. He asks exactly what's wrong and listens carefully as I report the doctor's diagnosis. "I want to give this some thought," he says. "Write down your address and phone number so I can get in touch with you before you leave."

What could he have in mind? I tried the watercress. It was very nice, but hardly the solution.

EACH MORNING I check the burden of fear weighing on my chest, making my heart pound. It's getting lighter. I'm leaving the fear behind a little bit at a time, emptying my sack in sleep, the grains scattered into oblivion with no trace to follow me by. Each day that I manage to continue brings a small accumulation of faith.

And one day brings a small white envelope addressed in an unknown hand, neat letters straight up and down, nondescript but self-assured. No return address. I open it and glance first at the signature. He's as good as his word.

"Dear Laura," the Tai Chi teacher has written. "I hope this reaches you before you leave for the seashore. Perhaps you know what the *Tao te Ching* says about the sea. 'All streams flow to the sea because it is lower than they are. Humility gives it its power.' I know a woman who might be able to help you with your ailment and restore your *chi*. No doubt you're unfamiliar with Chinese medicine and it may seem strange at first, but I urge you to try. It certainly can't hurt, as they say about chicken soup. I'll look forward to seeing you in class when you get back." Below are the woman's name and phone number.

Anyone else would have called. But he couldn't very well, without the interpreter. In this faultless, even graceful English, I sense the interpreter's hand and voice—correspondence, too? What a useful fellow!—and can only hope they're a faithful translation of the teacher's own. Did the teacher dictate in Chinese to be translated directly, or leave it to the interpreter to paraphrase his intentions? (Who's whose muse? The one with the words or the one with the thoughts?) Perhaps like an executive with a seasoned secretary, the teacher merely instructed, Write and give Laura the name of the Chinese-medicine woman, and while you're at it, mention her stay at the seashore. In that case, the curlicues and adornments, the *Tao te Ching* and the chicken soup, were courtesy of the interpreter. Did it make any difference?

THE WOMAN IS A NATIVE SPEAKER, with a voice that lilts over the wires in a young, bell-like tone. "Oh, yes, Frank told me you might be calling. What's the trouble?"

As I name my symptoms, the vibrations coursing back to me feel different from those I recall with doctors. Some pressure is absent. She is not in haste. She welcomes my answering her questions in complete sentences, even paragraphs. She listens as though my perceptions might be relevant and trustworthy.

"The worst of it, really, is that I can't think clearly. My mind doesn't feel like my own, if that makes any sense. It's as if I'm possessed. I'm angry at everyone and everything."

"Yes, well, that's not unusual," she says cheerily. "A common feature of this virus is brain fog."

"Brain fog?"

"The virus affects hormones and enzymes that go to the brain, so it's no wonder your thinking is clouded. I may be able to help you. I can't promise, but why don't you come in and I'll take your pulses and we'll see."

No waiting: an appointment the day after tomorrow. Can this be legitimate?

THE MEDICINE WOMAN'S DEN is in a stately brownstone several blocks from the river, on a tree-lined side street, cool and hushed on this steamy day. In the distance, over in Central Park, rise the unstirring tops of trees. The halls inside are dim, their walls stripped down to brick. Trudging toward the third landing, I meet a young couple, robust and breezy in jogging clothes, the woman carrying a small black terrier.

"Good-bye, Seth. Good-bye, Pat. And good-bye to you, too, Beaver," a light female voice rings out from above. If the voice had shape and texture it would be a big rainbow-tinted bubble. Seth and Pat smile as we edge past each other on the narrow stairs. At the fourth floor landing a door is open and the unmistakable sweetish odor of marijuana wafts toward me. A little party, I suppose.

"Hi, Laura," the voice calls from an inner room. "Make yourself comfortable. I'll be right with you."

I sit in a canvas director's chair. The room is large and airy, with hanging plants at the sunstruck windows and posters on the walls: a many-handed Indian goddess advertising a bio-ecology conference on saving the earth. A huge photograph of a famous rock formation in Australia, the rock, carved by millennia of wind, shaped uncannily like an ocean wave. A few of the usual Impressionists—sunflowers, water lilies.

A Chinese anatomical chart shows the fourteen meridians of the body running vertically and horizontally in dotted lines, an unfamiliar map of familiar terrain. It's as if the well-known perimeter of North America enclosed brand-new mountain ranges, rivers, lakes, and internal borders. Another wall chart is pentagonal: each point represents one of the five vital organs in living color, along with their corresponding elements, seasons, emotions, and colors, all linked by a network of arrows.

Opposite me are floor-to-ceiling wooden shelves, the top ones holding tall mason jars filled with herbs and labeled in Latin and Chinese, and below, thick tattered books bound in black leather with gold trim. It feels like a sorcerer's chamber or alchemist's study, except that on the desk across the room sits a state-of-the-art telephone and answering machine, and in between two jars of herbs, a radio is tuned to the yuppie classical music station (a station I shun because the DJs, dreading an instant's silence, break in before the last note of music has fully dissolved).

"Sorry to keep you waiting."

She appears from within, a goddess-like creature herself, tall, large-boned, with dangling earrings and waves of abundant black hair tumbling down her back. Young, I think. She's not Chinese, but like the Tai Chi teacher, her age is hard to fix. Thirty-one or two? An olive complexion, piercing blue eyes, full lips. Glowing with West Coast vigor and out-

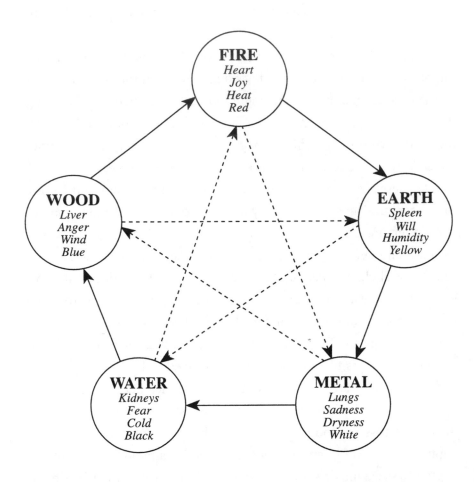

Another wall chart is pentagonal: each point represents one of the five vital organs in living color, along with their corresponding elements, seasons, emotions, and colors, all linked by a network of arrows.

fitted not as a goddess but suitably for a New York summer, in a short skirt and V-necked T-shirt. Strong, suntanned legs, Dr. Scholl's sandals.

The inner room where she leads me is smaller and its walls are bare white. On the floor is a mat covered by a striped Indian bedspread. She gestures to me to sit and kneels opposite me, flicking the hair off her neck. "So, tell me again how you feel." She rests back on her heels listening, nods, jots down a note now and then.

"Okay, I'm going to take your pulses." Not pulse, but pulses, up and down the inside of the lower forearms.

"Hmm, yes. Chinese medicine," she says, the searching blue eyes taking my measure, "is based on the movement of energy, or *chi*, through the body. It flows in patterns along the meridians. From the pulses I can tell if any of the organs are in an unbalanced condition, too active or not active enough. That blocks the energy. With the treatment I try to unblock it and get it flowing again. For instance, your spleen or pancreas energy is very low. Those organs help digest, so probably you're not getting all the benefit of what you eat. It's like the pilot light of a furnace is very low and doesn't always catch, so the fuel doesn't get burned. Also, the spleen corresponds to the will."

"Really?"

"Yes. So I would guess you have to push yourself to do everything. I'll work on that, this time. Since the virus is consuming your energy, I'll have to take energy wherever I can find it and get it moving. But basically you have a strong constitution."

"I do?"

"Oh, yes. You'll be fine, but it might take some time. We have to get rid of the toxins first. That means you could have some uncomfortable symptoms, but once those pass you'll feel better. Let me see your tongue. Yes, that's what I thought."

She tips a small brown bottle over her palm and a lush forest odor rises into the room. She massages the oil into my stomach and my legs. Her touch is warm. Then she presses her hands down hard all along my legs. "Turn over." She presses again. Laying on of hands. She's transmitting something through the hands; I only hope it's something good. When I turn on my back again, my body feels different, as if it's drawn something alien and interesting from the hands. She opens a package of long thin needles tipped with red plastic.

"Oh, needles," I say.

"Yes. You did realize that's part of the treatment, didn't you?"

"I don't know. I just came because the teacher told me to. At this point I'd do almost anything."

"It won't hurt, I promise."

"Do you sterilize the needles or what?"

"I use fresh needles for every patient." She holds up a miniature red plastic garbage can with a flip top, a cute gadget smaller than a beer can. "See, the old ones go in here. As you'll see, I open a new package each time."

I peer into the little can. Dozens of discarded needles. She must use hundreds, maybe thousands, each week. Someone is making a fortune on them. "What about these uncomfortable symptoms? I have enough uncomfortable symptoms as it is."

"Well, I can't always tell what they're going to be. That depends on your body. But sometimes after the treatment you might get a headache or a skin rash or a stomach ache. Or maybe muscle aches, a cold, fever, menstrual cramps."

"Great. You mean you can give me all that?"

She laughs. "That's not my aim. But as I'm moving out the toxins, they have to find a path to leave by, and there are only the obvious ways. Everything in the body moves in certain directions—from the organs to the skin, from the center to the extremities, from up to down. The particular path they take is your body's choice. Afterward, as I said, you'll feel better than before."

"I feel like a sewage disposal plant, with all those toxins."

"Don't take it personally. It's the body's natural process—taking things in from outside, using them, and producing toxins to be released. Okay, I'm going to insert the needles now. Breathe in."

They don't hurt. The thickness of a hair, she says. I crane my neck to study the landscape of my body, in bra and pants, punctured here and there by the long, red-tipped stalks. I look like an exotic planet growing hair-thin vegetation.

"They go in triangular patterns." As she inserts several more and twirls them a bit, she points out the triangles they form. So she's just another kind of performance artist after all, and I'm a canvas for her abstract art, an integral part of the project, like Grace's dentist.

"You see," she says, "how the ones on your stomach aren't standing upright but kind of leaning? That's because of the low *chi* there. As the treatments continue, you'll begin to see them stand up straighter."

"That's something to look forward to."

She returns an ironic flash of her blue eyes, then reaches over to a little witch's chest and brings forth an object resembling an extremely long cigar. She lights one end with a cigarette lighter and instantly the air fills with the sweet marijuana odor.

"Don't tell me you're going to smoke that!"

"It's not pot. It's moxa, a Chinese herb. Everyone thinks it's pot, the first time. Mothers in China still use this when their kids have colds or coughs. It's very healing. You hold it above certain parts of the body and the fumes penetrate." She holds the moxa over my stomach, which grows quite warm as I inhale happily.

"It smells good. It's a long time since I smoked any pot."

"It's terrible for the immune system, unfortunately," she replies. "One joint is equal to sixteen cigarettes. I'll give you a couple of moxa sticks to take home, and show you where to use it. Also, you should take baths in Dead Sea salts. They'll help release the toxins through the skin. You can buy them in the health food store."

"A whole new world is opening up." I wonder, in fact, if my body's inner map is shifting into the alien design I saw on the waiting room wall.

"It's very pleasant. You'll see your arms float. I think you might like that."

While the hair-thin needles are poised over my skin ("That which has no substance enters where there is no space"—I checked out the *Tao te Ching* after I got the teacher's note), and the drifts of pungent smoke move between us, she asks many questions. Where I was born, childhood diseases, eating and sleeping patterns, work, exercise, tastes and distastes. Not since I first met Q. has anyone taken such an interest in my personal habits. With each response she nods as if she figured as much, making an occasional note on the diagram of a nude body she holds on her lap, on which she's marked *x*'s here and there. After twenty minutes her knowledge of me is encyclopedic. Quite unlike Dr. A., the tongue doctor, whose curiosity was limited to whom I had recently sucked off.

"Oh, I forgot to tell you. I keep dropping things."

She explains this as a loss of yang, which she pronounces so as to rhyme not with "bang" but with "gong." "Health depends on the proper balance between yin and yang. If one or the other becomes too powerful, you're thrown off balance, and you can feel it." Yang, she says, is the grasping or holding-on faculty, as distinct from yin, the unfurling, receptive faculty.

"In other words, I'm losing my grip."

"You could put it that way. It could be you went through some experience recently—physical or emotional or even professional—that required you to hang on too tight in one way or another."

A witch.

"As a matter of fact . . ." Under the spell of the moxa—mock-pot—and the needles that sway like palm trees over my smooth terrain, I find myself telling her about the shoot-out on the Bronx street and the grand jury that refused to indict anyone.

"Ah," she says. "That could certainly weaken you. I'm so sorry."

"So how can I strengthen my yang?" I must be bewitched. If she tells me to avoid stress, though, the spell will be broken.

"There are exercises, but at this point I don't think you should try anything strenuous. The Tai Chi is enough. What you should definitely avoid are cigarettes, alcohol, sugar, and caffeine."

That sounds familiar. "All of them?" They always helped keep a grip on things.

My dismay amuses her. "As much as you can. Start with one or two. And you should eat foods that cohere tightly around a core, budlike foods. Brussels sprouts, cabbage. Tight foods."

"Tight?"

"Yes. Rather than foods that open outward, like spinach or kale."

"The Tai Chi teacher said to eat watercress."

"Watercress? No, I'd say just the opposite. Foods have certain proper ties, and when you ingest them you ingest their properties as well. I'm not suggesting you change your diet completely because I can see you're not the type who'll do it, but at least eat things that aren't too processed. The shorter the distance the food travels from its natural state, the better. It's the same as with people—the more you try to alter their nature by processing them, the less authentic they get."

Full of metaphors, no less. "Yes, well, I don't mind eating fresh vegetables. I like them. It just sounds . . . you know."

She smiles and leans over to remove the needles, which she drops delicately in the toy garbage can. Her fingers are long and thin, too, tipped with red. "You don't need to believe anything. Just eat the stuff, okay? Also, I'll give you some oils to rub in, and herbs which should improve your energy. They're in capsule form. I like to brew them myself, but not everyone has the patience. Oh, and another thing. Walk."

"Walk?"

"Yes, a little at a time. Walk where there are trees. For the oxygen."

"Can I move now? Are they all out? I feel a little spacy," I say, sitting up.

"That's the energy moving in unfamiliar patterns."

"You're the first person who's offered any real help." I toss the jars of herbs into my bag. "One of the worst things about this is that no one believes me, especially with so many people dying of AIDS and other terrible things. Well, almost no one. You know what people think—they make you feel like a fool."

"Yes, the virus that dares not speak its name."

A very literary witch.

"The lighthouse is falling into the sea," I told Jilly as she came panting toward me. I had driven over, while she chose a three-mile run through the fields and over the dunes.

"What do you mean? It looks perfectly fine to me."

It was our first full day on the Cape. We stood before the classic lighthouse, white with black trim. Beside it, the red-trimmed lighthouse keeper's cottage looked the same as when I'd last seen it three summers ago, the same as years ago when I'd first come, its yard still dotted with bicycles and toy cars and trucks as if the children had not aged, or else more children kept being born to inherit them. The only addition was a new red skateboard.

From the high dune we watched the black sea below, "graveyard of ships," as this patch was called before the lighthouse was built. The sea appeared secretive as befits a graveyard, and nonchalant about its own beauty. A half dozen or so surfers rode the waves, making patterns like a Busby Berkeley musical against the stately dance of ripples and foam.

"It's not falling right now. It's moving about three feet closer to the edge each year. Look, it tells you right here. Actually it's the cliff that's eroding. The ground is slipping out from under it."

We stood before the classic lighthouse, white with black trim. Beside it, the red-trimmed lighthouse keeper's cottage looked the same as when I'd last seen it three summers ago.

"I figured that out, Laura."

A hand-lettered sign appealed for help to save the lighthouse. In 1961 it had been two hundred thirty-two feet from the cliff and in 1990, one hundred twenty-eight feet. "At this rate it won't be long," I said.

In the museum down the road we bought raffle tickets, adding to the fund to move the lighthouse farther back on the dune. Given the nature of erosion, the venture would have to be repeated, but we needn't worry about that. Jilly's great-grandchildren would contribute to the next move.

"What's being raffled off?" Jilly asked the woman at the desk, an elderly pastel woman, all pink, white and blue.

"First prize is a copper rooster from the Town Hall Weather Vane and second prize is a picture by a local artist. The drawing is after Labor Day." She smiled with pink benevolence. "Good luck."

"I was hoping it would be something like a car," Jilly said as we trudged back up the hill. "I'll need a car in the fall to work with this theatre group in Center City. We want to rent space in a storefront gallery for a protest piece on the famine in Somalia. We'll take turns sitting there, two at a time, wearing rags and eating grains of rice with our fingers out of wooden bowls. Isn't that a great idea? Anyway, speaking of cars, I've got to bring Grandpa's old pickup back to life because, well, I have a job waitressing in Provincetown. Six days a week. You'll be alone a lot. Do you mind?"

"Of course not. I didn't expect you to baby-sit. How'd you manage that so fast?"

"I heard about this new upscale place, Chez Louise, in the East End, so I called and said I was an experienced waitress and almost a local person, my family was from here, and she said okay, come see her tonight. I'm pretty sure I'll get it. Those places are silly but the people are big tippers."

"You're very enterprising. The truck looks pretty dead to me, though."

"No problem." She waved a hand airily. "Jeff taught me a lot about engines. I'll make it run. Or I'll ask the guys at the station to come and help. I have to hunt up the keys. Oh, did you ever go to the health food store like I told you?"

"*As* you told me. Yes, I got the bee pollen." Got it but hadn't yet taken it.

"Good. I bet you'll improve up here. The sea air and all."

"Maybe." Meanwhile, I still felt filled with sand. If my skin were peeled off I'd be a shapely dune like the ones undulating around us. How well I fit in the landscape—sand washed over by tides of memory.

"I know lots of people who've had this, Laura. In fact it usually hits younger people, so you see, it took you for a young body. There must have been half a dozen in my dorm last year. It's like mono—you know how many students get mono from overwork or overexcitement or whatever? It could even be an aftereffect of mono. Did your doctor say anything about that?"

"I think so."

"Everyone I know got better. It just takes time."

"They were young."

"You're young, too. Forty is pretty young."

"Forty-one."

"Whatever. You feel old but that's the illness. Let's go get some clams for dinner. You rest and I'll cook."

SHE SET OFF THE NEXT DAY, the truck cleaned up, its engine thrumming. "Off to join the labor force," she called out the window.

Even though I'd watched her grow, I was always a little surprised at how lean and rangy Jilly had become, a firm-boned girl with long legs and large eloquent hands. With her tanned face and her dark hair in a heavy braid down her back, she might have been one of her Portuguese ancestors, a fisherman's wife, perhaps. Apart from her work outfit, that is, a denim miniskirt and white tank top.

Ev's family were among the many who came from Portugal a century and a half ago, some keeping their alien names, others lopping off a final vowel or shifting a syllable to transform them into Yankee names. Those who worked as indentured servants took their masters' names, so that reading a town roster today, you'd never imagine the names and their bearers had traveled so far. The language survived, though, with some families still speaking Portuguese among themselves. And in the groceries, even in convenience stores like the one Ev's parents ran at their gas station, amid the lackluster Protestant bread and canned tuna and sliced ham, you could find Portuguese breads and sausages, and on lucky days sweet *malasadas*, wanton, doughnut-like delicacies with no hole, whose racy spices melted on your tongue.

Jilly's eyes, though, were New England blue, earnest and serious. Her mother's, no doubt, the woman who admonished her children that every appetite passes in twenty minutes. Jilly had a streak of that unlovely stoicism, too.

After she left I visited the local library, a white frame house no larger than my apartment back home, to find books about the town and especially about its tides. The tides were mysterious and overdetermined. It was important to get a sense of their movements and rhythms, and not only for my languishing book. The mysterious thing that possessed me—virus, spell, or planetary decay—felt like a tide, too, advancing and receding, eroding then relenting, an inner flow and ebb that inundated then parched the cells. A tide of blood and heat.

Ask anyone what causes the tides and chances are they'll say something about the moon's gravitational pull on the earth. That was what Ev's father answered years ago on my first visit. When I pressed him for exactly how it worked, he put down his knife and fork patiently, cupped his gnarled hands before him and tipped them gently from side to side. "You've got to think of the ocean floor like a big bucket, or a basin," he said. "The earth spins around and the basin tips, just like if you were carrying it and running in circles at the same time. The water sloshes around. High tide here—" he nodded toward the hand tipped low, "and low tide there. You get it?" Yes, I nodded back, though I didn't see what that had to do with the pull of the moon.

I was struck, that first time, by the ugliness inside the house. The furnishings, that is. Not the dreary sort of ugliness that pains the soul but an amusing, senseless clutter that tried to cover every inch as in a primitive painting, perhaps in a misguided attempt to enliven or fill up the blank beauty of the surroundings. Every inner door had a doorstop against the constant winds, and every doorstop was a pug-faced porcelain dog. The large pair of lamps in the living room were, and still are, statuettes of fishermen wearing yellow sou'westers, braced for a storm. Each stout piece of furniture was robed in a print slipcover, and even the kitchen chairs wore seat pads decorated with tropical birds and tied to the chair backs with ribbons. The potholders and dish towels bore pictures of kittens, the curtains pictures of fishing boats. The oval hooked rugs on every floor were the colors of mud and old blood, while the chenille bedspreads were pastels. Yet for all that the house was lovable, the air blowing through it cool, fresh, faintly salty.

It was Ev's great-grandfather who built the house on a low rounded hill (truly in 1877 as I wrote in my tentative pages) for his growing family. He must have been grateful to have a family to house, for he was one of the few men of his line left after the great gale of 1841, known to this day as the October gale. It had sprung up unforeseen in midday, after an innocent morning promising fair weather and mild seas, and destroyed a fleet of seven ships. Fifty-seven fishermen, some as young as twelve years old, were lost at sea. An overwhelming loss for a small fishing town of several hundred people. Ev's great-grandfather had been an infant at the time and the family newly arrived. The storm took his father, two teenage brothers, two uncles, and three cousins.

"There had been gales before as there would be gales to come." These grandiloquent lines appear in my stack of pages. "Everyone knew, when the men and boys set out, that they might not be back, but never was there anything quite so ferocious and unheralded: no fair warning from the sea, only a squall like a maniac's tantrum, hurling waves so furious that just one young man was left to tell the tale, as though the storm were proud of its force and wanted the tale told. He lived into his eighties and was known thereafter as the single survivor."

I heard all this from Ev at night, after his father had cupped his hands at dinner to explain the movements of the tides. We lay in the narrow bed in Ev's old room, with the very moon that pulled the tides beaming in on us, lighting up the field of cabbage roses on the quilt.

"I still don't quite get it about the tides," I said.

"You get high tides at certain times of the month," he said, yawning, "just after the moon is full or new, and lower tides other times."

"Yes, but what about this bucket business?"

He pretended he was asleep, because he hated to be caught not knowing something precisely. Five minutes later he rolled over and said, "What do you think, seeing them in their own setting?" A direct question!

"I like them even better. But they seem just as sad as they were in the city. Maybe they're not keen on me. Do you think they're nostalgic for Margot?"

"No, they're always like that. It has nothing to do with Margot. They never especially liked her, as a matter of fact. They felt she was watching their every move, because she was a psychiatrist. But she wasn't interested in the least. She never liked the beach, either, so she didn't come here much. She didn't like sand in the bed."

"I love the beach. I'll come whenever you want. I don't even mind sand in the bed."

"I used to explain to them that she was a doctor—that was something I thought they could trust—but it didn't do any good."

"But why the sadness, then?"

"That's the gale. The history."

He told me about the eight members of his father's family lost at sea in 1841. It struck me as an exceedingly long time to mourn.

"I'll take you to the cemetery tomorrow and show you the stone," he said.

"All right." I didn't know what else to say. I began touching him—he seemed so remote.

"I don't think anybody's ever made love in this bed," he said.

"Didn't you and Margot, when you visited?"

"She never wanted to, here. Maybe it was the sand. She was right, you know. There are always a few grains in the sheets."

"Well, we can be the first."

He was ready but reluctant. "We'll have to do it quietly. They're right on the other side of the wall."

"What do you suppose they think we're doing? We're grown-ups."

"They're my parents."

I had a bad feeling then, a kind of presentiment. Maybe I shouldn't marry him, what with the gale and the sadness and this quiet love. My exuberant Q.—how different he was. If we had had to be quiet he would have made a game out of it. Let's make love like Trappist monks, I could hear him whisper. If I didn't want to play a monk he'd let me be a Carmelite nun. Or, Let's pretend we're deaf—we'll do it in sign language. Or, First one who makes a sound is the loser. And then, as I often did at that time of my life, I silenced Q. I shoved him into a hidden chamber of my heart where his voice was muffled.

The next day we went first to the local museum, housed in what used to be a hotel on a high dune overlooking the sea, close by the lonesome lighthouse with the small cottage and yard alongside, where children's bikes and toys stood disconsolate in the salty air like figures in a Hopper painting. In the museum Ev showed me a letter under glass from Daniel Webster, Secretary of State at the time of the gale. Webster was replying to the town selectmen's request for help for the widows and orphans "left in want of the most common necessaries of life; food, clothing, and fuel."

> Such a destruction of brave men far exceeds all the painful forebodings which I formed, when, at my home on the Coast, I witnessed the approaching fury of the gale. . . . I feel that I should ill requite the kindness, I have ever experienced from my fellow citizens of your part of the country, if I should let pass without notice, such a letter as yours.

Allow me then, to request your acceptance of the enclosed;
which, though small, may relieve some one of the unfortunate,
and I hope will at least serve as a proof of my sympathy and regard.

"They wrote so much better then," I said. "Imagine how a Secretary of
State would write today."

"Yes, you'd probably get something prefab from a computer, if at all.
On the other hand, there'd be disaster relief programs. I suppose substance is worth more than style."

"In this sort of case, I suppose. It was your father's family, wasn't it?
So why is your mother sad?"

"Her family lost people, too. Almost everyone did."

"And so is everyone sad? A century and a half later?"

"Oh, it's not at all a sad town. It's a very solid, energetic town. Just
certain types who like to keep the story alive. They feel it like a fate, you
know, a constant reminder. And when they marry each other, well . . ."

He took me to the church cemetery to see the memorial to the fifty-
seven men and boys lost in the gale. The carved inscription blurred with
moss read, "Man goeth to his long home and the mourners goeth about
the streets."

I squeezed Ev's hand. He wasn't going anywhere in a ship and even if
he were, now the lighthouse and the Coast Guard and radar would
guard him. He was safe, and with me. I had the audacity to think his
congenital sadness would burn off like the fog of the early mornings. I
was barely free of Q. myself, I wasn't even sure why I was marrying this
stranger, a Portuguese in Yankee disguise, as different from me as anyone
could get, but I trembled with the romance of making him happy. And
maybe I did, for a little while. A few minutes, here and there.

Late that night, after his parents had gone to sleep, I wandered into
the small spare bedroom neatly fitted out as a guest room, with a
salmon-colored chenille bedspread and flowered curtains, a scarred old
dresser holding a vase of artificial daisies, and a lamp whose base was a

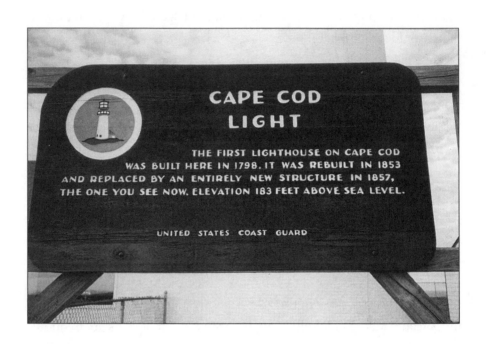

I squeezed Ev's hand. He wasn't going anywhere in a ship and even if he were, now the lighthouse and the Coast Guard and radar would guard him. He was safe, and with me.

clipper ship. From the neatness of the room and the stillness of its air, it seemed rarely used. On one shelf of a sparsely filled bookcase—mysteries, a half-dozen *Reader's Digest* Condensed Books, a few thin, outdated phone books—was a row of the annual Town Reports over the last few decades. I leafed through them, entranced at the story they told. Dirt roads were paved; civil servants got small raises; teachers complained of the crowded elementary school; Halloween dances were held at the high school and swimming lessons for children were offered at high tide at the bay. Tracts of beach were ceded to the meticulous care of the National Seashore.

"Look," I said to Ev back in bed, "for years the same three men were the Selectmen, the Assessors, and the Board of Public Welfare, except they're listed in a different order each time."

He peered over my shoulder. "Sure, I know them. I went to school with their kids."

The Police Department consisted of the chief and two patrolmen. Other town officers included the Tree Warden, the Shellfish Constable, the Surveyor of Lumber, and the Moth Agent. Ev was not amused. "That's what we've got here, trees and ocean and bay. They've got to be taken care of."

"Of course. I'm not laughing at that. It just seems so nice and simple. That a town's major problem could be moths."

I read to him from the most recent report of the Moth Agent, bemoaning the infestation of gypsy moths over the past four years. "Many conferences were held and surveys made. . . . An aerial spraying project was then planned. . . . It is too early to say how effective the spraying will control the gypsies, although results look fair to good. We will certainly know in the spring when the caterpillars emerge from their eggs."

He smiled unwillingly. "You think it's quaint," he said. "It's not. It's people's daily concerns."

"That's what I like. How come your father has all these reports? Does everyone get a copy?"

"Probably because he's been Harbormaster on and off for a long time."

171

"I thought he had the gas station."

"He does. Harbormaster isn't a full-time job."

"What does he have to do?"

"He collects fees from the boats moored down at the harbor, he goes out now and then to check that there's no speeding in the bay, or that boats aren't getting too close to swimming areas in the summer. I used to help him when I was a kid. After a storm there'd always be a few wrecks or boats that got loose from their moorings, so we'd go out with the Rescue Squad to get them back."

"Did you know everyone in town?"

"More or less. If I didn't know them personally I knew who their families were."

"So you know the Cemetery Commissioner and the Pound Keeper and Fence Viewer and the Inspector of Animals and the Wire Inspector—"

"You're teasing me," he said, knocking the Town Report out of my hand and vaulting over me.

"You're so easy to tease, it's irresistible. Hey, aren't we making too much noise? What about your parents?"

"They must be sleeping by now. You city provincials are all alike. No respect."

He was wrong. I was awed by the town, and it wasn't anything to do with quaintness. This glorious strip between bay and ocean was, in size and silhouette, uncannily like my own water-lapped island—long and narrow and tapering at the tip. Except much of its twenty-three square miles was sandy beach, and its affairs could be managed by a few dozen people (nearly all of them male back then, aside from the Library Trustees and the schoolteachers).

It was manageable: that was what drew me. At Town Meetings, citizens pondered not just the problem of gypsy moths, but how best to clean up the town dump and fight Dutch elm disease. They set speeding limits for motorboats, they tarred the roads and tended the beaches. They voted that yes, the new police cruiser should have a two-way radio but no, power steering was an unneeded luxury. They set rules for the dimensions of road signs, so as not to mar the town's beauty, and voted down any alterations in the dunes or the marshes. Time and again the selectmen rebuffed the notion of broader highways and development at the harbor, and bristled at the threat of a major airport at the nearby Air Force base.

Meanwhile, my hometown was growing less and less manageable. The whole country felt unmanageable. We had lately come, tattered and intemperate, from the jungle war Ev fought in and barely spoke two words about. Our history was looking like a series of gallant, doomed efforts to make order out of a stretch of land too large to govern, home to groups at cross-purposes. Much more locally, I was coming out of two years with Q., also unmanageable—that is, together we made an unmanageable situation. Ev and his town, I thought when I married him, were the opposite.

FIFTEEN MONTHS AFTER I MARRIED EV, Q. left Susan. He was madly in love. Or just plain mad, Mona reported over the phone. I tried to find out about Q.'s love—what she looked like, where she came from, how old she was, and had she any brains. But dear, terse Mona said only that the woman had been playing Sally Bowles in a summer stock production of *Cabaret*. I suppose she thought it would pain me to know more and she was right. Though it would have pained me less to hear it from Mona than from Q., which in the fullness of time I did. Why do you tell me these things? I'd say. What makes you think I want to know? Yet even as he gave me details—not so much sexual as intimate—making me the keeper of his life and his narrative, even as I cringed inside, every word like a surgeon's fingers on deep raw innards, I relished each convolution of the emotional drama. Here's something for your data bank, he said. He knew.

Q. left his wife. Q. was madly in love. Had there been a lull in the ongoing domestic crises? Carla drug-free, Renata over the abortion trauma, the drowned brother given belated artificial respiration, the entire family

1 7 3

as cheery and stable as at the close of a half-hour sitcom, meaning that my timing was wrong, I hadn't had enough patience? Or should I feel a certain pride that he fell in love on the rebound, banished by me, and knew enough not to make the same mistake twice? No, such fore-thought didn't sound like Q. Whatever the case, he left Susan and I was married to Ev. I had to do something for revenge, something short of killing Q., which I considered but abandoned.

"You know what?" I asked Ev one night after we made love and were sitting side by side, I with a magazine, he with mounds of newspapers in English and Spanish, for he was leaving for El Salvador in a few days. He looked monkish even though naked, paled after the flush of love, his rimless hexagonal glasses glinting in the night light, his beard in disarray. He put down the paper and turned with the half-smile.

"No, what?"

This was a routine of ours. I did it to make him ask a question.

"I'm pregnant."

He laughed and slid a finger up into the center of me, making me shiver and smile. "Isn't it a little early to tell?"

"Not from this time. I'm serious. From weeks ago."

"You really are?"

"I really am." His silence. This time I pushed. "Aren't you going to say anything?"

"Well, good. I'm surprised. But, good. If that's what you want."

"I guess I want you to be happy about it."

"I am. I mean I will be. I'm so preoccupied about this trip, I guess I . . ."

"Didn't this ever occur to you?"

"I'm not sure. Maybe not. I didn't know you wanted it."

I could have screamed at him for all the traits I had once admired and thought would be so easy to live with after Q. But screaming wouldn't change anything. I wanted him to be Q. and he never would be, and there was nothing to be done about it. If only I could have sobbed in his arms that Q. didn't love me, he loved someone else, how could that be?

How could he leave Susan for someone playing Sally Bowles when he wouldn't leave her for me?

"Laura, I am glad. It'll be fine. I don't mind at all."

"That makes me feel great, that you don't mind. I guess that's how you decided to marry me, too."

"That was different."

"Was it? In what way? Maybe it's time we figured that out."

He waved that away. "Look, you want me to tell you what I feel, you always say. This is important to you and I respect that. I just don't see my life as a drama the way you do. Dramatic decisions at every turn. It'll be fine." He reached over and touched my leg. The finger had long been removed.

"Never mind. Let's not talk about it anymore."

He picked up the paper, and three days later left for El Salvador.

It was bleak winter, the river frozen. I stared out the window at a ship that had been stalled for days in the ice. When I picked up the ringing phone and heard Q.'s voice I lost my grip. The receiver fell in my lap.

Sorry, I dropped you, I mean I dropped it, I told him.

He laughed and said, I've worked on my voice but I never knew it was so powerful.

I laughed, too, and so before I could remember to be enraged we were laughing.

I'm in town, Laura. I thought I'd see how you were.

In town from where? I'm not even sure where you live.

Minneapolis.

With that whatshername, the one you met in *Cabaret* and left Susan for, who played the Liza Minnelli part, Sally Bowles? Her?

Oh, God, no, that's been over for months. It was a disaster. You have no idea, Laura. She wanted to reconstruct me. She herself came from a family of alcoholics and was constantly—

You don't have to tell me.

No. Well, how are you?

Pregnant.

Pregnant! Laura, love, how wonderful! Somehow I never imagined you pregnant. I knew you had that great success with the novel. I read it. It was marvelous. I knew it would be, just from the bits I read way back.

You never told me you read it.

I'm telling you now.

You were right not to before. I probably would have spit in your face. I don't know why I'm not doing that now. But it's good to hear your voice, actually. (Now that I'm safe, I thought.)

It was a wonderful book, he said. I want to talk to you about it. We have lots to talk about. But pregnant! Well, I don't know why I'm so surprised. That's what happens when people get married. And you did that. You went and got married, he accused.

Yes, I said. I don't know why that should surprise you either. I'm the same as other women. The majority of women get married and pregnant at some point.

Oh, you're not the same, my love. You're very special. There's no one like you. Age cannot wither you, nor custom—

For Chrissakes, Q., I'm not even thirty.

Sorry, just a manner of speaking. I've lost track of time. I was so wretched with that Sally Bowles. Plus I was having periodontal work done all during it. I don't know which was worse. Best of luck, Laura. I'm happy for you. How about meeting me for a cup of tea?

I went.

You don't look pregnant. That was the first thing he said. Then he put his arms around me. We didn't know what kind of kiss to do so we devised, spontaneously, the unique kiss that we perfected later on for those ambiguous phases between us, something between a friends' kiss and a lovers' kiss, a kiss with slightly parted lips, a kiss bearing the richness and memory of loverdom but not the assurance, a tentative kiss, full of geniality and a touch more, but something short of passion, a questioning kiss, moist but chaste, brief but longer than a friends' kiss of greeting. . . . I wasn't swept away, only a trifle unsettled by it. Then I looked him over: coarse graying hair, tired eyes, old-fashioned tweed overcoat—

he might have been playing a bemused professor in a 1940s movie. I'm safe, I thought.

We sat down in a Greek diner—Q. can't stand anything even mildly fashionable—and started to talk about the book, but a troop of high school kids paraded in, turned on the jukebox and screeched over the music.

This is intolerable, he said. We can't hear each other speak. Come back to my place. I'm staying in Peter's apartment, you know, my ex-brother-in-law but we're still friends.

I don't think so.

Come on, there's no one home and it's too cold to take a walk.

But not to make love, I said.

Who said anything about making love? He laughed as he took my arm against the wind and pulled me close. You're the one who's always got that on your mind. We're old friends. Surely we can sit somewhere quiet and talk.

The apartment was full of Victoriana. Knickknacks. Fringed lampshades. Silhouettes on the walls. A velvet chaise.

I've always wanted to lie on a chaise, I said, and stretched out.

It suits you, said Q. He pulled up a chair and sat beside me.

We stared at each other and I felt the danger. Q. all over again.

How pregnant can you be? A few hours?

Two months. I've hardly told anyone.

I remember when Susan was pregnant. I used to put my hand on her belly and feel it kicking.

Well, this one's not doing anything yet so you can just stop. Really, Q., this is silly.

All right, but I have to kiss you. May I?

He slid down from the chair so he was kneeling beside me.

You're being adolescent.

You're quite right. When was the last time I asked permission to kiss someone? I think after the Junior Prom.

I touched his hair. I couldn't help it. Maybe you'll turn into a frog, I said.

Isn't it the frog who turns into a prince when she kisses him?

Yes. But with you it's the other way around. You're a frog disguised as a prince. All it takes is one kiss.

Ah, I see. He drew back. That is a very damning thing to say about a person, Laura.

I think you even look a little like a frog. I think you're beginning to get a little green around the eyes and mouth.

There's nothing I can say to explain, is there?

I can't imagine what.

Even though you were the one who got married?

What are you saying? You were married already.

Let's get back to kissing, he said. It's easier.

Let's not, I said a moment later. I don't think this will be good for my health. Not with a frog.

Why don't you move over and let me lie down. Maybe I can still add something to the gene pool.

I sat up. That's an awful thought. What's got into you? You were never awful before. In that way, I mean. I shouldn't have come here. I'm going home.

As you wish, said Q. with a sigh, and he stood up to let me pass. I'll call you when I'm back in town. We'll try again.

Meanwhile, why don't you fall in love just to pass the time?

That reminds me, I never asked about your husband. What is he like? Do you love him?

Why should you care what he's like? Of course I love him. Why else would I marry him?

Good. I'm glad. I want you to be happy, said Q. at the door.

Frog! I said. Just one step up from a toad.

A few days later I had a miscarriage. Cramps, blood, terror. My cousin Joyce, luckily in town and not in Africa gathering anthropological data on her chosen ethnic group, the Tsumati, took me to the hospital in a cab, towels packed between my legs. Ev was still in El Salvador. I could easily have invited Q. over that day but I was afraid. It had never occurred to me to be afraid of this. The baby I had barely welcomed into me was gone. I'd imagined there would be ample time to think about it and truly come to want it, and now there was nothing left. No baby. Ev away. No Q. Only books to write. I had already written about loss but overnight I became an expert.

I felt guilty, as if I had shaken the baby loose from its moorings by making love with Q. I had to keep reminding myself that I hadn't made love with Q., not at all, only kissed him a few times and thought about making love. What harm could that do? Still, I couldn't help connecting the two events, my kissing Q. and losing the baby. Once more I wanted never again to see him or hear his voice or his name mentioned, and if by chance I had come upon his face on the screen, as in that silly murder mystery where he appeared in the guise of a pastry chef, I would have climbed past the row of irritated people and fled the theatre to stumble about the streets until the fresh air dissolved his image.

In the end, I blamed him for the loss of the baby. I attributed to him great and impossible powers. Absurd. Whatever spells his gray eyes could cast, Q. wasn't that kind of sorcerer. He liked children. He had so many of his own; he would have liked mine, too.

Mona lived with three different men before finding Dave, her great love, at last. He was the reward after preliminary stages of lesser men, more troublesome men, just as the swineherd of fairy tales after many trials marries the king's daughter. Whether or not it would stand up to scrutiny, this private narrative satisfies her. An opposite narrative satisfies me. Q. was the first: everything since then is measured against the original enchantment, and is a falling off. We have not always been lovers. We've not even been friends, always. But we have always been.

I called mine an ill-considered marriage, a while ago. But perhaps it wasn't after all. It left ample room for Q. Apart from the baby I never felt guilty over him—how could I? It would have been like feeling guilt at looking in a mirror or at the negative of one's own photo. It's true I believe in lying in the bed you make. But I had made my bed with Q. long ago, and Ev never cared to know whether I had a bed elsewhere. Anyway, I was bound to it.

I never wished Ev would disappear. That he would go away, yes, and then return. He did often go away on assignment. I liked the solitude, smoother in texture than the abrading solitude I felt when he was home. Then after a while I would begin to miss his wraith-like presence gliding through the house, the precise, absorbed way he patted his trousers down on the hanger and ran a fingernail along the crease, and measured out his coffee, dreamily sniffing the aroma, and cleared his desk every night to leave a bare surface, and squinted to trim his beard, and rustled his newspapers in bed. Above all, I missed his embraces, slow, melancholy, and intense. Then and then alone he was fully present, fully mine. He gave all he had to give, his inscrutable sadness. It was as if all the sadness were distilled, at those moments, into physical yearning.

I never knew why he chose me, and only after he was killed and I could see his life as a completed span did I understand he hadn't chosen me at all: I was dropped in his lap. When I was introduced to him at the party, he must have had some vague, inarticulate sense of my readiness and diffidence, which suited his own readiness and diffidence well enough for him to take the next step and the next, until before he knew it he was married to me, and I suppose that suited him well enough, too. Perhaps his heart also was broken, and all during our marriage he remained in thrall to Margot, the psychiatrist, without knowing it. Perhaps we had more in common, Ev and I, than we ever dreamed, and if we could meet in some region where the happenings of this world are viewed from a great distance as the laughable nothings they are, we could tell our secrets and even smile ruefully at the companionable but silent life we led together. I could tell him—and he'd listen with interest—how Q. came back. And back. That that was my marriage, in its fashion.

Q. was even faithful, in his fashion. Not long after I lost the baby, the loss I blamed on him because we kissed, he called me, undaunted.

Laura, my love?

Q.! Where are you?

Downtown. Come see me in *Lear*. Please. I want you to be there.

Lear? You're playing Lear?

No, no. I'm not ready for that. It's years away. I'm playing Kent.

Kent? You can't be serious.

Why, what's so funny?

Kent the faithful servant? My God. No one could accuse them of type-casting.

He fell silent, which almost never happened.

Q., are you there? What's the matter? I'm sorry. I didn't mean anything.

You don't think I could do Kent? (Dear Q. It wasn't the insult to his character that he minded, but the inferred slight to his talent.) I can do Kent better than anybody. People understand their opposites best of all. Don't you know that, Laura?

Forget I said anything. Tell me where it's playing.

Like a child, he brightened up. He made a magnificent Kent. "Now, banished Kent," he addressed himself, full of dignified humility, "If thou canst serve where thou dost stand condemned, So may it come thy master whom thou lov'st Shall find thee full of labors." Trippingly on the tongue, no trace of the very faint accent that crept in when he was worn out or just waking from sleep or making love.

Kent is put in the stocks. "Some time I shall sleep out, the rest I'll whistle." Yes, that was very like Q. At the end he prepares for death: "I have a journey, sir, shortly to go. My master calls me; I must not say no."

I cried. As if he were my child, I was that proud. So what if he couldn't ever be a Kent, or only for a few days at a stretch? He could portray him. The real Kent might be charmless, a bit of a bore, even. You might not want him around all the time. By the final curtain I had convinced myself that the image, the performance, superseded the reality: a true child of my time.

I went backstage and threw my arms around his neck, and in his weather-beaten tunic he picked me up and twirled me in circles, exulting: I told you I could do it! I told you! Later, bending over me in his hotel bed, he whispered, What does it matter who we really are? I'm really the Fool. It's the Fool you love. *Il Matto*.

ON ONE OF HIS TRIPS TO NEW YORK we all found ourselves at a large party. Q. and I hid our astonishment and made ludicrously civil introductions all around. Our host, a doctor acquaintance of Ev's just back from a stint in Nicaragua, happened to be an uncle of Q.'s latest love, a vixenish Dubliner who sang Irish folk songs. While she was off helping her aunt remove a turkey from the oven, Q. behaved outrageously, stroking my hip as we were wedged together between the wall and a table laden with raw vegetables, stroking gently and unremittingly while we chatted with strangers who in the general crush could see nothing amiss. We were so cramped that I couldn't have stopped him even if I'd wanted to. I didn't want to. Ev was across the room with the doctor, talking no doubt about the scarcity of medical supplies in Nicaragua, his face intent and animated in a way it rarely was when he talked to me. I liked the secrecy and the bad taste of it, the idea of behaving so badly together with Q.

When we next met he told me he'd found Ev cold. Oh, not cold, I corrected. Withdrawn, remote; it was different. But nothing could soften Q.'s verdict. You only saw him that one time, I would protest years later. That was enough, Q. said. Besides, he had read Ev's book about Central America and seen him on a couple of television panels. Admit it, I said finally, you wouldn't like anyone I married. Not at all, he said, I'm capable of being objective. You could have married me yourself, I said. You got married first, he said. And so it went, everlastingly, the climax of the dialogue taking place in a shabby, enchanted Mexican restaurant a year and a half before Ev was killed.

I hoped Ev's first wife, Margot, would come to the funeral. You don't exactly issue invitations, but I told Tony and Jilly she was welcome. No need for animosity between us; it was she who had ended their marriage (and by now I understood why, even if Ev hadn't). I imagined we might compare notes as women do, and between us give him the weight he lacked, compacted out of our grieving breath and voices. We could summon into existence that part of him he had never allowed to exist, and thus complete him in death. But clearly she had no taste for that enterprise for she didn't come.

Q. came. Naturally. And how well he behaved on this occasion. Most people behave ineptly at funerals, as if some prescribed mode of behavior exists which unfortunately they haven't been taught, and so they concoct a somber, clumsy role. But Q., who concocts roles moment by moment, was perfect, blending easily with the large assembly. He modulated his billowing energy into an exquisite courtesy, just the sort of discretion Ev prized. I marveled while I mourned. With the others, he stepped up to greet me in my role of bereaved widow, took my hands and murmured the appropriate words. Sorry, sorry. Well, of course he was sorry, even if he hadn't liked Ev. Who isn't sorry at a funeral, most of all sorry that they have to attend.

So perfectly sorry that no one could have detected a trace of our streaky passion, or of our confusion, which I sensed drifting in on the vibrations of the future. What now? As the bereaved, I needn't think of that future for a while. But it would drift closer. Once, I had craved a life with Q. Now I wasn't sure we could exist in brightly lit reality. We had gotten so used to our shadow life together, alongside our ordinary lives which had been forms of faithlessness: for Q., falling in love, and for me, staying married to Ev.

Fragments of ambivalence, beads on a string. The hard question in telling any story is, Which are the beads and which is the string?

Very soon Jilly and I are settled into a routine. I'm alone much of the time and glad of it. My sack of fear is emptying, my heart beating almost at a normal rate. But a different kind of fear is replacing the old—a calmer, duller kind. That I'll get used to living like this.

Meanwhile, I work at taking things in for future use, absorbing data for the book. I stroll through the handful of shops and visit the museum displays: harpoons once used to spear whales from shore, antique hip boots, fishing rods and seafaring gewgaws, glass-encased yellowed clippings about storms and foundered ships. Diligently, I read the local paper, which shows civic life as quite eclectic, the Ladies' Aid church rummage sale and Rescue Squad bake sale alongside the writers' group and yoga classes, the recycling get-togethers and meetings of La Leche League ("children always welcome").

Mostly I sit on the beach for long spells—an observer might not perceive it as work—reading, dozing, watching the tides move up and back.

It's not only the moon that pulls but the sun, too, the library book explains. Each one beckons to the spinning planet. The land is firm, recalcitrant, but the water, ah, the fluid, responsive water leaps to the desire of the celestial bodies. The tides are the answer to that importuning call from far in space, the reaching up for the two lovers, sun and moon. The tides leap highest, reach farthest, when the sun and moon are aligned and pulling in the same direction, which happens, as Ev said, just after the new and full moon. Spring tides, they're called. Not for spring, the season, but spring, the response. At half-moon the sun and moon are at right angles to the earth, tugging in opposite directions; confused, pulled this way and that, the waters subside into stillness and lethargy. Then the tides are at their lowest: neap tide. Their apparent docility is the result of an impasse.

The newspaper prints a chart showing the times of high and low tides each day, with variations in minutes from beach to beach, ocean side and bay side, up and down the coast. It seems wondrous that this can be calculated—the exact moment the water will reach its highest and lowest points on the waiting tractable beach, whose task is to be covered and exposed, covered and exposed, through the rounds of darkness and light, as if a giant pair of hands on high were doing Tai Chi and by the force of their energy drawing up, then releasing the waters. Real masters can raise lakes and oceans by the movements of their hands, one of the Tai Chi teacher's parables says.

The passage from high to low tide takes roughly six and a half hours, but is sometimes closer to six and a quarter, sometimes seven. I couldn't find the clue that determined such small variations. The tides are predictable, but like everything in nature, regular only up to a point. I suppose that on the scale of the cosmic passion impelling the triangle of sun, moon, and water, irregularities of a few minutes hardly count.

I DRIVE FROM ocean side to bay side several times a day—only a couple of miles apart—marking the changes in water and light. The strip between them is the town, the safe haven, its geographical task to divide the waters.

I love the bay at low tide, when the water has retreated so far that you can walk out close to half a mile on the mud flats. Small children go chasing hermit crabs while their parents dig for clams and mussels, tossing them into the children's plastic pails. Sun-lovers set low beach chairs way out on the flats to bask for hours as the water slowly—but always faster than expected—comes lapping at their toes, soon to reach the slatted seats. There's something primeval about the scene: sun, dunes with their gray-green shrubbery, and vast stretches of mud covered by a shiny film of water. So it must have looked when that crucial wayward fish slithered in and gasped for breath.

Out in the distance sits the old blackened ship, its charred remains submerged then revealed at the whim of the tides, a permanent fixture in the landscape through endurance and longevity. At high tide it looks impossibly far, but at low tide it seems I might walk to it, if I had the strength. I can walk more easily here than in the city, ten or fifteen minutes at a time, once I get revved up. My body simply needs coaxing like an old car, like the pickup that resourceful Jilly got to move.

One afternoon I was seized with the desire to examine the ship close up, and impulsively set out. When I was tired enough to turn back, the ship seemed no closer. For several days I tried, checking in the papers for the hours of low tide. Each day I went a little farther out, but the ship got no closer. If nothing else, I was increasing my own endurance. Then I would rest on the beach, and drive over to the ocean to watch the waves.

My favorite ocean beach has huge dunes walling it off from the town, from the continent. At the approach, at the top of the dune, the expanses of sea and sand below are a discovery no matter how many times you've stood there. You climb down as if descending into an endless room, or onto a stage with the sandy hill as backdrop. On the beach, the rest of the world vanishes except for the swimmers and an occasional slow-gliding ship far out. Each time I climb down, I'm not sure how I'll manage the climb back up, but I don't care. Not a bad fate, to be stranded here on the welcome blankness of Long Nook. For aside from a few unobtrusive signs warning of loose sand on the dunes, there are only the God-given essentials: no snack bar, showers, changing rooms, toilets or drinking fountains, and now no lifeguard chairs either, since the selectmen have apparently cut lifeguards from the budget, leaving the tourists to fend for themselves.

A million years ago this unadorned stretch of beach, walled off by high dunes, was the edge of a mountain range, until a glacier slid down from the north and nudged the mountains about to form a curved spit of land. Later on, sand deposited by the currents and tides flattened the land and refined it into the familiar arc on the maps. But this bit of magnificence is only for today. Thousands of years from now, long after the lighthouse has fallen into the sea, this beach, worn down by the tides, may be the ocean floor. Instead of the arc-shaped spit of the Cape, there will be a string of islands.

It looks as if nothing is happening, a narrative without a plot, yet this patient shaping and transforming work of water—carving the shore, never satisfied—is the earth's real drama.

I WAS DETERMINED to get out to the ship. "I bet we can make it this time. I've been working up to it," I told Jilly. She was taking the night shift, so we set off on the mud flats after lunch.

"We'll have a nice walk, but I doubt if we'll get there. It's farther than it looks. Why do we have to get there, anyway?"

"I don't know. I like to have a goal. And I have a yen to see it up close. It's mysterious."

"They say it was sunk in World War II. Maybe it was headed for Europe. Or the Germans were offshore. Imagine, German subs in Cape Cod Bay."

It's always felt daring walking so far out, not dangerous-daring—the tide comes in slowly and the waters are calm and shallow—but adventurous-daring, walking on land usually covered over, secret land not meant to be seen or trod on. I kept my eyes on the ship, black, open and bare. Jilly unexpectedly proved to be an expert on the tides. She knew about the sloshing basin and the pull of both sun and moon.

"The sloshing around goes on all the time, plus you have the gravitational pull, plus the wind, which can whoosh the water forward or keep it back, depending. You've got all these factors and the slope of the land, too, working at the same time. When the pull of gravity and the sloshing are in the same direction, that's when you get tidal waves or huge high tides like in the Bay of Fundy, or else the opposite, very low tides, like in Nantucket. Have you ever been to Nantucket?"

"No. How do you know all this?"

"I took a course in oceanography last semester. We went to the Marine Observatory in Woods Hole, at the other end of the Cape. The Bay of Fundy, in Nova Scotia," she said soberly, like a child who's studied up for the exam, "has the world's highest tides. They can go up to fifty feet—the water just zooms in. Everyone knows it's coming so they keep away. The bucket is sloshing upwards just as the sun and moon are pulling. I'd love to see that someday. They have this neat way of fishing, because of the tides. They set up poles way out on the flats when the tide is out and string up nets between them. When the tide comes in it's so deep it covers up the nets and poles, and when it pulls back, the nets are full of fish. And, like, they haven't really done anything, just waited out the tide."

"Like loaves and fishes."

"I guess. How're you doing? Still okay?"

"A little tired. Does it look any closer?"

"Not really. I think the current's shifting, too. See, it's up to our ankles. You have to figure, Laura, once we get out there we have to come all the way back."

"Okay, let's turn around. It makes me feel like an old lady, though."

"Oh, cut that out. You're looking better already, not so sleepy. And you can swim. You didn't think you'd be able to."

"Anyone can swim in this water. It's all salt."

"Still. My next day off, we'll rent bikes and ride down to the harbor. It's partly a matter of will, you know. You have to push yourself."

Don't I know it. I was performing every minute. Back on dry land I stretched out on our waiting blanket. The beach was hot, the wind sultry; the sun turned the mud flats into a vast coffee-colored mirror. When I woke the sun was lower, pale and creamy in a graying sky with a breeze that promised rain. The beach was almost empty. Off in the distance, I saw Jilly bending down to pick up rocks. She would examine them, toss some away and stuff others in the paunchy pocket of her sweatshirt. She returned and sat brooding on the blanket, head bent, letting sand sift through her fingers.

"Is something the matter, Jilly?"

"Oh, I thought you were sleeping. It's nothing, just . . . I've been thinking a lot lately . . . about people dying and whether anyone even notices they're gone, after a while. I mean, after a while you start to live again and go on as if it never was?"

"But that's not how we feel. You know. We think about him all the time."

"It's not even so much him. I do think about him a lot. It's more . . . have you ever felt . . . it sometimes seems nobody cares if anyone else lives or dies? As if no one's connected?"

"What do you mean? We're connected."

"Not us. There was something in San Francisco." She flopped over alongside me on her stomach so our faces were close. "You're going to think this is ditzy, but . . . do you remember I mentioned Barry and I took his father's car one day and drove into the wine country?"

"Did something happen with the car? Were you hurt? Why didn't you tell me?"

"No, no, nothing like that. We just had some wine, and after that Barry decided to stay at a friend's house up there and I drove back myself. But this strange thing happened when I crossed the Golden Gate Bridge."

"Well, what?"

"Nothing really. Just a thought I had."

"Come on, what thought?"

"Well, I'm driving along with all this fantastic scenery and suddenly at the tollbooth I get stopped. I didn't know why. It was weird—I felt guilty, like I was in a stolen car or carrying drugs or something. I even thought for a minute Barry might have set me up. He's a pothead, who knows what else he might have in the car? I mean, I was pretty freaked for a minute. The attendant disappeared and I even thought of making a dash, but it's a good thing I didn't. Meanwhile, traffic was piling up behind me, all the Marin County types coming to town for the evening, you know? And being late for stuff? Honking away as if it was my fault. But what could I do? They saw me trying to hand the woman the money but they still honked. Then I saw cars at other tollbooths stopped, too, so I figured, well, okay, it's not me. Whatever it is, it's going to take awhile. I turned off the radio and the a.c. and the motor and rolled down the window and just sat there. Finally the attendant came back and I asked her what it was, and she said someone was trying to jump off the bridge and there were police cars and ambulances on their way to try to stop him or catch him or whatever. It's a great bridge for suicides. I think it has a world record. Well, after about fifteen minutes—all this time I couldn't see a thing, at least if I'd been able to see it might've been interesting—I thought to myself, I wish he would just jump and get it over with, or else not jump. Either way, so I could get going. I was tired of sitting there, you know? I mean, if people are considering jumping off a bridge they could at least have their minds made up before they cause all that disruption? But the next minute I realized, what a terrible thing to think. I mean, it's a person up there. Maybe somebody's father. How could I think such a thing? So I was sort of upset that I thought that. How could I forget what it feels like to have someone die?"

"It doesn't mean you forgot, Jilly. It's what anyone would think in that situation. You can't control those thoughts. Probably the other drivers were thinking the same thing."

"That doesn't make it any better. What I should have been thinking was how to save him. Why didn't anyone jump out of their car and rush over to help?"

"People tend to get paralyzed at those moments."

"I didn't feel paralyzed. The thing is, I didn't feel anything. Do you think it's modern life and alienation and all that shit, Laura?"

"I think it has to do with distance. If you had known him or if you were standing three feet away, you would have acted differently. There's no point agonizing over a thought. How can you censor thoughts? Well, you can, I guess, but would you really want to? It's not as if they affect what happens. What did happen, anyhow?"

"They finally let us go through after about half an hour. I suppose they got him down. Or her. There were no signs of anything except all the police cars—I don't know why they need so many for just one person. It might've looked the same if he'd jumped. In fact that idea has been used as a performance piece. Not the guy who jumped out of the window for the pictures. Another artist announced he'd really kill himself at the end of a year."

"Oh, was he planning to jump off a bridge?"

"No, he was going to shoot himself. That whole year he lived the way you would if your days were numbered. He got his affairs in order, he traveled to exotic places, he didn't bother getting his teeth fixed. He advertised the time and day he would do it and a big crowd came to watch."

"Don't tell me you actually witnessed this!"

"No, it was years ago. I was just a kid. I read about it. He came with his loaded gun. But in the end he didn't go through with it."

"I don't get it. You mean it was all a hoax?"

"Nobody knows for sure. Maybe he really meant it but at the last minute he just couldn't. I guess as a performance you'd have to call it a failure. But now I think, after you've been close to someone really doing it, like on the bridge, to do it as a display seems sort of . . ."

Yes, the line between life and art is not so fine after all. Arthur, in the hospital dying of AIDS, is not putting on a performance.

"Did the audience get their money back?" I asked.

She giggled. "I don't know. It might've been free, in a park or something. Can you imagine doing that, though?"

"No." I didn't tell her I'd thought of killing myself if I wasn't better in a year. Not in public, though. And not for art. "In a way it wasn't a failure," I said. "For the audience, that is. They paid for the thrill of anticipation, imagining someone act out their fantasies. They had that for a whole year."

"Well, you see, then thoughts *do* affect things, Laura. I really believe that. His thought made an audience feel and think, maybe changed their lives. And it could be this person on the bridge was surrounded by a lot of negative thoughts, negative energy, in his life. That can make you depressed or even sick."

If I agreed, I might shortly find myself discussing auras and crystals and asking the neighbors their zodiacal signs.

"My mother didn't like me to think bad thoughts," I mused, "but that was because they weren't nice. She never said they had any power."

"She might have been onto something. They have the power you give them. That could be more than we know."

"I hope not. I think bad thoughts all the time." I didn't mention handsome Dr. B., perchance a victim of my thoughts traveling on the vibrations of the universe. But I did tell her what I'd wished for the drivers on Broadway, especially the car with the blaring radio. "It was harmless resentment. Why should they be driving merrily along, inflicting their horrible music on everyone, while I can't dash across the way I used to? I didn't feel the slightest guilt. And they didn't die. I would have heard the sirens."

"I wish you wouldn't think that way, Laura, because Barry and I had the radio on very loud on that trip."

"In that case, I'll express my anger some other way. But you know, it is extremely inconsiderate."

"I suppose, but don't you think punishment by death is a little harsh? Like, you might be overreacting?"

"Naturally. That's what makes it fun."

On the way home the little white car's motor stalled, a recent ploy. The temperamental thing was protesting its exile. It missed the city and its old habits, moving from one side of the street to the other each day, seeing Luke and the neighbors. Never mind that back home it risked having its bumper or other parts knocked off. You can't explain nostalgia.

Late at night, in the spare bedroom, the old Town Reports felt familiar as I sat leafing through. After my first trip up here with Ev, I'd spirited home a few to read now and then in bed with him beside me. And so after his death, my vision of the town—rare in beauty, rich in water—was a patchwork of civic data mixed with scraps of memory that were mostly his, not mine. An outsider's vision, quickened by the ebb and flow of the tides and the disruptions of the gales, and defying the inadmissible fact of the body lying on an unlovely Bronx street, outlined in chalk marks that washed away in the first rain. That was not supposed to have been Ev's story. Nor mine.

I remembered now the way dramatic events were enshrined in lists, complete with dates and cost—dry statistical fodder to be kindled by imagination: fires, rescues, stray dogs returned by the Dog Officer, the earnest efforts of the Handwriting Committee, whose goals were "To teach the concomitants of neatness, clarity, and attention to detail" and "To achieve and surpass national norms in speed and quality." I could vouch for the program's success. Ev's handwriting was neat and legible, yet not without character: tall, slender, austere.

In 1971, a time of marches and protests throughout the land, a fifteen-man Auxiliary Police Force was recruited and trained in riot and mob control. Obviously the prudent selectmen felt it best to be prepared, especially given what a report the following year would call the town's "reputation of permissiveness."

It is regarded as a natural haven for the new generation, the members of the third culture. It also attracts a number of nudists, and the nudists, not surprisingly, attract a certain number of voyeurs. When all these factors are combined, it is little wonder that the community attracts an extraordinarily large influx of summer visitors! Nor is it surprising that the influx includes so many nonconforming persons who sometimes trespass on private property, sleep outside, park illegally, or break into parked automobiles or unoccupied cottages.

Nudists, voyeurs, nonconforming persons might come and go, but no native son or daughter slipped through the cracks: the arcs of their lives were traced and tallied from birth to marriage to death, with the deaths recorded in the biblical way—seventy-eight years, four months, three days. An anomaly among the ordinary deaths was a man of forty-seven—asphyxiation by strangulation, self-inflicted. That jarred my idyllic vision of the town and I felt a shudder of foreboding. Yet why not allow one such item, for verisimilitude? Certainly the town would have its private tragedies, but not, thanks to the lighthouse and the Rescue Squad and the Coast Guard, great communal tragedies like the October gale of 1841 in which fifty-seven men and boys were drowned on a day that began fair and mild. No, violence and tragedy would never be the theme of the town or any book about it.

The strict statistics embraced vast possibility, like the dimensions and texture of a canvas or the formal requirements of a symphony. A novelist would imagine the town's porous life within the hard shell of data, making up what the statistics didn't tell—how the wife of the Superintendent of Schools falls in love with the Civil Defense Officer, or the child listed as born to Vincent and Cheryl Delgado is really the love child of the Clam Constable, a bachelor who lives with his aging mother, a woman careless with matches—two small fires recorded in one year. Is that the Burial Agent's daughter who's so often stopped for driving under the influence, or the Town Accountant's son apprehended for breaking and entering? Was the boy who dropped out of school in eighth grade the one who hanged himself thirty-three years later?

You could chart a man's life by his appearance in the statistics, moving from his parents' marriage to his birth, his duly noted passage from elementary school to high school. He marries a classmate and serves on the Board of Health or maybe the Recreation Committee, supervising the swimming lessons at high tide. In a careless moment he's arrested for speeding or, if the cop is an old friend or distant cousin, given a verbal warning. After one beer too many while his wife is out at a Library Committee meeting, he causes a minor grease fire, fixing hamburgers for the kids. Their dates of birth have been appearing every few years and soon their names are listed among the high school graduates. Finally, at ninety-one, he dies quietly of coronary thrombosis. This might have been Ev. Yes, I could give him that. He'd teach school or edit the local paper or work in his father's gas station. His children might today be living off the tourists, working in the restaurants or motels, in the Provincetown shops or at the golf course.

Or I could even see him as a fisherman, sere, solitary, in heavy dark clothes, poised at the rail of the boat, eyes fixed on the horizon. There wasn't much fishing here now, though. The shift and churn of the tides, modeling the shoreline like a sculptor never satisfied with his work, decades ago filled the harbor with sand: ships could no longer pass. Those who still fished did so in Provincetown to the north, where Jilly served what they caught. The rest had gone the way of the whalers. It was here and not in famed New Bedford that whaling began, learned from the Indians. I couldn't picture Ev harpooning whales from shore, a common method over a century ago. Even for him, that would have been too direct a mode of slaughter.

I SLEPT A HEAVY, unbroken sleep that night. Eight-fourteen: the digital clock beside the fisherman lamp on the night table always surprised me. I would have expected something more old-fashioned of Ev's parents, a plain round clock with easy-to-read numerals and a shrill ring relenting only after you fumbled for a cold metal button on the back. (Elderhostels, color TV, microwave, what next?) The graceless clock quantified time in so artificial and linear a way, as if time were a series of static moments dealt out from a deck like cards. The old round clocks quantify time, too—how else to track it?—but at least the circle tries, ingenuously, to mirror the cycles of the day. The hour hand journeying around the face imitates the sun's slow journey over the face of the earth, ascending and descending like the arc of time.

The phone rang and I reached out quickly so it wouldn't wake Jilly. Who wanted what, so early? Had my mother finally totaled the car?

195

Laura, my love.

(Oh, no. I thought I was rid of him for a while. He almost felt like something I'd made up.)

I know it's early but I wanted to be sure to get you. I kept calling to say good-bye before I left. I thought you'd disappeared. Finally I looked up Mona and she gave me this number. You didn't even tell me you were going to the Cape.

That's true, I didn't. Anyway, I wouldn't have known where to find you. Where are you now, anyway?

In Washington. I stopped to stay with my father awhile on the way back. Well, it's not really on the way, but . . . here I am.

So where did you finally stay in New York? Peter's new place?

No, in the motel they booked for us in Queens.

Uh-huh. And the woman who was too young? Did she grow up?

Laura, surely you jest.

Why? People age quickly in the city, what with the pollution and tension and noise and all the rest.

I never thought you'd take that seriously. Don't you think I can go for three weeks without a love affair? At my age? You flatter me.

What about Arthur? How's he doing?

Hanging on. He's surprising everyone. Last I heard, there was a chance he could go home again.

Well, that's good. Though it's not the same home anymore. Do you think Peter's sorry he moved?

Frankly, it won't matter that much. I saw the new place when we un-packed. It's very much like the old one, the same kind of building, a similar layout, and Peter was arranging everything in the same way. Re-creating it. It kept him occupied.

So why are you calling me now when we're hundreds of miles apart and not when we were both in New York?

I did try, I told you. Anyhow, I had the distinct impression you didn't want to see me. Don't you remember you turned me away? No room at the inn?

I didn't want you to live with me. I didn't say I didn't want to hear from you at all.

I must have misunderstood. Look, let's not get into this. I really called to see how you're feeling. You were in bad shape last time.

I had some blood tests. I've got a virus that could go on awhile. My immune system has surrendered. It's been insulted once too often. I'm a miniature ecological disaster, reflecting the larger global breakdown. A walking metaphor.

(Only to Q. would I speak this way, from the place I write from. I also told him, in plain English, what the doctor said.)

The good news is I won't die of it, like Arthur, just sort of drag around indefinitely.

I'm so sorry, *mia cara.* I know how you hate being sick. You could never bear having to stay in bed. By yourself, that is.

Well, that's changed. Now I'm in love with my bed. And I'm supposed to avoid stress. The only effective way I can think of is suicide.

They always tell you that. Avoid stress, as if it were fried foods, said Q.

Yes, I said, and I keep scoring so high on those quizzes in the magazines, you know, where you count up your stress in points? I go right over the top.

Everyone does, Laura. How could we not? The things they list are just ordinary life—trips, paint jobs, illness in the family, death of loved ones, heartache, unemployment, no money. What else is there? Still, you've got to try. I wish there were something I could do for you.

(Love me, I thought. Change history.)

I know. Thanks anyway. How's your father? I thought he was still in the nursing home.

No, I guess I didn't tell you. They gave him shock treatments a couple of months ago. It was extraordinary. He came back to life and went home.

How horrible, though. Shock treatments.

I know that's the liberal line but the fact is, Laura, they work. You should have seen him before. *Più morto che vivo.* The living death.

I remember your description. So is he okay now? This isn't another crisis, I hope?

No, just a visit. It hasn't been too bad, this time. I've been cooking and putting it all in the freezer for when I'm gone. I got him new under-wear and shoes, vacuumed, changed some bulbs. He must have been sitting in the dark. He can't get up on a ladder anymore and maybe he doesn't care. Still, he's doing all right, relatively. He doesn't have a lot to say—well, that's putting it mildly. He spends most of the time in his radio room puttering with—

Where?

His radio room. Didn't I tell you about his radios?

No.

Oh. What he does is, he goes around to flea markets looking for old radios. They have to be early, prewar is best, he says, and he buys them for two or three dollars, though he once went as high as twenty. They don't work, you understand. He takes them apart. He sits in this little room upstairs that my mother used to use as a practice room, with all the disassembled parts around him, and puts them back together lov-ingly. *Come mai funziano*—I mean, how he gets them to work is beyond me, but I swear that when he finishes, voices come out, real live voices, Laura, from these antique radios. I always expect to hear those famous old radio voices—Fred Allen, Jack Benny—you're too young to remem-ber and I just got the tail end of it, but no, it's those flat, smooth voices of today. Always cheery. Anyhow, Aldo seems happy enough up there, although since I'm here he brings whatever he's working on downstairs in the evening and does it at the kitchen table, so we keep each other company. I read the paper and he tinkers away. We don't talk much. That is, he doesn't, and you know I require a response. But it's nice, watching him putter.

Do you talk Italian with him?

What else? *Senz'altro*. I sometimes think, here we are in this town house in Georgetown surrounded by politicians, movers and shakers—they're probably planning the new world order within fifty feet of us—

and we sit like two old men, reading the paper and fixing radios. We could be back in his village in Tuscany, sitting in the piazza.

Did he do this when you were a boy?

Oh, no. Just since he's been alone, in between going to the hospital, though now he tells me he fooled around with ham radios as a young man. I only found out about the radios a couple of years ago. I was cleaning up while he was in the hospital and I discovered cartons of radios and radio parts in this former music room. After he does the insides and gets them to work again, he cleans the outsides. He refinishes the wood and spray-paints the plastic and metal parts until they look like new. You must have seen those prewar radios in fancy antique shops. They can be quite beautiful.

Is that what he does with them? Sells them to antique shops?

No, at least not yet. He didn't use to do anything, just resuscitate them, but the last couple of years he's been subscribing to antique radio magazines. You'd be amazed how many people read those things— there's a whole world of radio cognoscenti out there. He reads the ads for radios wanted and he's started advertising his own for sale. A few months ago he made his first sale—ten dollars. It was to a small theatre in Maryland where they needed a 1930s radio for a play. Unfortunately, in the play, what they do with the radio is throw it across the room.

But it could be destroyed in one performance. After all his work.

Maybe they were very careful. If they wanted an authentic 1930s radio and they were running for more than one night I suppose they would be careful, wouldn't they? One of the few things he said to me this week, after he told me about this sale, was that I should keep an eye out for any plays that might need a radio as a prop, so I said I would. And that's not all. Last week, right after I arrived, he sold one to an Australian in Adelaide who's a collector. That's getting into the serious big time, so *chi lo sa*? Maybe he'll be getting more business. It's a lot better than sitting in a stupor in front of the TV, so if it takes shock treatments . . .

I suppose so, I said.

He enjoys his radios. I see him fussing over them at the kitchen table after supper while I do the dishes, and I think how peaceful he looks. More peaceful than any other time since he retired, and certainly more than when he was at the embassy. Oh, and besides that, he has his ham radio, which is another thing entirely. Sometimes while he's fixing or painting, he listens to foreign stations. Strange languages, not Italian or French or anything he might understand. Hungarian, Turkish, I can't tell, but it doesn't seem to matter. Maybe he's tired of hearing English, or he just wants to hear a human voice without the burden of having to understand what it's saying. After all, he spent his whole working life being careful about what he heard and what he said. It could be he's had enough of words but still needs the voices. At least that's what goes through my mind when I watch him. He'd rather listen to those strange languages than to me, *magari*. . . . Laura, are you there? Tell me, do you still love me?

What a non sequitur, I said. I'm unprepared.

I need you to still love me. I have my doubts. Say you do.

Okay. I do.

Say it with some feeling.

Some feeling.

Oh, come on.

I love you with some feeling.

He made me promise to call soon. He'd done all the calling lately—now my turn. Okay, okay. I hung up slightly feverish. Not a fever of lassitude but of excitement. I could feel my eyes glinting. It wasn't Q.'s voice this time, still live in my ears, that excited me so. It was the story. The radios. I sat very still, breathing the way the Tai Chi teacher taught us, feeling the outgoing breath leave its wake of energy, and waited. Something was there for me, in those radios. My fingers curled, trying to grasp it, the thumbs stiffening. The thumb is the grabber, the Tai Chi teacher said. Let it relax. Don't grab. Keep the hand open.

The newest Town Reports on the shelf have changed with the times—
more so than the town itself, whose concessions to fashion are few, no-
tably one gourmet food store selling fresh-ground coffee and tortellini
salad. These stylish volumes are as large as popular magazines, with matte
covers and subtle photos. Inside, the language is streamlined, bureaucra-
tized. Since time in the 'nineties is measured in microchipped incre-
ments, sound bites, syllables, the Finance Committee is called Fincom; it
includes women now, as do the other committees. The Rescue Squad has
begun handling "environmental injuries." The Recycling Committee, too,
has expanded its operations, and the new elementary school is built at
last. No more complaints of overcrowding. Handwriting is forgotten.

Alcoholics and drug addicts, battered women and rape victims claim
a good share of the budget. It's jarring to see, on the police listings, rape,
arson, bombing, crimes that never appeared in the old days. "The Town
is now growing at an unusual rate," reports the Chief, "and we ask all citizens if at any time a citizen sees, hears, or finds anything out of the ordinary, that the Police be called immediately." The Police Department
itself has grown at an even greater rate than the town and, fittingly, is
computerized.

Among the couples joined in wedlock are quite a few out-of-town-ers. They've discovered the romance of marrying by the beautiful sea; it will become a piquant note in their family mythology, something to tell the children. Ev and I were married here, too, but I don't feel like looking it up for confirmation. I do check under deaths, where I find more suicides than before. The birth and death dates of the deceased are given in businesslike fashion now, no more biblical years, days, and months.

His name isn't there. No, of course not, it happened elsewhere.

The tides alone are unchanged, still moving in and out, shaping the shore. The Conservation Committee reports, I daresay to no one's surprise, that "the forces of nature are altering the coastline."

Again the phone jolts me from my reverie. "Tim, I've been meaning to call you. How're you doing?"

He's feeling lonely. Unloved. Visiting in the Hamptons on weekends. Could I save a weekend right after I get back? We were invited to his friends Hal and Celia's house at the shore. I vaguely remembered hearing about Hal, one of Tim's many friends involved in real estate. They all joked wryly about the sorry state of the market without suffering much, so far as I could tell.

"I'm at the shore right now. I think I might like some city streets for a change."

"Is it doing you any good?"

"Yes, I think so."

"Then a few more days will be even better."

"Okay, as long as they won't expect me to do anything. Sports or parties, I mean."

"They're very easygoing people. All we'll do, probably, is eat and drink and lie on the beach. Or at the pool. They have a beautiful pool right in back of the house."

"Sounds good."

"I should warn you, though, they're having a few people over Saturday night."

"Well . . . no. I don't think I'm up for that."

He cleared his throat at length. He found me difficult. So did I. I had no choice, but why did he put up with me? I almost wished he wouldn't, for I could see the era of Tim the benevolent drawing to a close. Better for both of us to do it soon, but I dreaded it. It takes energy to do real, as distinct from imagined, damage to others.

"It's not as if you have other plans, Laura. It's professional snobbery. If it were your writer friends you wouldn't feel this way."

"It's nothing like that. I'm tired, that's all. I'm feeling lousy."

"It's two weeks away. Think about it. By the way, you're missing an unbelievable heat wave. Four straight days in the high nineties."

The forbearance ploy. He understood me, I had to admit. The less he pressured, the more I'd come round. And why couldn't I take some pleasure in a group of people eating a well-prepared meal in fairly elegant surroundings?

He was mistaken, however, about my snobbery; it wasn't professional. I liked his cronies' talk of deals and stratagems, warlike aggressions and gallant defeats, the boasts of hours put in at exorbitant rates, of corporate hanky-panky and legal skulduggery. Stories of how the world works are always worth listening to. It was the rest, what goes by the name of "socializing." The health club, the margarine, the ozone layer, the aimlessness of the young. . . . The issues. Plus the meal would be so well-prepared, the surroundings so elegant. Like an ad in a slick magazine, airbrushing out reality's pockmarks.

To top it off, there'd be someone with a pungent anecdote, urging me to turn it into a story.

Our time here feels sadly short—more days behind us, now, than ahead. Jilly gets in late, going out after work with new friends from the restaurant, I suppose. When we're together she's affectionate but still brood-ing. I know the silence that seals her like a coat of varnish. I hope it's not her failure to play the saint on the Golden Gate Bridge.

I keep reading the local paper, but with a gnawing dismay. For it's hardly different from the city. Groups meet regularly for adoption heal-ing, skin cancer education, gay male alcoholics. . . . There's the stroke re-covery club, the cancer support group, the AIDS support group, and one Dina, no last name, wants to start a support group for brain-tumor and seizure sufferers. Twelve-step programs flourish at various accommodat-ing churches—Narcotics Anonymous, Overeaters Anonymous, Sex and Love Addicts Anonymous, and Parents Anonymous; that must be quite a trick, being an anonymous parent. The Attention Deficit group sup-ports parents of children with the eponymous problem, while Province-town/Truro Mediation Services offers constructive ways to resolve disputes.

A regular little magic mountain, only sea level. What a far cry from 1965, when the Board of Public Welfare had a caseload of sixteen and the Board of Health fretted over a few animal bites and the controversial fluoride clinics.

I'm a realist, not a utopian writer. How can I show the seaside town as an idyllic haven, while the buzz of countless support groups drifts to-ward me on the vibrations of the air?

I ponder this as I walk in the bay, the water up to my hips. I want to feel its texture and resistance, so that at home when we practice swim-ming in air, I'll remember.

ON HER DAY OFF Jilly and I sit at the edge of the sea while surfers like shiny devils in their slick black wet suits ride the wild waves. She studies them keenly. Then we return to the bay where the wind is calm, and watch the tide retreat.

"Jilly? Want to have another try at the ship? It's almost all uncovered. It's a good time, if we're ever going to do it."

She sits up and gazes out, shading her eyes with her hand. "You don't give up, do you? What's out there that you need?"

"I'd just like to accomplish something, I guess. Don't you ever get this need to do a certain thing for no good reason, or you forget whatever reason you once had?"

"Sure, but you've picked something impossible. I keep telling you it's farther than it looks. I'd have to carry you back."

"You could leave me clinging to a mast and go for help. Come on."

Other people are ambling aimlessly on the flats, but we head straight out, with purpose. Jilly is pensive; once or twice she looks up as if about to speak, but doesn't. Finally it rises to her lips.

"Laura, do you, um, think it's very, like, fickle to go out with someone when you're involved with someone else?"

"It depends on the circumstances."

"Well . . ." She takes a deep breath and we go on in silence. When Jeff was in the motorcycle accident a year ago, she said she'd die of grief if he died. He's all mended now, teaching summer classes on an Indian reservation in New Mexico. She hasn't seen him in two months, but after midnight, curled up in the wing chair, she murmurs into the phone.

"I met someone at the restaurant. We got to talking and he said he'd come back but I didn't think much of it—lots of them say that. But then he did. So I've seen him a few times since."

Aha, a trial run for my stint as Juliet of Verona. She'd certainly be sympathetic. "That's not so terrible. If he's a nice person, I mean. Who is he? What does he do?"

"That's not the point, what he does. You sound as bad as my mother. The point is Jeff. We're supposed to be going out."

"I understand. But it's still important to know something about this one. After all, he just appeared out of nowhere, more or less."

"All right, he's a grad student at Michigan. And a surfer. He's sharing a house with three other guys. They couldn't find anything on the ocean side so they drive over every day for the waves."

"Like us."

"Not exactly. I mean, they're serious about the tides and all. Anyhow, what do you think? About Jeff, I mean. Why are you grinning?"

"Not at you." I tell her about the retiring Juliet and her many corre-spondents seeking help with *problemi di cuore*.

"Her parents were forcing her to marry the first guy, weren't they? My mother would kill herself if I ever married Jeff. Not that I was particularly planning to, I never—"

"Look, Jilly, this could pass, just a summer romance, and then Jeff won't have to know a thing about it. If it develops into something more, well, you'll tell him then. You're not locked into anything. . . . Even if you were . . ." Juliet wouldn't say anything of the sort. I'd be disqualified at once.

"God, you older people can be so . . . immoral."

"We do have to be flexible. So much has happened to us."

She laughs uneasily. "Why, did you ever feel you could like two peo-ple at once?"

"Sure."

"You mean when you were my age?"

"And older."

"So what did you do?"

"Well, I've always been a very practical sort of person."

"Meaning what?"

"Meaning I did what would work. Sometimes the best thing is to do nothing. Just let things . . . take their course."

"I don't think I get it." When I don't clarify, she asks shyly, "Were you really in love with anyone before Dad?"

"Yes." We've come quite far and the ship does seem a trifle closer. The sun is declining, the water halfway to our knees and rising. We might have to swim part of the way. How would I get back? Another Rescue Squad statistic?

"So what happened?"

"It didn't work out."

"And then you met Dad?"

I nod.

"So is it, like, if you start to love a new one you stop loving the old one?"

"Not always. Certain people you don't stop loving. You might not want them, but you love them."

She's horror-struck. "You mean you kept loving him while you were married to someone else? To Dad? I never thought of you as. . . . Are you saying you put on some kind of act the whole time you were with him? Is that what you're telling me?"

"Of course not. I didn't put on any kind of act." It wasn't necessary. "No, what you saw was exactly the way it was between us. Look, Jilly, this is about as far as I think we'll get today. I'm tired. Let's turn around."

"Okay. But tell me. About the other one."

"There's not much more to tell. Some love you just . . . put away somewhere, in a quiet place."

We walk in silence, the sun on our backs now. If I'd said any of this before her *problema di cuore*, she would have been more vehement. Now I can feel her sifting through it, seeking a new pattern. Q. didn't like my shooing him out of the house when he came faithfully to care for me after Ev died. Not at all. I can't help it, I said, she might very well turn up. Couldn't you tell her I'm a friend, Laura? I'll act like a friend. No. He packed sullenly. If he didn't return, so be it. I couldn't risk Jilly. After he left for Peter's place I went around clearing up coffee cups, wine glasses, every trace. I shelved the tapes, removed stray hairs from the tub, changed the sheets. I scoured the apartment like a duenna alert to signs, far more carefully than I would have done for Ev. It wasn't guilt. Protecting what was mine. And he did return, late Sunday night. That was when we danced to the Jamaican music, then collapsed on the living room sofa and soon he was making love to me, seizing the moment of animation. I didn't even cry at the end: it was a new sofa where I had never lain with Ev. It bore no memories.

Don't move, I said. Oh, it feels so good. I wish I could keep it in me forever.

Q. smiled. They all say that, he said.

Really? Well, if it's so universal there ought to be some way. Maybe it could be detachable. I mean, you could have it back, I know that terrifies men—but just so I could walk around with it for a few hours. That would feel nice.

I'd help you if I could, said Q. But it's a lot to ask.

I dozed off briefly. He was still holding me when I woke, big and heavy and patient. How many is all? I asked.

What, all? What do you mean?

You know, altogether.

My whole life?

Mmm-hmm.

He was quiet for a long time, with the distracted, sober air of a woman making a grocery list for a large dinner—don't forget the olives to start, and the cooking sherry, better check the butter and ginger ale and toilet paper, too. . . . I can't say, he said finally.

Why, is it too many?

No, I just can't remember. What's the point?

You could fill rooms with them, I bet.

Oh, I doubt it. I wonder if they're all still alive, mused Q.

I heard of a man who did that once, I said. Filled a room. Mona's first husband. She had left him and gone off to live in London with the baby. Two years later, after he kept urging her, she came back and he gave a big party to welcome her. He invited all their old friends, she told me. New people, too. A very nice party. A year later, when she left him again, he told her he had invited all the women he'd slept with while she was away. Five. Why do you think he did that? I mean, besides having his little joke on her. Is it some kind of thrill for men to see them all at once? To be surrounded?

E chi lo sa? Q. shrugged. That's pretty mean. Mona, eh? I never knew that.

She only told me after I'd known her for years. Mona's very tight-lipped.

Kiss me, said Q. I want to see if you're tight-lipped.

"Where is he now?" Jilly says at last.

"Oh, quite far."

"Is he married?"

"No, I don't think so."

We walk slower all the time. "So have you ever thought . . . now, you know?"

"I'm not thinking about any of that now. I feel too sick."

"You know, Laura, sickness can be used as an excuse for not taking the next step in your life."

I give her a withering glance.

"Okay, okay. So who was he? What did he do?" She mimics my tone perfectly.

"He was an actor."

"Was he anything like Dad?"

"Nothing like. He . . ." As we splash back through ankle-deep water, I rein in the urge to tell her about the many ways Q. was not like Ev, how he made me excited and exalted, to talk about him as if I were her age, in that bubbling, tipsy way girls do. But I can't use her for that. Not yet. Not ever. "He was a very different sort of person."

"Well, now you've got Tim," she says with bland scorn. The revival of an ancient flame, lovers rejoined after tragedy, might appeal to her as a story. Tim, an example of my practicality, does not.

"Tim is something else altogether."

"That's for sure. You know, Laura, maybe you should think about moving. Change your life. Go someplace where it's not so stressful. San Francisco, even Santa Fe. You can write anywhere. Except for the downtown scene New York is the pits."

"Oh, but I love it, Jilly. I have the river. . . ."

I have it all there, I didn't say aloud. My past, your father. That Bronx street—Spanish movie house, supermarket, botanica, OTB parlor . . . I even feel my lost energy is there somewhere, if only I could locate it. Not to mention the beds around town where I slept with Q., the places we ate and walked. There's that Mexican restaurant, and the motel we checked into for an hour, and the place near the Marina where we parked and groped in each other's clothes and came in two minutes and had a fit of laughter. There's my old apartment in the Village where he used to come see me, where I threw him out one day and he went, closing the door so silently. . . . The day-long walk I took after he left, up the whole length of the island, wearing out a pair of sandals.

"No, I couldn't leave the river. My friends. My Tai Chi class. My parking spaces."

"You're so weird, Laura." She pokes me gently in the arm. I hope that means it's all right between us.

We stumble to dry land across a stretch of sharp rocks, and at the water's edge cross paths with a young woman in a bikini, who stops and smiles.

"You look very familiar," she says to Jilly. "Haven't I seen you around somewhere?"

"I work at Chez Louise. Maybe you ate there."

"Oh, that must be it. Just the other night. Sure, I remember you now. The mussels were great. How do they do them? It tasted like cumin or chilies or something like that."

WHILE THEY CHATTED ABOUT FOOD with the epicurean seriousness of the twenty-somethings, I had a sensation of mist rising and air clearing. Not outside—the sky was already blue and the air quite clear—but in my head. It was as if someone had wiped off a window pane and all at once I saw what was outside. My brain cells felt fresh and crisp, their damp fog burned off, even my fear almost evaporated. I took a few deep breaths to test the feeling. The synapses clicked nimbly along, registering and filing perceptions as they used to do. I could see as plainly as if they were declivities in the landscape of my future, certain things I would never do. I would never understand Ev the way I wanted to, from the inside, or understand us together. My curiosity, my need to dwell on the town and reinvent it, was more for me than for Ev, and it was too late. Too late to give him something I'd never given, and that he wouldn't have accepted if I had. No amount of staring at the landscape from which he sprang would bring me closer.

I would never write the book about the seaside town, and as those words landed in my inner ear with a soft thud, a lightness came over me. Beautiful as it was, there was nothing I needed to say about the town. It, too, had its arsons and rapes and would have its murders, and there was nothing to say about that either—nothing except the obvious. I might write out of love, for I did love the feel and smell of it, the shape and sky and terrain. And the data. Each new fact, each glimpse of the town in a new wash of light or shade of weather, was rimmed by my projected love. I doted on the town the way mothers dote on children or artists on their work, as if I had invented it. I wish I had invented it. But with love, often, not a lot needs to be said. You can only write to perfect and fulfill things, and the town in my vision was perfect already.

Another thing I would never do was walk out to the ship. It was just too far. It receded as I approached. Whatever treasure it held was out of reach.

"You should definitely try the Key lime pie," Jilly was telling the woman. "I think it's our best dessert. It's what we all eat in the kitchen."

"I almost had it the other night. I was torn between that and the Mississippi mud cake. That was good, too, but it's always so heavy. Well, it was nice talking to you."

"Come again. The specials keep changing." Oh, my Jilly. She would go far.

The beach was dotted with colorful umbrellas. Clumps of people lounged on blankets, some reading fat summer novels. Children ran here and there with water sloshing out of their buckets, and a few sunbathers still sat in chairs out on the flats, the water lapping about their feet.

"Why don't we go over to the ocean and have a real swim?" I said. "Then later we can come back here for the sunset."

Jilly laughed. "This is crazy. Do you think other people go back and forth like we do?"

"Who cares? We don't have too many more days to do it. Come on, so we get back in time."

It's a ritual: people take their places on the beach like spectators watching a performance, on some evenings showy and dramatic, on some understated, and on foggy days the show is canceled altogether or takes place behind a curtain that stubbornly refuses to rise. Today's sunset is the flamboyant kind, as if a daredevil magician behind the scenes were whirling giant colored scarves about the sky, seeing how close they could get to the wheel of fire without being burned. With the others, we stare in awe. Once the orange wheel drops into the water, the ship, rainbow-tinted, reverts to its usual blackness. Then comes the best part, the scarves subsiding, pulled slowly back up the magician's sleeve, the afterglow and curtain calls. A special-effects sunset. Just last night I read that the sunset truly is a special effect, an atmospheric effect made possible by the layer of air cocooning the vulnerable planet. "The blue of the sky, the white fluffs of clouds, and the rosy glow of sunset," the library book says (with a hint of the spoiler's satisfaction, like telling little kids there's no tooth fairy), "are all atmospheric effects, produced by the bending and scattering of light rays as they pass through the filter of air." Well, so what? Isn't everything an atmospheric effect, even love? "If there were no atmosphere, daylight and darkness would appear suddenly, almost as though an unshaded lamp were being switched off in a room." Yes, we all know what that's like, no need to rub it in.

SOON IT'S OUR LAST DAY. Typically, Jilly is working until the very end, and will go out afterward for a farewell fling with the graduate-student surfer. I spend the day at the ocean watching the tide carve the shore, its rhythm precise but seemingly capricious, sweeping in from the stretch of sea once called the graveyard of ships. I'll never possess the town, as I had hoped, by a story that would change Ev's life and mine—at least in a world translated into words. But I'll possess the tides. I'll feel their reach and retreat on my private terrain, covering then exposing, back and forth, world without end. World without Q.

Though maybe not world without end. At least not according to the books about the tides. They say that millions of years ago the earth spun much faster on its axis, rotating every four hours. It's tidal friction, slowing things down, that has given us our more leisurely twenty-four-hour day. As the friction continues, the earth will drift into lethargy, rotating once a month, once a year. What long days to anticipate. And nights. Until, I read with some trepidation, "billions of years from now, the pull and haul of cosmic forces will be in balance, and the tides will be still."

I PACK AT NIGHT so we can get an early start, and put the Town Reports back on the shelves in proper chronological order. I won't be needing them anymore. But once I go to bed, my last night in Ev's parents' house among the sweetly ugly trinkets, I open the library books out of habit. Most of what I read I already know, the much-advertised historical high points: the Pilgrims' first drink from the inspiriting springs, the Indians, the whaling and shipbuilding, the ships lost at sea, the October gale. And then I discover one item I never knew or else forgot: the nineteenth-century harvesting and processing of salt.

Salt was an urgent need back then, not just for ordinary use, but to preserve the catches of fish that were the town's livelihood. People would arduously pump seawater—with all its healing powers—into huge kettles and then boil it off until a residue of salt was left, a process which not only took enormous time and effort, but destroyed the surrounding forests. Great heaps of wood were hewn to build the fires that heated the kettles that boiled off the water and left the salt. Finally in 1876, a Captain John Sears from a neighboring town hit on the idea of using the sun's heat to evaporate the water. Solar energy, we'd call it. From then on, a windmill pumped the sea into vats which stood in the sun until the water was gone, leaving the precious salt. One of those simple ideas that sounds obvious as soon as someone has thought it up.

Deep in his ingenious New England soul, Captain Sears must have grasped the Eastern principle of *wu-wei*, or non-action, that is, waiting until the right and natural action arises spontaneously, of its own accord. The end result—useful, healing salt—is the same, but one way requires hard labor and ruining the forests, while the other requires nothing but sitting in the sun.

Jilly was out of sorts on the ride back to Boston. Farewell to the generous diners at Chez Louise, to me, the good stepmother, and above all, to the surfer. They'd agreed to keep in touch, and he might even try to see her on his way back, but she suspects that phrase "try to," and I suspect she's right. Keeping in touch would be iffy, with him at Michigan and Jilly at Penn. At least her cozy arrangement with Jeff had been shaken up.

After I dropped her off, the car ran friskily toward home, eager to return to its street life. Grateful, I murmured to it with affection. Animals and plants, the ancient Taoists believed, could respond to the vibrations of love and could even develop individual souls if they were loved sufficiently, the Tai Chi teacher once told us slyly. Why not cars?

Just outside of Providence I switched on the radio, which obliged with James Galway playing a Schubert flute sonata. During a pause between two notes, almost long enough for a rest area to zoom by, slipped a hasty intake of breath, James Galway's breath, like a surreptitious gasp; without the music I might have heard it as a gasp of fright. A gasp revealing that behind the illusion of effortlessness is effort of the human breath, the breath the Tai Chi teacher calls spirit and which inside the body is transformed into energy, then into audible sound shaped in the patterns that make music.

Where was that puff of air now? In the same place as my unwritten book, a small pause between tangibles, something meant to go unobserved, yet sustaining. Necessary.

The quantity of energy in the universe is fixed, they tell us, endlessly transformed and transferred. That puff of air, the flutist's furtive intake of breath, long ago wended its way across continents in who knows what guise, yet was not lost like Marcel Duchamp's casual breaths. Preserved. And multiplied hundreds, thousands of times on tape: immortal spirit, or art, as Duchamp the surrealist would have it, challenging the laws of physics.

And the quick opening of the throat, the little rise of the chest—all this was done by cells sloughed off by now, yet they too lived on. That the music should be preserved was not startling: that was music's life, to be heard again and again. But this preservation of the solitary, secret breath between notes seemed a true miracle. When the flutist was dead, the breath that flew through the aperture of his throat, infusing each cell with spirit to animate his song, would remain. More powerful than a voice preserved on tape, this was the thing behind the voice, as my unwritten words might be the book behind some other book waiting to be translated.

It was then that I remembered Q.'s story about his father bringing the old radios back to life. I felt the same excitement, the same warmth. And this time the fever focused, like concentrated heat erupting into fire. Like a green flame springing from the dark carcass of the earth, a familiar impulse rose with the force of a command, and I knew exactly what I must do. Write it down. Write down everything he said about the radios. And more. Write it all down.

If the sounds humming over the radio wires were Aldo's lifeline, slim strands binding him to the world, then all the words borne on the telephone wires or vibrating face to face these last months were mine. I would make them—clothed in the human voices of loved ones bringing the news—the story of my life, tinkering, restoring and refining. I would write for my life, a life lived through the air and the ear. Too late to save Ev's.

The course of the illness, traced and punctuated by the voices, would take on a shape. Whatever possesses a shape is less terrifying than the amorphous and unbounded. Not the comforting, self-possessed shape of a weathered Cape Cod house near the sea, but one of those unsettling latter day buildings which in a fit of aesthetic despair exposes all its dynamics and private parts—pipes and plumbing, supporting beams and electrical lines—like a crude Madonna of architecture.

I would put despair to work, using a pen the way prisoners use a spoon—stolen at great risk from the cafeteria—to dig a tunnel through the dirt barring them from freedom. Slowly, how slowly, a few scoops every night while the guard is nodding. And as the prisoner's digging toward daylight becomes a passage out, writing through the sickness meant it would have an end. When I came to the end of the book, the sickness would be over. Or when I came to the end of the sickness, the book would be over. Whichever came first. Until I could say, It is over, I am well, like a Taoist prayer, vibrations on the air becoming a declaration of what is.

I would have pulled off the road and begun right then, but I was too eager to get home. In my reverie I'd been doing over eighty. The light was just fading as I pulled up. Luke, folding his chair for the day, waved and came to the car window.

"Laura, where'd you disappear to? You done took that kiddie car and gone off without a word."

I told him about the Cape. "How're things here? I've missed it."

"Here? Nothing much. No big crimes, fires, or accidents, so we're calling it a good month. They's diggin' up part of the Drive to shore up the retaining wall. I'll fill you in on the gossip later—I want to go watch the ball game. You're looking mighty good. Darker."

"How can you tell in this light?"

"I can tell. You're gettin' there, Laura." As he left he pointed out a better parking space, under a streetlight. The air was muggy and sweet. Home.

Up on the Cape I had rarely thought about the squirrel and when I did, I felt indifferent to his fate. I was even a bit proud of my detachment. But the sages tell you never to be proud. Enlightenment itself is to be taken in stride and not marveled at. The goal is a leveling of emotion. Indeed, with enlightenment even great natural wonders cease to amaze: it's simply their nature to be wondrous, as a famous old Chinese poem shows:

> *Mount Lu in misty rain; the River Che at high tide.*
> *When I had not been there, no rest from the pain of longing!*
> *I went there and returned. . . . It was nothing special:*
> *Mount Lu in misty rain; the River Che at high tide.*

But I wasn't indifferent at all. I dropped my bags and went straight for the window ledge. Could he possibly be alive, waiting for me? Or would I find his decaying body? Broom, dustpan, paper bag, trip to the basement.

Gone. Nothing but the familiar curved hollow in the tamped-down bed of ivy. I missed him the way you might miss an old friend who's moved unexpectedly with no forwarding address. I felt almost slighted, and yearned to know his fate. Had he gone off to die elsewhere or recovered? Would he be back? In the meantime, I packed up the messy nest and brought it downstairs.

The spell of clear inner weather I felt on the beach hadn't lasted. Fog and weariness were settling in again, thick as ever. Outside, a car alarm yelped in the gathering dark. No matter. I found a fresh composition book—exactly the kind in which I'd written my first stories while the teacher explained long division on the blackboard—and obeying the command, I recorded my conversation with Q. about Aldo's radios, writing with the surreptitious glee I knew in school, the glee of writing what I was not supposed to, what was not the work assigned to me. I transcribed our dialogue using the reliable and efficient mechanism lodged in my ear, a faculty like Aldo's inborn skill with the radios that allowed him to revive aerial connections otherwise fated to dissolve in the world's great heap of transience, making old filaments transmit new, living vibrations.

But unlike Aldo who liked strange tongues on his ham radio, I wanted words in a language I could understand, even words which might seem useless on first hearing. In the transcribing they would yield up a pattern. A design made of scraps of memory, disassembled then cleaned, varnished, and reconstituted. And like the unwritten book about the seaside town, this, too, would have its regular yet unpredictable tides moving across the landscape, with now and then sudden gales.

I would have no design but make opportunity my design. I wrote quickly, almost illegibly, dropping the pen and routinely picking it up. If I stopped I might forget. Memory loss, Hortense had said. What I lost might be the best.

The pen rushed across the page, leaving segments of ransomed conversations. Q.'s sister Gemma and her doomed love affair. Evelyn's snatches of old songs. Llamas, breeding, females expensive, trip around the world, meditation, tie it to a tree, wool for a sweater, manure dry and cohesive, Santa Fe shit. There, I had it. Never mind Hortense. Possibly what memory retained was meant to be included, while the forgotten was ill-suited for the unknown design: a survival of the fittest theory for the scrappy story.

Above all, what I wrote must not be too determined. Like being sick, the story made in its image must be a marriage of submission to data and management of it. And wrought in the dark, like the prisoner's tunnel. He might dig along a number of possible paths. It hardly mattered so long as he dug past the fence and up into the light.

Do I bless the fact of Q. or curse it? A capricious muse, he'd given me another book.

AT LAST THE IMPETUS RAN OUT and I stopped for the night. My bed received me warmly, forgiving my long absence as generous lovers do. And

I sank into its embrace with the ardor of a prodigal. One can be promiscuous, but home is best.

I had a splitting headache as once more I climbed the stairs to the witch's office, the pungent *faux*-pot smell drawing me on. I had burned a moxa stick, too, lying in bed. I couldn't vouch for its healing properties but it smelled nice and warmed me at the points the witch had marked on the diagram. Below the navel, alongside the knees and ankle bones, near the big toe: I felt like a priest administering the last sacraments in blasphemous places.

The door was open. "Come on in, Laura," her voice bubbled from within. "I'll be there in a minute."

In the waiting room I studied the chart of the five organs—liver, heart, spleen, lungs, kidneys—and their corresponding elements, seasons, colors, and emotions. A complete metaphorical system, the body as microcosm with its procession of climatic moods. Suddenly from behind the closed door came a series of small yelps. Silence again, then more yelps, and the witch's soothing murmurs. What if I heard piercing screams? Do I call 911? What did I know about her, anyway? Did she really believe in the network of arrows moving clockwise on the chart: wood makes fire makes earth makes metal makes water? Just as I was tensing with doubt, the door opened and she emerged, followed by the couple I'd seen on the stairs last time. The man held the small black terrier, who seemed subdued and peaked, his head lowered despondently.

"Hi, Laura, good to see you. These are my friends Seth and Pat. And this is Beaver. Isn't he sweet?" As the witch spoke his name, the dog looked up and leaned toward her the way a baby will stretch out to the arms of someone he trusts. "Ah, yes, come here, come on," and she took him from Seth like a baby. Beaver perked up in her arms, barking with what eagerness he could muster.

"What's wrong with Beaver?" I asked after they left.

"He has arthritis. I'm treating him." She sat down opposite me on the mat.

"With acupuncture?"

"Yes." She laughed, then sipped from a mug of the foul-looking tea she brewed in the kitchen. Black twigs and dried leaves floated at the top. "Seth and Pat are old friends of mine from college. They begged me to treat him. I'd never treated a dog before, but the only other recourse was to put him to sleep. He was in a lot of pain and the vet said there was nothing to do. He had no energy, no *chi*. I couldn't refuse. I've been treating him for two months now. He's gotten used to me."

"How do you keep him still for the needles?"

"At the beginning he was so listless that he just lay there. It seemed to calm him, the way it does with people. Then later, as he improved, he got more frisky, and Seth or Pat might have to hold him down. But most of the time he let me do it quite readily. I'm so pleased. If not for the treatment he wouldn't be here. I saved him. I only wish I could do as much for my AIDS patients."

"You treat AIDS patients?"

"Oh, yes, that's the main thing we do here. A group of us run a free clinic twice a week. The patients see Western doctors, too, but the drugs usually make them feel worse, so we try to relieve some of the symptoms. The acupuncture stimulates the immune system and regulates the whole body, so the organs function better. Anyway, Beaver is almost finished with his treatment now. It's great—he looks at me with such infinite love, more, actually, than any person ever has." She chuckled again—a witch with a sense of humor—and took a swig of her muddy brew. "Do you know, the vet wouldn't believe it when Seth and Pat told him he was better. He had to see for himself, so they brought him in. He thought there was no hope. There's always hope."

"How did you know what to do for him? Were dogs part of your training?"

"No. I played it by ear. I figured it out the way I would with any pa-tient. The first time, Seth and Pat told me he was eating feces."

Feces. Anyone else would have said "shit." Very professional, this witch. Performs her role to the hilt.

"Eating shit?"

"Yes, his own and anyone else's he could find. Any dog's, that is. There's a word for that, I can't recall it at the moment."

"Coprophilia," I said. "Love of shit."

"That's it. You writers know everything. Well, I gave this some thought. It's very unnatural, and when an organism exhibits unnatural behavior there's usually a logical reason. I looked it up in my books and wouldn't you know it, it turns out there's a component in certain feces that cures arthritis. In other words, he was trying to cure himself. If left to themselves, all sick creatures instinctively seek a cure. So I read some more and found that there's something you can make up from silkworm feces, and I called someone and had it made for him. . . ."

She has a network, I thought, a coven. One weird sister gathers the herbs, another distills the oils, another hones the needles to the thinness of a hair. . . .

"The first week or so there was no change. So I decided to administer it the way homeopathic doctors do, in minuscule doses. For a few days nothing happened, but that's not unusual—it can take the body that long to register when something new is being taken in. Then sure enough, he started to improve. In a couple of weeks, Seth and Pat told me, he stopped looking for feces. Meanwhile the acupuncture was help-ing as well. And there we are."

"This could be a first in medical history. Curing animals with acupuncture, I mean. You could write a book about it."

"Oh, no, it's been done since way back, in China. You can do it for plants also."

"Really? I wish I'd known you when my husband died. All his plants withered, too. I suppose you'd say they missed him."

"That might well be. Seth and Pat were so grateful that they got me a wonderful book, *Veterinary Acupuncture*. I was quite engrossed, and then unfortunately I lost it. In a Chinese restaurant, I think. It had pictures of animals with all the acupuncture points clearly marked. Roosters, camels, everything. And you know something about the camels? None of the points are on the hump."

Even with the headache, I was feeling more lively than I had in weeks, sitting on her mat, the two of us tittering like girls in a freshman dorm. "You might start a special practice, treating animals. Even one day a week, you could make a fortune. You know, those people who get their pets decorative haircuts and manicures? It could support your other work. The AIDS work, for instance."

"I hate to spoil your fantasy, Laura, but it's already being done. There are a handful of acupuncture vets. But as it turned out, even though I didn't charge Seth and Pat, they made a large contribution to the AIDS clinic, so the guys have this joke about it. They say their needles are coming to them courtesy of Beaver the terrier. Let me look at your tongue now. Hmm. Not so bad."

"What's so important about the tongue? I don't have a sore throat."

"In Chinese medicine, the tongue is the one internal organ we have ready access to, and since all the organs are interrelated, you can use it to infer the condition of the others. You go by the color, and whether it's coated, whether there are fissures and where . . ."

"The last doctor who looked at my tongue asked me what he termed an odd question."

She was amused by the story of Dr. A. "You could have told him they're all strange."

"Exactly."

"Still, he probably had something legitimate in mind. You shouldn't be too hard on doctors. They do their best, considering the context they work in. You know, in ancient Chinese medical practice, the doctor's job was to regulate the energy through the meridians and keep the organs in balance. If the patient got sick, it was considered that the doctor had created or allowed an imbalance, and he wasn't paid. If the patient was very sick the doctor might even be fined. So there was a certain degree of humility, of necessity."

"But you get paid either way, right?"

"I'm afraid so. Believe me, if I had other means of support I'd be more than willing to work that way. But I'd need a sugar daddy."

"I take it you're not married."

"No. I was for eight years, when I was living in France, but we divorced."

She must be older than I thought. A broken-down crone disguised as a beautiful young woman, perhaps? A fairy tale reversal. "Was he French?"

"Yes, a molecular biologist. We met in the halls of a scientific institute. He was working on genetic repression in protein production and I was there studying a new theory of auricular diagnosis. It seemed romantic at the time."

"So you must speak French."

"Oh, sure. I make some extra money translating at scientific conferences. I just went to one in Quebec last month, on healing the environment."

"Another translator," I muttered. "So, you're alone now?"

"Yes, but . . ." She hesitated, lowering her gaze. "There may be somebody appearing on the horizon. I'm not exactly sure. He's a rabbi."

"A rabbi and a witch. Together you could work miracles."

"I think he may be living with someone, though. It doesn't sound kosher to me."

"I'd be careful about that."

"You have experience in that area?" she asked.

"Sort of."

"Let me take your pulses now. How have you been feeling?"

"Up and down. My energy was a bit better—I walked a lot up on the Cape, as you said. Here I can't go as far, but the other day I managed four blocks without stopping."

"That's very good. The herbs must be starting to work."

"But the symptoms are changing. My stomach's been upset. I get headaches, in fact I have a headache right now. And I've got a rash on my stomach."

"A rash? Really?" She seemed very pleased. "Let's see."

I showed her the pink splotches and welts. "It itches. It's just the last few days. At least I didn't look hideous on the beach."

"Oh, but this is an excellent response. I told you there was lots of stuff that would rise to the surface, but sometimes I work for months before I manage to bring out a rash."

"Congratulations," I said. "But I'd like it to go away."

"Well, sure. I'll give you some oils to rub in. I'm feeling a lot of heat in your body. The body operates between extremes of hot and cold, damp and dry, and you're hot and damp."

"How sexy," I said. "I wish I felt that way. It sounds like the old theory of the humors. Remember, sanguine, phlegmatic, choleric and melancholy? Of course that was medieval pseudoscience. I assumed it was discredited."

"I know. But there was some truth to it," she said blithely. "The parts of the body have temperaments just like the mind. And the temperaments interact. Western medicine isolates the organs and treats each separately, as if they had no effect on each other. But actually it's surprising how close together they are, and extremely porous, with the blood and lymph flowing around them. It's so clear, when you look inside a body, how every function is connected." She sounded rapt at the vision.

"Why, have you looked inside bodies?"

"Of course. I went to medical school for several years. I bet you thought I was just an ignorant witch, right?"

"Yes," I confessed. "Why did you stop?"

"I knew I wanted to be a healer, but I also knew I could never practice medicine the way we were being trained to do. I didn't enjoy it, and I couldn't get into that mode of thinking. Not only because it's unrealistic to separate the various functions. Western medicine is based on aggression. The aim is to kill the invading organism, and it's had most of its spectacular successes that way. Chinese medicine has a different approach to the body. It creates an environment that's inhospitable to the intruder. If the organs are well-balanced and the center is strong, an invading organism can't find a vulnerable place to lodge."

"Like in Tai Chi."

"Yes, just like that. You use your energy in such a way that the opponent can't find a place to attack. So in medicine we focus not so much on the outside threat but on supporting the righteous."

"The righteous?"

"The righteous is the natural, healthy state."

"I don't think I'd like looking at innards. Years ago, when I needed money desperately, I got a job proofreading something called the *Herpes Handbook*. It was right before AIDS. Everyone was worried about herpes. They sent the photos, too, because I had to proofread the captions. Those close-ups of body parts infected with herpes were so revolting I hated to look at them. But I also couldn't take my eyes off them. I know it sounds paradoxical. I'd stare, and then I'd suddenly have to look away."

"It's always more difficult," said the witch, "to study organs when they're detached from the people they belong to, which is the way you're taught in medical school, examining discrete parts. It becomes simpler and easier when you look at each part as belonging to an organism. A real person. You'd be amazed at how it stops being revolting."

"It's all very mysterious, isn't it? The body, I mean."

"The body," she said, crossing her legs Indian fashion as she reached for a fresh package of needles, "is a black hole. Now, for this headache. I'll work on it, but I have to warn you, if the headaches go away you might get other symptoms. The heat has to come out one way or another. Once it does, though, you'll find you have more energy."

"So what can you offer me? What are the specials today?"

"Well, we have a kind of smorgasbord—fever, nausea, diarrhea . . . I really can't predict. Show me where the headache is. Okay, turn over, please." She inserted three needles in the back of my neck, no doubt in a triangular pattern, then pressed her hands to my lower skull. "Do you feel anything?"

"The headache is moving around. Now it's here." I pointed.

"Better or worse?"

"Better."

"Okay, I'll try a few more." She put in three more needles and pressed again.

"Now it's moving to here. Now it's getting less. Shit, you're giving me the creeps, you know? You're moving my goddamned headache around. You could get burned at the stake for this."

"I know," she laughed. "So don't tell anyone."

When I got dressed to leave, she said, "See you next week, Laura. Keep walking."

The next day when I boarded the bus to meet my cousin Joyce for lunch, there she was, halfway to the rear. No great coincidence—she lives eight blocks north and we were headed for the same place—yet unsettling. Joyce is the sort of person who's hard to imagine alone. She responds so powerfully to others, it's as if she wouldn't exist without them. Her un-projected self was a stranger—bright red lips pursed somberly, dark eyes muted, gazing inward.

I approached and she leaped up, throwing her arms around me and exclaiming in her tremulous musical voice like liquid gold. Everyone turned to watch. Joyce was notable even when quiet—almost larger than life at close to six feet and outfitted to make heads turn, today in a longish white dress splashed with flowers. Masses of untamed curls trickled from beneath her wide-brimmed straw hat and fell to her shoulders. How people had prized those curls when she was a child, as if curly hair were the ticket to life's most splendid offerings. I was struck with stage fright at the exaggerated scene she was making, yet childishly pleased, too. After all, she acted in good faith. Life is small, I imagine she thinks. Let's help it out a bit.

Just as we broke from our embrace the bus veered, and the contents of Joyce's enormous tote bag poured out and scattered on the floor: books, papers, pens, wallet, tissues, makeup kit, comb, glasses, pillbox, cough drops, keys, address book. Joyce was notoriously sensitive to subtle vibrations. Could she have caught my symptom so fast?

"Look at this mess," she groaned as we crept around gathering things up, the nearby passengers pointing out strayed objects. At noon the bus was never crowded. The travelers were mostly old people, some with canes, walkers, or caretakers. I bent to retrieve a ballpoint pen that had rolled behind a woman's feet. "Excuse me," I said, but she sat impassive, not moving aside to ease my groping. When we finally had the bag reassembled, Joyce hugged me again, less vigorously.

"You look fine, Laura. Not sick at all. I thought you'd look worse."

"Thanks a lot." I laughed. "It's the suntan. And I'm getting plenty of sleep."

Soon she was waving at the restaurant owner, sitting at the bar reading a copy of Variety, and then at the waiter. "Lorenzo! How are you, my dear!" I was afraid for the bag if she hugged him, too, but she merely engulfed him in her smile. The owner sent complimentary glasses of wine to our table.

As we picked up the menus, my shoulders tensed. Joyce has always had an odd habit in restaurants. She liked to order the same dish as me. What are you going to have? she'd ask casually, and I, just as casually, would say, I think the spinach salad. Oh, that sounds good, I'll have that, too. Something would clutch at me, as if a choice to which I was exclusively entitled were being taken from me. I wouldn't have minded had I thought Joyce really wanted the spinach salad. But no. She chose it, I was convinced, only because I was having it, thereby making it less my own. It was perplexing, especially as Joyce didn't have an envious nature, and moreover what was so enviable about spinach salad? It wasn't as though it were filet mignon or pheasant.

I used to mull it over. Maybe Joyce wanted to create, in a public place, the illusion of an intimate at-home lunch where everyone eats the same thing. No, I definitely sensed a boundary infringed upon. I began trying to outwit her, adopting the strategy of asking her first, forcing her to choose. So what are you going to have, Joyce? Well, she'd say, I'm not sure. Either the mussels or the shrimp salad, maybe. What about you? as if offering me a choice between those two. The linguine with clams, I think. Oh, I didn't notice that, she'd promptly chime in. Maybe I'll have the linguine, too.

It was a difficult game to win, a game of pursuit and evasion, and I wasn't even sure Joyce was aware of being a player.

"So, Laura, what have you decided on?" she asked.

"I don't know yet. It all looks good. What about you?"

"Well," she said reluctantly, "I'm torn between the tabouli and chick peas with eggplant and the grilled salmon."

"Hmm." I perused the menu some more.

"What are you in the mood for?" she urged.

"Let's see, I think I might have a mushroom omelette."

"Actually that sounds very good. Light. I ought to have something light, too. Let's have the mushroom omelettes, then."

"You don't have to have it just because I'm having it," I said a bit testily.

"I know. Of course not. It just sounded good."

The waiter, Lorenzo, appeared.

"We'll have the mushroom omelettes, Lorenzo," said Joyce.

"I've changed my mind. I think I'll have a cheeseburger. Medium rare."

"That's an idea," she said, brushing her curls off her face. "You know what, Lorenzo? Forget the omelettes. Bring us two cheeseburgers, medium rare."

Foiled again. I never thought she'd stoop to that, and in front of Lorenzo, too.

"Tell me," I said when he'd gone, "why do you always like to order the same thing?"

"Why, do you mind? I didn't realize you minded."

"I'm curious."

"It's nice to order the same thing. Why not?"

"But why is it nice? I really don't get it."

"Because then we're, well, we'll be having the same experience."

"But why is it nice to have the same experience?"

"It just is. Don't you think so?"

"I knew a man like that once. I don't mean he liked to eat what I was eating. Nothing like that. But he . . . we felt as if we were always having the same experiences because inside our heads, or our guts, it was the same. The same chemical components or something. Oh, he was different in many ways—he was older, he had a different background, he wasn't even American, really. But we had this feeling you seem to crave, that there were no boundaries, that we felt everything in exactly the same way. It was, I think, sick."

"Why sick? It's a certain kind of romantic ideal. It's not realized very often, but still . . ."

"Yes, and it's obvious why. It's madness. Was, I mean. We couldn't be together and we couldn't be apart. Or he couldn't. I could have managed—to be together, that is. But he needed the Other. With a capital O. He knew too much about me, from the inside, because he was the same. He wanted mystery. But he also couldn't . . . can't . . . couldn't let go either."

"When was this?" Joyce asked cannily.

"Oh, long ago. Long, long ago. It was like a fairy tale, and they're always long ago, aren't they?" I hesitated as she stared. "I was young. I was like someone entranced, I don't mean by sex, I mean by this crazy way of being with a person."

"In the fairy tales," said Joyce, "when the princess is carried off it's always from being asleep or doing housework—sewing shirts out of nettles or minding the geese or being a drudge like Cinderella. Were you asleep?"

"No, I wasn't asleep. And it was not exactly like being carried off. It made up a little world, like a trick with mirrors. We could see each other in the mirror. I also think it made me sick, frankly."

"What, years later? Nonsense. You've got a virus. You told me so your-self. Didn't you have lab tests?"

"Yes. I mean it left me open to this . . . thing. I don't know. He was like a virus himself. He got into my bloodstream and has to work himself out." I lit a cigarette even though I could see Lorenzo at the far end of the room gliding in our direction bearing the cheeseburgers, shoulder height. "No two people can have the same experience of anything, can they? Because even if the thing is the same, the people having the experience are different. Look, never mind all this, Joyce. I don't know what's come over me. I'm not used to drinking wine at lunch. Don't pay any attention. I'm sorry about the omelettes. It's not important. This virus has probably gotten to my brain."

"I believe it has. Thank you, Lorenzo. That looks lovely." He blew her a kiss as he left. "The Tsumati think that any man and woman who have been together, even if only once, leave a trace of themselves in the other person, so that you can carry around traces of any number of people, and they influence your thoughts and speech and actions. They shape you and change you."

It was a pleasure to listen to Joyce when she got going, and to watch her mobile face mirroring the vivid workings of her mind. "That's why you have to be careful whom you sleep with," she continued. "Not for old-fashioned morality, but to choose what will become a permanent part of you, which is actually a higher form of morality. You know how old married couples get to talk and look like each other. Well, this is the same idea, only scaled down. But that's just one kind of explanation for the general phenomenon of influence. Personally, I think you've just got a bug, Laura. Even more to the point is that the major diseases of our age involve the immune system defecting or turning on itself. It's obvious from what you read in the papers that we're into self-destruction on a global scale. Why wouldn't it be happening on the individual level, too?"

"Maybe I should join this tribe of yours."

"The Tsumati are an ethnic group. When you say tribe, it conjures up images of savages dancing around the campfire with tom-toms. Have you noticed that the fighting in what used to be the Soviet Union or Yugoslavia is always between ethnic groups, but in Africa it's tribes? And yet these groups have exactly the same distinctions. So how long ago did you know this man you mentioned, again?"

"Long ago, I told you. How is Roger, by the way? It's odd that since you two got married I forget to ask. I wonder what that could mean."

"He's fine. Same as ever."

"So it's working out?"

"So far."

After eight years of indecision and moving—her apartment, his apartment, together, apart—Joyce and Roger married last year. More sensible and convenient, they decided, to continue their struggles under the official rubric. At their wedding, a colorful, mellow affair, the eyes of the bride and groom shone with relief: at least they'd no longer have to worry about whether to spend their lives together. Their gestures had the blissful serenity of people who have accepted the world and their fate in it, Buddhist monks, for instance. The only one who didn't seem entirely content was Joyce's cat, and with good reason. The cat was her confidante about intimate matters, especially this long back and forth romance with Roger. The creature sensed she was losing her *raison d'être*.

"Do you still talk to the cat as much?"

"No. It's too bad, and she really feels it. She was heavily invested in that closeness. But with Roger around all the time we can't really have the same long talks. And there's not that much left to say."

"Why don't you get her a cat for company? It might be more appropriate."

"I've thought of that. Except it means when I go to Africa there'd be two cats to take care of. I don't know how Roger would like that."

I left half my cheeseburger—I hadn't really wanted it. I would have preferred the tabouli salad with chick peas and eggplant that Joyce was considering in the first place. The chair was stiff and unyielding. I imagined my soft bed awaiting me, calling, Lover, come back. It was hard to keep talking amid the buzz of voices and clink of silverware, and hard to attend to civilized table manners. To close down, not feel anymore, what heaven that would be.

"Joyce, I have to go home. I can't sit up anymore. That cheeseburger did me in. It was overdone and greasy. How was yours?"

"Mine was fine."

Of course. Joyce rarely admitted to disappointment. Willfully upbeat, she'd hardly uttered a bitter word through two divorces. That must be how she kept the good vibrations rolling in her direction, as in a Taoist prayer. The Taoist prayer, as the Tai Chi teacher often says, is not a request for the future—Make me happy! Make me well!—but a declaration of what is in the present: I am well. I am happy. Such declarations attract the vibrations of wellness, as the great symphony of the universe unfurls. Fine, is Joyce's prayer, her declaration of what is. No complaints whatsoever.

Outside, the sun was blinding, like coming out of an afternoon movie. Two fire engines screeched down the street with an ambulance in their wake. Against the sirens' treble came the petulant continuo of a car alarm—existential dread made audible, worthy of one of Dante's deeper circles. The strollers on Broadway didn't seem to mind, though. So inured, or so acquiescent, they accepted it as readily as birdsong.

"Just a second," Joyce said. "My bag feels very light. I think I'm missing something." She rummaged with one hand while looking skyward as if for assistance. "Oh, God. I think it's my notebook with all my notes. I was going to the library. This is awful. I can't lose that. It has everything about the lineage system for my article. Maybe I left it inside."

Lorenzo searched. We all searched under the table and retraced the path to the door, but no notebook.

"It must have been when everything spilled out on the bus," I said.

"Oh, right. I forgot all about that."

"Someone might have picked it up and given it to the driver. Call the lost-and-found at the MTA. It's a long shot, but still."

This was not idle encouragement. Years ago I had lost a precious notebook, too, and gotten it back. But this didn't seem the moment to tell

Joyce. Besides, it was another Q. story, and I'd said more than enough about him.

"I'll try that. This is why people keep everything on a computer. That's what Roger'll say, anyway." She sighed. Her eyes looked teary; even her springy hair seemed to droop.

"If I hadn't gotten on the bus just then it wouldn't have happened."

"Don't be silly, Laura. It was just a coincidence."

She didn't understand. It was my dropping things. Porous Joyce must have absorbed it. Did I also spread loss: husbands, health, work? What would the Tsumati have to say about that?

We kissed good-bye and went in opposite directions. I have no friends, says the Samurai creed. I make my mind my friend.

I follow the witch's advice about walking. I drag myself out to Riverside Drive, the sinuous, leafy stretch Q. called Lungohudson, after Lungarno in Florence and Lungotévere in Rome, to walk it off the way you might walk off a drunken stupor or an overdose. Or a fit of rage. The way long ago I walked off Q. I used to be a good walker. I urge the muscles on like coaxing out a lost language I once spoke fluently.

Swimming in air. The city heat continues; the viscous air resists my movements. Without the faraway ship to lure me, without the salt air, I can't go more than a few blocks before I'm felled by weakness and sink onto a bench, like the old people with their visibly bored caretakers.

Thank goodness I don't need a caretaker, though several friends have volunteered to walk with me. Mona entertained me with tales of last-minute shopping expeditions with her newest Let Me Dress You clients, members of a Czech mime troupe whose bags were lost in transit. She recited several phrases in Czech, such as "How much?" and "When can we eat?"

"I really mean it," she said. "I'm starved."

We passed the defunct Café Athena, its windows sealed by a corrugated tin panel on which vandals had spray-painted clumsy scribbles. Sheets were spread on the·sidewalk with old shoes, magazines, and kitchen appliances for sale.

"Let's try the place two blocks down," said Mona, turning away from the pitiful scene. "Can you walk that far?"

The walls were bare, the floors were dusty, there was no music; the service was as lackadaisical as in the Athena but charmless. "This isn't going to work. I'll have to keep looking." Her only sign of disappointment was the faint heave of her chest as she inhaled, hinting at secret weariness: all those husbands, children, gourmet dinners.

"How's Evelyn doing?"

"Oh, the same," she sighed. "Singing a little less, watching more TV."

Tim, who was taking a few days off, was always ready to walk. He lives along the Drive, too, half a mile south of me, in a ground-floor apartment. "Ring my bell, or just knock on the window. If I'm there I'll come out and keep you company." He walks fast, with long purposeful steps. He likes to have a goal. "We'll go as far as the flower beds." Or, "We'll go down to the Marina. Can you do that?" "Not without stopping. Do you mind stopping every couple of blocks?" "No, I'm used to it. It's the way I walk with my father, except he's eighty-one." It won't be long now, with Tim and me. He must sense it, too. But we've got that weekend coming up.

In the end, it's better to walk alone. "I have no friends; I make my mind my friend." I invent little games—how far can I go without stopping? One good day, achy but no fever, I go for five blocks. I pretend this strip of the Drive is my estate and walk through my land as Tolstoy used to do, checking on the serfs, asking about the crops and the families' health, noting repairs to be made on the hovels. Bringing small items of charity and accepting small items of tribute. I record snatches of talk caught in my ear as I pass, and sometimes unreel the tapes in the data bank, listening until I have them by heart to write down later: Jilly and the suicide on the Golden Gate Bridge. Grace's projected show of dental equipment. The witch's success in treating Beaver.

The best my estate has to offer, its centerpiece, is an enormous tree trump, almost four foot in diameter, that stands like an august sculpture guarding a popular sandbox. The tree didn't topple in a storm but was deliberately cut, for its surface is entirely flat and smooth as a bench, though no one ventures to sit on it. Too high, for one thing, nearly three feet above the ground; too hard to scramble up the sides of rough, tortuous bark coiled like gargantuan innards. And it looks very forbidding, a throne for larger-than-human royalty, elephants or dinosaurs. It must have been the familiar tree men who cut it. For years I've seen them on the Drive, ascending into the upper branches in their metal seats to lop and prune, bend and straighten. What happy work, up amidst the leaves doing arboreal housekeeping, seeing from on high the curving Drive and broad river. The Tai Chi teacher told a story once—or the interpreter told it for him—about a friend who worked up in the branches and one day slipped from his seat. Because of his practice of Tai Chi, he didn't resist the twenty-foot fall but yielded to it, landing soft and unharmed on the waiting earth. But maybe it was more than that. Maybe he had breathed an invulnerability that rides only on the tides of the upper air.

When I stop to rest on a bench, I study the motley parade of joggers, all panting like dray horses in the service of a pitiless master. I listen to the tinkling tune of the Mister Softee truck, the shrieks of the children, the shouts of people calling their dogs with absurd names, Abélard, Sebastian, Hector.

I find all this very soothing. I trust the walking more than any other remedy. I walked off Q. and it worked, at least long enough for me to marry Ev. Q. couldn't leave Susan, not just yet. It wasn't the children any longer—they were finally all right, Jessica attending Wesleyan, Carla doing well in a detox program. But Susan had thrown her back out carrying a carton of old papers down to the basement storage room. She was in pain and couldn't manage alone. She needed his help.

It'll just be a few weeks, he said. How can I leave her flat on her back?

Flat on her back, I repeated. Flat on her back.

Yes, what's so odd about that? It's the only tolerable position. That or standing up. Sitting is unbearable.

Why didn't you carry the goddamned carton yourself?

I wasn't home. If I had seen her lugging it, of course I would have. . . . Why are we even going into all this? It's not the issue.

That's just it. If it weren't this it would be something else. I'd like to see you flat on your back. I swear if I were a man and could knock you out I'd do it.

(That was before I took up Tai Chi. Had I known Tai Chi I would have drawn close to him in a pretended embrace, then stepped aside and let his own erotic energy hurtle him to the floor.)

If you were a man we wouldn't be in this situation. But go ahead. Swing from the shoulder. I won't hit back.

Don't give me any of your lame wit, Q. You'll never leave her. You're lying. You've always lied, whether you know it or not. At this point it's fine with me if you don't leave her. Actually I find it disgusting when men leave their wives for younger women, did I ever tell you? Do you think I like my part in this vile mess? Stay with her, just tell me the truth.

I'm not lying. I—

I hit him on the shoulder, trying out how it felt. I hadn't hit anyone since I was seven years old and knocked out a boy's loose baby tooth in the schoolyard; he was hogging the ball. Q. was jolted but didn't lose his balance. I know now what I did wrong, relied on upper-body strength. Now I could throw him off balance with a touch.

I'm not lying, he repeated, straightening out his shirt. It was gray-and-white-striped. I have many faults, he said, but I'm not a liar. I love you and I want to live with you. You know that.

I don't know any such thing. What I do know is that you're a weak overgrown adolescent and I don't want to see you ever again or hear your name mentioned. I don't want to feel you touch me or hear your voice or—

You can't mean that, Laura. I can't believe you mean it.

It was his steady gaze and tone that incensed me. His coarse hair was brown then. He needed a shave. Did he have the mustache? It came and went.

I do, I want you to get out of my house. Stop looking at me like that. What role are you playing now, Svengali? Cut it out. Just go.

All right. All right. I can't talk to you when you're like this. You should have done this onstage. You would have been very successful. Okay, I'm going. I'll call tomorrow.

Didn't I made it clear? Don't call tomorrow or ever. This is ruining me. I don't want you in my life.

I'll call in a few days, when you've calmed down, said Q.

I thrust his sweater at him and pushed him toward the door, but the touching was a mistake. I turned away and the door opened and closed. So quietly, as if he were afraid to wake someone. A temperate man.

I called in sick the next morning—I was teaching at a private school while I worked on the novel, as Q. had urged. He was the guardian of the novel, he liked to joke. (The muse, I thought but never said aloud, maybe because I knew I'd have to finish it without him.) The late September day was warm and bright. I put on a pair of new sandals and started up Sixth Avenue—I was living in the Village then. I walked to Fourteenth Street, turned west and went up Eighth Avenue until I got to the sleazy section in the Forties, then turned west again and up Ninth. I walked for a couple of miles, not seeing much around me except that I'd reached Riverside Park. Soon my eyes focused. I watched a barge make its way downstream. I passed the Marina with its houseboats bobbing in the water. A few bicycles skimmed by, a few mothers wheeled strollers, but mostly I was alone. Everyone was at work or school, keeping the city's life going. My legs and feet ached but I forced them on as if guards in shiny boots were prodding me with rifles: Into the woods! Hand over your valuables! Onto the train! After a while I stopped to sit on a bench, but only briefly. It was wonderful how my brain was numbed; I had almost forgotten why I was walking. At some point I went over to Broadway and stopped at a hot dog stand, eating as I headed back to the river.

I passed the high towers of Riverside Church and followed the river up to the George Washington Bridge, where I thought of crossing over to New Jersey—not jumping, only crossing—but didn't. I wanted pavements and wasn't sure I'd find them there. It was six-twenty when I got back home. Just as I unlocked the door the strap on my right sandal broke. How lucky, I thought, it waited till this minute. The sandals had been brand-new in the morning. Now the heels were worn down and there was a small hole in each sole, precisely in that place behind the ball of the foot where (the Tai Chi teacher would explain years later) we take root in the earth from which our strength rises. The rushing spring, it's called, because the earth's energy bubbles up through it to diffuse through the body. But you have to allow it in, make way for it and welcome it.

I tossed out the shoes and looked at my streaked, sweaty face in the mirror and said, Good, I've walked him off. I've thrown him away like an old shoe. I didn't see him again for three years.

I'm not asking for forever. Only for the way things are and must be. If I can walk this thing off and get my strength back for three years, I'll take it gladly.

After the noisy, foul-smelling highways, Tim and I drove through prettified towns bustling with shops and framed by commercial strips and billboards. Between the towns stretched acres of potato fields; farm stands along the road displayed robust fruits and vegetables. At last we turned off toward the ocean, its salt smell wafting through the car windows, and passed through flat, empty land barely graced by a tree. New gray-shingled frame houses sprang up haphazardly, as if someone had scattered a handful of Monopoly houses on a board. This strange pattern, or nonpattern, arose, Tim explained, when real estate was in its palmier days. People bought up sections of the potato fields one by one to build summer homes.

He swung the car easily around a few bends—Tim drives with grace, the way some men dance—and onto a dead-end street. We pulled into the driveway to find ourselves secluded by high dark hedges suggesting a sanitarium or an expensive boarding school. The house and its surroundings felt isolated, and then a couple appeared to greet us.

The first thing they did, laughing wryly, was show us the pool, which was about half an acre down a slope of sunny, manicured lawn. The pool was empty, or nearly empty. A little past its center, toward the deep end, lay a green hose from which a thin stream of water trickled.

"What happened, you're wondering, right?" said Celia.

"What happened," said Hal, "is that the pool people were supposed to clean and refill the pool last week while we were away but they obviously forgot to finish the job."

"They didn't forget," said Celia. "They've got a lot of pools to do and they neglected this one. Like triage. Or it might be that you forgot to pay them."

"Well, whatever," Hal said mildly, untouched by the sharpness of her tongue, even smiling with a kind of familial pride. "The point is, this is where we are with it. But it's okay, there's always the ocean."

"Yes, I hope they remembered to fill it," Celia said.

The pool was long, elliptical, and walled in slate, not the usual blue-green that suggests a Walt Disney movie where fabulous sea creatures might suddenly cavort onto the scene.

"When it's filled," said Tim, "it's very beautiful. Have you ever seen a slate pool? It's dark, like a pond in the forest. Sort of mysterious."

I looked at him with surprise. That was very poetic, for Tim.

The four of us stood at the edge of the pool as on the lip of a canyon, contemplating its emptiness. There was nothing mysterious or forest-like about the sloping lawn and handsome low house up the hill with its deck and tubular furniture, or about the navy blue webbed reclining chairs on the concrete border of the pool, affably waiting to receive idlers. On a small Lucite table were newspapers, glasses, an ashtray. Evidently before we arrived, Hal and Celia had been enjoying their summer retreat, watching the pool fill.

Seeing me glance around, Celia waved at the chairs. "Yes, we were watching the pool fill up. It's going to be our weekend activity."

I smiled, though I didn't wish to be seen as partaking in her amiable scorn—for her husband, the pool, the world? She was compact and athletic-looking, with auburn hair tied back in a pony tail. She seemed forever on the verge of moving or speaking, every cell alert, a step ahead of the moment. She wouldn't be shocked by my wishing all the drivers on Broadway dead. She'd probably wished much worse.

"How long will it take to fill up?" I asked. "A few hours?"

"Oh, no, much longer," said Hal, his mustache dancing as he spoke. He was tall and fat, his round genial face shrouded in a dark beard, a cigar stuck between his lips. He wore a blue short-sleeved shirt and powder blue shorts that reached nearly to his knees and swelled alarmingly at his middle. "The water has been running like this since last night, that's Friday. Let's see, the pool is sixty feet long by twenty feet at its widest, that would be twelve hundred square feet. To get the volume you'd have to make allowances for the gradation in depth. . . ."

The two men calculated, with mathematical precision, the volume of the pool, taking into account its elliptical shape and the gradation in depth, then factored in the rate of the water trickling from the hose, which they deduced by dividing the volume of the pool which was already filled by the number of hours the hose had been trickling.

"The pool will be filled," concluded Tim, "by Monday morning."

"No, Sunday morning," Hal corrected. "In practical terms, that is, because it doesn't have to be completely filled in order for us to swim in it."

Celia laughed her sharp laugh and tossed her head disdainfully. "Not before Tuesday, I'm willing to bet."

It appeared that Hal and Celia were performing a teasing script in which Tim and I were required to speak our lines without knowing the larger themes and references of the play, just as some choreographers, Q. once told me, prefer that their dancers be ignorant of the mythic sense of the work and simply execute the steps. As always, when Q. came to mind lately, a little blob of elation and despair thumped around my solar plexus but I paid it no attention.

"Not Tuesday, sweetheart. How can you say that?" Again, her taunting didn't seem to bother Hal. Nothing seemed to bother him except, I later discovered, the state of the real estate market. "It's much more full than you imagine. It's up to six feet at the deep end. In fact you could probably swim at the deep end right now. It's very deceptive, an optical illusion."

This struck me as highly unlikely, little as I knew about pools or optical illusions. From where we stood it looked as though roughly two feet of water covered the deep end, while the shallow end was not yet wet.

"No, Hal," said Tim in his judicious way. "I doubt if that's six feet deep."

"I'll give you a demonstration." With his lit cigar in his teeth at a jaunty angle, Hal strode to the shallow end of the pool and stepped suavely down the stairs. He walked across more than half the length of the pool before his feet got wet. As he advanced further, water enveloped his legs at a surprising rate. Water is deceptive. And the angle of the pool floor at the deep end was evidently steeper than it seemed from the rim. Hal walked until the edges of his blue Bermuda shorts were wet, then glanced our way for acknowledgment. The day was very fine. The leaves of the shrubberies glistened, the flowers in the flower beds stirred softly in the breeze, the sky was blue, the light radiant. Not so hot yet. Not hot enough to swim.

"Six feet, ha," said Celia.

Ignorant or not, I would enjoy this performance. Too bad Q. wasn't here to watch—he would appreciate Hal and Celia as much as I did. They played their roles well, like Pinter characters.

Hal kept advancing. When the water reached the crotch of his shorts a shiver rippled through his vast body and he glanced up again and chuckled. Ungainly, no question about it, yet not unattractive. I wouldn't mind at all, despite the weight. I mean I wouldn't mind aesthetically. Certainly Celia wouldn't have taunted were she indifferent. Probably quite the contrary. He kept walking, holding aloft the lit cigar, until the water reached the breast pocket of his shirt, which contained two ballpoint pens, and still he was not at the deepest point, where the drain was.

"Hey, I wish I had a picture of this," said Tim. "I didn't think of bringing my camera."

"Is it cold?" I called out.

"Not too cold," Hal called back. "Come on in."

I took off my shoes and walked the length of the concrete border,

"Hey, I wish I had a picture of this," said Tim. "I didn't think of bringing my camera."

down the steps and into the shallow end of the pool. Not until I was at the center, near the green hose trickling out water like a burbling brook, did the soles of my feet get wet. The water was so cold that a chill shot through my spine to the back of my neck. I walked on, up to my ankles. At the far end, Hal stood immersed up to his shirt pocket, his arms held above the water with the fingers of one hand lapping tenderly at the ripples as one does in a canoe, while he puffed on his cigar and gazed fondly around at his property. From down in the pool the property took on a majestic aspect: the trees were higher, their swaying tops closer to the azure sky, the spreading house set regally on the crest of the slope. Tim and Celia, standing at the edge and laughing at us, appeared elongated and powerful.

"This is so cold," I said. "And it's such a trickle, too."

"We could turn on another hose," said Hal, "but then we'd have no water in the house. We did that last night, actually, had both hoses going in the hope that it would fill up in time for you two. We should have factored that in, Tim, both hoses overnight. But then in the morning we wanted to take showers and make coffee and so on."

"Yes, you wouldn't want to come out here for a shower," said Celia. "A bath, it would have to be. Like the British. It forms character. We could offer character-forming baths for children of the local landed gentry."

The matter of the water being connected to the house confused me. I hadn't thought of where it might be coming from. Didn't water in the country come from the ground? A well?

"If it's coming from the house," I said, "then why can't you turn on the hot?"

Everyone burst out laughing, Tim loudest of all. Tim delights in what he considers my impracticality, my remoteness from the nuts and bolts of daily life. A writer, he thinks, deals in fantasy and abstraction. I cannot convince him that I'm an extremely practical person, that writers have to be close to the daily nuts and bolts. This example of my plumbing ignorance would only reinforce his feelings.

I laughed, too—I felt comfortable enough with Hal and Celia—

though I wasn't sure what the joke was, only that I had said something ludicrous.

"The water isn't coming directly from the faucets," Hal explained gently, "but from the well which feeds the pipes which supply the house. The well water is cold, naturally. Inside it gets heated up by the boiler."

Standing several yards from me, in water up to his chest, he spoke with professorial earnestness about the nature of wells, especially artesian wells which go deep into the ground. Meanwhile, Celia took Tim to see the vegetable garden. As Hal went on I retreated a few feet onto the dry part because the water was too cold to stand in.

"Underneath the land we stand on, there's water," he said. "Water, water everywhere. What we call the earth is mostly water. In fact, the only reason we have dry land at all is that the earth's crust is uneven and buckles in places, so it juts out. If the globe were quite smooth, without any warps, there'd be water all over it, a couple of miles deep."

For some reason this information left me appalled. "I knew there was a lot, but not that much."

"Yes, wherever you dig you'll eventually find water, since the earth, the globe, is made of a series of alternating concentric spheres of land and water."

"That is a very striking image," I said. "If that's so, what holds it all together? Why doesn't the water seep through?"

"Well, it does, in the forms of lakes and springs and so on. It holds together because the layers are very thick. And then, factors like gravity and centripetal force enter into it."

"You seem to know an awful lot about this for someone who's in real estate."

"What I'm telling you is not very arcane knowledge." He chuckled again, as he had when the water hit his crotch, and added, "I wanted to be a geologist at one point, but I got sidetracked into making money."

"If I were a Tai Chi master," I said, "I could make the water rise simply by standing here and slowly raising my arms. It would be the force of my inner energy. They call it *chi*."

"Why don't you try? Who knows? It might work."

I shook my head and smiled as I backed out of the pool. Concentric spheres. The notion made me feel a little less secure. The Tai Chi teacher had told us our strength came from the earth, so that we must root our feet firmly to receive its energy. Feel the rushing spring rising, he said, into the point just behind the balls of your feet. And we did, or thought we did. But if beneath the earth was water, then earth, then water all over again? That made the source less stable. No wonder it was called the rushing spring, though. The Tai Chi masters must have known about the alternating layers of water.

Which was at the very center, the innermost sphere, water or earth?

"The obvious thing to do under the circumstances," said Celia, strolling back with Tim, "is to paint murals on the walls of the pool. I've always felt they needed some decoration."

"Celia is a painter." Tim turned to me. "Did I tell you that?"

"I'm not a muralist, though. Few people are these days. The demand is slight, except down in SoHo. Still, here's my chance to do something big, like Gulley Jimson."

"But the pool is so dark when it's filled," Tim said. "You won't be able to see the pictures."

"You'll see the tops. Anyway, you'll see them when you're underwater."

"No, sweetheart," said Hal, emerging from the pool and wringing out the bottoms of his shorts, "you won't see them when you're underwater. There's less light there, not more."

"There's only one way to find out for sure," she said. "Either way, we'll know they're there."

"I'll paint," I heard myself say. I hadn't held a paint brush since Ev and I moved into the apartment on the river years ago. Painting the pool seemed a lark, even though I had no scientifically based opinion on whether or not one would see the murals while swimming underwater, and if I had I would have been hesitant to offer it after my misguided comment about the well and the faucets. "I like that idea."

"If you really want to do it right," said Hal, "we should drain the pool so you can cover all of the walls."

"Oh, Christ, Hal, let's not drain the pool! Not when we've gotten this far."

After lunch Celia and I drove into the chic little town. "What would you recommend for the walls of a pool?" she asked at the hardware store. She conversed knowledgeably with the clerk, who didn't seem to find our project at all odd. I suppose the locals were used to city folk performing their frivolities in the potato fields, like colonizers building on sacred graves of the ancients.

Back at the house, she gave me an old pair of shorts and one of Hal's T-shirts, which I had to knot up at the waist, it was so large. We traipsed out with our paint cans, passing the men on the deck drinking beer.

"You look very fetching, Laura," said Tim in that sober way I liked.

"I bought that row for three-quarters of a million," Hal resumed, "and now I don't think I could get rid of it for half of that. Make sure to leave a strip unpainted above the water level, sweetheart," he called after Celia, "because the tide will be rising and your work could get ruined."

"I will. But I got quick-drying paint," she retorted. "Quicker than our rising tide."

"What are we going to paint?" I asked as we set up our equipment in the shallow end.

"Sea creatures. Fish. Mermaids. Anemone."

"I really can't paint anything. I can't even draw."

"That's okay, I'll sketch it all out and you can fill it in. Like paint-by-number."

Celia moved rapidly along one long wall, outlining a pair of mermaids seated on a rock, combing out their tresses. Her own hair was covered by an aquamarine scarf that caught the light as she zipped back and forth sketching schools of bright fish, fantastically tentacled coral and anemone, outlandish ferns, and a sunken treasure chest spilling out gold coins. We didn't do the wall at the deep end since neither of us wanted to walk through the icy water. "I should really make Hal do that," she

said, "but never mind." The wall at the shallow end was too low for anything elaborate, so Celia assigned me the task of painting it sea-green,
like Rubens with a beginning apprentice. From time to time she in-
spected my work, deftly adding ripples and shadows that transformed
my flat surface into a credible representation of water. While she did the
mermaids' iridescent scales she asked questions about my life, as women
do, and I gave her the broad outlines, omitting Q., of course. At such
moments, when people become acquainted and give their data, it was as
if Q. didn't exist, was a fantasy I had made up, though without him any
impromptu sketch was as incomplete as her quick outlines on the walls.

"You're very good," I said as I filled in some shellfish. "How can you
do it all so fast?"

"I do everything fast, that's my trouble. For example, marry in haste,
repent at leisure."

"Really? That's not the impression I got. I thought it was more of a . . .
a kind of number you've both developed."

"Oh, you mean a couples act? Stiller and Meara? Nichols and May?
Life imitating art. That's an interesting angle." She didn't go on, though,
but daubed at a black hulking shape.

I could understand her silence. It's one thing to offer the bold outlines of one's life on first acquaintance, as I had done, and something
else to fill in the shadows and ripples that make the story a credible representation.

Before long we were finished, having left a careful margin for the rising
tide, as Hal advised. Our creation—Celia's, really—was an undulating
blue-green, orange-pink sea dream where everything shimmered, a
whimsical wet paradise whose only object of menace was a large gray fin
disappearing into a corner.

"It looks like a stage set," I said. "I almost feel we should put on a play
or something." Or string up nets like the fishermen at the Bay of Fundy,
though we'd never catch anything: we hadn't even attempted realism.

"On the off chance that it fills up soon we can do an Esther Williams
routine."

Celia stepped away from the wall to reveal the black shape behind her, tilting toward the water line. I was startled to see the eroded frame of a sunken ship. It was superbly done, eerie yet full of promise. I was about to remark on the coincidence, telling Celia how much it resembled the ship I'd tried to reach in the bay, but with her suddenly enigmatic eyes on me, I said nothing. I walked up to it, as though here on the wall it might finally yield up its treasure, but of course it was only two-dimensional, a representation.

"Free time!" she announced, ripping the scarf off her hair and striding briskly to the house. I went in, too, to take a nap—it was amazing I'd lasted so long without one. Tim followed me into the bedroom and wanted to make love. Just a quickie, he urged, but I was worn out from my artistic endeavors. He left grumpily with a book under his arm, a lawyer thriller he found on the shelves, about Claus von Bülow.

BEFORE THE DINNER GUESTS ARRIVED we checked on the water level in the pool.

"I can't see any difference," I said. "Except for the murals, I mean."

"Look at the margin you left under the pictures," said Hal. "Don't you see that it's narrower?"

As a matter of fact it was about an inch narrower. And three-quarters of the pool floor was now wet, or at least dark with dampness.

"Tomorrow, mark my words, we'll be able to swim. Meanwhile, we're going to be pressed into service this evening," he said. "Our friend Steve is bringing over another game."

"Oh, not again," said Celia. "The last one, the fairy tale game, was a real bomb. I could have told him that before we began. In this day and age, any game that requires reading is not going to sell."

"Well, he must know, sweetheart. He's made a fortune on them. Our friend Steve," he said, turning to Tim and me, "is a game originator. Yes, that's a profession. Look, someone has to do it. He invents games and toys. Little robots who perform simple tasks. Electronic-doll kinds of things. Some are doing very well. One doll, Harriet Hermosa, paid for

251

their new house in Water Mill. You should see this place—the living room shelves are lined with his toys. Now he's into board games. You'd be surprised how much intellectual effort goes into working out a board game."

How wrong I was in every way about the dinner party. Nothing fancy or *nouvelle* to eat, for one thing. Hal played man the hunter at a huge open hearth on the lawn, poking at steaks with the sweet ingenuous pride of outdoor chefs, while the rest of us carried out mounds of potatoes and onions wrapped in tinfoil. I was so starved at this fashionably late hour that I could hardly keep from grabbing the meat off the grill with my bare hands. I'd forgotten to eat a banana beforehand, as Jilly had ordered.

No fancy clothes either. The men wore shorts and the women were casual. One, a very pregnant dress designer, wore her own creation, a white linen tent printed with black half moons. Nor was the talk what I'd envisioned. An inevitable swipe at the sluggish real estate market and some brief dismay at the hole in the ozone layer, but nothing serious. There was a risky moment when Steve, the gamesman, remarked on the cholesterol content of the double Brie, but Hal diverted the subject. "My grandmother used to make me drink heavy cream to build me up," he said. "I was a very puny kid, can you believe it?"

"So was I," said a grizzled, bearded man close to sixty, the oldest man present. He had a young wife, probably his second or even third, while the other two couples, in their late thirties, appeared to be on their first go-rounds. "I was spoonfed for years. I remember as a boy in Washington Heights I would sit on the floor after dinner listening to the radio and my mother would sit on a chair near me with a bowl of apples on her lap and a knife. She would cut an apple in half, then core it and scrape at it with a spoon so it flaked off. All I had to do was open my mouth periodically and I had instant apple sauce."

"How old were you when she did this?" I asked.

"Oh, I don't remember."

"Well, for example, two, three, six?"

"Older than that."

"Fifteen?"

"Twenty-one?" put in Celia, passing around the salad.

"Was it before or after your bar mitzvah, Harvey?" asked his wife.

"Oh, come on, I'm pretty sure it was before that."

I was hard at work recording what I heard, silently echoing the phrases and cadences so I'd have them exactly right. Tim glanced across the table and smiled with triumph at my rapt attention. You see, you had a good time, he'd tell me later. And you didn't want to come. I was in fact enjoying the party, though it took effort to smile and talk and eat properly all at once: I'd hardly ventured into polite society of late. Mona's party didn't count as polite society.

During coffee, the pregnant woman eyed me with a mixture of wariness and grudging awe. "You're a writer, aren't you? I thought so. Well, I don't know where you writers get your ideas, but I have a story for you. Someone really ought to write this down."

It was my turn to smile triumphantly at Tim, for I had bet him on the drive out that I would be offered a story that had to be written down.

"This is a story about my great-grandfather on my mother's side. He came to New York from Poland as a boy, around the turn of the century. But then he did an unusual thing for an immigrant back then. He turned right around and went back, I'm not sure why. Maybe he found the life too different and missed the old ways, maybe he couldn't make a living, nobody in the family really knows. Anyway, he went back, not to Poland but Paris, and there he started making women's capes. That was how he earned his living. The special thing about his capes was the fantastic colors. They were made of different colored strips of fabric sewn together in the strangest combinations, very flamboyant, not like any capes anyone had ever seen. And these capes of many colors, strange as they were, were worn mostly by the working-class women who were his clientele. Until one day Sarah Bernhardt happened to see one of his capes, maybe on her cook or seamstress, and took a fancy to it. She bought one and started wearing it, then she bought another, and before you know it the capes became all the rage among fashionable women and my great-grandfather became very rich. Eventually he returned to America and married and raised a family. But the point I want to make is, it turns out that these capes of flamboyant strips of color stitched together in such odd combinations were that way because he was color-blind. I mean, he didn't really know what he was doing. It's passed on, you know, through the female line to the males—my brother's color-blind, too. And if I have a boy—" she looked down at her hard belly—"he might be also. Now isn't that a story for you? You really should write that down."

(And so I have. The thing these storytellers don't grasp, however, is that to write down a story the way it was told, as I've done, honoring her request, is to embalm it. To understand what the story might mean or give it a meaning, you'd have to break it into its component parts—the immigrant, the return trip, the capes, Sarah Bernhardt and her cook, the success, the color-blindness—then shake them up and rearrange them in a new pattern, thereby sending life—or *chi*, the life force—through its frame. Sarah Bernhardt's cook brought the capes to America, where she met a desperate young immigrant, color-blind. . . . A poor young Parisian finds the cape tossed out in the great actress's garbage and sells it to a seamstress for barely enough money to get to America, not realizing its worth because he's color-blind. . . . Something along those lines.)

Soon the dining room table was cleared and ready. Steve set out a square plywood board, two packs of homemade cards, dice, and a hand-ful of colored tokens and disks.

"Remember this is still in an embryonic stage," he said. "I haven't got all the kinks worked out yet. Comments are welcome. The game is played pretty much like any other board game, Monopoly, for instance. You shoot the dice, you have your various options about where to move, you get directions to follow, which are more or less your fate. Like any really good game, it's a metaphor for life. What's special is that this is a better one than most. It's a perfect replica of our time, which is why I think people will relate to it. I mean, what is the central experience of our era? Catastrophe, right? That's the name of the game."

Catastrophe, complete with Reversal of Fortune cards, Survival Credits, and twists of fate, proved lively: shrieks and groans as players confronted catastrophes on a global to personal scale, from Lethal Toxins Found In Drinking Water to Favorite Son Joins Cult. I couldn't seem to get into the spirit, though. I dropped out early and went to bed, a king-sized bed every bit as ardent as my own, and fell promptly asleep despite the Walpurgisnacht down the hall. Tim woke me later to report that he was the winner. The game wasn't bad technically, he said, despite a few snags. Some people felt the theme was too much of a downer to be commercially successful. "What do you think, Laura?"

"People love that kind of thing. I think it'll be a big hit."

"Me, too. The sicker the better, these days."

Then he had a minor personal catastrophe, at least he thought so. He couldn't get an erection. "Shit, what does this mean? This never happens to me. It must be the beginning of the end."

"No, stop worrying," I soothed him. "I'm sure it's a passing thing. You're tired and you probably had a lot to drink. That's all it is."

"Is this the price of victory?" he groaned, then put his head on my chest and was fast asleep.

WHEN WE SAUNTERED OUT to check on the pool the next day, the water was considerably above the margin we had allowed when we painted. Exactly how far it had risen was hard to judge since, as Hal had predicted, the dark walls obscured the murals below the water line. Still, their shimmering evoked something mysterious stirring beneath the surface, as in the ocean itself. Perhaps that was the effect Celia had intended. The ship had sunk lower, as if the tide had risen; only the top of its mast and stark black frame was visible.

"Aha! Half full!" exclaimed Hal.

This seemed impossible. The deep end still didn't look full enough to swim in even if the weather had been suitable, which it wasn't—brilliant and sunny, but cool. The shallow end was barely covered by a thin film of water.

Once more the men reviewed the rate of the trickle, the number of hours passed, and the present water level, concluding that regardless of appearances the pool was indeed half full.

"It's irrelevant anyway," said Celia, "unless you want to freeze your ass off."

We drove to the beach, where there was no water problem. The ocean was full, at high tide. Waves surged up the wide beach to what my Cape Cod library book called the "splash zone," hitting with great force as sometimes happens on radiant days, and dragging back clots of pebbly sand. A wave of tiredness broke over me, not quite knocking me down but making me sway. I lay down beyond the splash zone while the others went walking.

Only a few people were around. A pair of aging men in rolled-up white trousers strode through the surf, one gesticulating and talking excitedly, perhaps about the ebb and flow of money, while the other listened with arms folded as if for protection. A couple with a small child kept digging a hole and watching the water fill it as each wave rolled in. The child was surprised every time the hole filled up, and the parents pretended surprise. Way out at sea was a large white ship, not moving.

With each hurtling wave the tide crept up imperceptibly, like the water level in the pool, though with far more energy and inspiring greater confidence. The others receded in the distance—Hal and Tim side by side and Celia a bit apart, stopping to examine shells or rocks cast up in the foam.

When I woke I was alone with the ocean—no one in sight. The hole the young family had dug kept filling and emptying; the white ship sat stationary on the horizon. The only movement was the water's assault and fierce retreat, as if it could not resign itself to being forever yanked back. This was just a passing mood, of course—two weeks ago I'd seen the same ocean graciously yielding to the inevitable.

After a while the others reappeared as specks and grew slowly into human form, then into generic identities: end-of-the-century Americans who played games that mocked their condition, as if a playful dose of catastrophe, like a homeopathic cure, could bring relief. Tim's sister had been abused by an uncle and later was beaten by her husband, giving birth to a retarded child as a result. Steve's parents had died in a hotel fire just last year, I'd overheard Hal saying to Tim. Celia's parents had lost their farm in Illinois, she'd told me as we painted. Not to mention Ev.

Reaching life size, they came and retrieved me. Too chilly for the beach, we all agreed.

WHEN NIGHT FELL we ambled down the dark road, Hal and Celia up front leading the way. Tim took my hand. His hand was firm and warm, perfect for handholding, a comfort. So much so that tears came to my eyes. As I blinked them away I saw bright white lights moving through the trees, or rather through the bulbous masses, dark shapes against the dark, that the trees had become. Could the lights be my tears projected, aglow in the black night? How unscientific, how Tim would have laughed. Or stars magnified and made mobile by my tears? But the lights remained even when the tears were gone, dispelled by curiosity.

"Look at that." I squeezed Tim's hand and he squeezed back. "They can't all be shooting stars, can they?"

He didn't laugh or suggest anything logical. He looked, as more and more lights encircled us. The thick darkness annihilated all depth—one moment they seemed near enough to touch, and the next, they were off in the cold spatial reaches.

"Or UFOs?" I whispered, only half joking.

"More likely shooting stars," but his tone was uncertain.

Twinkle, twinkle, little star, I remembered Evelyn reciting. Like a . . . Like a . . . Mona urged her on until finally she got it. Like a diamond.

"Fireflies," said Hal, turning around. We'd been talking so softly, I didn't realize he could hear.

"They can't be. They're so high," I said. "And big and white. In the country, when I was a kid, they were yellow. It was easy to catch them and put them in jars."

"They're fireflies. Last of the season. It's the dark that makes them big and white. You'll see when we get back to the house."

He was right. As we approached the lighted house the white glows deepened to yellow and shrank in the middle distance. Attached to the yellow flickers, dark bodies appeared. Ordinary fireflies. Tim kissed the inside of my wrist before we came into the full light.

We walked down the lawn for a last check on the water level. With the garish pool lights turned up, the grass looked fake, like Astroturf. The shrubs flashed an unearthly sheen and the slate walls painted just yesterday, though it seemed longer ago, were lurid and ominous. The water level was more than halfway up the deep end, possibly high enough to swim in. At the shallow end, a thin layer glistening like ice coated the bottom step. The trickling hose was covered.

"Well, so much for your luxurious backyard swimming," said Celia.

"It doesn't matter," said Tim. "It was too cool anyway. Thanks for a great weekend."

"Come again soon," said Hal. "Next time I promise there'll be water."

I must have fallen asleep before we hit the highway and didn't wake until we pulled up at my building.

"Did I sleep the whole time? Not sparkling company, am I?" As I sat upright my canvas bag fell from my lap and its contents, including an unused bathing suit, spilled to the floor. "Oh, sorry. How clumsy." I gathered up the things and stuffed them back in.

"Laura, we're not teenagers out on a first date. Stop apologizing."

"Was I? I only meant it must have been dull for you. Do you want to come up?"

"I'd better not. I've got an early morning meeting and I'm exhausted. So, did you have a good time?"

"Very. I liked them a lot. You were right, it was a good idea to go." Good data, too.

Inside, I checked the window ledge. Still no squirrel, but wonder of wonders, the nest was back, bristly and ragged in the glow of the street lamp, like a building under construction. Recently slept in, I'd say. With a surge of relief, I pictured him fully recovered and out carousing, coming home to sleep in the wee hours. It might have been some other squirrel, yes, but I chose to think it was the same one, coming and going, keeping his death at bay. Too tired now for rubber gloves, broom, dustpan. Let him have a night of comfort.

DAY ANNOUNCED ITSELF BY the hellish grinding of the garbage truck just below my window. From bed I could envision the scene. I'd watched it often enough, like a diffident witness to urban crime. The black plastic bags which last night lined the side street were being hurled mercilessly into the maw of the truck, where giant teeth pierced their thin skins and sank to the innards, *fee, fi, fo, fum,* chomping up the trash (though not yet the squirrel) like huge gobs of food.

I pried my body from bed, pulled on shorts and an old shirt of Ev's, and walked around to get my blood moving. The Tai Chi class was out of the question, but I might get a slight hit by watching them from the window. I was absorbed in following a shabby barge haul itself up the river when the phone blared over the grinding trash.

"Laura? This is Celia. You're probably working so I won't keep you. I got your number from Information. I had to let you know that when we left for the city early this morning the pool was not yet filled. I'm thinking of writing up the whole process for the *Journal of Higher Mathematics.*"

I liked her. I would have liked to know her better, but that might be awkward since our connection was through Tim, and very soon I'd be saying good-bye to Tim. If Verona had hired a new Juliet by now, she might help me find a tactful way. He'd be vexed and querulous. Tell me exactly what the problem is, he'd say, and I'd have no quantifiable answer.

The witch is an artist of the most radical kind. She overturns the usual configuration of fairy tales, where it's the Prince who appears in the nick of time to break the spell. With her laying on of hands, her unobtrusive needle pricks ("That which has no substance enters where there is no space"), and her captivating company—nearly as captivating as Q.'s— she's making an upside-down story, undoing his spell with one of her own.

She offers me spells to work at home, too. I light up the moxa stick and the apartment smells like a marijuana den. I rub the aromatic oils into my skin, conjuring forests and fields: pine, eucalyptus, rosemary, fennel, caraway, lavender. . . . I practice deep breathing. The air disperses inside to become tingling energy—the Tai Chi teacher's beloved elixir, the flutist's preserved breath that will outlast him and even his music— and then spirit, an amber glow like inner sunlight. I watch my arms float in baths filled with salts from the Dead Sea; I could almost levitate in the water. I can't swear any of this will cure me, but I follow her instructions on faith, the way you have to do in a story.

And yet, and yet, she hurts. In her effort to make me well (I do feel some energy returning, it's unmistakable), her potions and treatments make me sick. She sets me painful trials, like sewing shirts out of nettles. The skin rash alone would have been sufficient. The skin rash and fever would have been sufficient. The skin rash and fever and sore throat . . . But like God raining down plagues on the Egyptians, she's unleashed the whole arsenal.

One afternoon as I lay on her mat in the cool, quiet room, she began her performance by pricking my ear with needles.

"Hey, wait a minute! That one really hurt."

"Sorry," she said. "That was for the kidneys, where your energy is weak today. That's why you felt it."

"The kidneys? So why make my ear suffer?"

"The meridians of the body pass through the ear, so by inserting needles in the proper ear points you can influence different organs."

I gave her my skeptical look. She knew it well. She merely smiled the virtuous California smile and carried on.

"The ear is shaped like a fetus. Have you ever noticed?" she said. "Picture the fetus lying upside down in the ear. The acupuncture points correspond to where the various organs would be located in that position."

The ear is shaped like a fetus? "It is, isn't it? Those photos of fetuses always reminded me of something. Or maybe it was the ear that reminded me."

"Chinese medicine has used acupuncture points in the ear for centuries, but the analogy to the fetus was just noted and tested in the 1950s. It was a French doctor, Paul Nogier. It's not witchcraft, I assure you. You can read about it in respectable books. That's what I was studying in Paris when I met my former husband. A whole new set of ear points was developed as a result. What's uncanny is that many of them correspond to the old Chinese points."

"What a nice image. The fetus lying upside down in the ear."

"It's more than an image. You can treat incipient cataracts through the ear, and cardiovascular disease, and lots of other things. Okay, I'll do the other. Is it still hurting?"

"Not as much. Ow! The kidneys again?"

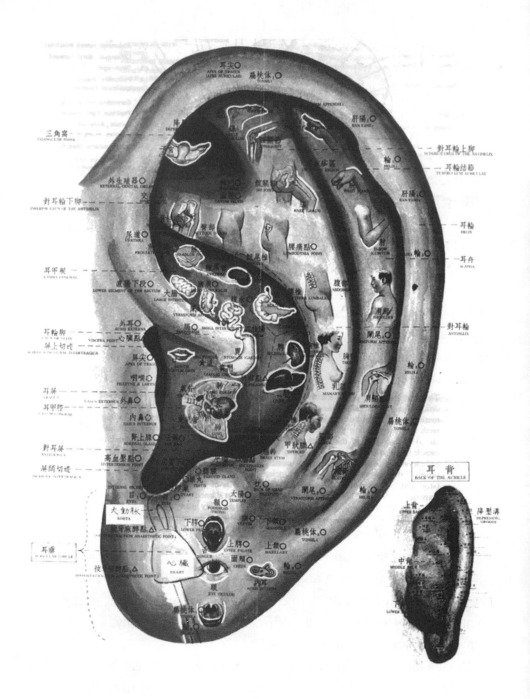

"The ear is shaped like a fetus. Have you ever noticed?" she said. "Picture the fetus lying upside down in the ear. The acupuncture points correspond to where the various organs would be located in that position."

"Sorry. Your ears seem very sensitive."

"Maybe because I've been exerting them. Listening."

"To what?"

"Oh, everything. Conversations I overhear as I walk. What friends say over the phone. They call to see how I am, but they don't quite believe I'm sick. And if I tell them I'm seeing a witch, I hear this strange veil come over their voices. But they humor me. I even write down things you say that interest me. No wonder my ears are sensitive."

"That may be." I'd never known her to deny any possibility, no matter how farfetched, but she looked dubious. She was scientific, in her way.

"The ear and the fetus," I mused. "Maybe that's why lovers like to lick ears. They could be licking points that correspond to sex organs."

"Funny, I never thought of that." She began pressing her hands down hard along the length of my legs. "I'd like to check it out, but unfortunately no one's licking my ears at the moment."

"What ever happened to the rabbi you mentioned a few weeks ago? Is that progressing?"

She sighed. "Slowly. It's up and down. He called once or twice, we met for a walk, we had coffee. There's definitely a strong attraction, I know that much. If this weren't such a puritanical age we probably would have made love by now. Ten, twelve years ago, well . . . But I'm glad we haven't, because I'm not about to get all involved while he's living with someone, and I as much as told him so. I also ran into him on the street several times—he lives in the neighborhood. But I think the fates had something to do with that."

"Which fates?"

"Well, a couple of weeks ago, before I knew for sure about his girlfriend, I cast a spell with my mother."

"Your mother? Didn't you say she was in California?"

"She is." She grinned as she pressed down on my ankles. "We did it over the phone."

"Oh, is she a witch, too?"

"No, a computer programmer. But she's very supportive. We lit can-

dles simultaneously and offered up dried flowers at little altars we im-
provised. Some real witches have elaborate altars to goddesses in their
apartments, but I don't go that far. We told each other how the candles
were flickering, and they seemed to be making similar patterns. Three
thousand miles apart. I think something powerful must have been passing through the air. Then we both whispered some wishes, and over the
next few days I met him twice on the street. By accident, so to speak."

"I hope your phone isn't tapped."

"No kidding, there are covens that do witchcraft over the phone, goddess and spirituality stuff. Conference calls. You know how hard it can be
to get a bunch of people together in the city. But I'm too busy working
and keeping up with the scientific literature. . . . Well, since that first
spell seemed to work, I tried again with a friend, not on the phone. We
lit the candles and we also offered up some pieces of very expensive
chocolate. Godiva. I figured, if I were a goddess, I'd have high-class
tastes. What would induce me to grant someone's wishes? The thing I
came up with was Godiva chocolates."

"And did that work?"

"I think so. It was right before we had a date to meet in Central Park.
We had a lovely time, I thought. We talked, we held hands, we sat on the
grass and kissed a little. But that was over a week ago. Since then things
have cooled. I ran into him on the street last Friday and he was very casual, as if nothing had ever passed between us. So I'm beginning to think
he's just a playboy, the kind who acts very seductive and then when
they're sure they've got you interested, that's the end of it. Do you know
the type I mean? They can be pathological, especially when they don't
even realize what they're doing."

"Yes, I do."

"He got what he wanted, which was to get me hooked. On the
other hand, he might have changed because I asked him to please
clarify for me what is going on with his girlfriend. If we're going to be
just friends, then why doesn't he invite me over to meet her, I said.
And if we're going to be more than friends, why is he still living with

her and deceiving her? I think I might have frightened him off."

"I bet you did. You're too much for him. It stands to reason—a witch, and he's a mere rabbi. He must be scared to death and I don't blame him."

She reached over for a small, ornately carved brass box covered by wire mesh. "Your abdomen feels cold. It's partly the change in weather, but I think I need to send some warmth there." She placed a gauze pad on my stomach. With a small knife, she scraped some muddy stuff from inside the box and deposited it on the pad to form a little mound.

"What's that?"

"It's just moxa in a different form." She flicked her handy cigarette lighter and applied the flame to the mound resting on my stomach. It sent up plumes of smoke like the warning signs of a volcano. "Tell me if it gets too hot."

"What kind of spell is this? What horrible symptom will I get now?"

"Nothing from this. The symptoms you're referring to are a result of the herbs and the acupuncture doing what they're supposed to. I told you I'd be releasing heat and toxins to free up your energy. They have to come out in some way. What have you had this week?"

I gave her all my complaints.

"I'm not sure what to do, Laura." It was the first time she'd shown a trace of exasperation. "You can't tolerate the skin rashes or the stomach cramps or the fever. If you find it all unacceptable, then my hands are tied."

"Your hands are tied?"

"Yes. Why, what's so odd about that?"

"Nothing. It's just . . . you know how sometimes you hear expressions literally, as if for the first time? That happens to me lately. Knowing you, I can't imagine your hands are tied. You'll find something. How about a vaginal infection? Yeast or whatever. That's not so bad, and I'm not using it at the moment."

"I can try, but I can't promise. It's your body that chooses how it responds to the treatment."

"This potion on my stomach is heating up," I said sullenly.

She quickly removed the gauze pad, grasping it deftly in her long fingers. "You are getting better, though, Laura. Don't you feel it? Over and above the transient symptoms?"

"It could be. But the doctor said I might get better in a few months anyway. Who knows? I'm just tired of feeling this way. My patience is wearing down."

When I was dressed, we kissed good-bye and hugged. She was large, and her body felt hard and supple as a palm tree. "Hold on," she said.

Through summer's ebb I keep walking along the river, Lungohudson, mostly in the late afternoons. Play areas with benches appear at five-minute intervals as if designed for my walking habits—and why not, if it's my estate?—though my favorite is the sandbox where the huge tree stump sits serene amid the children's rumpus, its bulging whorls of bark like the muscles of a tangled wrestling team. From exposure, the stump's round-table surface has been bleached to a gray-beige color, with rivulets of yellow and brown and rose streaking through it as through marble. Even with its cracks and fissures, it looks as smooth as if a sculptor's hands had stroked it patiently over and over until it became like the down of a peach. I imagine it would feel peachy to the touch, and porous, like downy human contours. I don't touch it, though. I feel a bit of the awe we've been taught to feel in museums, and in fact the stump looks eerily man-made, iconic: nature copying primitive art. I've never seen anyone else touch it either—it's so sublimely indifferent.

I like sitting where mothers and children congregate. I study the toddlers wobbling down the slide and rummaging in the sandbox, some of them bellicose, hurling sand as a weapon, others already accustomed to insult. The dreamers sit apart letting sand sift through their plump fingers, while the budding movers and shakers mark off their territory and busily organize equipment—pails, shovels, sieves. On the benches are mothers in varying degrees of attentiveness and an occasional father, but most of the watchers are black or Latina women whose children must be across the city with still other baby-sitters or grandmothers.

The plastic pails these days are notched at the bottom, for instant crenellations. What's happened to craftsmanship? Jilly and I made our own crenellations, those long-ago summers on the beach, while Ev and Tony dived into the waves. We'd cut them out with sharp shells or with a tarnished butter knife from the house, suiting their size to the grandeur of the castle.

Over on the grass, a few small boys, barely old enough for school, are learning to swing their plastic bats. Each mother or baby-sitter stands six feet away and aims the ball slowly and directly at the bat. The boys swing out wildly the moment the ball leaves her hands. Their bodies are firm, rubbery, and energetic as the Tai Chi teacher urges us to be. Be like a child, he says, or rather the interpreter says. An infant. An infant is infused with energy and moves spontaneously, without tension or stiffness. See how firmly he grabs things in his fist. See how he falls so loosely, he doesn't get bruised.

About one time out of five, the ball glances off the bat. One time in ten a boy will actually hit the ball, at which the mother sends up great cheers. The boys' persistence in the face of such a high failure rate is admirable. It seems a marvel that they ever learn to hit the ball, yet they do, for only a block down the Drive, not much bigger boys, with no mothers standing by, are pitching, hitting, running, the whole ball game. At some mysterious point, the nerves connecting brain and hand draw up a contract, and bat smacks ball. Is all the practice necessary or would it happen in any case, like menstruation or erections or death?

A few seven-year-olds are learning to ride bikes with the training wheels removed by eager parents who trot along behind, one hand steadying the back of the seat. At some arbitrary moment the parents let go. Immediately, the children feel the withdrawal of the hand anchoring them to the earth, rooting them, and they hastily concentrate all their efforts on keeping the wheels balanced. Their blood turns to fear; they can't relinquish their concentration and let the wheels roll, and yet it's the surfeit of concentration that undoes them. No longer spontaneous, like infants, they're sabotaged by effort, the mind turned in on itself. The bicycle starts rocking from side to side while the parents shout encouragement in English, Spanish, and Chinese: Just let go, relax and pedal. But the weight of concentration collapses in on the children; their panicky feet abandon the pedals and grope for firm ground. There they stand, shaky and forlorn, as the bicycle clatters to the pavement between their spread legs.

Yet how persistent they are, how bravely willing to climb back on, because for one immeasurably small instant between the removal of the steadying hand and the blood turning to fear, they felt the exhilaration of balance in motion, the blissful absence of effort, the joy of doing without doing. For this immeasurably small instant, they keep trying until one time, caught in the forward impulse, they fail to notice the removal of the steadying hand. They're carried along, skimming through air for fifteen or twenty feet before the shock—I'm riding the bike, this is the whole idea!—jolts them into concentration once more—Can something so wonderful feel so natural? No, I must earn it!—and once more the bike rocks, this time with a loose, merry abandon. Again it clatters to the pavement, but this time the children stand above it triumphant, like heroes.

One afternoon I felt a spurt of energy, possibly the energy freed up by the low-grade fever *et al.*, which were appearing as promised. This witch delivers. Enough of my own performance. I'd go across town and look at some real art.

A stab of guilt reminded me I was passing Tim's building. Tim's familiar window on the first floor, where he told me to knock if I passed by and wanted company. I'd ended it, finally, after our visit with Hal and Celia. Dismissed him, as he put it, slapping my extra set of keys down on his coffee table.

"Sure, I'm not serving any purpose anymore," he said. "Don't you think I know that? You're not the only one who notices what's going on. You're not feeling sexy and you're busy with your notebooks, so what do you need me for?"

"I'm very sorry," I said, and picked up the keys. "I certainly wouldn't put it that way. I don't want to hurt you but I just can't. . . . It's not a good time for me to be with anyone. This illness is messing up my head. I need to sort things out."

I said other embarrassingly lame things, but he was right to feel dismissed and we both knew it. Still, he wouldn't be lonely for long. A couple of Saturday afternoons in the Museum of Modern Art should do it. Naturally I didn't say anything so crude. Businesslike people like Tim are more sensitive than the arty types I'm used to: emotional violence and crudity are our raw materials, our daily bread.

Broadway was thick with strollers, shoppers, panhandlers, and neighborhood crazies cursing their unseen enemies. Tables of secondhand books and racks of clothing stood brazenly on the sidewalks, hot dog vendors dipped their tongs in the simmering vats, as a passing ambulance casually wailed and the Mister Softee truck piped its tune to scurrying children. So dense that I could feel the texture of the air. Practice swimming in air, the Tai Chi teacher said. This air felt more like soup. Thick, rich urban soup. Swimming in soup.

As I boarded the bus that swooped through Central Park, I clutched my bag closer. Joyce's dismay as she rummaged through her purse was still vivid. I carried my composition notebook everywhere now, to jot down sentences as I unreeled the tapes: Joyce's eating habits in restaurants, the subtle beliefs of the Tsumati, the witch's supportive mother lighting candles in California. I couldn't afford to lose it—I might not be as lucky as once before. There'd still be the typed sections on my desk, but I'd have to reconstruct the newer bits from memory, arduously piecing things together. A rough framework was already taking shape. If memory failed me I'd be forced to fill it in with invention, the way you make substitutions in a recipe when you've run out of the real thing. But I was low on invention, too.

Aside from typing faster and holding the notebook tight, I could only trust that the thing would shape itself with what was at hand, making opportunity its design, even making sense of loss, incorporating lost with found. And that the vibrations my ear picked up on the air would pipe a melody to charm me back to myself.

The museum had the look, feel, and smell of a major airport. Getting to the paintings required a great deal of waiting in line. In front of each painting were half a dozen people moving along in the slow, submissive fashion of passengers assembling to board the plane.

"I can't understand why would he want to paint the same haystacks so many times." The voice rose from a group leaving the Impressionist room, all similarly dressed for a cultural outing. They thronged the already crowded space.

"Carolyn, Carolyn," came another voice a few feet off, near a Gauguin. "What say we take this one home?"

I inched on to a Vuillard painting wider than it was high.

"Can she cook and serve, though?" asked a woman edging up beside me.

The painting was in tones of red, burgundy, and maroon, merging into one another. Hues of blood.

"She cooks but she doesn't serve," a voice behind me replied. "But she's very good, very thorough."

Only gradually could I discern the figures of several women, Vuillard's mother and sisters, according to the card on the wall. They seemed part of the richly patterned background rather than discrete entities.

"I have to have someone who can serve. The cooking alone is no use to me. Jane can cook all right but she can't serve. She's never been trained and she doesn't have the finesse."

Vuillard's mother and sisters sewed at home for a living, the fact-packed card explained, and he painted them over and over, working at their machines. Sometimes he put himself in the paintings, too, a melancholy, bemused presence, but not in this one.

"Well, you can't expect them to do everything. That's how it is. If they can clean they can't cook, and if they can cook they can't serve."

Vuillard's mother and sisters emerged more clearly the longer I looked. It was up to the viewer to find them and dislodge them from their setting, as if they were reluctant to show themselves.

"That's the hardest thing to get right, the serving. Since Dorothy went back to Barbados I haven't had a single one. . . . By the way, this is gorgeous, isn't it? Just gorgeous. I wish I could find drapes that color."

I tired quickly and took a cab home to the waiting embrace of the bed. Near midnight I woke, tingling and restive. Another spurt of energy—the magic herbs, no doubt, coursing through the channels.

I sat at my desk and wrote down what I'd heard in the museum. Just to clear it from my ears—it was too obvious to be of any use. Next I typed up some pages from the notebook: the water level in Hal and Celia's pool, the story of the color-blind immigrant and his capes of many colors which appealed to Sarah Bernhardt, as well as Harvey's being spoonfed applesauce at an indeterminate but definitely inappropriate age. Simple enough work, but my fingers had a different agenda. Typos, misspellings, and homonyms appeared. Familiar phrases ever so slightly off. Shades of Hortense! Had my fingers forgotten the layout of the keyboard? Protesting this project made of scraps? They preferred the small seaside town.

I paced through the apartment as if taking inventory, putting errant things in place. Restoring order may be the tangible expression of panic, but it's also the remedy. I stared out at the night and checked on the river, always reliable. The squirrel hadn't appeared for a while but the nest was there—I'd grown careless about cleaning it up. It had come to seem a natural growth on the ledge, like the ivy of which it was made. My heart pulsed, craving action. Again I tried to type my notes, but hands and brain refused to cooperate, as if they'd never been properly introduced, as if I were one of the small boys wildly swinging a plastic bat.

On the desk was a letter from my editor, no longer Gretchen, alas. A couple of years after introducing me to Ev at that book party, she'd joined a group of radical activists bound for Central America and stayed. Somewhere in Guatemala, she was teaching children to read. The letter slipped through my fingers to the floor. I picked it up and gripped it firmly with both hands. He'd had no luck reaching me by phone, he wrote, and politely chided my not using the answering machine. What about lunch someday soon? Oh, and he was enclosing the galleys of a hot new novel of disaffected, coke-snorting youth, hoping I'd supply some words of praise to help sell it. How was my work progressing, by the way?

It would be politic, to say the least, to reply. Keep the show going. Grace once mentioned a performance artist who sent his friends post-cards announcing what time he got up each morning, and occasional telegrams saying, "I am still alive." After a while these were collected and hung in a gallery, making a statement of sorts. A document.

Dear Colin, Am I correct in interpreting your six-month silence as a faint brushoff, a sign that my stock is sinking, or am I being oversensitive? I knew a man once who used to say I was very touchy, but never mind. Yes, probably you were on vacation, or in a meeting. . . .

No, no, no, that would never do. What's gotten into you, Laura? Delete.

Dear Colin, Yes, I'm starting a novel. I do appreciate your interest, but in all honesty, I suspect it's not going to be any more "commercial" than the last. Probably less so. At least with the way it's shaping up I can't see . . .

Out of control. Is this what Hortense meant when she said she couldn't sew properly? Delete, and fast.

Dear Colin, Yes indeed, there's a new book in the works. And what a blockbuster it will be! Victorian neurasthenia, origins ambiguous. Or call it immune-system breakdown, sign of the times. Action-packed thrills on every page: fevers, vertigo, muscle aches. Long walks along bodies of water. Oh, yes, and a love triangle. Well, not exactly a triangle but something or other. And much, much more. Maybe not quite blockbuster material, come to think of it. Maybe a trifle self-involved, as my late husband used to say, if that isn't an oxymoron . . .

The poor computer was perplexed. Are you sure you wish to delete? it kept asking. You are deleting more than can be retrieved. Well, yes, I've made that mistake before. I took pity on it and got a grip on my wayward fingers.

Dear Colin, I'm sorry I missed your calls. Yes, I'd love to have lunch but I'm very tied up with work at the moment. How about in a month or two, when I've gotten things organized. I'll give you a call then, and look forward to seeing you. Warmly, Laura. P.S. The galleys look intriguing—I'll have a look as soon as I can.

There. An impeccable performance. So lifelike, you could hardly call it a metaphor. Simply the cry we all utter behind each small, ritual inter-change. "I am still alive."

Save. Print. Bed.

I haven't made it to the Tai Chi class since I returned from the Cape, but I'll get there this morning no matter what. I wake early to allow time for the somnambulistic rites. Raising shades, opening windows, check-ing the squirrel's empty bed and greeting the river, this cool, crisp morning streaked by silver light with lime-green patches like splashes of Pernod.

Going down the hill to the park I meet Grace, looking morose. "Hi. How's your dental performance shaping up? I hope I didn't miss it while I was away."

"Don't worry," she mutters. "It's off."

"Really? That's too bad. What happened?"

"The dentist made a pass at me."

"Oh, for Chrissakes. I thought you knew him. He was interested in the project, wasn't he?"

"Yeah, well, I see what he was interested in. I don't know him that well—I've seen him maybe three or four times. And he did it in such a canny way, too. Yuck."

"During the root canal work?"

"No, it wasn't a regular visit. I stopped in to pick up some insurance form. Just as I was leaving, at the door, he bent over fast and kissed me on the lips and cupped my breast with his hand. The hand that wasn't holding the doorknob. I swear, it was so quick I couldn't do a thing. In an instant he had the door open and there I was facing a waiting room full of people."

"Couldn't you make a scene?"

"Who would believe me? He'd say I was a hysterical woman. Anyway, it's hard to make a scene when you're flabbergasted. Before I could even grasp it, it was over. A guy in his sixties, married. Grandchildren, I bet."

"Did he have his mouth open or closed?"

"I don't remember. Partly open, I guess."

"Did he press his body against you?"

"No, I don't think so. What is this anyway, Laura? The Spanish Inquisition?"

"Sorry. It's too bad about your idea."

"I'll have another idea. There's no shortage of ideas. More important at the moment is my teeth."

"Why don't you make some kind of complaint? Tell the insurance company. Or the dentists' association."

"Are you kidding? They'd laugh. No, no complaints whatsoever. It's not like I'm scarred for life or anything. And you know how those bureaucracies work—I'd be embroiled forever. I should have told him, Doc, I'm a dyke. That might have scared him off. Or I wonder if I could have used Tai Chi. What do you think the teacher would say? Yield and be soft? Imagine where that would get me!"

"I somehow don't think that's the sort of situation the old masters had in mind."

"No," says Grace. "He says they were fearless in the face of ferocity. But the dentist wasn't what I'd call ferocious."

"No. Oh, that reminds me. I went to the Fauves show at the Met the other day and thought of you. What you said about museums not being the right place to show art. I thought I'd wandered into a suburban shopping mall. I tell her about the woman in search of a maid who could serve as well as cook.

"Well, those women have a right to look at paintings, too. That would be okay, to hang work in shopping malls. The paintings could be part of daily life, next to the Taco Bell place or the merry-go-round. Or between the ATM machine and the ice-cream bar. In the Middle Ages the art was in the cathedrals, which were gathering places, and you'd see it whenever you passed through. Of course that was a holy atmosphere, but nowadays shopping malls are holy, so it comes to the same thing. Or else hang them in the subway. That would be ideal. Other countries have art in the subways."

"It would certainly look better than ads for acne, warts, and anal fissures." We've reached the park now and can see the others standing around in clusters, waiting.

Grace shakes her head sadly. "They should think of those ads as our public art, then see if the Moral Majority would make a stink. Or if the NEA would fund them, not that those guys need funding. Listen, twenty-odd years ago there were these hordes of hippie couples coming to the museums in their tie-dyed uniforms with babies on their backs and toddlers trailing with sticky lollipops. They'd put the kid in front of a Picasso and say, So, Jason, what do you think of that? And the father would whip out a notebook to preserve Jason's opinion for posterity. Meanwhile people are standing there trying to get a peek at the painting. So, is that any different from busloads of suburbanites getting culture?"

"Maybe not. I was in school back then. That all seemed very exotic and free."

"Yeah, well, I dropped out," says Grace. "I happened to be one of those counterculture types with the sticky kid holding my hand. But even then I knew that parading through those huge overheated rooms with one great picture after another lined up on the white walls was not the way. People get the idea that art has to do with self-improvement, you know, take your regular doses, like vitamins. And now, between the cards on the wall and the tapes you plug in your ears that tell you what to think, how can you see or feel anything? Those tapes should be bombed out of existence."

I've never heard Grace so irritable. "How many kids do you have?"

"Just the one."

"Where is he? Or she?"

"He. Don't ask. He's a schoolteacher in Memphis. He married a born-again Christian and he became one, too. It's his personal backlash, my punishment for giving him a disorderly childhood. What did I know? I thought he'd be a free spirit. He thinks I'm a disgrace, my work, the fact that I live with a woman, everything about me. You know, I think he'd prefer it if I were really militant, heavily into gay rights and stuff. Then I'd have a kind of religion. He could relate to that. This way, he thinks I'm just perverse. I've told him it's not that I didn't like men per se. I had my share. Only after a while I just couldn't take all the shit that goes along with it."

"I don't suppose he appreciated that."

"No."

"But I know what you mean. I've thought the same thing. Believe me, I've often considered . . ."

"It's not something you consider, Laura. You just find yourself doing it."

"I guess I never met anyone who's my type."

"Why, what's your type? Oh, don't get alarmed, I'm happy with Irene. I'm just curious."

"My type? Big shoulders, hairy chest, scratchy cheeks . . ."

"Uh-huh." She nods as we take our places in the assembling group. "I can see your problem. But I'll keep my eyes open. You never know."

"Good morning," the teacher says. "Continue."

"He could change," I whisper halfheartedly.

"He'd have to," Grace whispers back, "because I can't."

Then it's business as usual. Relax, sink, keep the breath thin, long, quiet and slow. Spine straight—it's the Pillar of Heaven. Joints loose. Feel the weight of the air, feel the arms encircling the ball of energy. Like Mount Lu and the River Che, nothing much.

"In the olden days," he says, as he has said often before, "the masters used to teach at the shore of a lake. The students would raise their arms and with the invisible strings at their fingertips pull up the energy of the water. When the water level began rising, ha ha, they knew they were doing Tai Chi. Here we have the river. See what you can do." He glances in my direction and the interpreter's gaze follows along. "A parable, Laura."

"Ha ha," I reply. Could the interpreter do all this by himself, maybe? Surely he knows the images and parables after so much translation. Unless the teacher's presence and voice are needed for the efficacy of the words. Is there an original that the teacher translates from?

We do the arm-raising movement five, ten, fifteen times—why keep track? We've done it many times before. We know the repetitions are a test of endurance, and by now we've mastered the unspoken secret of endurance, which is not to long for the test to be over. The teacher himself has no sense of time, or I should say feels no pressure about time, though the lessons begin unfailingly at the appointed moment and end exactly an hour later. How he manages this is unclear. Perhaps he goes by the progress of the sun, scaling the sky from the east or heading down to rest overnight in the river.

"All right, enough. Now we'll do a little exercise. Rooting the feet."

We've done this little exercise before. We stand with one foot forward and the other slightly behind and pointed outward, like fourth position in ballet. We place all our weight on the front leg for two or three minutes, then switch to the back leg. Very simple, back and forth for an eternity. The faint of heart, or of leg (in Chinese medicine their strength is interdependent, linked by the circulation), drop out quickly. I endure out of pride and habit, though this may well cost today's quota of energy.

"If you do this for a few minutes each day, growing your root deep into the earth, nothing will throw you off balance."

He calls me over to do push hands with Marvin, who seems preoccupied. Maybe video rentals are in a slump. He teeters off balance again and again. The teacher lectures him about adhering. To me he says, "I see you're listening to him."

"I don't know why it's happening. I'm not even trying."

"Not trying is good. But something is different," he insists. "You've started to listen. To listen." He says those last two words in English and ears perk up all around: What's going on here—the teacher spoke in English!

He fixes me with a penetrating look. Of course. "You're right, actually. I have been listening."

He's satisfied. I've given the correct answer.

Afterward, the students sit or lie on the grass, limp, the two stock-brokers resting their heads on their attaché cases. The teacher comes over to ask, through the interpreter, how I enjoyed my vacation. I'm glad to see that at least he acknowledges my words directly, without having them translated.

"Have you seen the woman I suggested? Carol?"

I always forget she's only human and has an ordinary name.

"Oh, yes, thanks again. You did get my note? That was very kind of you."

"Is she helping?"

"I think so. At least I feel better for a couple of days after I see her. She's a bit of a witch, isn't she?" Carol the Witch.

"A wise woman."

"That's what I meant. A good witch. Can she make the waters rise?"

"Yes, I think she can. It's nice to have you back, Laura."

"Thank you." I look the interpreter squarely in the eye. "Nice to see you again, too." An experiment.

He nods blandly as they turn to leave. Has he nothing to say for himself?

"Laura? You'll never guess what happened with my notebook. Just listen to this. I took your advice and called the MTA but no luck, and then one day—"

"Joyce, could you hang on just a minute? I want to turn on the light and find a cigarette."

"Oh, God. Smoking. With the way you feel . . ." The liquid voice on the phone congealed in disapproval. "I only smoke one cigarette a day. There's no reason you can't do the same."

"You're right, I'll do that. Wait just a second. Okay."

"I'm sorry if I woke you. It's only nine-thirty. You usually stay up late."

"It's fine. I was up." Lying in bed with the moon out my window, I was off on a trail of speculation in the thicket between waking and sleep. What would it feel like to live this way forever? Never to walk fast again, never again to run for a bus or spring out of a chair or dance (raucously with Q. or sedately with anyone else)? Never to glide easily through space, always to be swimming in air. Always to calculate, then assemble the energy needed. If there were reincarnation, I'd do best returning as a tree. I could stay rooted in place century after century, bare or lush as the climate dictated, learning the tides of the upper air, willingly enduring sun, wind, rain, so long as I needn't budge.

"So what were you doing, sitting in the dark?"

"Just thinking."

"What about?" Joyce through and through. Gathering data from her informants.

"About smoking, Joyce. About how nice it was when we could smoke with impunity. So what happened?"

"I couldn't get resigned to losing it, not only because of the notes but because Lizzie gave me that book for my birthday last year. She got it when she was in Siena—they make beautiful paper in Italy, beautiful designs and textures. Anyway, I called the lost-and-found and got this charming man on the other end. We had such a nice talk. It turned out his son-in-law is an anthropologist, too, and is in West Africa for two years, so he understood, I mean the MTA man did, how important the notebook was. He told me how he missed his daughter and grandson and kept bemoaning the way young people travel constantly nowadays. He longed for the old days when families stayed close to home. I could've told him there were really never such days, there've always been migrations though not always by the same groups, but I left him with his illusions. Well, with all that talk, he still didn't have the notebook, so I was very disappointed, as you can imagine. But then the other day I happened to get on the Broadway bus around the time we did on that fateful day, noon, and guess what? The driver was the same one as when I lost the book."

"Really? I didn't even notice what he looked like."

"She, not he. That's why I noticed. A small dark woman, about in her mid-thirties, with her hair in a braid."

"It's amazing you remembered."

"I got on the bus before you, so I had a chance to look around. But I do tend to remember people. It's a habit, from being in the field. So I asked her about it. You'll never believe this, Laura, but the woman had my notebook. She found it at the end of her shift and left it in her locker down at MTA headquarters. She said to call her there at six and describe it to her. Well, I ask you, how many people would be carrying around a notebook exactly like that one, with the Italian floral pattern. But I suppose they have their procedures. . . . Anyhow, I said not a word, I didn't want to push my luck. I told her I remembered her because you don't see that many women driving buses. She said it wasn't easy to get the job. They make you go through so much training—I must say you wouldn't think it from the way most of them drive. She's Mexican, and before this she worked on a farm in California, driving a tractor, she told me, so she's used to handling heavy vehicles—"

That was the last I heard. I was listening, I was even visualizing as Joyce spoke. Too well. In my visions the small dark Mexican woman climbed down from the bus driver's seat to clear a path in the underbrush of memory. I traipsed off behind her, and when I reached the end of the path I dug a hole and sank in.

The trail she led me through began in Penn Station, four years ago. I was meeting Q. He was perpetually in transit, always disembarking. The Metroliner, that day, after settling his father in a Washington hospital.

Why don't we have lunch right around here? I suggested. I know a place.

He peered in and said, Laura, my love, this is one of those yuppie places I cannot abide. Do you mind if we go elsewhere?

No, wherever you like. But your suitcase?

I can manage. It's light. You're looking splendid.

And you too, I said.

That was unusual. Lately he'd been looking haggard. When he wasn't sleeping enough or eating right, when he was working too hard or ravaged by love, his shoulders drooped and the hollows in his cheeks grew shadowy, until he resembled a medieval saint carved in stone. Today he stood up straight and his hair was becalmed, almost long enough to gather into a little ponytail like Jilly's motorcycle boyfriend, Jeff. The mustache, yes, I think so. He was grayer, but thank goodness would never look distinguished. No, rather the aging outlaw who'd seen plenty of hand-to-hand combat—nerves of steel, heart of gold. Not a mean bone in his body. Sure. Could he help it if the effects were virulent?

We walked more than half a mile before finding a place that suited him, but I didn't mind. We had a history of indulgence. Hadn't he spent many an afternoon, long ago, listening to me hopelessly recite lines, then wandering up and down Eighth Street for shopping therapy? He finally fixed on a cheap Mexican restaurant on a shabby side street. Two small rooms, both empty. We sat in the inner room, away from the door. Checkered tablecloths, dinky metal chairs, green leather banquettes. Posters of slinky matadors waving red cloths at bulls, of sultry señoritas in ruffled V-necked gowns. Linoleum tiles on the floor and red café curtains hanging from tarnished brass rings. Q. was in an exuberant mood, casting his spell. Beaming on everything, especially on me.

And because of his visible beam and mine in response, the waitress or proprietor—hostess, really, for she welcomed us as graciously as if it were her home—assumed we were lovers, which at that juncture we technically were not, or lovers only in spirit. I read somewhere that experienced waitresses can always tell the nature of their customers' relations. She was a short, sturdy, honey-skinned Mexican woman neither young nor old, wearing a plain black dress and white apron, not beautiful but emitting a benign glow, an allusion to the idea of beauty. Her presence was evocative, like those ancient statues of goddesses recently rediscovered and prized: squat women with inscrutable but comforting faces and abundant breasts and hips, who seem to have grown from the earth like palpitating, fruit-bearing plants. She called us Señor and Señora and smiled down at us knowingly, with the wry amusement bestowed on couples who are blatantly, comically in love, enjoying a rendezvous. Did we truly look that way? It was an easy pose for us to fall into; once it had been reflexive.

She cooked everything herself, she said, recommending what was best. Q. engaged her in detailed discussion of the menu, and in her resonant voice, the names of the common dishes became archetypal, Platonic ideals of Mexican foods. I was intending to eat very little, keeping my participation minimal and my stance remote, for safety's sake. But Q.

urged me to eat and I succumbed. The food arrived, steaming and aromatic. We bit into it. Home-cooked and succulent as our hostess had promised.

Mmm isn't this nice! said Q. Isn't this better than one of those awful yuppie places?

I had to agree.

We talked, bringing each other up to date. There was a lot to say, for it had been a while since the last time, perhaps there'd even been a quarrel, I can't remember. But we carefully skirted the subjects of my husband and of Q.'s romances.

Suddenly Q. put down his glass and said, I have sometimes thought that our relationship is like one of those old Hasidic tales, where I go looking and looking all over the world for something that's right there before my eyes.

I've often told you that in one way or another. You don't need to go to a Hasidic tale. Oh, what a fool you are.

Yes, perhaps you're right.

One of Q.'s virtues is that he absorbs such insults without anger or defensiveness, as if they're simple observations about the weather. The underside of this virtue is a certain patronizing: he knows words are my only tools, so he won't protest my using them.

Perhaps you're right, he said. But as I've said before, I can't help what I do.

Of course people can help what they do, I replied evenly. That's what civilization is all about.

He tilted his head and frowned as if to say, So much for civilization.

The trouble, I mused aloud, was way back. (It was the food, so warm and spicy, loosening my tongue.) Not when I got married, but before that. Not when you didn't leave Susan, as I used to think, but even before. The trouble was that at the time you loved me you didn't really want love but a way out. I was your tunnel to freedom. You dug your way through me. You're still digging.

Loved you! Q. burst out. Loved you! *Ma cosa stai dicendo?* What are you saying, Laura, as if it's past? I still love you and always will.

Ah! My frail efforts to keep things—Q.—at a distance collapsed. He loved me and always would. True, they were words that came trippingly off the tongue, especially of one who'd uttered them so often in costume, behind footlights. But I knew my Q. He had an air of authenticity. Perhaps only for the moment, in this enchanted little dive, but how permanent was anything? He loved me. And I? Could I call "love" the sulky feeling I kept for him, locked in a drear chamber in the vicinity of my heart like a chained attack dog drugged by time and disillusion, rendered harmless, dormant? While it slept in chains I carried on my life well enough. I could never get rid of the dog—that was too much to hope for, you never completely get rid of anything organic that once lodged in you—but it might well sleep forever. If nudged awake, though, it could yank on its chain and spring up with all the old ferocity, baring its pointy teeth.

I tried to eat my burrito as if nothing were happening, but with each swallow I felt the chain shifting, its links softly clanking as the dog stirred.

As if alerted by Q.'s outburst, the fertility goddess came over to ask how everything was. Q. praised the food; she had fulfilled her covenant of a bountiful harvest. She brought us more beer and said how pleased she was to have us in her restaurant, and how lucky Q. was to be with so beautiful a woman. He nodded abstractly. Surface beauty was not our issue.

You love me, I repeated at last. Loved me, love me. I don't know what to make of it. Sounds like a game or a riddle.

Q. stared in surprise. I can't see anything puzzling, he said. It's what I've always told you. You're a married woman, *cara*. Do you expect me to be the faithful lover of a married woman living in another time zone? You've never mentioned leaving him. Look, Laura, let's order something more to eat. I'm suddenly ravenous. I had no breakfast. There was nothing decent in my father's house—I cleaned out the fridge because he'll be in the hospital a few weeks—and the train was so crowded I couldn't fight my way to the snack bar.

It was a long lunch. Our personal Ceres kept bringing food while we talked about our love. I felt the dog grunting awake, uncurling his stiff limbs. He wanted food, too. He'd been asleep for so long that he was voracious. He wanted hope and agitation. Turbulent feeling was what nourished him best. Pleasure or pain, it didn't much matter. It was emotional foreplay that he craved.

With the spices on my tongue, I talked. I told Q. things I'd never told him before, or never as intensely as I felt them. What he had meant to me all those years ago. How it had been when he vanished after I sent him away, the door closing so gently, a muted clicking into place. And as I heard the words forced out, the dog's hungers translated into speech, I thought maybe it was my great error not to have spoken them before. Maybe, like a woman, Q. needed to be seduced and held by words. He was listening intently. He was more of a woman than I'd thought.

The trouble with you, he said ever so kindly, is that you are too proud. Or reticent, or something. You never told me what you were suffering or how much you felt. You hid it in anger. You remember the awful things you said. *Arrivederci e basta*. You threw me out. You have no idea what women do. They tear their hair and scream and implore. Not just women. Men, too. When I was twenty years old and my girlfriend dropped me, first I banged on her door for an hour, then I stood in the shower and bawled at the top of my lungs and jerked off for all I was worth. I had the water running so no one would hear. You don't do that.

I should hope not. But it doesn't mean I don't have the same feelings. What an image. You never told me that before.

Well, it's not something I like to remember. Don't go telling anyone.

I suppose I can't help what I do any more than you can. You know what they say about narcissists? When you love one, I mean? My cousin Joyce told me, she knows all about psychology. Give them a hard time but never threaten to stop loving them. Do you think that's good advice?

Yes, said Q. That is very astute.

So you're saying I fucked up?

Don't take it personally, love. Everyone does, with me.

Q.'s face was suddenly so bare and ragged that I almost reached out to smooth away the lines with my fingers. There was a long pause, an impasse of pain. He drained his beer and grinned sadly. We're so close to the bone, he said. It's all so raw.

So if you love me, now what? What happens next?

Here? he said, gazing around at the bullfighters and señoritas on the walls. What can happen here? Under the watchful eye of Isis or whoever she is?

You know what I mean, I said. You throw everything into turmoil, then get on a plane and leave me with the mess.

But how could he know what I meant? That I was thinking we might begin all over from this raw but exhilarating place. Which suitcases and books should I take? I'd fill out those little change-of-address cards from the post office. Could I stand his noise, his early rising, his housewifely love of order? How much would Ev miss me? Passionately, tenderly, moderately, not at all, as French children chant, plucking the petals off daisies. But I said none of this. I waited.

Well, before we do anything let's have coffee, Q. said, and the woman appeared promptly, with prescience.

Thank you so much. Wonderful food. And that coffee smells good, he told her. So, Laura, I'm staying at Peter's. Do you want to come back there with me?

Our hostess saw us to the door. She wished us well as though giving her blessing before a perilous journey, and as a matter of fact we decided the subway would be quicker than a cab in midtown. Amid the dirt-streaked tiles and debris, the hunched addicts and beggars holding out Styrofoam cups, we walked hurriedly, holding hands, frightened of what we had come to. Q. opened the apartment door and we fell against each other. He dropped his suitcase and his hand was under my skirt in one motion.

Please close the door, I said.

Oh, I forgot.

Is anyone home?

I hope not. God, it's been a long time, Laura.

Wait a minute, you're strangling me. It doesn't open like that.

He pulled back, holding my hand as in a dance, and gave an antic bow, an Elizabethan courtier's bow. I await your pleasure, he said.

By the time the sun was slanting down toward the river I had had my fill of him. The dog nestled back in his chamber in the vicinity of my heart, not drugged but sinking into a sweet, snug sleep.

And now? I thought. Do I await his pleasure? Lying warm in his arms, I knew. We'd continue our meetings, parting miserable or parting, as today, ecstatic, full of mindless hope, wild as weather. Yes, we'd think in our separate ways, perhaps we were fated to be together. Yet somehow, perversely defying fate, we weren't. Lying in his arms, I was warmed also by a thrill of triumph. Whatever else, I had shown him the truth. Shown myself, too. He had a poor memory, short and selective. He would remember it only until the next event to engage his attention—phoning his father, seeing Peter and Arthur when they came home. Our lunch and our truth would recede to a remote cranny in his mind. But it would be there.

What a blow, early this summer, when he suggested going back to that restaurant where so much—and so little—had happened. Had he forgotten utterly? Or did he want to make it happen again? Didn't he know such things never happen twice in the same way? To attempt it again would be to write over it, as the computers say. !Attention! If you continue, your experience will be overwritten! Do you wish to continue? No, no, never back there.

I WOKE WITH THE RECEIVER ON MY LAP, emptied of Joyce's voice, the curly cord limp on the sheet. If only I'd drifted off like this when Hortense told me about the three worst years of her life, or even better, during Q.'s tale of Nadine, the sexual savage from El Paso.

The moon was gone from my window, risen high above the roof. I must have slept for nearly two hours. Every joint and muscle whined, an aching cacophony. I wandered around the dark apartment to get unknotted. At the front window, straining to make out the river, I felt a vibration. That eerie feeling that you're not alone. Could it be? Yes, who else would crouch in exactly the curve I knew so well, the hairs of his tail stirring and reflected in the window pane: wearier, sicker, oblivious to my taps on the screen. "Love calls us to the things of this world," a poet wrote. But the squirrel no longer heard or heeded the call. Perhaps, like a saint or a Buddhist monk, he had passed beyond desiring the things of this world. *Maya*, illusion, nothing. He was curled up in his nest like a young bird. By tomorrow morning he'd surely be dead. The corpse, the orange gloves, the brush and dustpan, the trip to the basement with the bag oozing the stench of death.

Meanwhile, if I didn't call Joyce back she'd have the police at my door, their sirens wailing for me this time.

"I'm really sorry, Joyce. Something made me drift off and the next thing I knew, I was asleep. I mean, the next thing I knew, I woke up."

"Thank God you weren't murdered in your bed. The phone was off the hook, the operator said. I nearly called the police, but Lizzie always tells me to lighten up, so I controlled myself and figured I would have heard any struggle."

"Well, you can relax. So what happened with the Mexican bus driver? I was left hanging. Unless it's too late and you're in bed."

"Not at all. This is a good time. I'm here in my study, totally naked. I'm feeling great, especially now that I know you're okay. I just took a bath with Vitabath bubbles. The room is dim and I'm burning a stick of incense. I had my first and last cigarette of the day in the tub, listening to Billie Holiday, and before I go to bed I'll do the *Times* crossword puzzle. An evening of bliss. It almost beats sex."

"Where's Roger?"

"Roger is sleeping. Roger is a morning person. You know how men have their favorite hours, and what can we do?"

Ev was a night person. Q. was an afternoon person. Unless afternoons are in the nature of love affairs. Had we lived together for a long spell he might have settled into a more conventional routine.

"Frankly," Joyce added, "at the moment I'm more involved in Lizzie's sex life than my own. Not that I choose to be, I assure you, but she tells me. We never told our parents in such vivid detail, did we? She tells me, but she doesn't want to hear what I have to say. Then what is she telling me for, I'd like to know? You know how Lizzie's been running around with boys and men since she was thirteen years old? Love is just one chapter out of many, I keep telling her. But she thinks it's the name of the book. What do you think? Laura, are you there?"

"Yes, yes, I'm here, Joyce. I don't know. I'll have to think that one over."

"Well, now, out of the blue, she wants to settle down. She's gone and gotten involved with a man who's divorced and has a ten-year-old daughter. They're madly in love, she says, they talk about marriage, but he doesn't want any more children and she wants babies. Mad for babies, suddenly. Knowing Lizzie, I could wind up taking care of it. I could always bring it to Africa, to the Tsumati. They don't mind extra babies. They're considered community assets."

"Joyce, the notebook," I prodded. "The Mexican woman who moves heavy vehicles."

"Oh, yes. So I called her and described the notebook. Naturally the one she had was mine. I never asked why she kept it in her locker instead of bringing it to the lost-and-found. Why take chances? Probably she forgot. Anyhow, she was in a hurry to get home and said to call again at night to arrange when to meet. So I did. I would have done anything she said. She's bringing up two kids on her own in the Bronx, scraping by on her bus driver's salary. She must be a strong woman. Carmen, her name is. We had a long talk about this and that, raising children, mostly. I even told her about Lizzie, because it's weighing on my mind so. Carmen said any man who doesn't want to have children with the woman he loves is no damn good, but I realize that's just her opinion. I don't really know where she's coming from. . . ."

"Joyce! Joyce, you astonish me sometimes. This Carmen is a complete stranger. She may know how to maneuver heavy vehicles but she's hardly an expert on Lizzie's future."

"Okay, don't scold me, Laura. You know I can't bear to be scolded. I guess I can't contain myself. There's no harm done, is there? After all that, we arranged to meet on the bus today at noon. They run on a schedule, though you'd never know it. I went out this morning and got her a little gift, a beautiful alabaster egg, and wrote her a card to go with it."

Joyce's cards are the stuff of legend. She chooses handsome reproductions of paintings, extravagant paintings, Caravaggio, Fragonard, El Greco, and writes with a thick-nibbed black pen, every letter perfectly formed to make certain her message gets across, every line of script as regular as a child's drawing of ocean waves. Classically legible. She would have won the approval of the Outer Cape's Handwriting Committee. And yet the communiqués themselves are florid. Never one for minimalism, Joyce loves all adorning accretions of punctuation: hyphens, commas, and exclamation points wherever feasible. She labels the pages of her cards with a numeral and period, and draws an arrow at the bottom of page 1., along with "continued" in parentheses, to ensure that not a word or sequence will be missed. She shuns abbreviation and writes out the words Street and Avenue on the envelope, as well as New York, New York. Everything conceivable is done to enhance the reading experience and ward off the possibility that life is just not all that much.

Beyond birthdays, holidays, or visitations of good fortune, she can make an occasion out of anything. "Dear Laura, What a nice surprise, running into you in Urban Outfitters yesterday. I realized how long it's been. You were looking radiant. . . ." That was after an exquisite afternoon in bed with Q. in Peter's apartment, a while after I lost the baby. Let's run away, he kept murmuring. To an island with a beach. All islands have beaches, silly, I whispered in his ear. Would you, Laura? Can you see yourself doing that? Oh, I can see it very well, I said. I'd get to the airport with my bags and you'd have forgotten all about it. I'll tell you what. Call me when you have the tickets in your hand. Meanwhile . . . Q. looked down at me and sighed. Meanwhile, he said, you be the island and I'll be the explorer.

I'd almost drifted off again. "So right at noon," Joyce was saying, "the bus pulled up and sure enough, there was my precious book, exactly as I last saw it! I stroked it. I pressed it to my bosom. Carmen was very touched. She couldn't open the gift right then because she was driving, but maybe she'll call. So how do you like that, Laura? My notebook is back!"

"I like it. I like it a lot." I also understood her relief better than she could know.

"You're very patient to bear with me. How are you feeling? I'm almost afraid to ask, you don't seem to like it. . . ."

"Fine, thanks. Pretty good." Anything to avoid another unsolicited opinion. Sugar, my dentist claims the universal culprit. Tests show women who get this are highly suggestible, the psychiatrist upstairs volunteered when he found me swaying dizzily at the mailboxes. Dr. Atkins, my mother keeps urging over the phone.

Besides, my ailment per se no longer interests me. It's tolerable only as I keep finding metaphors and stories to wrap it in. These I enter one by one in the composition book—a patchwork stitched together by touch, unruly as the capes of the color-blind cape-maker—risking my fortunes, as he did, on the hope that it will make a garment against the elements.

Past Labor Day and the temperature back in the nineties, the river shining with reflected heat. Dusk was coming down like soft mosquito netting. From my window, the benches lining the Drive looked inviting. If I could transport my body with a click of the heels and a wish, I'd sit under the trees alongside the old people taking the air, watching the dripping joggers in disbelief and the few children still languidly playing on the grass. But I was achy and feverish, inert; the desire refused to blossom into the act.

As the precious light slid slowly down, I tried conjuring up an image of myself sitting outside gazing at the river. And my visualizing practice paid off: a phantom me appeared on a bench, yet the real me still refused to move, rooted at the French doors where once a rat had skittered past and I'd hardly blinked, because of Q.'s sustaining voice on the phone.

The traffic patterns on the Drive below were mesmerizing. It's a two-way street divided by a strip of cobbled pavement barely wide enough for a pedestrian caught between zooming cars on either side. They rush toward the bridge to escape the city as though this undulating, leafy, river-hugging stretch graced with old stone buildings were one of their freeways. At this hour, though, traffic was sparse, a trickle of cars on the voyage out and even fewer headed downtown. The occasional bus lumbered by, usually without stopping; the occasional biker in slow motion, subdued by the heat.

Suddenly, without my thinking, the impulses coalesced and this alien body jerked into motion. Sandals, keys, mugger money, and I was at the door—an electronic toy guided by remote control.

"Hi, Luke." He sat on a plastic lawn chair alongside his parked car, the last three fingers of his left hand wrapped in a bandage stained a brownish color. With him was Vernon, a younger, stockier super from around the corner. "What happened to your hand?"

"I was settin' over by the park eating my lunch and a squirrel come over and bit me."

"People like to feed them," Vernon remarked in a melodic West Indian accent. "They shouldn't. The squirrels get the idea they can come and eat out of your hand. Eat your hand, too."

"Have you seen a doctor?" I never thought I'd hear myself asking that. But squirrels were said to carry rabies. Luke must know. He was from rural Alabama; he knew more about animals than I did. In some parts of the South, I'd heard, they hunt squirrels and eat them.

Before he could reply, my downstairs neighbor, Helene, approached, dragging her loyal shopping cart. "What happened to your hand, Luke?" she demanded in her brisk way. She was taking his ailment far more seriously than she had taken mine. "Really? You must see a doctor for that. Some squirrels are rabid."

For an instant I thought she said some squirrels were rabbits. I had to deconstruct the phrase in my ear.

"I had a shot," said Luke patiently, to the relief of all.

"Why is your bandage that funny color?" I asked. "Is that old blood?"

"No, iodine. It's no big deal, Laura. I'm gonna live a long while yet, you'll see. The good Lord ain't ready for the likes of me."

"Some folks shoot squirrels," said Vernon, "and the Humane Society people don't like it. But to my way of thinking they've got the right idea."

"There was a sick one on my window ledge all summer," I said. "I had the hardest time getting rid of him—he made himself a little nest and every time I expected him to die there, he disappeared. But I think he's finally moved out."

Helene shrank back in disgust, and with good reason. She lived one floor below. Any creature evicted from my window ledge might well migrate to hers. Well, let her cringe. I still hadn't forgiven her for that schoolteacher's rebuke at the elevator three months ago.

"I wonder," I went on, "if it could have been my squirrel that bit you."

All three turned to me. Helene's face was a caricature of droll shock—raised eyebrows and parted lips; even her tight gray curls seemed to stiffen. Luke arched his neck in a pose of dry amusement. Heat's got her, I saw in their eyes.

"There's lots of squirrels," said Vernon gently, as if speaking to a slow child. "Hundreds around here. They breed like rabbits."

Rabbits? They breed madly, being rabid.

Luke grinned and winked at me. "And they all look alike, too."

At such moments he reminded me of Q. Possibly not even Q. could muster such ironic gallantry.

Another super appeared, a gangly white man whose blue uniform hung loosely from his bones. He was about to pass with a wave, when he caught sight of Luke's bandaged hand. "Hey, Luke. What's with the hand?"

"Yeah," said Luke wearily. "I was settin' over by the park keeping an eye on my car and eating my lunch and a squirrel come up, just like that, to get some food, and bites me."

"D'jou get a shot? They can be rabid." He pronounced it "ray-bid."

"Got me a shot, yeah."

Was it really such an absurd notion, about my squirrel? Had I driven him to vengeful acts against humanity?

We drifted off, leaving Luke to read his *Amsterdam News* and perhaps work out tomorrow's parking pattern, like a chess master. Sitting on a bench across the street, I relished the oncoming cool of evening, exactly as

I had envisioned from the window. A vision come true. A little triumph.

Down the block I spied Philip, the professor from next door whose wife and daughter had been sick last winter. He leaned into the window of a gypsy cab, talking exuberantly to the driver, the briefcase dangling from his hand making an odd contrast to his shorts and T-shirt. All at once his wife, Brenda, came darting from their building to run across the street, dodging traffic. How she ran—light, mercurial on sneakered feet, gliding compactly through the air. Did I ever run like that? She must have recovered from the mysterious disease. The daughter, too—no anxious mother would move so jubilantly.

Brenda joined him at the cab window. When the car drove off a moment later, they headed in my direction. How was I, they asked cheerily, and I told. Too tired to pretend.

"That's too bad." Philip turned to Brenda. "It sounds just like what you and Lisa had. It was really frightening to watch."

"Yes," Brenda said, "dreadful. I know how you must feel. But you'll get better."

She sounded very sure, so sure that I felt a bit better on the spot, and not quite so ashamed of my lassitude. "You certainly seem fine," I said. "I haven't seen you around in ages."

"Oh, yes, we both came back to life. But for a while there—" A dramatic moan. "We didn't know what was wrong and it seemed it would never go away. I thought, okay, my life was over, but I felt worse for Lisa because she'd hardly lived yet." She smiled and shook her head. "We'd lie around watching soap operas on TV and sometimes even that was too strenuous."

"Well, I'm not quite that bad."

"Believe me, you'll get better. It took us a few months. Sort of like a pregnancy, you know? The beginning is the pits, then you gradually pick up and feel more like yourself, only a trifle slow. I started going to work half days and Lisa went to school half days and we rested the other half. Little by little we worked our way back."

"You have no idea how encouraging that is. Some people really scare me, you wouldn't believe. . . . You didn't get injections of vitamin C by any chance, did you?"

"No, we just waited."

"Well, thanks, I mean it. It's a great help. I must tell you, when I saw you run across the street just now, I was thinking how energetic you looked and feeling envious."

"You'll be doing that soon. What it was, I was rushing to have a look at that nice cab driver before he went away."

"I left my briefcase in that cab this afternoon," said Philip, "and the driver found my name in it and called up and came all the way back to give it to me. Isn't that amazing? I had everything in there, lecture notes, student papers. I never thought I'd get it back."

"You're lucky," I said. "Something like that happened to me too, years ago. I lost some work in a taxi, an old journal I'd kept in college. I was frantic, but then the taxi company looked me up in the phone book and called. They didn't bring it the way yours did, though. I had to go to Brooklyn, the end of the subway line, to pick it up."

Q. went with me. He didn't want me going out there alone, he said, to who knew what kind of neighborhood. You outlanders always imagine the worst, I said. The place is right near Brooklyn College. I know the area. Well, I'll go anyway, he said. I want to make sure you don't lose it on the way back—I don't trust you. Besides, I've never seen a taxi depot, or whatever they call it. It could be useful some day.

On the train he told me, You see, Laura, you're fated to write this book. It's not just me urging you. Your subconscious can resist with every weapon it's got—what do you think losing it means?—but in the end you'll have to drop the acting and give yourself to it.

Years later, under the eye of the goddess in the Mexican restaurant, as the dog stirred from sleep and I forced out one truth after another, I said, You didn't want me traveling to the depths of Brooklyn by myself, you didn't trust me to write the book without you, but you didn't mind leaving me to live the rest of my life without you. Did you think that was any easier?

"When I got to the taxi place," I told Philip and Brenda, "I found this huge room with old wooden desks and half a dozen burly guys sitting on top of them, looking as if something was very funny. One of them said, 'So, you must be the writer.' I remember I was so embarrassed thinking maybe they'd read my sophomoric drafts. As if they cared! Anyway, I got it back."

And someday, playing a taxi driver, Q. would use the look and feel of that room and think of me. How could we exorcise each other, with so many details stored in the cells?

I guess I went on a bit too long. Brenda's body made small twitches of leave-taking. "Well, try to have faith that you'll get better, Laura. I looked a lot worse than you do and I got better."

I envisioned her lying languidly on a sofa in an old bathrobe, her Afro in disarray, her eyelids heavy, watching a soap opera and finally murmuring, No, turn it off, it's too much of a strain. I wished she would stay at my side indefinitely, repeating, You'll get better, at five-minute intervals. A taut, dark savior in running shorts.

"Laura, if you're going to be sitting here awhile, could I leave my briefcase with you? We were just going to do our evening run."

"Sure." They were off, slowly, then picking up speed, joining the sweaty parade, as the fiery sun was extinguished in the river leaving a trail of lavender smoke. Like a pregnancy? I couldn't say. I never got far enough, but I felt fine while it lasted. This was my fourth month; with luck I would be delivered of a book.

The oncoming cool felt good. I gave thanks, the sort of gratitude old people whose evenings were numbered might feel, the very people on the neighboring benches, some with paid companions: whatever our terrors and infirmities, for the moment it suffices to sit in the draining pinkish light, in the filtering cool, with the trees, the river, the sailboats aglow.

On the bench opposite sat a pair no younger than the others but different, not passed over into static anonymity, still in the process of becoming. Like a couple in love, they seemed, their bodies listing toward each other, eyes brightly rapt in a dialogue spiced with gestures and touches—listening, responding, listening again—a spontaneous, skilled *pas de deux*. Could it have been this way for fifty years? Or had they only just met, having divorced or buried earlier mates? Had they been happy with the others, too—willfully happy people—or had the others been preparation for this evident romance, the way Mona sees her patchy erotic past?

The man was tall and sinewy, with a burnished face, craggy nose and fine lips, his hair the pure white that looks soft as silk and strong as steel. He wore tan Bermuda shorts that showed veiny, muscled legs, and he held a cane. Not the newfangled chrome kind with ugly claws for balance, but a wooden cane with a curved handle. Through will or luck, he had ceded nothing essential to age. No withdrawal on his face. Even if his blood at this very moment was gathering to flood his brain and sweep him off to his long home, he was not offering valedictions.

The woman's girlish sandals were very like the pair I wore out fourteen years ago, walking off Q. as if he were a bad trip. Her tanned legs were admirable. (The legs are the last to go, my mother often said, looking down at her own with wry pleasure.) She had on a denim skirt and a loose white shirt, maybe one of his shirts—the collar had that starchy men's look. Her oval face was lively, the face of a sober young woman who lightened in spirit as she aged, though thin lines etched a dimension of wisdom. And her full lips had no sour downturn at the outer edges, so common in old people, signifying disappointment with the return on one's investment. In my father's family, we age first around the mouth. The lips narrow and sink at the corners in rancor, settling, day by day, into permanent brackets, so that a smile requires coaxing the drooping muscles. I'd seen the start of it, these last months, on my own lips, and would stand at the mirror forcing the corners up in an artificial smile. When I let go they slipped back down in the rancorous curve.

The old couple was so absorbed and alone, I might have been peering through the slatted blinds of their bedroom. Now and then they paused in their talk to glance at the kids on the grass. Not minding grandchildren, I was sure, or seeking easy sentiment. Registering life, taking in data. Ev and I grown old might have strolled along the Drive, too, even watched children at play, but not in such intimacy. We'd have looked like two solitaries who agreed to walk in step for company's sake. We'd never had that look of belonging unmistakably together. No. No party guest scanning the room and figuring out pairs would ever have matched us.

They got up—not creaking but calmly unfolding—and walked on hand in hand, the man setting the cane lightly down at every other step. Who were they? How did they do it? If not for their net of privacy, the invisible cords linking them (though unlike Grace's couple tied together, they were surely permitted to touch), I might have gone up and asked. How come you have what we all once wanted but learned the hard way is impossible, an illusion? How dare you show it?

The light was nearly gone when I handed Philip back his briefcase and went inside. Thanks to Brenda and the river, I was feeling slightly better. I even had feeling to spare.

"Peter, it's Laura," I said, settling into the chair with the phone. "I wanted to see how you were, and how Arthur's doing."

"He's about the same. Maybe a little weaker. Some days he's lucid. Right now he has an ingrown toenail that's bothering him."

"An ingrown toenail?"

"Yes, and he insists he wants a podiatrist to come over and take care of it. It's strange, he never saw a podiatrist in his life. Now he's fixated on this toenail. I get so harried, I can't think straight. Maybe I should find someone to come and treat it, though I doubt if any doctor would want to. Still, if it would relieve a minor pain . . . Does that strike you as absurd?"

"No, why not? If that's what he wants."

"He also has a cataract."

"Isn't he a little young for that?"

"Everything deteriorates faster with this illness."

"You're not thinking of a cataract operation at this point, Peter? I mean . . ."

"No, no, of course not. But one does begin to lose one's bearings. How are you feeling, by the way? All better, I trust?"

"Yes, thanks," I lied. Someday it might not be a lie.

"Have you heard from Quinn lately?" he asked.

"He called last month from Washington, visiting his father. He sounded fine. I should give him a call, I guess. I promised."

"I haven't heard a thing since he left, not that I expected to. You know Quinn. Out of sight, out of mind. He didn't use to be that way when he was married to Susan, at least not until the end. I oughtn't to complain, though. He was a tremendous help when I moved. I couldn't have done it without him."

"Yes, I know what you mean. Q. can be very useful. But as they say," I added breezily, "nobody's indispensable."

"I find Arthur indispensable."

"Of course. That was thoughtless. It's just a stupid cliché. Please give him my love, and let me know how—"

"He doesn't want a regular funeral service, he told me long ago. Just a few close friends. He has no family except a sister in London."

"If there's anything I can do to help . . . ," I said lamely.

"If you really mean it, there is something. I need people to cover for me in the store so I can tend to him. I can't afford to hire anyone else at the moment. Even a few hours a week would make a difference."

I couldn't hesitate. People really mean it, or they don't. "Sure. I don't know much about rare books, though."

"It doesn't matter. There's a full-time clerk who'll show you what to do. Just sound literate."

"Okay, tell me what days would be best."

After I hung up, I went to the window. I didn't expect to find him anymore, and he was so inert, I thought he was dead. (Rabies?) But when I knelt down I could see his back rising and falling ever so slightly, in a rapid rhythm. Small animals breathe very fast, Jilly told me when she had hamsters. This must be how mothers felt, checking on a sick infant. Still breathing? Thank God! Hanging on.

Something loosened in me. Let him be. Let him live here, even die here. He's chosen this place, he's made himself mine. I yield to the Tao of squirreldom, as the Tai Chi teacher might say. No more rubber gloves and paper bag and scissors for cutting away the tough-stemmed ivy. Not until I had to carry his body to the basement and stuff it in a black plastic bag to be tossed into the maw of the garbage truck that awakened me at six-thirty every other morning, chewing thunderously under my bedroom window, *fee, fi, fo, fum.*

With luck he might not die on my window ledge at all but curled beneath a tree in the park, or wherever squirrels ought to die. Odd that you never see their remains, the way you see dead pigeons on the streets, often flattened to two dimensions under the wheels of traffic and etched into the asphalt like fossils. Squirrels, no.

I knelt at the French doors like someone at prayer. A Taoist prayer, an affirmation of how things are: He is still alive, we are all still alive. He might even recover, it's not out of the question. If he's the one who bit Luke, there's some spirit in him. Maybe all he needs is to rest undisturbed, not having his bed destroyed each time he creeps off to forage for food.

Whatever his fate, I withdrew from it, leaving my window ledge to his discretion.

"So, what did you have this week?" The witch's greeting. "Did you get the vaginal infection?"

"No such luck. I've been having trouble sleeping. At night, that is. During the day I sleep fine. Some nights I woke every hour with my heart pounding and a weird kind of energy. I had to get up and move around."

"Sleep disorders. That's common when the immune system is off."

"I also kept breaking out in a sweat every so often. It felt like what my former editor described when she went through menopause. You're not going to cause menopause, are you? Because I'm far from ready."

"No, no," with a merry laugh. "There are ways to make you stop menstruating, but don't worry, I haven't gone near that. Let me see your tongue. Oh, it looks much better. Less heat. And your pulses?" She pressed her fingers into my inner forearm. "Have you had any alcohol lately?"

I gasped. Mona and I had met in another local café yesterday in our continuing quest to replace the Athena. I'd been in good spirits; during my insomnia I'd managed to type up everything in my notebook, making a nice stack of pages. When I paced around in the dark hours, I felt myself warming up to write. My mind moved nimbly, rubbing against the contours of words and phrases, shaping sentences, sound molding itself to syntax like clay on an armature. To celebrate I'd risked a glass of wine.

"How did you know?"

She smiled. "Oh, I can feel it in the liver pulses."

"You know, sometimes you really scare me."

"It's nothing special. Anyone could learn. It feels like you're doing better. Have you felt any different?"

"Yes, I must admit."

"Admit?"

"God, did I really say that? I hate to think what that might mean. Could I be adhering to it the way you adhere in Tai Chi?"

"No," she said firmly. "It's adhering to you. In any case, that's altogether the wrong image in this case."

"Yes, let's forget it before I get interested. The other day I walked six blocks without stopping. I'm not as tired as I used to be. Or not in the same way. It's not the kind of tiredness where I feel I'll topple over before I make it to the bed."

Or where I sink into the bed like a sack of sand. Not the kind of tiredness that feels beyond death.

"On the other hand, I'm dropping things more, the way I did at the beginning. Last Sunday I dropped the entire *New York Times* right on the street. It caused quite a scene. A few people came rushing to help before it blew away, including one very attractive man who I think owns a new Greek restaurant at the corner of . . . Well, anyway, that's not a good example, the Sunday Times is absurdly heavy, but other things, too. I've been helping out in a friend's bookstore and I drop the rare books. Also pencils, envelopes, keys."

"That's not surprising," she said, placing a needle in my bare stomach. When has she ever been surprised? "The way these viruses work is, they often go out the way they came in. As you get stronger, they can't find as many vulnerable areas to lodge in, so they look around desperately, so to speak, and try the old familiar paths they used when they first started in on you."

"Have you ever thought of writing poetry?" I asked.

"I used to as a teenager, it so happens. But I don't have a musical ear. I am writing a novel, though."

"About love."

"How did you know that?"

Ah, for once she's surprised. "Look at those needles," I said. "They're standing up straighter, aren't they? Remember you said that would happen when I was a little better?"

"Yes, they definitely are. There's a lot more chi there." She inserted another, and another. "But how did you know?"

"About writing," I told her, "I'm the witch. So bring me up to date on the rabbi. Have the spells been working?"

She hesitated. Her radiant face dimmed as she leaned down to twirl the needles. "I was having grave doubts, and now . . . He came over last Sunday. It wasn't a romantic date—I think he understood I wasn't getting into that unless he cleared up his situation. But we were having a nice time, talking about one thing and another, mildly flirting, you know how it is. Until he said something that disturbed me very much. I have a new kitten, she's so lovely, a white Siamese, and she was climbing all over us on the couch, so I very gently brushed her away to teach her not to climb on the furniture, and accidentally knocked her to the floor.

When he saw that, he said, Cats are like women, a little abuse goes a long way."

"Uh-oh," I said. "Uh-oh."

"Yes," the witch agreed, her mouth grim. "When I heard that, something turned over inside me. I withdrew, sort of curled up in a corner of myself, and he left pretty soon after. Do you know, the next day I was so sick—I haven't felt that sick in years. It was the realization that this is no good. He's really no good for me."

"I didn't think you ever got sick."

Again she looked surprised. "Me? I'm susceptible like everyone else. The only difference is, I stay in good shape, and when I feel something coming on I can usually head it off. I've got every kind of herb out there on the shelves. Actually I'm always trying them out to feel the effects, so I'll know what I'm letting people in for when I prescribe them. It's true, everyone responds differently, but I need to have some idea. It's only fair. Sometimes I'm not happy with what I find out and I have to look for other remedies."

She used her own organs as a medium, then, the way some artists paint their skins. Or the way actors like Q. use their bodies as instruments. In her kind of witchcraft, the viscera were the experimental field, through which nature's green bounty worked its charms.

"I can't imagine regular doctors doing what you do. It would never occur to them."

"You can hardly blame them, can you? Their techniques are so invasive, from surgery on down. . . . I wouldn't subject myself to any of that either, if I were a doctor."

"So what did you do as an antidote to the rabbi?"

"Well, Monday was my night for the AIDS clinic and I didn't know how I was going to get myself over here, I felt so rotten, but I knew I had to. Anyhow, it's always better, with that kind of misery, to get outside yourself. The first patient I saw was so scarred, his body looked so . . . mauled, that I sat here studying him, wondering where I could find an opening. And as I concentrated on how to approach him I suddenly felt better, so glad I had useful work to do in the world, and glad I hadn't gotten too involved with this rabbi, so that all I had from it was a day's sickness and a little misery but not years of anguish, which was what I had the last time I knew a man like that, when I was very young. After that relationship I married someone else, the French biologist I told you about—a quiet marriage, we were good companions, but it was hardly a wild passion. I think it took me the eight years of my marriage to . . . to kind of recover my balance after that man."

It was then that I told her all about Q. Everything I've set down earlier, pages and pages ago, about how I met him in the theatre and he urged me to write the first novel, and how he wouldn't leave Susan until it was too late and I couldn't trust him ever again, and how I lost the baby and blamed him but that wasn't his fault, and how he played Lear's faithful Kent and took good care of his own father and came to me after Ev was killed but the timing was wrong—all the years and years of him in my head and in my body. While I talked she removed the red-tipped needles and dropped them delicately, one by one, into the little plastic garbage can, then sat cross-legged on the mat with her hands folded, listening.

"However," I wound up. "However, about this rabbi. That's another story altogether. You could still have a fling with him if you really want to. You say you're very drawn to him. What's the harm, as long as you know exactly what you're doing and do it for fun without expecting anything, then end it when you've had enough. What I'm saying is, try using him for a change. A little exploitation goes a long way."

"You can't do that if you do my kind of work. It's not even a matter of principle. Just in practical terms . . . no."

"Why not?"

"Because the kind of energy I need, which is physical and flows through the body and into the hands, gets depleted very fast if you engage in a meaningless affair that gives you nothing except sex, which this would be. It's different with something that gives you real sustenance, like what you told me about, but the other, no. I can't afford the expenditure of energy. I need it for my work."

"The expense of spirit in a waste of shame, eh?"

"Exactly," said she.

A very literate witch indeed, and a translator as well, besides which, she's working on a novel, God help her.

"Carol," I said as I hugged her good-bye in the waiting room, "you're an inspiring witch and I love you."

"I love you, too, Laura. But I must tell you, you're really not a very good candidate for acupuncture."

I let go. "Why do you say that?"

"You don't have the patience for the symptoms."

I looked at the wall chart of the five vital organs and their corresponding elements, emotions, colors and weather, so I would not have to see her transform before my eyes into a nasty old crone.

"You're a pretty young witch, Carol. You have a lot to learn about patience."

"Well . . . See you next week, then?" Hesitantly.

"Yes."

Seven blocks without stopping. I walked them with Luke, who caught up with me on the Drive one breezy Saturday afternoon. The air was clear, the leaves crisp; before long they would start to turn.

Luke's hand was all healed. He showed me the scar, two tiny specks, dark against the skin, like a fragment of a Morse code message. He was on his way to get fluid for the power-steering mechanism of the Cadillac, he said. All the fluid had leaked out overnight.

"These cars. If it ain't one thing it's another. You got to mind them like babies. Turn your back one minute and they get themselves in trouble. Lord, I remember those times. . . . You never had none of your own, did you, Laura?"

"No, just my husband's."

"Well, you got a real fine little girl there. Your boyfriend gone, eh? Gave him his walking papers?"

I paused. On a bench sat the old couple I'd seen two weeks ago, still absorbed in talk, their bodies listing toward each other as before, legs crossed and feet nearly touching. They were more warmly dressed today, in sweaters and sneakers.

"He wasn't right for me," I said as we moved on.

"I could've told you that from the start, if you asked me. Your husband neither, not meaning no disrespect to the dead."

"That's possible."

"So here's a good-looking woman like you all by yourself."

I gave him back his own teasing grin. "There's nothing unusual about that. It happens all the time."

"Nah, you can't fool me. You ain't been the same these two years. You're waitin' for that other one to come back again."

"God Almighty, you notice everything, don't you? You're worse than the CIA."

"I got to notice. That's my job."

"Mine, too." A small girl on a bicycle wobbled past, her gray-haired father puffing as he ran along behind, clutching the back of the seat. "But it happens you're wrong. That's not what I'm waiting for. Anyway, he's been back."

"So what are you waiting for, then?" asked Luke.

"I haven't been feeling right for months. See, there's something you didn't notice. I hardly think about that stuff lately."

"I can't believe that, I mean that you don't think about it. What's troubling you? You look fine to me."

I told him. We had reached the playground with the tree stump. Crowds of children and parents were out seizing the bright day—the sand-throwers in the sandbox, the incipient ballplayers, small girls jumping rope. "I'd better stop now. I can't walk too far. I have to sit every few blocks like an old lady."

He walked me to the nearest bench. "Take care of yourself. And you let me know when you're feeling up to a nice Chinese dinner. How's that? My treat."

"Oh, the last time I had Chinese food they sent the wrong order. Can you believe it? It's those computers."

"I meant out, Laura, not in. I'll take you to that new place on Broadway. Cheer you up. Listen, if there's one thing I know, it's how to treat a lady."

"I'll bet."

I watched until he disappeared in the parade of walkers, the mourners going about the streets, though in fact they all looked quite lively. Then I turned to the stump. I could have studied it forever without wearying, tracing the gnarls of bark curving up its sides. Centuries old, maybe. It was hard to tell. The last time I went up close, its rings appeared to be worn away, as the striations of seashells are worn away by the battering of the waves. Surely it had learned all it needed to know, mutilated and exposed, sitting at the river's edge enduring endless cycles of the sun's toil and slide, watching the generations amble by, the children timid, violent, and brave.

Soon the old couple passed holding hands, the woman gesturing as she told what seemed an elaborate story. At one point the man threw back his head and laughed, and his white hair shook in the sunlight. They moved slowly through the clutter of toy cars, strollers, and bikes, then stopped to sit on a bench half a block south. They were like me, resting every few blocks, only they'd had time to ease into it.

On bright weekends like this one lots of fathers are out in the playground, a number of them fiftyish men. They have grown children, too, by the wives of their youth, some already raising families of their own, but the little ones hurling sand are from younger wives, women drawn to them by their money or power or mellowed sexuality. The men have more time now. They're established in some business or profession and don't need to hustle quite as much as twenty years ago, when the wives of their youth sat at the sandbox. Or else the new wives insist that they make the time. Besides, it's a different era. It's acceptable, more than acceptable, desirable, for fathers to show a tender interest in the sweet details and paraphernalia of childhood—the crenellated pails, the ritual removal of the training wheels. They hover about the playground idly chatting, settling disputes, chasing balls. Exactly like women. At this late date, they want to be women. What kind of mirage are they living in? These children, emblems of their pride, teetering on the bikes, so coddled they don't even need to carve their own crenellations, will face much harder tasks. They'll struggle for balance, concentrating with all their might, missing the steadying hand that let go too soon. And the young wives, those innocent twenty-eight-year-olds? What's in store for them?

Sour grapes? I can imagine Q.'s voice. Get down off your high horse, *cara*. Then he'd give a sad smile: You see, at least I saved you from that fate.

CROSSING THE DRIVE AN HOUR LATER, again I hear a voice, quite real this time. "Laura, how're you doing?"

I pass Tim's building so often on my walks that I hardly register it lately. He's standing at his wide-open, first-floor window with the requisite iron bars, holding a brush and dustpan in his right hand. He doesn't look angry anymore. He looks boyish and appealing in his college sweatshirt and cutoffs, his fair hair slightly mussed.

"Pretty good. Not bad at all. How about you, Tim?"

"Good. Fine." He rests his free hand on the ledge, palm down, half in and half out.

The silence, for a few seconds amiably familiar, quickly turns awkward. There is nothing to say. "So what are you doing?" I ask.

He waves the brush; it's obvious. "Cleaning the window sill. It's all sooty. The wind here on the river."

We need just five minutes of small talk to get us through, a civil tribute to our connection, but we're both at a loss. "By the way," Tim says, "there was something I meant to tell you."

I brace myself for recriminations. Tim broods over things, preparing his briefs point by point. "What?"

All at once, as if misguidedly coming to our aid, the open window falls with a crash onto his wrist. Behind the glass, behind the bars, he grimaces in pain. He tries to pull his hand out but can't. I push at the stuck window from outside, but before I can loosen it, he manages with his other hand to force it up two inches. With a deft, athlete's motion—the reward of countless hours of tennis—he flips his trapped left hand over and tugs it back. Before the hand is completely free, the window drops again, and only by a swift yank does he get his fingers out in time. Now the window is closed tight, and behind it Tim holds his wrist, his face stunned with pain. Buzz me in and I'll help you, I mime, pointing to the door. He shakes his head, no, and feebly signaling good-bye, turns away to vanish within.

His stunned face behind the glass haunts me all the way home. I think it was the most intimate glimpse I've ever had of him, and I find it uncomfortably, perversely interesting. I should have gone in even though he didn't seem to want my help. A neighbor could have buzzed me in. As soon as I'm home I call to see if he's all right.

"Sure, fine," he says. Not broken, only bruised. He's got it in a bowl of ice. "But what a shock. The chain snapped. I'll have to get it fixed. Oh, what I was starting to say . . . You'll get a kick out of this. Hal called the other night. He discovered that the reason it took so long to fill the pool was that the pump was broken. It was pumping only a fraction of what it should."

It's a relief to laugh. "That would never happen with the moon and the tides, I bet. So your calculations might have been correct after all."

"Yes. I had a feeling something was wrong. But it was too cool to swim anyway."

"Yes," I agree.

"Well, thanks for calling, Laura." He knows how intimate that glimpse of his pain was, perhaps even how interesting I'd find it, and hastens to restore formal relations. Smart. He always was very smart.

I can feel the bed longing for me, and I go like a complaisant wife. Not as tired as before, when I went like a famished lover. I know why I was reluctant to tell the witch I was feeling better. Superstition, nothing more. If tempted, the virus could rouse itself in spite, for a fresh assault. I'll always be afraid at the slightest symptoms—these viruses stay in the system forever. Impossible to dislodge. Like a lover who forever disappears and returns, waning and waxing, an inner moon pulling the tides of emotion.

I haven't tried any new-agey visualizing in some time, have almost forgotten those blue and red warrior cells rampaging down my bloodstream. It's not the eye that will see me through but the ear, which holds everything curled in embryo. Even so, as I lie on the bed waiting for strength to return, a kind of vision comes unbidden.

It is a dozen years into the future. Q. is aging. Passing him on the street, small children like the ones I watch in the playground would see an old man. Big children like Jilly might, too. In truth he's not exactly old, not old-old, but still . . . Let's say that now he's ready to do Lear, with the proper makeup. He's crossed a subtle border, on the far side of which his former way of life is no longer, let's say, feasible or expedient. To put it bluntly, he might just look a bit of a fool trying to get away with it. Even more bluntly, he wants me. For his old age. He himself isn't clear why, after everything. . . . Maybe he's just practical. Maybe, as he said in the Mexican restaurant, he realizes he's been errant all along, seeking me elsewhere in vain. Or perhaps it's what he's been saving me for, a final haven, the way a selfish Victorian paterfamilias might make sure one daughter remains at home to look after him. In any case, at this point it's pleasant, easy, it makes sense to him. He comes to claim me. He importunes as never before. So what do I do? Spit in his face? Ask how much money he's got? Test him to see if it's still working, all systems go? Or simply acquiesce.

We fade out into a Technicolor sunset, strolling hand in hand down my favorite beach, the one whose high dunes wall it off from the rest of the world. The surf trips about our ankles as we breathe in the salty spirit of the air. We're wearing shirts and hats to forestall skin cancer—we take the warnings seriously now. We don't smoke anymore, or eat red meat, or do any of the bad things. Utterly absorbed in each other, we emit a rare, invulnerable intimacy that makes the oiled young people lying on their blankets murmur, Look at that nice couple walking by—they seem so serene, like people who've grown old together. How do they do it? Do you think we'll last like that? (She's not really old at all, a few discerning ones note. She a lot younger, isn't she?) Q. still looks with interest if a sleek, long-legged bikini passes, but I don't mind, it's only force of habit. I look too, for that matter—a purely visual pleasure. . . .

Back at the rented cottage, he goes over his lines for *Lear*, slated for the fall. I cue him. I'm Kent, Oswald, Goneril, Regan, Cordelia, the Fool. He goes to bed early, can't take the late hours anymore. I know by his heavy, even breathing that he's in a deep sleep. Nevertheless, when the phone rings I snatch it up quickly and whisper, "I told you not to call me here. I can't talk. Yes, I'll be back in two weeks. Yes, yes, of course I remember. Yes, me too. You know I do. . . ."

I WOKE WITH A SHUDDER in the dark and reached for Ev beside me. Only a split second. That hadn't happened in a long time. It was because I felt like my old pre-murder self, my mind lithe and agile. It, the thing, seemed to have left me with that shudder, the way you shudder off a nightmare. My eyes adjusted quickly to the dark and I made out the shapes of things—desk, chair, window edged by light from the street lamp. The inner fog had lifted, as it had for those few hours up on the Cape, when I could see out and saw clearly that I would never write the book about the seaside town.

The night was very still. No car alarms or sirens, no sounds of traffic or a car door slamming somewhere, not even a faraway voice in the street or a baby's cry or anxious footsteps hurrying home. Not a rustle or a rattle, not a creak in the old uneven floorboards. So hushed it was as if the cosmic forces had finally ceased their friction, as the library book predicted, and the tides were still. The earth would be moving in slow motion, the days and nights unthinkably long. Ev's town would long since have sunk into the ocean, leaving a scattering of islands. The only stirring was my breath, thin, long, quiet and slow. Almost out of place in the silence, like the flutist's little gasp between notes, but sustaining, necessary, the spirit behind sound.

Suddenly out of the silence broken only by breath, scenes and dialogues from the new book came to me, swift and hard as a tide sweeping in. I rushed after the words, clinging to key phrases—bits of flotsam—repeating them like a litany so as not to forget. The more I memorized and catalogued, the more kept coming. And it was like coming, like sex, that feeling of pitching through space borne by something untranslatable; the infinitesimal hesitation—a kind of terror, a kind of bliss—and for salvation you give in and take the hurtling, even become the hurtling. Soon I wasn't chasing the tide of words but was the tide itself, mercilessly carving the shore and giving it a new shape. When it receded, I knew I would have nets full of fish.

I leaped up, turned on the light, and grabbed a pen. Lines skimmed unevenly across the page, threads seeking their tapestry.

THE CRISP, clear feeling was gone the next morning, leaving me the familiar sack of sand. I couldn't even remember getting back into bed. But when I looked over at the desk, the pages were stacked there; thank God it hadn't been a dream.

Last night, writing feverishly, I'd had the opposite notion: that the inert summer months might have been a bad dream. One of those harrowing stories that pulls you in, then backs you into a corner with no way out, until at the last minute the author reveals it was only a dream. A dream within a dream, giving the eerie feeling that every layer might be a dream, the author herself a figment of imagination—but whose, and where?

And though you're relieved for the dreaming heroine, you're resentful, too. You've been tricked, your feelings somehow exploited. As if it were revealed that all of the above, say, were the stratagem of a woman lying on a couch in a room overlooking a river, fighting boredom by transforming it into stories of a life she never led, while in the dim reality are the husband going to the office and the children to school, lunches to be packed, jeans to be hemmed, and the class play tonight—she's got to rouse herself, the kids are counting on it.

Well, no, I wouldn't dare. Anyway, it's been no dream for me. Here I am, in the usual morning struggle to free my body from the bed—the kind of lover who hates to let you go, who plays at keeping you pinned down. This thing will not leave with any simple shudder. But more such shudders will bring longer respites of clarity, at closer intervals, reversing figure and ground as the fog burns off to a smaller and smaller patch on the landscape.

Meanwhile, I'm waiting, as Ev's ancestors waited, once they learned not to deplete the forests but to pump the sea into vats, where in time it would leave them the precious salt.

Meanwhile, everything I've reported is real, down to the last headache. Moreover, Joyce is off to Africa next week to spend two months with the Tsumati, gathering data on rituals connected with agriculture. She's leaving the cat with Roger but is concerned about Lizzie, alone and depressed since she broke up with the man who didn't want more children. Mona's latest client is a hot new women's rock group noted for its outrageous outfits, so as we sit in the neighborhood cafés, none as satisfying as the Athena, she tells me about their jaunts through the thrift shops. Otherwise she continues faintly benumbed in her happy marriage, or so it seems—who am I to judge? Luckily Grace found an excellent woman dentist, so the root-canal work is proceeding apace; the downside is that this dentist has no interest whatsoever in the performance art project. Instead, Grace is toying with the idea of a miniature model of the Museum of Modern Art, floor by floor, complete with wee guards, gift shop and cafeteria, and scaled-down replicas of all the paintings. Obviously this will take a great deal of time. I'm having fantasies about getting Carol the Witch and the Tai Chi teacher together. They have only a nodding acquaintance at this point, but I suspect more could develop. Carol could do wonders for the teacher's English. Unless he and the interpreter . . . ? No, I never got that impression. It was all words and spirit between them. Anyway, just a passing fancy. Oh, and I've had a card from Tony. He's coming East for Thanksgiving at his mother's and could easily take the shuttle to New York. How would I feel about a visit from him and Sophie? Her mother, Hortense, incidentally, is all right. Struggling with the chemo, but the prognosis is good.

And Jilly? I was just wondering myself, when the phone rang.

"Laura? I hope this isn't too early. I meant to call before but my schedule is wild. I'm taking five courses, plus we're in the middle of our famine piece. Remember I told you? We take turns sitting in the gallery window eating bits of rice on and off all day. It really works well during rush hour when lots of people pass by. And we don't cheat, either, I mean, like go out for pizza afterward or anything. We just have the rice."

"But you must get pretty hungry, don't you?"

"Laura," she groaned, "getting hungry is the whole idea! But don't worry, my turn only comes two days a week and I eat enough on the other days. If we get more people involved we'll only have to do it once a week, and maybe—"

When she paused for breath, I asked, "What ever happened with Jeff and that other guy, the surfer? I can't remember his name."

"Zack." She grunted. "He never made it to Boston but he did write, once. He's one of those people who shouldn't write. He does better in person. He's not such a hot speller, either. I don't know how he got into Michigan. I haven't thought about him lately. And Jeff, well . . ." Another grunt. "After all that, it turned out he got involved with someone on the reservation. And I'm sure he didn't agonize over it the way I did! The funny thing is, Laura, when he told me, I wasn't even that upset. I mean, I acted upset and I suppose I was for a little while, but it was more like I was supposed to be? Because we'd been together almost three years, you know? But after a week or two I realized I didn't even mind so much. I was even, like, relieved? Does that sound weird?"

"Not at all. I'm a little relieved, too, frankly."

"So was my mother. Listen, one reason I'm calling . . . you'll never guess what happened."

Oh, not another one. A hang-glider? Bungee-jumper? "What?"

"I won the raffle. Not the first prize, the copper rooster. The second prize."

"What raffle?"

"The lighthouse. Don't you remember? It's falling into the sea? We bought tickets so they could move it back from the edge."

"Oh, yes. Well, congratulations. You're the first person I ever heard of who won a raffle. So what's your prize?"

"A painting of the lighthouse by a local artist. I can't remember his name. I wrote it down somewhere. It's nice, but I'm going to give it to you because I don't have any room. My walls are crammed as it is."

"You might want to save it for later, when you've got an apartment. . . ."

"No, it's not my thing. But you'll like it, I know. I want you to have it."

"Thanks."

"You don't sound very enthusiastic. How are you feeling?"

"Good. Better. Yes, sort of better."

I told her about Carol the Witch and her various spells and potions. I thought that would please Jilly and it did. She sounded proud of me, as if I'd passed into a new phase of maturity and accomplishment, probably very much the way I sounded when she was seven and learned to ride her bike without the training wheels. Ev and I had each run behind her with a steadying hand on the seat, but Jilly was having none of that. "Give it to me," she said, tugging at the bike. "Just leave me alone and I'll figure out how to do it. And don't watch." She dragged it off to a far corner of the playground. We did as she ordered, only peeking now and then to make sure she wasn't kidnapped. A half hour later she was back. "Now you can look!" She got on the bike and rode so far down the Drive that Ev took his bike to go after her—she was almost out of sight. "How did you do it?" I asked when they returned. She only smiled slyly and flounced off.

"Laura, the other reason I called is, I was thinking of coming up for a weekend soon. Maybe next weekend, if you're free. How's that? I can bring the painting."

Yes, yes.

I had barely hung up when the phone rang again.

Laura, my love.

(Oh, no.

Oh, yes.

And now what?)

A c k n o w l e d g m e n t s

Many thanks to Wolfe Lowenthal, a different sort of Tai Chi master from the one portrayed in the novel, but equally fine. Some of the principles and practices of Tai Chi were drawn from his book, *There Are No Secrets* (North Atlantic Books, 1991). I also drew on *Tai Chi*, by Cheng Man-ch'ing and Robert W. Smith (Charles E. Tuttle Co., 1967).

My grateful appreciation goes to Rachel Koenig for much of the information about Chinese medicine, though naturally any errors or misinterpretations are my own.

I used Stephen Mitchell's translation of the *Tao te Ching* (Harper & Row, 1988). The story on p. 27 about "no complaints whatsoever" comes from a footnote in Mitchell's translation (pp. 100–101), which he adapted from Zenkei Shibayama Roshi's *A Flower Does Not Talk*.

Information about the tides comes from Joyce Pope, *The Seashore* (Franklin Watts, 1985), and George W. Groh, *Land, Sea and Sky* (Collier, 1966).

Quotations about the seaside town are from the *Annual Reports of the Officers of the Town of Truro, 1965–1990*.

Many of the examples of performance art are taken from Marcia Tucker's book, *Choices: Making an Art of Everyday Life* (The New Museum

ACKNOWLEDGMENTS

of Contemporary Art, New York, 1986).

Quotes from the Samurai's creed are from Alan W. Watts, *The Spirit of Zen* (Grove Press, 1958), p. 120. The poem quoted on p. 218 is taken from Alan W. Watts, *The Way of Zen* (Vintage, 1989), p. 126.

"Love Calls Us to the Things of This World," referred to on p. 288, is the title of a poem by Richard Wilbur, from *Things of This World* (Harcourt Brace and Company, 1956).

ILLUSTRATION CREDITS

Pages 6, 162, 170, 245: Photos by Harry Schwartz

Page 80: Photo by Ani Mander

Page 154: Chart by Zecky P'tank

Page 262: Chart courtesy Japan Publications, from *Acupuncture Medicine: Its Historical and Clinical Background,* by Yoshiaki Omura (1982)